"It doesn't matter that I'm your usual type, because I'm still the wrong woman."

"You got it." He flashed a half smile that melted that ball of ice in her stomach. "But then, I'm the wrong man for you." No half smile now. "And I'm pretty sure that makes this one of those irresistible situations we're just going to have to resist. Or at least keep reminding ourselves to do it."

Yes. She wondered, though, if a reminder would be just wasting mental energy. "I don't want to find you attractive." But she did. Mercy, did she. On a scale of one to ten, he was a six hundred, and even with the danger, he fired every nerve in her body.

D1149971

JUSTICE
IS COMING

BY
DELORES FOSSEN

MILLS &
BOON®

All the characters in this book have no existence outside the imagination of the author, and have no relation whatsoever to anyone bearing the same name or names. They are not even distantly inspired by any individual known or unknown to the author, and all the incidents are pure invention.

All Rights Reserved including the right of reproduction in whole or in part in any form. This edition is published by arrangement with Harlequin Enterprises II B.V./S.à.r.l. The text of this publication or any part thereof may not be reproduced or transmitted in any form or by any means, electronic or mechanical, including photocopying, recording, storage in an information retrieval system, or otherwise, without the written permission of the publisher.

This book is sold subject to the condition that it shall not, by way of trade or otherwise, be lent, resold, hired out or otherwise circulated without the prior consent of the publisher in any form of binding or cover other than that in which it is published and without a similar condition including this condition being imposed on the subsequent purchaser.

® and ™ are trademarks owned and used by the trademark owner and/or its licensee. Trademarks marked with ® are registered with the United Kingdom Patent Office and/or the Office for Harmonisation in the Internal Market and in other countries.

First published in Great Britain 2013
by Mills & Boon, an imprint of Harlequin (UK) Limited,
Eton House, 18-24 Paradise Road, Richmond, Surrey TW9 1SR

© Delores Fossen 2013

ISBN: 978 0 263 90385 0

46-1213

Harlequ...   ...ural, renewable an...
recyclab...   ... sustainable forests. The
logging   ...onform to the legal environme...al
regulati...   ...y of origin.

Printed
by Blac... ...rint CPI, Barcelona

MORAY COUNCIL LIBRARIES & INFO.SERVICES

20 36 43 14	
Askews & Holts	
RF	

Imagine a family tree that includes Texas cowboys, Choctaw and Cherokee Indians, a Louisiana pirate and a Scottish rebel who battled side by side with William Wallace. With ancestors like that, it's easy to understand why *USA TODAY* bestselling author and former air force captain **Delores Fossen** feels as if she were genetically predisposed to writing romances. Along the way to fulfilling her DNA destiny, Delores married an air force top gun who just happens to be of Viking descent. With all those romantic bases covered, she doesn't have to look too far for inspiration.

Chapter One

Marshal Declan O'Malley eased the saddle off his chestnut stallion. He tried not to make any sudden moves, and he didn't look over his shoulder, though Declan was pretty sure someone was watching him.

That "pretty sure" became a certainty when he spotted the footprints on the partially frozen ground.

What the heck was going on?

Since he'd been a federal marshal for nearly six years, he was accustomed to having people want to do him bodily harm, but threats like that rarely came right to his doorstep.

Or rather to his barn.

Declan put the saddle on the side of the watering trough and adjusted his buckskin jacket so he could reach the Colt in his belt holster. He gave the chestnut's rump a gentle slap, and as Declan had hoped he'd do, the stallion headed for some hay in the side corral. If there was going to be a shootout, Declan sure didn't want his horse caught up in the gunfire.

He stepped to the side of the barn door. And waited. Listening.

But the only thing he could hear was the bitter December wind rattling the bare trees scattered around the grounds. He didn't mind the cold when he was on his daily ride, but he minded it a lot when he was waiting for something bad to happen.

Or maybe not bad.

He looked at the footprints again. Small. Like a woman's. He hadn't been in a relationship in the past three or four months, but maybe this was an old girlfriend come to visit. Still, it didn't feel like something that simple.

Or that fun.

His house wasn't exactly on the beaten path, not even by rural-Texas standards. He was literally on the back forty acres of his foster family's horse-and-cattle ranch. A good ten miles from the town of Maverick Springs, and with not even a paved road leading to his place. Besides, there wasn't much of value in his small wood-frame house to make it a target for thieves.

Declan glanced around. Kept listening. And when he was finally fed up with the cold, he drew his Colt and moved away from the barn door so he could follow those footprints. From the looks of it, the prints started at the back of his barn, and that meant somebody had probably walked in from the pasture and checked out the barn itself.

Maybe looking for him.

Or looking to make sure he'd indeed gone on his daily ride.

And then the trespasser had made her way to the back of his house. Declan went in that direction now, using the trees for cover.

Finally, he saw something.

Or rather *someone*.

There was a person dressed in dark clothes and equally dark sunglasses peering around the edge of his back porch. Judging from her size, it was probably a woman, though he couldn't be positive since his visitor was wearing a black baseball cap slung low on her head, and the brim covered most of her face. Declan expected her to duck out of sight when she spotted him.

She didn't.

She put her index finger to her mouth in a keep-quiet gesture.

What the hell?

And just to confuse things even more, she motioned for him to come closer.

Declan debated it. He debated calling out to her, too, but she frantically shook her head and made that keep-quiet gesture again.

He looked to see if she was armed. Couldn't tell. But since she'd had ample opportunity to shoot at him and hadn't, Declan decided to take his chances. He didn't put his gun away, but he went closer.

Yeah, it was a woman all right. About five-six, with an average build. Judging from the strands of hair that had slipped out from the back of the baseball cap, she was a brunette.

"Inside," she whispered and tipped her head to his back door. *"Please,"* she added.

Well, if she was a criminal, she was a polite one, that was for sure. The *please* didn't sway Declan one bit, but her shaky voice did. There was fear in it. Or something. Something that told him she wasn't a killer.

Well, probably not.

He'd been wrong before. And he had the scar on his chest to prove it.

But did that stop him?

Much to his disgust, nope, it didn't. He'd never been a cautious man, and while this seemed like a really good time to start, Declan went even closer, still looking for any sign that she was armed.

Okay, she was.

Without any prompting, his mysterious visitor opened the side of her jacket to show him the gun—a Glock—that she had tucked in a shoulder holster. Since she made no attempt to draw it, Declan walked even closer, up the side steps. He also tapped the badge he had pinned to his holster, just in case she didn't know she was dealing with a deputy U.S. marshal.

She kept her head down so he still didn't have a good look at her face. "I know exactly who you are, Declan O'Malley," she whispered.

Well, that wasn't much of a stretch. Everyone in Maverick Springs knew who he was. He and his five foster brothers, who were all marshals, too. Anyone could have found out his name and where he lived within minutes after arriving in town. Heck, he didn't even have a burglar alarm because he figured no one would be stupid enough to do what this woman was apparently trying to do.

"Inside," she repeated.

It wasn't caution but rather common sense that had him staying put when she turned toward his door. "I want answers first," he insisted.

"Shh." The fear in her body language went up a significant notch, and she fired a few nervous glances around his yard.

Confused and now somewhat riled at, well, whatever the heck this was, Declan followed her glances but didn't see anything out of the ordinary. Only the woman.

He cupped her chin, lifted it.

And groaned.

Yeah. He recognized her all right, and it wasn't a good kind of recognition, either.

Eden Gray.

What in the Sam Hill was she doing here at his house?

He opened his mouth to demand some answers but her hand flew up, and she pressed her fingers to his mouth. Cold fingers at that.

But soft.

And she smelled like some kind of girlie hand lotion. It definitely didn't go with that Glock she was carrying or the fact that she was trespassing.

"They might hear you," she whispered. "Inside," she insisted again.

"They?"

She eased down her fingers, stepped back and yanked off her glasses. Those eyes caught him off guard for just a moment. Ice blue but somehow without a hint of cold in them. Definitely memorable, but he hadn't needed to see her eyes to know this was a blast from his past that he didn't want or need.

Well, a blast he didn't need anyway.

For a split second, his body overrode his brain, and that whole *want* thing came into play. In those brief moments, he didn't see Eden Gray, a person who despised him, but rather a hot woman. One who just happened to be armed and acting crazy.

She swallowed hard.

Something different went through her eyes. Not fear, but Declan recognized the look. It was the quick glance that a woman gave a man when she was interested but didn't want to be.

Declan was afraid he was giving her the same look right back. *Oh, man.* One day he was going to learn to think with his head only and not some other body part that often got him into trouble.

She swallowed hard again. Turned. And she eased open the door. *Sorry,* she mouthed.

Declan didn't ask for what. He didn't want to know. He only wanted answers, and that was why he followed her inside to his kitchen.

"Why are you here?" he demanded.

But she still didn't answer. She hurried to the window over his sink and looked out. She did another of those shifty glances that he often did when he was doing surveillance or in the presence of danger.

"You obviously remember me," she finally said.

He gave her a flat look. *"Obviously."*

"This way," Eden added. "I have to show you something." And she headed toward his living room that was only a few yards away.

She would have made it there, too, but Declan snagged her by the arm and whirled her back around to face him. "Remembering you doesn't tell me why you're here. Now spill it, or I'm tossing you out."

"You can't." Eden was breathing through her mouth now, and her pulse was jumping in her throat. But that didn't stop her from shaking off his grip, catching his arm and pulling him into the living room.

"Stay away from the windows," she warned.

Just on principle and because he was now about twelve steps past being ornery, Declan considered doing the opposite of anything she was asking. "Give me a reason why I should stay away from my own window."

"There's a tiny camera attached to the big oak on the right side of your front porch." Her breath trembled in her throat. "And they're watching the front of the house. Maybe trying to listen, too."

Declan shook his head, stared at her and made a circling motion with his gun for her to continue. He needed more. A lot more, but he needed that "a lot more" to make sense. So far, that wasn't happening.

"Did you miss a dose of meds or something?" he asked.

"No." She stretched that out a few syllables. "I'm not crazy. And I have a good reason for being here."

He stared at her, made the circling motion with his hand again.

"I got here about a half hour ago, while you were out riding," she said. "I've watched you for the past two days, so I know you take a ride this time of morning before you go in to work."

Well, it was an answer all right, but it didn't answer much. "You watched me?"

She nodded.

"Really?" And he didn't take the skepticism out of it, either.

Until this morning when he'd reined in at the barn, he hadn't felt or seen anyone watching him yesterday or the day before. Of course, he'd had a lot on his mind what with his foster father, Kirby Granger, battling cancer. The thought of losing Kirby had been weighing on him. Maybe enough for him to not notice someone stalking him.

He looked her straight in the eye. "Are you going to make me arrest you, or do you plan to keep going with that explanation?"

She made a soft sound of frustration, looked out the window again. "I'm a P.I. now. I own a small agency in San Antonio."

She'd skipped right over the most important detail of her brief bio. "Your father's Zander Gray, a lowlife swindling scum. I arrested him about three years ago for attempting to murder a witness who was going to testify against him, and he was doing hard time before he escaped."

And this was suddenly becoming a whole lot clearer.

"He sent you here," Declan accused.

"No," she quickly answered. "I'm not even sure he's alive."

Okay, maybe not so clear after all.

"But my father might have been the reason they contacted me in the first place," Eden explained. "They might have thought I'd do anything to get back at you for arresting him. I won't."

He made a sound of disagreement. "Since you're trespassing and have been stalking me, convince me otherwise that you're not here to avenge your father."

"I'm not." Not a whisper that time. And there was some fire in those two little words. "But someone's trying to set me up. Earlier this week someone broke into my office, planted some fake financials on my computer and changed the password so I can't delete them from the server. That someone is trying to make it look as if I'm funneling money to a radical militia group buying illegal firearms."

Declan thought about that a second. "Lady, if you wanted me to investigate that, you didn't have to follow me or come to my ranch. My office is on Main Street in town."

Another headshake. "They didn't hire me to go to your office."

Mercy. It was hard to hang on to his temper with this roundabout conversation. "There it is again. That *they. They* put up the camera that you don't want me to go to the window and see. So who are they?"

"I honestly don't know." She dodged his gaze, tried to turn away, but he took hold of her again and forced her to face him. "After I realized someone had planted that false info on my computer, I got a call from a man using a prepaid cell phone. I didn't recognize his voice. He said if I went to the cops or the marshals, he'd release the info on my computer and I'd be arrested."

And maybe she would be. Because some cops might assume like father, like daughter.

But was she?

Declan pushed that question aside. Right now, that didn't matter. "This unknown male caller is the one who put the camera outside?"

"I think so. If not him, then someone working with or for him. All I know is it's there because I saw a man wearing a ski mask installing it right after you left for your ride."

He shook his head. "If they sent you to watch me, why use a camera?"

"Because the camera is to watch *me*," she clarified. "To make sure I do what he ordered me to do."

"And what exactly are you supposed to do?" Declan demanded.

Eden Gray shoved her hand over her Glock. "Kill you."

Chapter Two

Declan O'Malley came at her so fast that Eden didn't even see it coming until it was too late.

Even though he was tall and lanky, he still packed a wallop when he slammed into her, knocking her back against the wall. In the same motion, he ripped her gun from her shoulder holster, tossed it behind him and jammed his own weapon beneath her chin.

"Kill me?" His teeth were clenched now. Jaw, too. And even though there were no lights on in the living room, she had no trouble seeing the venom in his eyes.

Eden was certain there was no venom in hers. Just fear. It'd been a huge risk coming here. From everything she'd read and heard about him, Declan could be a dangerous man. Still, she hadn't had a choice. If she was going to die, she'd rather it be at his hands than others'.

"The man who called me on the burner cell ordered me to kill you," Eden managed to say. Though it was hard to speak with the marshal's body pressed against her chest. It was hard to breathe, too.

But maybe Declan himself was responsible for that.

Eden had known that he fell into the drop-dead-hot category. Tall, dark, deadly. However, what she hadn't known was that despite the danger and this insane situation, she would feel the punch of attraction. She'd never expected to feel it for this man, but it was there.

You're losing it, Eden.

Declan O'Malley was the job. For some huge reasons, especially one, he couldn't be anything else.

"Why does he want me dead?" he demanded.

"I don't know. That's the truth," Eden added when he made a "yeah, right" sound. "He just told me if I didn't kill you that he'd release the info he planted on my computer."

No "yeah, right" this time, but his left eyebrow lifted. "You'd kill me rather than risk charges for funneling money to a militia group?"

Eden lifted her own eyebrow. She wasn't feeling especially brave, definitely not like the cocky man looming in front of her. The seconds were ticking away, and with each one of them, the risk got higher and higher. Someway, somehow, she had to get this hot cowboy marshal to go along with an asinine plan that had little or no chance of succeeding.

Still, little was better than zero.

Without warning, he yanked the baseball cap from her head and threw it in the direction her Glock had landed. Her hair was in a ponytail, but it dropped against her shoulder. He studied it. Then her eyes. Every inch of her face. Maybe trying to figure out if she was telling him the truth. Or maybe he was just giving her the twice over as she'd done to him.

She hoped not.

They didn't need both of them feeling this involuntary heat.

"You sure this isn't about your father?" he pressed.

"I'm sure. I haven't heard from him since he escaped from jail."

And she didn't want to get into that sore subject now. Declan had arrested her father, and then her father had escaped. It wouldn't do any good to mention that she believed her father was innocent of at least the most serious charge—attempted murder. That really wouldn't help in getting Declan to cooperate if she questioned his lawman's skills of apprehending a guilty suspect.

"Could you at least move the gun?" Eden asked. "Because we need to talk. I figure at most I've got twenty minutes left before someone will want to know why I haven't fired a shot."

She was being generous with that timeline. The mysterious caller had told her to show Declan ASAP what she'd been sent. Why, she didn't know, but it seemed as if that was only to taunt him.

Or rile him even more than he already was.

Like poking an ornery rattler with a short stick. It hardly seemed wise, but she would show him. And hope for a way out of this.

Declan slid his intense green eyes to the gun, then back to her. "Yes to the talking. No to moving the gun."

There was just a touch of an Irish brogue beneath that Texas drawl. A strange combination. And one she might have enjoyed hearing if his finger wasn't on the trigger of the gun pressed to her throat.

"I agreed to kill you because I didn't have a choice," Eden explained. No beautiful lilt to her words. Her voice was strained like the rest of her. One big giant nerve. "If the planted info had been leaked, it would have set off an opposing militia group that would in turn kill me, the rest of my family and anyone they thought might be a friend of mine."

Finally, he let up a little on the pressure to her chest and eased back a fraction. Still close. Still touching. He probably hadn't realized that he had his right leg shoved between hers. Eden's gaze drifted in that direction. Then back up at Declan.

Correction. He'd noticed.

But clearly he didn't plan to do anything about the intimate contact between them.

"I have two sisters," she added. "They're nineteen and twenty. Barely adults, and they've been through more than enough with my father's arrest and disappearance. They don't deserve to die because someone's targeting you."

"You could have arranged for them and you to be protected," he pointed out.

"I did the best I could, but there's no place to hide from these men. Eventually they'd get through any security I could set up. They proved that by hacking into my computer and leaving that bogus info."

Declan made another sound that led her to believe he was making fun of her.

"You ever killed a man before?" he challenged, but he didn't wait for Eden to answer. "My guess is no."

He put his face right next to hers. So close that the brim of his midnight-black Stetson scraped against her forehead. It was hard to tell where the Stetson ended and his hair began, because they were the same color.

"And my second guess is that you can't kill me," he went on. "Of course, that's not really a guess since I wouldn't let you get the chance."

"I wasn't planning to kill you," she said, but had to clear her throat and repeat it so it'd have sound. Great. She was acting like a wuss rather than a P.I. with her family's lives, and hers, at stake.

"You're here with a gun," he reminded her.

"I didn't intend to use it. Well, not to shoot you anyway. I will have to fire, though, because I want who-ever's on the other end of that camera to believe you're dead. And to make sure that person doesn't come in here and try to do the job himself, I need to fire soon."

With his gaze still pinned to hers, he backed up again. "Maybe we should do just that—let the person come in here and try to kill me," he suggested. "If he's really out there. He won't get far. I'm thinking a step in the house. Two at most. And I wouldn't let him get off the first shot."

"I don't doubt it. But I can't risk that. His death could start a chain reaction that'll get my sisters killed."

Thankfully, he didn't disagree with that. Well, not verbally anyway. "Tell me everything you know about the person who hired you to do this."

"There isn't time." Eden tried to look out the win-dow to make sure no one was coming, but the angle was wrong. "He said I had to have the job done by seven-thirty. It's seven-twenty now."

"Make time," he countered.

Eden huffed and tried to think of the fastest expla-nation. It wasn't too hard because she didn't know a lot of facts. "I don't have a clue who he is. As I said, he used an untraceable cell phone. It's the same with the info he emailed me about you. I tried to track down the source, but it led me to a coffee shop in San Antonio where hundreds of people use the internet each day. There aren't any security cameras and no surveillance feed from nearby businesses."

He gave her another hard look. "What info about me did he email you?"

"It's on my phone."

Eden glanced in the direction of her pocket, where his hip was still brushing against hers. She waited until he nodded before she reached between them, and the back of her hand did more than brush. She had no choice but to touch him in a place that she shouldn't be touching.

He still didn't back away.

But Declan did make a slight sound of discomfort.

Eden knew how he felt. This wasn't comfortable for her, either, and it was even worse because touching him wasn't nearly as unpleasant as it should have been. After all, he was holding her at gunpoint.

Still, it was time to poke that rattler.

She went through the emails on her phone until she reached the first one the man had sent her. It was a series of photos with just four words: Your target, Declan O'Malley.

She went through the shots, the first a recent one of him wearing his gun and badge and going into the marshals' building in Maverick Springs. It appeared to have been taken from a camera with a long-range lens.

Eden showed Declan the photo and went to the next one, a close-up of him at the diner across the street from his office. Probably taken with the same long-range camera since it had a grainy texture.

"Did you have any idea you were being photographed?" she asked, hoping that maybe he'd seen the person who'd snapped these shots.

Declan shook his head, and while his expression didn't change much, Eden figured that had to bother him. It was a violation, something she knew loads about since this whole computer-hacking incident.

She clicked to another photo of Declan in his truck, turning onto the road that led to his foster family's ranch and to his own place. The next shot was of his license plate.

And then Eden got to the last one.

The puzzling one.

It was an old wedding photo of four adults and a young boy. Even though the person who'd emailed it to her hadn't identified by name all the people in the group shot, he had said that the child was Declan. He was about four years old, dressed in his Sunday best, and the people surrounding him were his parents, an uncle and the uncle's bride. They were all smiling. A happy-family photo.

It didn't make Declan happy now.

He closed his eyes for just a split second, and then he cursed, using some really foul language. And Eden knew why. She, too, was personally familiar with bad memories. And despite the smiles, this photo was indeed a bad memory, because in less than twenty-four hours after it'd been taken, Declan's life had turned on a dime.

Or rather turned on a different kind of metal.

Some bullets.

"The information this hacker gave me was that the photo was of your family in Germany," Eden said. "They were all murdered when you were four years old."

Declan took a moment, inhaled a slightly deeper breath. "Why the hell did he send you that?"

Eden shook her head. "I was hoping you could tell me. The person also said your name had been changed after the murders."

"It was. Twice. But as far as I know, no other living person has that specific information. Except maybe my family's killer."

Was that it? Was that the connection?

"What does this photo have to do with the order the hacker gave me to kill you?" she asked.

He snatched the phone from her, backed up, but he still didn't lower his gun. He kept it aimed right at her while he glanced out the window. Maybe to see if the camera installer was returning. He apparently wasn't, because Declan's attention went back to the photos. There weren't more to see, but he paused for a long time on that last one.

The bad-memory one.

"I've been digging, but I don't have many answers," she admitted. "Still, I have to believe that picture has something to do with all of this or he wouldn't have sent it to me."

Eden paused, hoping Declan didn't shoot her for asking what she had to ask. "What do you remember about your family's murders? Who killed them? Because the person sent me links of the old crime, but all the articles said the culprit was an unknown assailant."

A sterile term for something far from sterile.

"I don't know who killed them." He was in control again. The tough cowboy lawman, and he was glaring at her, maybe because he didn't believe she was innocent in all of this.

And maybe she wasn't.

Eden didn't know if she was one hundred percent blameless, but that was what she intended to find out—after she bought herself and her sisters some time.

"I don't have any memories of the attack," Declan finally added. "According to the shrink the cops made me see, I blocked them out."

Too bad. But Eden cringed at the thought. Maybe blocking them out had been the only way Declan had survived. That and being hidden in a cellar while his family was murdered. If he hadn't been in that cellar, he would have been killed, as well. In fact, Eden was afraid that Declan was the reason they'd been killed in the first place.

Judging from the look in his eyes, he thought so, too.

He groaned, dropped back another step and shoved her phone in his front pocket. Maybe so he'd have a free hand to scrub over his face—which he did.

"What's the first memory you do have after the murders?" she asked.

"A few days later." And that was all he said for several long moments. "The local cops put me in protective custody, gave me a fake name and eventually sent me to a distant cousin, Meg Tanner, in Ireland. I lived on and off with her and then some of her friends in County Clare for eight years before she brought me to Texas."

Yes, because Meg had learned she had Parkinson's disease and could no longer take care of Declan. Or at least that was the info Eden had been given by the mystery person who'd orchestrated this visit to Declan's place.

"Eventually your cousin took you to the Rocky Creek Children's Facility," Eden supplied. "Why there?"

"She just said I'd be safe there. I got another name, the one I use now, and Kirby said I shouldn't talk about my past to anyone. So I didn't."

Eden took up the rest of the explanation. "The facility didn't normally take boys your age, but they made an exception. Actually, someone there faked the paperwork so you could be admitted."

Declan glared again. "How do you know that?"

"Despite what you think of me, I'm a good P.I. I know how to find information, even when someone wants that information hidden."

Though it had been especially challenging to get any records from the notorious facility because of an ongoing investigation into the murder of the orphanage's headmaster, Jonah Webb. According to what she'd learned,

Webb's wife had murdered him sixteen and a half years ago when Declan was just thirteen years old and his five foster brothers had all been living at Rocky Creek.

And Webb's wife had an unknown accomplice.

Declan and all five of his foster brothers were suspects. So was their foster father, Kirby Granger, the retired marshal who had "rescued" Declan and his foster brothers and then raised them on his sprawling ranch.

That led Eden to her next question. "Is this connected to Jonah Webb's murder investigation?"

Declan certainly didn't jump to deny it, and coupled with that photo of him as a child, this might be one very complex puzzle. Something they didn't have time for right now.

"I need to fire the gun," Eden reminded him, checking the time again. "The person who set this up needs to believe you're dead."

"So you've said," he argued.

Eden was sure her mouth dropped open. "You don't believe me?"

"Why should I?"

It took her a moment to get control of her voice so she could speak. "Why else would I have come here? Why else would I have those pictures of you?"

Declan gave her a flat look. "You tell me."

Oh, mercy. She hadn't expected Declan to blindly go along with the faked-death plan, but Eden had figured the photos would have at least convinced him that he was in danger. And not from her. But from the same person who could get her and her sisters killed the hard way.

She walked closer to him. "Look, I don't want to be here, and I darn sure don't want to be involved in this mess. I have enough going on in my life—"

"Enough going on that you could have cut a deal with someone to kill me. I've made enemies."

Yes, he had made enemies. Plenty of them. For whatever reason, maybe old baggage from his childhood, Declan volunteered to take the worst cases. Scum of the scum. And men like that didn't forgive and forget easily. They would often try to take revenge against the lawman who'd arrested them.

"I'm not disputing that people might want you dead," Eden said. "But why come to me? Why involve me in this other than because you arrested my father? I think even you have to admit that's a thin connection."

"Maybe." Clearly, he wasn't admitting that at all. He reached down, picked up her gun and shoved it into the waistband of his jeans. "Come on. You're going to the marshals' office with me so I can take a statement."

Eden held her ground when he latched on to her arm. "Someone wants to kill you." Though she'd already made that point several times. Either he didn't believe her at all or he was ready to risk his life and hers by walking out that door.

"Think of my sisters," she said, and she was ready to beg if necessary. "You know what it's like to lose someone close to you. Don't make my family go through that."

Eden didn't see what she wanted in his eyes—any indication that he was considering what she'd just asked. But then Declan turned his gun toward the floor.

And fired.

The two shots blasted through the small house, the bullets tearing into the wood floor. The sound was deafening. Unnerving.

But a relief, too.

"Thank you," Eden managed to say despite her suddenly bone-dry throat. "Now, for the next step. While you pretend to be dead, I'll leave and contact one of your brothers. I'm thinking maybe Harlan McKinney." She'd researched them all, and he seemed the most levelheaded.

He shook his head. "I'll call Wyatt. Harlan's tied up with some personal stuff right now. Wedding plans," he added in a mumble. His gaze shot back to hers. "I've got no intention of playing dead for long. You cooperate with Wyatt and me, and we'll get to the bottom of this."

Before she could agree, Declan got in her face again. "Here's the only warning you'll get from me. If you're lying about any of this, I *will* make you pay."

She nodded, knowing that this was far from over. It was just the beginning, and Eden prayed they could all get out of it alive.

Using his left hand, Declan took out his phone from his pocket. Hopefully to call his foster brother Wyatt McCabe, but he didn't press any buttons or numbers. Declan froze for a moment before his gaze shifted to the window.

Eden's heart went to her knees. "Did you hear something?"

"Yeah." He hooked his arm around her and shoved her behind him.

That only made her racing heart worse, and she came up on her toes to try to look over his shoulder. She didn't have to look far.

Eden spotted someone beside the tree where that camera had been mounted. A man. He was peering through a scope on a rifle.

And he had that rifle aimed right at Declan O'Malley's house.

Chapter Three

Declan backed Eden deeper into the shadows and took aim out the window. The guy didn't appear to be on the verge of shooting, but Declan didn't want to take any chances. If this moron fired, it would be the last shot he'd ever take.

Without moving his attention from the man with that rifle, Declan pushed the button on his phone to call his foster brother Wyatt.

"You still at the ranch?" Declan asked the moment Wyatt answered.

"Yeah. About to leave for work now. Why?"

"I got a problem. Several of them, in fact." He spared Eden a glance to make sure she wasn't ready to do anything stupid. Her attention, too, was staked to the guy outside, and judging from her reaction, his being there wasn't part of her plan.

Whatever her plan was.

Just in case her plan was to still kill him, Declan repositioned her so that she was hip to hip with him. He didn't want her in his line of sight in case she tried to grab her Glock from his jeans.

"A man has a rifle pointed at my house," Declan explained to his brother. "I need you out here, but make a quiet approach from the back. I'd do it myself, but I have another unexpected visitor. This one's inside, and it's Zander Gray's daughter."

Wyatt cursed. "What the hell's going on?"

"Not sure yet, but I'm about to find out." Declan used the camera on his phone to click a picture of the guy, and he fired it off to Wyatt. "Send that to Dallas and see if we can get a hit on facial recognition. I need it fast. Oh, and if possible, keep the guy outside alive. I need to question him."

"I'll try," Wyatt assured him.

Declan had no doubt that Wyatt would indeed try, and it shouldn't take him long to get to Declan's place, since the main ranch house was less than a mile away. Wyatt would hurry, too. No doubts about that.

"You recognize that man with the rifle?" Declan asked Eden the moment he ended the call with Wyatt.

"No." She didn't hesitate, either. "But I warned you that someone was likely watching."

Yeah, someone who wanted to make sure she murdered him.

But there were some huge holes in her story. For instance, if someone had wanted him dead, why send a female P.I. with a goody-two-shoes voice and a body that could distract a man? A face, too.

Maybe that was exactly why someone had sent her.

Declan had never hurt a woman, even one that he'd butted heads with. And it could be the person behind all of this thought Eden might be able to pull the trigger before he even saw it coming.

Declan motioned for her to take out her phone when he felt it vibrate. She pulled it out, and her breath stalled when she saw the screen.

"The caller blocked the number," she relayed.

The guy with the rifle had both hands on his weapon,

so he wasn't making the call, but it could be coming from the person who'd hired this would-be triggerman and Eden, as well.

"Answer it," Declan insisted. "And put it on speaker."

She nodded, and her hand was trembling when she clicked the buttons. Eden didn't say anything. She just waited for the caller to respond, and she didn't have to wait long.

"You there, Gray?" the caller asked her. A man.

Declan used his phone to record the call so he could have it analyzed. Hopefully it wouldn't be needed as part of a murder investigation—Declan's own or Eden's.

"I'm here," she answered. "I'm sure you heard the shots. O'Malley's dead, so give me the password to delete the lies you planted on my computer."

That request meshed with the story she'd told Declan, but he wasn't ready to believe her just yet. For reasons he didn't yet understand, all of this—including her response to this call—could be part of her plan.

"Can't give you anything without proof," the caller argued. "I'm sending in someone to see the body."

"There's not enough time for that," Eden answered before Declan could coach her on what to say. "O'Malley managed to get off a call to the marshals. They're on the way. Best if we all get out of here now."

Declan gave her the worst glare he could manage, because that was not the way he wanted this to go down. He wanted the gunman to come inside the house. Or rather he wanted the gunman to try. Then Declan could have disarmed him and arrested his sorry butt so he could interrogate him. He darn sure didn't want the guy running off.

"The marshals?" the caller growled. "How much time before they arrive?"

Maybe the glare worked, because she hesitated. "I'm not sure."

Declan pointed toward the rifleman and then toward his front door. "Tell him to come in," he mouthed.

After a long hesitation, she gave another shaky nod. "You should have time to check the body if you make it quick."

But the caller didn't jump at the chance to do that. "I have a better idea. You go ahead and get out of there, and I'll verify O'Malley's dead once you're gone. Wouldn't want the marshals to catch you."

There was a taunting edge to his tone, but he didn't give Eden a chance to come back with a response. "Leave now," the caller said. "Walk out the front door and head straight for your car that you left on the ranch trail. If you go anywhere but there, our deal is off." He ended the call.

Eden pulled in a long breath. "I'd like my gun before I go outside."

Declan looked at her as if she'd lost her mind. "The caller doesn't believe you killed me," he pointed out. "And the moment you walk out that door, his hired gun will bring you down before you can blink. You're a loose end, and he's not going to let you live."

In fact, that had maybe been part of the plan all along. Somehow, convince Eden to kill him and then they'd kill her. That didn't answer his question of why, but Declan figured he could get to that soon enough.

If he kept them alive, that is.

"He'll try to kill me," Eden agreed. "But I'm not a bad shot. Plus, I know he's out there. I can fire as soon as I step on the porch."

"Even if you're the best shot in the state, that's a stupid plan. He's already got the rifle aimed and ready, and you don't even know if he's alone. If he misses, which I doubt he will, he could have a friend or two ready to make sure you die."

Her eyes practically doubled in size. "Oh, God," she mumbled.

Yeah. *Oh, God.*

Thankfully, Wyatt would be expecting the worst and knew how to sneak up to the house without being seen.

"So what do we do?" she asked. "We can't just wait. He'll be expecting me to walk out there."

"Then he'll be disappointed, won't he? If he wants you dead—and I'm pretty sure he does—then he can send his lackey in to do the job."

She mumbled another "Oh, God," and practically slumped against him. "This could have been all about me. Maybe to set me up for your murder. Maybe *I* made the wrong enemy."

"That's one real good possibility. Or it could be he wants us both dead. A two-birds-with-one-stone kind of deal. Maybe we both made the wrong enemies."

But why had this moron sent her the pictures of him? Especially that one photo of him and his family? The image of it was branded into his head, but seeing it again had brought the nightmare flooding back.

Hell.

After all these years, the nightmare was still there even though he had no memories of the day his family had been murdered. No clues to give the cops to help them find the person or persons responsible. Ironic, since his life now was all about finding justice for others, and he hadn't found it for his own kin.

"When the person called you to set all of this up, did he give you any other details about my family?" Declan asked.

"No." Eden made a soft sound of frustration. "But I did a background check to see if I could find any connection. I couldn't." She paused. "I couldn't even find a record of your birth parents."

Because there wasn't one, and Declan should know because he'd searched for it for years. His cousin, Meg, had disappeared after she'd abandoned him at the Rocky Creek facility. That meant Declan had no idea if he even had any living relatives.

"When I was a kid, I asked anyone who might know something about my mom and dad," he told her, "but I never got any answers."

"Maybe the person who killed your family is behind this."

Yeah. More of the nightmare. The killer returning, and this time there'd be no cellar. No place to hide. But he wasn't a little boy any longer. He was a federal marshal who'd been trained by the best: his foster dad, Kirby. Declan could take care of himself, but at the moment, that wasn't his biggest worry.

The killer could go after his family again.

His new family. The one he'd had since he'd left Rocky Creek sixteen years ago.

His brothers—Dallas, Clayton, Harlan, Slade and Wyatt—could also protect themselves, but Kirby was another matter. He was weak from chemo treatments and couldn't fight off a fly. His long-time friend, Stella, was in the same boat. No chemo for her, but Declan figured she wasn't capable of taking on hired guns, especially now. Both Kirby and she were no doubt still at the Maverick Springs hospital for an overnight stay, where Kirby was getting his latest round of treatments.

Just the thought of someone hurting Kirby had Declan reaching for his phone again, but it buzzed before he could make a call and have someone go to the hospital.

"You've got more than two problems, little brother," Wyatt immediately greeted him. "In addition to the rifle guy out front, there's another one on the west side of the house, right by the road that leads off the ranch."

Oh, man. One gunman and a P.I. that he maybe couldn't trust were bad enough, but now there was a third piece in this dangerous puzzle.

"Clayton's on the way," Wyatt added.

Declan didn't want that, even if he might need the extra backup. "Send him to the hospital to guard Kirby."

"You think he's in danger?"

"Could be." And it sickened Declan to even think that.

"My sisters need protection, too," Eden blurted out. "Trish and Alice Gray. They're both students at the University of Texas. I have a bodyguard watching them, but it might not be enough."

Her plea certainly sounded convincing, but Declan wasn't about to give her blanket trust just yet.

He heard Wyatt make a call and request the protection for all three—Kirby and the Gray sisters. Declan was hoping it was overkill, but he had a sickening feeling that this situation had already gotten out of hand.

"Try to neutralize the guy on the road," Declan instructed his brother. "I'll deal with the one out front." He didn't wait for his brother to agree. Wyatt would.

Declan shoved his phone into his pocket. "Wait here."

Eden was shaking her head before he even finished. "I can give you some backup."

"No. You'll stay here." Declan didn't leave much room for argument, though he briefly considered returning her gun just in case the guy managed to get in the front door. However, there was that part about him not trusting her.

He took her by the arm and practically shoved her behind his sofa. "Stay put, and that's not a suggestion."

Whether she would or not was anyone's guess, but Declan couldn't worry about that now. He had to take care of this situation and then check on Kirby.

Declan locked the front door, though it wouldn't stop a gunman from shooting through the wood and getting inside.

With Eden.

And that was what Declan couldn't let happen, especially if it turned out that she was just a pawn in all of this. Even if she wasn't a pawn, she could still have the answers he needed to figure out what the heck was going on.

He grabbed some extra ammo for his Colt from the top of his fridge, crammed it in his coat pocket and headed to the back door. He looked out to make sure there wasn't another gunman lying in wait.

The backyard appeared to be empty, so Declan eased open the door and stepped onto the porch. He took a moment, listening, but didn't hear any unusual sounds.

He hurried down the steps and to the side of the house. Using it for cover, he looked out and spotted the tree with the small camera mounted on the branch. The rifleman was there, beneath that camera, and he still had both his gun and attention fastened to the front of the house. Declan had a clear look at his face, but it wasn't familiar. Maybe they'd get lucky with the recognition software or the interrogation he planned to do once he had these dirtbags in custody.

Declan froze when he heard something. Footsteps.

But not from outside. They were coming from inside the house, and he cursed Eden for not listening to him. Maybe, just maybe, she wouldn't do something stupid like walk outside.

The thought had no sooner crossed his mind than he heard the back door open, and he saw Eden step out onto the porch. She had a gun. A little Smith & Wesson that she'd probably had concealed somewhere on her body. He cursed again. Damn. He should have taken the time to frisk her.

Too late for that now, though.

Declan caught the movement from the corner of his eye. From the guy with the rifle. The man stood. Not slow and easy, either. He flew to a standing position, and with that same lightning speed, he pivoted directly toward Declan.

And took aim.

"Get down!" Declan yelled to Eden.

He dived back behind the house, toward the porch and Eden, just as she dropped to the weathered wooden planks. She hadn't even gotten fully down when the sound blasted through the air.

A shot.

And it hadn't come from the direction of the rifleman but rather the west side of his property.

Where his brother had spotted the other gunman.

A jolt of fear went through Declan. Not for himself but for Wyatt. Maybe his brother had been ambushed, because that wasn't a shot fired from the Colt that Wyatt would almost certainly be carrying.

Declan turned and tried to pick through the woods to see if he could spot the shooter. But there came another blast. And another. Not from the west this time.

The shots slammed into the side of his house and porch.

Hell.

Eden and he were caught in the crossfire of a gun-fight.

Chapter Four

Eden's heart slammed against her chest. The blasts from those shots roared through her entire body. And she wasn't sure what she should do to get herself out of the line of fire.

Declan made the decision for her.

He took hold of her arm and dragged her off the porch and onto the steps, just inches from where he was trying to watch both the back and side of the house. Eden kept a firm grip on her backup weapon, and even though she landed in a sprawl, she levered herself up enough so that she could take aim.

"Don't shoot," Declan snarled, snagging her hand again. "My brother's out there."

Yes, but out there where? Eden's gaze fired all around them, but she couldn't see his brother or the shooters, only the bullets as they pelted into the frozen ground and porch.

"How soon before your brother can move closer and help us get out of this?" she asked.

"Maybe not soon enough." Declan turned slightly and fired a shot in the direction of the gunman in the tree. "Why the hell did you come out here anyway?"

Her heart was pounding in her ears, and it took her

a few seconds to actually hear that question. "Because I don't trust you."

The glance he gave her could have frozen fire. "The feeling's mutual, darlin'."

That wasn't exactly a surprise—and *darlin'* wasn't a term of endearment—but Eden had had no choice about what she'd done. If she hadn't come here, the man behind this would have no doubt just sent someone else. Someone who would have gone through with the job, leaving her in danger with the militia groups.

"And I came out here because I thought I could help," she added. "I didn't think it was fair for me to be tucked away inside while you fought this fight for me."

He made another of those sarcastic sounds. "I'm not doing it for you. Might not have noticed, but they're shooting at me, too. And my brother. That makes this my fight." And he fired another shot.

The gunman retaliated. His next shot smacked into the corner of the house, causing Declan to curse and haul her closer to him. He practically climbed on top of her, shielding her with his body. It was his training that'd kicked in, no doubt, because after everything that'd just gone on inside his house, there's no way he'd truly want to protect her.

Unless it was just so he could interrogate her.

Yes, that had to be it.

He'd want the truth. Heck, so did she, and he wasn't going to be pleased when he realized she didn't have it. First, though, they had to survive this, and the way the bullets were coming at them, that might not happen.

The new position with Declan was far from comfortable. Her pressed against the icy ground. Him pressed against her. Every muscle in his body was tight and primed.

The shooter in the tree fired more shots, but in the mix of those battering sounds, Eden heard a different shot. Declan no doubt heard it as well, because his attention shifted from the front to the back. He didn't fire. He just lay there, waiting.

It didn't take long for Eden to realize the gunman at the back of the property was no longer firing. Unlike the tree shooter. That guy picked up the pace, the shots coming at them nonstop.

Declan and she needed to move, since the bullets were tearing their way through the side of the house. Soon the wooden planks wouldn't provide any cover for them at all. But they probably shouldn't move onto the porch, not with the other gunman still out back.

Except he wasn't shooting.

No one back there was.

Still, Declan didn't budge. Didn't return fire, either. Maybe because he was running low on ammunition.

His phone buzzed, and without taking his attention off the gunman, Declan pressed the button to answer it. He didn't put the call on speaker, but Eden was close enough to hear his brother Wyatt.

"The gunman back here is down," Wyatt said. "I'm moving closer to check and see if he's alive. Don't think he is, though."

Declan clipped off most of the groan that left his mouth. "Get to him fast, and if there's an ounce of breath left in him, make him talk. I'm moving my *visitor* back inside."

And that was exactly what Declan started to do the moment he ended the call. He fired a shot at the gunman, hauled Eden to her feet and they scrambled across the porch and back into the house. Once they were inside, he pointed to the sofa.

"Get behind that and stay there," Declan ordered, and there was no mistaking that it was an order. He hurried back to the window, the broken glass crunching beneath his boots.

Eden did get behind the sofa, but she hated that Declan was the one taking the risks here. They were in this mess together, and she only wished she'd been able to figure out a way to diffuse this before it had ever started.

She thought of her sisters. Of the danger they were in, too. They didn't deserve this. Neither did she. The sins of the father were coming at them with a vengeance.

Maybe.

And maybe this had more to do with Declan.

Maybe this had nothing to do with her at all. Or her father. Maybe there was some other connection between Declan and her that she'd missed. Once they were out of this, she had to beef up security for her sisters and do some more digging, because there were a lot of unanswered questions.

"Hell," Declan grumbled. He fired out the gaping holes in the window where there'd once been glass. And he cursed again. He shot her a glance from over his shoulder. "Stay here, and this time you'd better do it."

Eden shook her head. "You're not going back out there."

"The gunman's getting away."

No, that couldn't happen. Especially if the other gunman was dead. They needed this one alive so they could question him and learn who'd hired him to do this. And why. If he got away, Eden figured it wouldn't be the end of it. The guy's boss would just regroup and launch another attack. And this time, she might not be able to protect her family.

Still, she didn't want Declan shot, or worse.

She was about to offer backup again, which she knew he'd refuse, but Eden didn't even get to make the offer. Declan ran out of the room, and a moment later she heard him leave through the back door.

Eden held her breath and tried to pick through the sounds around her—the ticking clock on the mantel, the wind outside, her own body shivering from the cold that was pouring in through the window—and she heard footsteps on the back porch. In case it wasn't Declan, she turned in that direction. Aimed her gun. And tried to brace herself for whatever might happen.

It was entirely possible that the gunman wasn't getting away at all but would backtrack and come through that front door. She knew for a fact that it wasn't locked. Neither door had been when she'd arrived at the place earlier. Obviously, Declan hadn't been concerned about security.

He would be now.

If he survived this, that is.

The sound of the shot blasting through the air caused her fear to spike. She was pretty sure it hadn't come from Declan's gun but rather their attacker's. And it sounded close. That meant the man likely hadn't escaped after all, that instead he'd just changed positions so that he could ambush Declan.

"You okay, Declan?" someone shouted. Probably Wyatt.

Declan didn't answer, and that didn't help the fear roaring through her. Despite his order for her to stay put, Eden stayed crouched down, but she made her way to the window. It took her several heart-stopping moments before she caught just a glimpse of Declan. He peered around the edge of the house before he snapped back out of sight.

For a good reason.

Another shot. This one took out a chunk of the house right where Declan was.

Eden got her gun ready, and her gaze fired all around in an effort to see what she could of the house and grounds. She still didn't see the shooter, but judging from the angle of that last shot, he was somewhere near Declan's black truck. It was certainly large enough to conceal a man and give him decent cover, but the guy might also use it to escape.

She caught some movement from the corner of her eye. Not Declan. Not by the truck, either. This was on the other side of the yard near a cluster of cottonwoods with their winter-bare branches. Someone was behind the trunk of the largest tree, and even though she only got a glimpse of him, she thought it might be Wyatt. She hoped so anyway.

The shots stopped, and quiet settled in. Declan didn't come out from cover. Neither did the shooter or the other man behind the cottonwood. The deafening shots had been bad enough, but the silence allowed her to think, and the only thing she could think about was just how deadly this had turned and how much worse it could get.

And then the silence shattered.

Declan shouted something, and he bolted out from the side of the house. Not standing up, either. He was on the ground and slid forward on the ice-crusted grass. Aiming low, he fired.

On the other side of the yard, the man behind the cottonwood did the same.

Both shots went in the direction of the truck. But not through it, beneath it. She heard the gunman howl in pain.

"Drop your weapon!" Declan shouted. He got to his feet and, using the trees for cover, he made his way closer to the truck.

It seemed to take an eternity, but the gunman finally limped out while he held on to the truck. Probably because, from what she could tell, he'd been shot in his lower left leg and upper right thigh. He threw his rifle onto the ground and lifted his left hand in the air.

"I need a doctor, quick." The gunman's voice was a hoarse growl and didn't mask the pain.

His injuries didn't seem to be life threatening, but he was bleeding. Eden didn't have much sympathy for someone who'd just tried to kill them, but she wanted him alive. And talking.

The gunman was wearing dark clothes and a stocking cap, but she could see his face now. He was heavily muscled and had a wide nose that appeared to have been broken a couple of times. Part of her had hoped she might recognize him. A former disgruntled client, maybe. Or someone associated with her father. But no. He was a stranger.

"Call an ambulance," Declan instructed Wyatt.

His brother stepped fully out from the cottonwood and took out his phone.

"Why are you here?" Declan asked the man. He kept his gun trained on him and walked closer.

"I'm on orders." The man caught onto the truck with both hands, and that answer seemed to take a lot of effort. But at least now they knew he was a hired gun.

Well, unless he was lying.

Declan inched closer to the man. Wyatt, too, after he put his phone back in his pocket.

"The ambulance is on the way," Wyatt relayed. "But my advice is for you to start talking."

The man glanced around as if trying to figure out what to do. She prayed he didn't try to pick up his gun and attempt an escape. It'd be suicide with two armed marshals closing in on him.

"Talking wouldn't be good for my health," he answered. "Call that ambulance and tell them to hurry up."

Wyatt didn't make an attempt to do that. Both Declan and he moved forward, both still using the trees as cover until they reached the clearing between the truck and them. The gunman didn't appear to have any other weapons, but maybe Declan and Wyatt would stay put until the ambulance arrived. The thought had no sooner crossed her mind than she heard the sound.

Another blast.

Definitely a gunshot, but this one seemed to come out of nowhere. Eden shouted for Declan and his brother to get down, but her warning wasn't necessary. They were already headed to the ground anyway, but they hadn't managed to do that before there was another shot.

Then another.

Eden sucked in her breath hard, and with her gun gripped in her hand, she pivoted from one side to the other, bracing herself to see the shots slam into either Declan or Wyatt. Or both.

But that didn't happen.

The gunman by the truck lurched forward, the impact of the bullets jolting through his body. It all happened in a split second, but he crumpled into a heap on the ground.

"Someone shot him," she mumbled. And that someone wasn't Declan or his brother.

"Who the hell fired those shots?" Declan asked.

But Wyatt only shook his head. "Not the guy in the back, because he's dead. I had to shoot him."

Eden got ready to return fire. Wyatt and Declan did the same, but there were no more shots. In fact, there was no sign of the person who'd just shot the gunman.

But there was another sound.

The roar of a car engine. It was on the west side of the property. Probably on the old ranch trail. Eden knew it was there because that was where she'd left her own vehicle.

"He's getting away!" Declan shouted, and he raced in the direction of the sound.

That brought Eden back onto the porch, and she eased out into the yard, following Wyatt.

Toward the downed gunman.

Wyatt made it to the man first, and he stooped down, put his fingers to the man's neck. Because of the angle of his face, Eden couldn't see his expression, but she got a clear view of Declan's when he started running back toward them.

Declan kept watch behind him, but he took out his phone and requested assistance. The ranch trail led to the main road, and he asked for someone to respond to that area immediately. He didn't stop there. He hauled her behind the truck. Probably because he didn't want her out in the open in case that gunman returned.

Wyatt met his brother's gaze before he moved away from the man on the ground. "He's dead."

Declan mumbled something she didn't catch, but she didn't need to hear it to see the frustration in his eyes and face. "You're sure the other gunman is dead, too?"

Wyatt nodded. "There was no ID on him. Nothing except extra ammo…and a note."

That snagged both Declan's and her attention. "What kind of note?" Declan asked.

Eden figured that whatever it was, it couldn't be good. Hired killers didn't usually bring happy news.

"It's a single sheet of paper, folded. It was sticking out of the guy's pocket, but I looked at it when I saw Kirby's name scrawled on the outside."

"Why would a hired gun have a note addressed to your father?" she asked at the same time Declan asked, "What did the note say?"

Wyatt pulled in a long breath. "It didn't make sense. It said something like, 'This is just the beginning. You can't save him.'"

Declan shook his head. "Who's *him?*"

Wyatt met his gaze. "*You,* Declan."

Chapter Five

Declan slipped on the latex gloves that he'd taken from his equipment bag at his house, stooped down and pulled the note from the dead man's pocket. Yeah, it was addressed to Kirby all right.

"Is it really a death threat?" Eden asked. She was right behind him, peering over his shoulder. And she was shaking. Not just her voice, her whole body was trembling.

He figured Wyatt hadn't gotten the contents of the message wrong, but Declan had to see it for himself. There wasn't much to read.

This is just the beginning, Kirby Granger. You can't save him. O'Malley's a dead man.

It'd been handwritten almost in a childish scrawl with green crayon. Maybe as an attempt to disguise any handwriting characteristics. But Declan would have it analyzed anyway. He slipped it into a plastic evidence bag.

"Why does someone want you dead?" Eden asked.

She'd only been around him for the past couple of hours, and she'd already asked him that several times. Too bad it was a question he didn't have an answer for.

He stood and started back toward his house, where

the chaos was in full swing. A different kind of chaos from the attack. The crime-scene folks had arrived. Two of his brothers, Dallas and Slade. Sheriff Rico Geary and his deputies, too. It wasn't exactly a local case what with the attempted murder of two federal marshals, but Geary had people in place to preserve the crime scene. Plus, the sheriff wouldn't do anything to keep Declan and his brothers out of any part of this investigation.

Not that he could have anyway.

Declan wasn't sure what'd happened here, but he would find out, one way or another. Apparently, Eden had the same idea, because she'd been on and off her phone since the attack. All of this was just for starters. Declan wanted to question Eden a lot more so he could try to pinpoint the person who'd set all of this in motion.

Maybe she knew.

Maybe she didn't.

He was leaning toward *didn't* since she'd nearly been killed. Most people didn't protect a person who wanted them dead. And besides, she was genuinely worried about her two sisters, since most of her calls had centered on arranging extra protection for them. Declan would add his own layer of protection soon by calling the marshals in that area.

"This is connected to your foster father," Eden said, falling into step beside him. "The note proves that."

"No. The note proves nothing. Someone could have written it to muddy the waters."

She made a slight sound of surprise, then frustration. Maybe because she hadn't thought of that angle first. Still, Declan couldn't take his muddy-water theory as gospel, and that meant talking to Kirby. Maybe there was something that connected all three of them— Eden, Kirby and him. Something linked to the photo of

him and his family back in Germany. And Declan had
a sickening feeling that it was a connection he wasn't
going to like.

"Thank you," she said in a hoarse whisper. "For saving my life."

Declan just gave a noncommittal grunt. He couldn't
issue a standard "you're welcome" without choking on
it, because he'd told her to stay put and she hadn't.

Yeah, she was hardheaded all right. And up to her
pretty neck in danger. A real bad combination. She had
just enough guts and skills to get herself killed. Him,
too, since his stupid body had decided to protect her.
But then, protecting her was the only way to get those
answers.

When they reached the front of his house, he saw
the medical examiner's crew loading the dead gunman
into their van. The guy had the two gunshot wounds to
the legs that Wyatt and he had given him. But it was the
gaping hole in the back of his head that'd done him in.

"Not an amateur's shot," Declan mumbled.

Wyatt nodded in agreement and pointed to the woods
directly ahead. They were thick and dark despite the
lack of leaves. "Dallas and Slade are down there having a look around."

Because it was probably where a rifleman had positioned himself to kill the gunman.

A hit man for the hit man.

Sometimes, karma worked. But in this case, it hadn't
worked in Declan's favor.

"Any sign of the shooter?" Eden asked.

"None." Wyatt clearly wasn't happy about that, either.
Neither was Declan. But they'd gotten someone out to
the area as fast as possible and had simply missed the
guy. Of course, if he was a pro, and Declan was pretty

sure he was, then he would have had his escape route well planned out.

"There are some tire tracks," Wyatt went on. "We'll do castings of those."

It was all standard procedure, but standard didn't seem like nearly enough.

"Maybe we're dealing with two factions here," Eden said. "Someone's trying to kill Declan and someone else is trying to protect him."

"Or someone didn't want the gunman to talk," Wyatt supplied.

Declan was leaning toward that theory. And it meant the person behind this really didn't want his or her identity revealed and wasn't willing to risk a hired gun running his mouth.

"I'll do mop-up," Wyatt assured him, and the sheriff added his nod to that. Wyatt motioned for Declan to hand him the evidence bag with the note inside.

Declan hated to leave his brothers with the chore of processing a crime scene this big, and this personal, but there were other things that needed to be done. Plus, Eden's trembling was getting worse with every passing second, and soon the adrenaline crash would hit her hard. Him, too. But at least he had some experience dealing with it. He was betting she didn't.

"Come on," Declan insisted.

But Eden held her ground when he tried to help her into the truck. "My car's on the back trail, and I need to leave to check on my sisters."

He looked her straight in the eye. "And what happens if the gunman comes after you when you're with them, huh?"

She flinched, then quickly recovered. "The gunman will more likely come after you."

"After *us*," he corrected. "For whatever reason, someone involved you in this, and you're not leaving my sight until I find out why. There's also the part about you coming here to pretend to kill me."

She budged, but after he practically pushed her into the cab of his truck. "You think I'm lying about being blackmailed into doing this?"

Declan shrugged, got in and drove away. "Not lying exactly, but maybe not telling me the whole truth."

"I don't know the whole truth," she practically shouted. She groaned, a sound of pure frustration, and she yanked on her seat belt. "I just know I don't want to be involved with this. Or with you."

She stumbled over the last word, causing Declan to glance at her. There was just another of those disturbing split-second glances where he saw the unguarded expression in those baby blues. There was fear in her eyes. But something else.

Great.

It was the kind of look a woman gave a man. Not one she was hired to kill, either. It was a look that smacked of attraction, and it made Declan curse.

Because he was feeling it, too.

As soon as he figured out how, he was going to make it go away. He didn't need the kind of trouble that Eden Gray brought with her. Especially since he'd been the one to arrest her father. Even though she didn't appear to be holding any grudges about that, maybe those blue eyes were concealing things well hidden.

She looked away from him. "Where are you taking me?"

"Since the EMTs are going to be tied up with the gunmen for a while, first stop is the hospital. You should be checked out by the doctor, and Kirby's there. He was a little weak after his last cancer treatment, and they decided to keep him a day or two."

"I'm sorry. How sick is he?"

"Sick," Declan settled for saying, and it was all he intended to say on the matter. Kirby could be dying, and there was nothing he could do about it.

"Maybe questioning him is a bad idea then," she added.

Yeah, it was. Kirby didn't need this while he was trying to recover, but there was no way to keep the news of the gunfight from him. Even while he was in the hospital. Someone would let it slip, and Kirby would be furious that he hadn't heard it from Declan. Besides, Kirby might be able to shed some light on the note.

"I don't need to see a doctor," she said. She reached out and touched his chin. "But you should."

Declan hadn't been expecting that touch, and he actually flinched. First, from the contact. Then the little zing of pain as her fingers grazed his skin. When Eden drew back her fingers, he saw the blood.

"You might need stitches," she suggested.

He jerked down the visor with the vanity mirror and had a look. Yeah, his chin was cut all right, but there was no way he'd take the time to get stitches. He reached over to the glove compartment, the back of his hand brushing against Eden's jeans-clad leg, and this time she was the one who flinched.

"Good grief," she mumbled. "What's wrong with us?"

Oh, she knew what.

So did he.

"My advice?" He took some tissues from the glove compartment and pressed them against his chin. "Pretend it's not there." Since she didn't question what *it* was, he figured they were on the same page.

Talk about lousy timing.

And bad judgment.

Of course, that idiot part of him behind his jeans' zipper was a bad-judgment magnet. He had a way of hooking up with women who could give him the most amount of trouble in the least amount of time.

The most fun, too.

Still, this went beyond his fondness for bad girls whose middles names were Trouble. Because this bad girl had been sent to kill him.

"Any chance your father's behind this?" Declan came right out and asked. He expected her to have a quick denial and figured she wouldn't admit that Zander Gray would try to kill his own daughter.

"There's no way he would put me at risk like this." She paused. "But he hates you. A lot. And he blames you for his arrest."

"He should blame himself. He's the one who tried to murder a witness."

"He said he was innocent and I believe him."

Not exactly a surprise. "Well, I'm just as adamant that he's as guilty as sin." Declan took the final turn toward town. "Would he include you in any plan to get revenge against me?"

He looked for any signs that she'd been lying, that she'd been in on this plan from the beginning—all to help her father get back at him.

"No." There was just a slight hesitation before she repeated it.

Maybe she wasn't as certain as she wanted to seem. Declan sure wasn't, and her father gave them a starting point. But before trying to track down the man who'd been a fugitive for months, he needed to deal with the note.

Well, maybe.

It was possible that Kirby would be too weak to talk. Still, he could at least have Eden checked out to make sure she was okay. He didn't see any cuts or bruises, but she'd hit the ground pretty hard when he had dragged her off the porch and away from those bullets.

He pulled into the parking lot of the hospital and looked around to make sure they hadn't been followed. Something he'd done on the entire drive. The missing gunman probably wouldn't choose Main Street for an attack, but Declan didn't want to take any chances.

"This way." He led Eden through a side door for one of the clinics located in the hospital. It was an entrance he and his brothers had been using a lot lately so they wouldn't have to go through the newly installed metal detectors and disarm. With Kirby's frequent stays in the hospital, it saved all of them some time.

Declan wound through the maze of corridors, and when he got to the wing with Kirby's room, he spotted his brother Harlan in the hall. He was pacing and talking on the phone, but he ended the call when he saw Declan.

"My brother, Marshal Harlan McKinney," Declan said, making introductions. "And this is Eden Gray."

"Yeah. I just did a background check on her." Harlan stared at her. Nope, glared. "She's a P.I. all right, but she's also—"

"Zander Gray's daughter," she finished for him. She extended her hand, waited, until Harlan shook it. His brother was intimidating with his linebacker-size shoulders and dark, edgy looks, but Eden didn't back down. Maybe because she'd already faced worse today. Even Harlan wasn't worse than flying bullets.

Harlan's gaze shifted to Declan, and he took out his phone to scroll through what was on the screen. "She's twenty-nine, single, owns the Gray Agency, but she's the only full-time employee. Last night, she went to the prison to visit her father's former cellmate."

Now it was Declan's turn to glare at her.

"I didn't speak to him," Eden quickly explained. "He refused to see me. But I wanted to ask him if he knew my father's whereabouts. I wanted to find out if my father knew anything about the bogus info planted on my computer."

Since Harlan likely didn't know anything about that yet, Declan finished the explanation for her. "We need to get a tech into her computer system."

She was shaking her head before he even finished. "If you do that, the info will be leaked, and it'll cause the two opposing militia factions to come after me."

Harlan looked at him to no doubt see if he was buying this. Unfortunately, he was. It wasn't that hard to hack into a computer, plant info and change the password. It wasn't that hard to rile militia groups, either. But the problem was that still didn't give them answers about who was behind this and why. It was a lot of effort, and it'd taken money to hire a computer hacker, the photographer who'd gobbled up those pictures of him and the three gunmen.

"I need to talk to Kirby about the note on the dead gunman," Declan said. Yeah, he was avoiding any further discussion about Eden's innocence—or lack thereof—so he could move on to something that had to be done.

Harlan nodded eventually. But Declan could tell his brother didn't approve. None of them wanted to do anything to make Kirby's situation worse, and this might qualify as worse.

"And I'll see what I can do about getting the info erased from her computer," Harlan offered.

"Thanks. Could you also take Eden to Dr. Landry so she can be checked out?"

"Eden?" Harlan obviously didn't like Declan's use of her given name, either.

But Eden clearly didn't like the checkup suggestion. "I want to hear what your foster father has to say."

Declan would have given her a firm no, but the door to Kirby's room opened and Stella Doyle stepped out. She was a fixture around Kirby these days.

"I heard voices," Stella said, and her attention zoomed in on the cut on Declan's chin. "Are you all right? Were you hurt?" And that concern extended to Eden when Stella's gaze shifted in her direction.

"We're fine," Declan lied. As he'd done with Harlan, he made introductions.

"You worked at the Rocky Creek Children's Facility," Eden said to Stella. "I read through everything I could find about you, and the others."

"I did work there," Stella confirmed. "A bad place. Bad times, too."

Harlan's phone buzzed and he stepped to the side to take the call. A moment later, he took out a small notepad from his pocket and started writing.

Stella glanced behind her at Kirby. Declan glanced, too, and didn't like what he saw. Kirby was hooked up to several machines, and he seemed paler than he had been lately. And he'd been pretty darn pale. His eyes were also closed, and his breathing was shallow.

"How is he?" Declan asked.

Stella studied his expression. Then Eden's. "Not strong enough for bad news. Is that what you brought with you?"

"Maybe. There was a note addressed to Kirby in the dead hit man's pocket. It said 'This is just the beginning,

Kirby Granger. You can't save him. O'Malley's a dead man.' I need to ask Kirby if he knows what it means."

Stella's hand moved to her mouth, but he still heard the sharp gasp she made, and her eyes widened. For just a second. Then she cleared her throat. But Declan didn't think it was his imagination that she was fighting to hang on to her composure along with something she didn't want him to know.

Hell.

He was tired of people keeping things from him. First Eden. Now, apparently, Stella.

"Who wrote that?" Stella demanded. She stepped out into the hall and shut Kirby's door.

Declan shook his head. "I don't know. That's why we're here."

"You can't ask him." Stella said it so fast that her words ran together, but then her demand came to a grinding halt. "If Kirby were to find out that someone wants you dead, it might break him. He's barely hanging on now, Declan. Fighting, yes. But I don't have to tell you that it's a fight he might lose."

No, she didn't have to tell him. That fear was always there, not on the back burner but rather in the front of his mind. However, he still had the feeling that Stella wasn't telling him everything.

But what?

He trusted her. Well, for the most part. He had yet to rule her out as a suspect in Jonah Webb's murder. All of them had motive, since Webb was physically abusing Declan and plenty of the other kids. And with Stella working there and seeing the abuse, she might have helped Webb's wife murder him and hide the body.

Of course, Kirby could have done it, too.

Or any of his brothers.

Still, Declan wasn't about to press them on that subject. Webb had deserved everything he got, and if Stella had helped deliver the fatal blow, then he wasn't going to be the one to arrest her.

"When Kirby wakes up," Stella said, her voice a little uneven, "I'll tell him about the note. But I'll leave out the part about your being a dead man."

"Thanks."

Even though it was the best they could do right now, Eden looked as if she wanted to press matters. She volleyed her attention between Stella, him and the door to Kirby's room. But she finally just huffed and dropped back a step.

"You look tuckered out," Stella said, giving Eden's arm a gentle rub. "Why don't you have Declan take you somewhere so you can get some rest."

Eden shook her head. "Thanks, but I don't want to rest."

Yeah, but Declan figured she needed it. After the hellish morning they'd had, they both needed it, but getting it probably wouldn't happen.

"Who's at the ranch?" Declan asked.

"None of the family," Stella answered. "Everyone's either tied up with the shooting or with other work. Lenora, Joelle, Caitlyn and Maya all went to San Antonio for a big Christmas-shopping trip. They took the babies with them. Won't be back until sometime tomorrow."

His sisters-in-law and three nephews. And it was good that they weren't at the ranch, since that was where he might eventually take Eden to regroup and try to figure out who'd put that information on her computer. That was the starting point anyway.

"I should go back in with Kirby," Stella added. "I'll

let you know what he says when I can ask him about the note."

Declan nodded, thanked her. Her offer seemed right, but there was something a little off with the tone of her voice. Maybe because she dreaded telling Kirby about the attack. And she would have to tell him. It didn't matter how little info Stella gave him, Kirby would piece it together, and he would demand to know everything that was going on.

Harlan finished his call, and before he made his way back to them, Declan knew something was wrong. Harlan always wore a bad-news expression, but it was even worse now.

His brother pulled in a long breath. "First, the FBI techs used remote access from Quantico and managed to get the planted information off Eden's computer. Well, actually, they confiscated everything on the hard drive and server so it can't be leaked."

That was better than good news. They darn sure didn't need the militia groups adding more danger to this already dangerous mess.

"They managed to do that fast," Eden said, shaking her head. "If I'd called them first—"

"These men would have just hired someone else to come after me," Declan interrupted. Besides, he didn't want the FBI involved other than to erase the computer info. Not with so many clues pointing right back to Kirby.

And possibly the Webb murder.

"And what's the bad news?" Declan asked his brother.

Harlan didn't deny there was some, and his mumbled profanity confirmed it. "We have the identities of the two dead gunmen. Howard Starling and Neil Packard."

Declan looked at Eden, but she only shook her head. "I don't recognize either name. Who are they?"

"Hired muscle." Harlan looked at his notes. "And they've worked for a variety of criminals in high and low places."

"Anyone we know?" Declan asked.

"Yeah." He turned the note for them to read. There were nearly a dozen names on the list, but Harlan tapped the last one. "But I think you'll agree that this is the man who hired them to kill you."

Chapter Six

Eden braced herself for the name of the person that Harlan was pointing out to them, but when she saw it, she had to groan. "Leonard Kane."

Unfortunately, it was someone she recognized. And one she didn't want on that list because it was a connection that led right back to her.

"He was your father's former business partner," Harlan said, and it sounded like some kind of accusation against her. Declan didn't echo the accusation, but he did stare at her, and he obviously wanted yet more information that she just didn't have.

"My father had a lot of business partners," she explained. "And besides, Leonard and he had a major falling-out years ago. Long before you arrested him and his escape from jail. Leonard believes my father backstabbed him on a business deal, one that ended up costing Leonard a great deal of money."

Declan's stare didn't let up one bit. "Rifts can be mended, and they could have teamed up to put together that attack today."

But that didn't make sense.

"Why come after us now?" she asked. "I mean, Declan arrested my father over three years ago. Why wait all this time to settle old scores? And why include me in any part of it? I didn't have anything to do with those business dealings."

"Maybe Leonard didn't have the resources in place three years ago to do this," Declan readily answered. Then he shook his head. "But it feels like more than that. If the idea is to get even with both of us, why not just shoot and kill us?"

That sent a shiver through her. It wasn't exactly a comforting thought that someone could have put a bullet in her at any time. Declan, too. After all, those pictures someone had taken of him could have been a gunman firing bullets. But while there was bad blood between Declan and her father—Declan and her, too—her father wouldn't do this.

Leonard was another matter.

"Maybe this is Leonard's way of getting back at my father. He could be trying to torment us," she suggested. "A cat-and-mouse game."

"But the game could have ended today with those shots," Harlan pointed out.

Declan shook his head again. "I'm not sure the attack was supposed to go down like that. Maybe that's why someone took out the shooter."

It made sense. Well, as much sense as this whole puzzling situation could make. But if the intent was only to torment them, why link Declan and her together? The torment could have happened without hacking into her computer and blackmailing her into attempted murder.

"I'll see about getting Leonard in for questioning," Harlan volunteered. "I can run a deep background check, too. What about Dr. Landry? You still want her to check out Eden?" He said her name with slightly less disdain this time. Perhaps because Declan's brother was beginning to believe she was innocent in all of this.

And Eden prayed she was.

She hadn't done anything intentionally to make this happen, but the connection to Leonard and her father was just plain unnerving. Especially since Leonard hated her father and vice versa.

"I don't want to see the doctor," Eden insisted. She had much more important things to do, so she took out her phone. "I do want to check on my sisters, though. And my car, which I left near Declan's."

"I'll arrange to have the car brought to the ranch," Declan told her. "After it's been checked for bugs and tracking devices."

It was a good idea, and something she wished she'd thought of. Her mind was so fuzzy now. Definitely not what she needed, because a fuzzy head could get her killed. Declan, too.

"And as for talking to your sisters, don't use your cell," Declan went on. "If the hacker was skilled enough to get into your computer, he could just as easily trace your phone. It's probably not a good idea for that missing gunman to be able to keep tabs on you."

Something else she hadn't considered but should have.

"I'll have someone check on the security arrangements for her sisters," Harlan continued. He glanced at the exit. "Best if you two don't hang around here much longer."

Because the gunman could track them there. If that was indeed what the missing man wanted to do. But something else occurred to her. If the gunman did track them here to the hospital, then it could put other members of Declan's foster family in danger. She didn't want that. There'd already been enough danger for one day.

"I'll take Eden to the marshals' office so we can make

our statements about the shooting." Declan looked at her. "After that, we'll go to the ranch."

"No," she immediately protested. "No need to take this fight there."

"It's the safest place to take it." But then Declan shrugged. "Maybe. I guess that depends on what we learn in the next couple of hours."

Yes, and she prayed there wouldn't be another attack on them or on anyone else. But she had a horrible feeling that the attacks would just continue until they stopped the person behind them.

"I'll keep you posted on whatever I get," Harlan added, and Declan led her back down the hall and out the side door where they'd entered.

The blast of cold hit her the moment they stepped outside, and Eden started shivering. By the time they'd made it across the parking lot to his truck, she was past the shivering stage, and her teeth were chattering.

"It's the adrenaline crash," Declan said, and he turned the heater on full blast. He also looked around. One of those sweeping glances that cops did when they were making sure everything was safe.

Of course, everything wasn't safe.

The realization of that hit her hard, and the sound of those gunshots started to roar through her head. That didn't help the shivering, either. "Just give me a second. I don't want to go into the marshals' building like this."

"Everybody there has seen worse." Declan rummaged behind his seat and came up with a plaid wool blanket. "It's probably been on the horses, but at least it'll keep you warm. Or not," he added when she just kept shaking.

She hugged the blanket to her. Yes, it'd been on the horses. She didn't mind the scent, but the extra layer of warmth still gave her no relief. Even worse, her eyes started to water.

Good grief.

She didn't need this. Neither did Declan. Falling apart would only make things worse.

"Hell," he said under his breath, and he hooked his arm around her and dragged her closer to him. "There's a middle seat belt. Use it."

She did, somehow managing to get it on while Declan drove out of the hospital parking lot. He kept his arm around her. Kept her close, too. Shoulder to shoulder and so snug against him that she caught his scent. Not the horse scent on the blanket, but Declan's. It sent a trickle of heat through her that her body welcomed but she certainly didn't.

Because that heat was a huge problem.

He glanced at her. Frowned. "Now you're breathing too fast and your face is flushed. If this keeps up, I'm turning around and taking you back to see the doctor."

"You're causing the fast breath." She kept her voice at a whisper, but he heard her anyway.

His frown got worse. His eyes narrowed a bit. "I think we can both agree that nothing should happen between us."

She nodded. But that *should* was still lingering in the air between them. The heat from the attraction, too.

"I don't have sex with women like you," he added. Then cursed. "That's a lie. You're exactly the kind I take to my bed."

Her breathing went from fast to warp speed. That wasn't the right thing to admit to her. Especially not now. "It doesn't matter that I'm your usual type, because I'm still the wrong woman."

"You got it." He flashed a half smile that melted the

ball of ice in her stomach. "But then, I'm the wrong man for you." No half smile now. "And I'm pretty sure in a stupid-sex world, that makes this one of those irresistible situations we're just going to have to resist. Or at least keep reminding ourselves to resist."

Yes. She wondered, though, if a reminder would be just a waste of mental energy. "I don't want to find you attractive." But she did. Mercy, did she. On a scale of one to ten, he was a six hundred, and even with the danger, he fired every nerve in her body.

"Ditto," he snarled. "Don't want it, but you are. In fact, you've got those bad-girl eyes."

She frowned. "They're blue."

"They're bedroom eyes. But it's not the eyes that have me cursing. It's the rest of you." He glanced down to where they made contact. Specifically at the way her breast was right against his chest.

"Yes," she agreed. Even though it was something she should keep to herself, she didn't. "The rest of you is causing problems for me, too."

And that was why Eden leaned away from him. She instantly felt the loss of warmth from his body, but she kept the inch or so of space between them.

Declan didn't say another word, and didn't move her back toward him, either, thank goodness. He just drove down Main Street until he turned into the parking lot of the marshals' building. He looked around again, and Eden ditched the blanket before they hurried inside.

Bedroom eyes, indeed. Better than his bedroom body. And she pushed that uneasy thought and images aside so she could face what would no doubt be another ordeal.

They went through security and reception, then up the stairs to a maze of office cubicles and desks. The moment they stepped inside, Declan's attention zoomed across the room to a tall, lanky marshal who was on the phone. She recognized him as Marshal Dallas Walker, Declan's foster brother. He held his finger up in a wait-a-second gesture and then quickly ended the call.

"Please tell me someone caught the gunman," Declan said.

But Dallas only shook his head. "No gunman, but I just got an earful on our suspect, Leonard Kane." He stopped, looked at her. "Zander Gray's daughter, huh."

Not a question, and he didn't wait for her to confirm it. Eden could tell from his brusque tone that here was yet another foster brother who didn't like her. Or trust her.

"What about Leonard?" Declan prompted when his brother's glare lingered on her.

Dallas's gaze came back to Declan. "Over thirty years ago Kirby shot and killed Leonard's son, Corey, when he was evading arrest. Leonard vowed revenge and said he'd make Kirby pay by killing a son of his." Dallas looked at her again as if he expected her to have more information.

She didn't. "This is the first I'm hearing about this. But then, I haven't had any reason to dig into Leonard's background. Well, not before now anyway."

If either of them believed her, there was no sign of it in their expressions.

"Over thirty years ago?" Declan asked. "That's a long time to hold off on taking revenge."

"Yeah," Dallas agreed. "Leonard just got some bad news. He's dying. And not like Kirby's cancer. This is an inoperable brain tumor. He's got less than six months, and according to a criminal informant, Leonard's been cleaning house and tying up old loose ends. One of his former business partners was found dead a week ago."

Eden's stomach knotted. The news just kept getting worse. "Any way to link it to Leonard?"

"None so far. The man has plenty of money to cover his tracks." Wyatt paused. "I think Leonard's threat is clear, though, about going after Kirby's son."

"But he has six foster sons," Eden pointed out.

"Technically, Kirby has just five. He had to adopt one because of some legal technicalities that had to do with all that mess that happened at the Rocky Creek Children's Facility."

"Which one?"

"Me," Declan answered.

He didn't add anything else, but it was clear to Eden that there was something to add. She didn't like these secrets, whatever they were, but they had bigger fish to fry, and that fish's name was Leonard Kane.

"So Leonard wanted me to kill Declan to get back at Kirby," she concluded.

Dallas lifted his shoulder. "With your father, Zander, either dead or unwilling to surface, it's my guess that Leonard will want to take his revenge out on you."

That ice knot in her stomach returned with a vengeance. "Me?"

Dallas held up his phone for her to see. "The CSI found this on the windshield of your car."

Both Declan and she leaned in, their attention zooming to the photo of the message. It was short but definitely not sweet.

Your life for hers, Zander. Time's running out.

Chapter Seven

Declan downed the rest of his coffee and poured himself another cup. It was strong, but he wished it were a whole lot stronger. Because he was no doubt going to need it to get through this day.

"That was the crime lab," Wyatt said the moment he finished his latest call. He was at the kitchen table at the ranch with Declan, both of them with laptops in front of them while they read over reports and updates on the attack. "The only prints on the threatening notes were those of the dead gunmen."

It was exactly what Declan had expected. This had been a well-planned attack, and the person who'd orchestrated it wouldn't have wanted to leave incriminating evidence behind. Well, unless it incriminated the wrong person.

Is that what'd happened with the note left on Eden's car?

Your life for hers, Zander. Time's running out.

Even though it seemed to be a challenge for Zander, he could have written it himself to throw them off his trail. If there was a trail, that is. Even with all the resources of the FBI and the Marshals' Service, they hadn't been able to find hide nor hair of the man.

"No sign of the missing gunman," Wyatt added,

"though they're running the tire tracks to see if they can come up with a vehicle match."

They might get lucky. *Might*. But he figured they'd need more than luck to break this case.

Declan heard the sound of someone moving around upstairs. Eden, no doubt, since he'd given the house-keeper the day off. And with Stella and Kirby at the hospital and his sisters-in-law on their extended Christmas-shopping trip, Wyatt, Eden and he had the place to themselves. Best if it stayed that way for a while.

If he could convince Eden, that is.

She hadn't exactly been thrilled that he'd taken her to the ranch for the night, but after they'd given their statements about the shooting, she'd been past the point of exhaustion. And the bottom line was, the ranch had a decent security system and was well guarded by the ranch hands who knew how to use a gun.

"What are you going to do about her?" Wyatt asked, his attention drifting to the footsteps they could now hear on the stairs.

"Not sure." In fact, Declan wasn't sure of anything when it came to Eden, except that she seemed to be in as much danger as he was. Even if she hadn't been the target of yesterday's attack, those bullets could have killed her.

"You trust her?" his brother pressed.

"No." But then he stopped. Rethought it.

Hell. Yes, he did.

He didn't want to trust her, but apparently that whole damsel-in-distress, bedroom-eyes thing was playing into this. As was the attraction. He reminded himself that at-traction shouldn't equal trust. But it might take another bullet or two for that to sink in.

Eden hurried into the kitchen. Practically running.

And she also practically skidded to a stop when her gaze landed on Wyatt. Maybe because Wyatt was glaring at her again.

"Sorry," she mumbled. "I didn't mean to sleep in."

Since it was barely seven-thirty in the morning, that hardly qualified as sleeping in. Especially after everything they'd been through.

She was wearing jeans and a dark blue sweater that she'd obviously taken from the overnight bag Wyatt had retrieved from her car. No ball cap today. Her hair fell in a shiny tumble on her shoulders. She looked darn good for a woman who clearly hadn't rested as much as she should have. There were still dark circles beneath her eyes that her makeup hadn't hidden.

Declan caught a whiff of that girlie scent she'd had on the day before. "You okay?" he asked.

She nodded. "You?"

He returned the nod, though they both knew the nods were huge lies.

Wyatt's phone buzzed, and he frowned when he looked at the caller ID. "It's a personal call," he said, and he stood and left.

Declan flexed his eyebrows. "Personal," he repeated. He hadn't realized Wyatt was involved with anyone. But then, Wyatt had the rock-star looks of the family, so it wasn't exactly a surprise that he was in a relationship.

"What's going on with the investigation?" She motioned toward the coffeepot, Declan nodded and she poured herself a cup.

"Not much. What's going on with *your* investigation?" Declan waited until her gaze met his before he continued. "I heard you talking on the phone last night."

Actually, he'd heard a lot, since he was listening to make sure she didn't try to sneak out. He hadn't pegged her for reckless, but people did all sorts of crazy things when their lives were on the line.

"I didn't use my cell," Eden said a little defensively. "Just the landline that you said was secure." She paused. "I tried to track down my father."

"How? Because you said you had no idea where he was."

"I don't, but I have the names of the people he's done business with in the past. Plus, the names of a couple of old girlfriends." She shook her head. "All claimed they didn't know his whereabouts."

"You don't believe them?"

She took a big sip of the coffee as if it were the cure for all ills. "Hard to say. One of them might know, but I have to wonder why my father would let someone in on his location when he hadn't told his three daughters."

"Maybe he did tell one. Not you," he quickly added when she shot him a glare. "But one of your sisters."

Eden was shaking her head before he had even finished. "Too risky. They're young and might let something slip. No, if he'd told any of us, it would have been me."

Maybe Zander hadn't wanted to involve any of his girls. Of course, that was something a good father would do, and Declan wasn't about to put that *good* label on any part of Zander's life.

Declan took a notepad and pen and moved it to the empty space at the table that was nearest Eden. "Write down the names of everyone you contacted. I want to press them for info, too."

Her glare morphed to a flat look. "If they wouldn't tell me, they won't tell a marshal."

"I can be charming when I have to be." He let the sarcasm drip off that, but it had an unexpected response.

The corner of Eden's mouth lifted just a fraction. "Yes, you're charming all right."

The smile stayed in place for just a few seconds and then faded. She huffed and dropped down in the chair to start writing on the notepad. "Even if your charm works on these contacts, I don't want my father drawn out just to be killed. And I think we both know that's what this note writer wants to happen."

Oh, yeah. If the person who wrote that note was anyone but Zander, that was exactly what the threat had been designed to do. Draw him out. And not just Zander but Kirby, too.

That wasn't going to happen.

Kirby wasn't strong enough to face down a killer, and even if he were, Declan wouldn't let him. Still, that did lead to some interesting conclusions.

"Whoever wrote the two notes probably knows both Kirby and your father," he pointed out. "And the person wants to use us to get to them. *Us,*" he repeated. "Not your sisters and not my five foster brothers. Because so far, none of the others has been mentioned in any kind of threat."

Eden stopped writing. Met his gaze. "So that's where we start digging. Something that includes me, you, my father and Kirby."

Declan had already been thinking in that direction and had come up with nothing. But there was a long shot that might give them the connection. Or rather might give them Zander. "I want the press to publicize the last note, to bring your father out in the open. Wait," he had to add, because she started to object. "Not so he can be gunned down but so he can help us figure out who's behind the attack."

"And so you can arrest him."

Declan lifted his shoulder. "That, too. He's a fugitive, Eden. If he's alive, I can't just let him walk away."

"I can't let you use me to get to him," she argued.

"Too late." And yeah, this was about to get uglier. "The threat's going out." He checked his watch. "Has gone out," he amended. "The news shows and the papers have probably already picked up on it."

If looks could have maimed, he'd be hurting right about now, because that was how hard her glare was. She was no doubt about to give him a piece of her very angry mind, but Wyatt came back in the room. He glanced at both of them and could probably feel the thick tension between them.

Wyatt shook his head as if disgusted with both of them. "My advice? Stay away from each other."

Obviously, his brother thought this was about the attraction and not the press release. Declan was about to correct him, but Wyatt took his coat from the peg near the back door.

"I've arranged for relief for security detail for Kirby and Stella," Wyatt continued.

Good. He wanted the hospital manned 24/7 until Kirby was home. Then the extra security would be moved to the ranch. "You're not anticipating any trouble at the hospital, are you?" Because something had put that grim look on Wyatt's face.

"No. No problems there. But I need to go into the office and look at some reports." He paused. "Remember the fertility clinic where Ann and I stored our embryos before… Well, before?"

Ann was Wyatt's late wife, and she'd died two and a half years ago. And the *before* referred to when they'd stored the embryos before she'd started her treatment for a rare blood disorder. Treatments that could have left her infertile. Instead, the treatments had failed, and Wyatt had lost his wife.

"There was a theft at the clinic," Wyatt continued. "Several batches of embryos were stolen, including ours."

"Mercy." Eden stood. "Who'd steal embryos?"

Wyatt shrugged, and even though he looked calm on the surface, Declan could tell this was eating away at him. "Some of the embryos were being contested as part of a divorce settlement, and the San Antonio cops think maybe someone was hired to steal them but got ours instead."

So all a mix-up, except this mix-up was massive, since Wyatt had planned on hiring a surrogate so he could finally become the father he'd always wanted to be.

"You need help?" Declan asked.

"No. You've got enough on your plate." He gave them one last glance, and though Wyatt didn't say another word, Declan could hear the repeated warning: *Stay away from each other.* To start, Declan locked up behind Wyatt, and while keeping some distance between them, he looked at the list of names that Eden was writing. She hadn't jotted down her sisters, but he made a mental note to have someone question them about their father. Even if they didn't know anything directly, they might have pieces of info that could lead them to the truth.

"Those are my father's business associates that I called," Eden said, handing him the list. "Well, except for the last one. Janet Klein is an old girlfriend, but she said she hasn't seen him since he was arrested."

Declan knew the woman. He'd interviewed her numerous times after Zander's escape and had even put her under surveillance for a while. And though he believed

Janet was capable of lying—anyone close to Zander could be—he hadn't thought she was hiding her lover.

"All of this could be for nothing." Eden's voice dropped to a raspy whisper. "My father's probably dead anyway."

He was about to remind her that the threat indicated otherwise, but he rethought that. Any part of this could be designed to throw them off track. Like the picture from his childhood. Or the notes themselves. Someone might want them to believe that Zander was part of the danger, but he might be innocent.

Of this anyway.

She stood, brushed past him and went back to the coffeepot to refill her cup. Her hands still weren't too steady. Neither was the rest of her. And it might stay that way until the danger had passed.

"Maybe this is just about you and me," he said. "If someone wanted me dead, then they could have set up this plan to make sure it happened."

Eden sipped her coffee and looked at him from over the rim of her cup. "Same here. If I'd killed you, then I would have ended up in jail. Or killed by the militia group." She paused. "But both of us were supposed to have died in your house. Those gunmen were hired to kill us."

Declan groaned, scrubbed his hand over his face. "Yeah, and that brings us right back to square one."

Well, almost. The investigation was a wash, but now Eden and he were more or less joined at the hip. For him, it was more because he wanted to keep her close in case her father resurfaced.

Or the gunman.

But Declan knew an "or else" look when he saw it, and Eden was no doubt trying to figure out how to ditch him. Maybe because she didn't trust him. Or maybe because if given the chance, he would indeed arrest her father.

Their gazes met. Held. And not just a little holding, either. She finally huffed, "What will it take for you to believe me?"

Declan thought about it a moment. "It's not a matter of belief. It's a matter of whose side you'll choose when and if you figure out your father's behind this."

"If he's behind this, then I'm darn sure not choosing him." She paused for a heartbeat. "But he's not behind this. What if it were your father?" she added before he could answer.

She had a point. He'd never believe that Kirby was guilty of putting him in danger. Or lying about his whereabouts. Lying, period. Kirby wasn't the same sort of man as Zander Gray.

"We need to declare a truce," Eden continued.

That sounded reasonable, and Declan was about to agree when he saw the slight tremble of her bottom lip. Okay, so they were back to that. Her having a normal response to danger. Him having a bad response to her normal one.

Great.

"Truce," he said. But there might be a time limit on it if anything changed in the investigation. Especially if they found anything to implicate her father.

They stood there. Gazes connected again. And with things warm and not so cozy between them. The heat was there all right, but nothing about this felt comfortable. Everything inside him was on alert, and not in a good way, either. For some dumb reason, his body was ignoring the danger warnings and moving right on to the really bad suggestion that he do something even dumber.

Like kiss her.

She didn't back away. Neither did he, and even though he tried to keep the kissing thoughts out of his head, they came anyway. His thoughts were pretty good in that department because he could almost taste her, and it was the prospect of that taste, of the kiss, that had him stepping away just in the nick of time. Of course, his body protested, but that was a mistake he couldn't make.

"The last time I trusted someone I shouldn't have," he said, unbuttoning his shirt, "I got this."

Her eyes widened, and a little burst of air left her mouth. Maybe because she hadn't expected him to bare his chest. But he did that so she could see the scar.

"I slept with a suspect once. Didn't believe she was a suspect until I got between her and her escape vehicle. I learned the hard way that she was not only guilty, she was a decent shot with the .38 she had hidden in her purse."

The look in her eyes changed. No longer truce-like. She reached out as if to touch the scar on his rib cage, but then she jerked back her hand. "Sorry."

He wasn't sure if she was apologizing for the old injury or for the fact she'd almost touched him.

"I've got my own set of baggage," Eden said.

Yeah, he was betting she did.

His phone buzzed. Thank goodness. Well, Declan thought it'd been a good interruption until he saw that the call was from Wyatt. Since his brother had barely had time to get to work, this couldn't be good.

"Eden and you need to get down here right away," Wyatt said the second Declan answered.

Declan put the call on speaker so Eden could hear. "What's going on?"

"You guys are popular today," his brother said. "We

just had not one but two suspects walk in, and both are demanding to talk to the both of you."

"Two?" Declan asked.

"Yeah. And they're already at each other's throats. My advice, get here fast before they try to kill each other. It's Leonard Kane and a guy name Jack Vinson."

Of course, he knew the first one. Leonard was indeed someone Declan wanted to question. But he knew the second name, as well. It wasn't someone he had associated with Zander Gray or the shooting, though.

However, he did have a connection to Kirby.

"Jack Vinson," Eden repeated. "Years ago, he had some business dealings with my father." She shook her head. "But would Jack have anything to do with you or your family?"

Declan tried to keep it short. "Remember the body that was found at the Rocky Creek Children's Facility?"

She nodded. "Jonah Webb, the dead headmaster. Kirby... All of you are suspects as accessory to murder."

"Yeah. And the rangers are also questioning Jack Vinson. He was acquainted with a lot of people connected to Rocky Creek, and he and Webb had had a recent falling-out over the way Webb was running the place."

Last Declan had heard, there was no evidence against the man. So why was he here in Maverick Springs?

"Jack Vinson says he's got information about yesterday's shooting," Wyatt explained. "Says he knows why somebody's trying to kill you."

Chapter Eight

Two suspects. Eden wasn't sure if she should be relieved or suspicious. Either way, this was a strange development, but if it panned out, it could save Declan and her some time. Maybe even their lives.

If the suspects truly cooperated, that is.

Just because they'd arrived voluntarily didn't mean they were at the marshals' office to do anything other than muddy already muddy waters. But then, sometimes people said things they hadn't planned on saying. Maybe that would happen this morning.

"Leonard Kane," Declan repeated, glancing at the two names that he'd jotted down after Wyatt's call. He dropped the notepad with the names on the truck seat next to her, and he drove away from the ranch. Heading into town, where they'd hopefully get the answers they needed.

Yes, Leonard was definitely a suspect since he had a grudge against her father. And against Kirby for killing his son. He'd probably come in because if he hadn't, the marshals would have hauled him in.

But the other suspect was, well, unexpected.

"How much do you know about Jack Vinson?" Declan asked, tapping the second name. He was all lawman now. No trace of the heat that'd stirred between them over coffee in the kitchen. And that was good. They didn't need that interfering with what they had to do.

Eden repeated that to herself.

"As I said, Jack did some business with my father," she explained. "In fact, he was in on that deal that cost Leonard so much money. I can't be sure, but it might have cost Jack money, too." She certainly hadn't known about his connection to Rocky Creek.

"But he wasn't on the list of people you called last night."

She shook her head. "No. I tried, but he wouldn't take my call. But I did speak with him shortly after my father disappeared." She'd contacted anyone and everyone who'd had an association with him. "Like everyone else, Jack said he had no idea where my father was."

Declan made a sound to indicate he was thinking about that. "So why would Jack show up now out of the blue?"

"I don't know." And she didn't. "Your brothers will run a recent background check on him." That was a given. But it might take more than a mere background check to discover why the man had just shown up, claiming to know why someone wanted to kill them. "Do the rangers believe Jack had something to do with Jonah Webb's murder?"

"I'm not sure. They're working with a long list of people they're questioning—including all the former residents and employees of the facility."

Declan was also on that list. Webb's wife had been the one to murder him, but she'd had an accomplice, and that was the person the rangers wanted to identify. So far, they still had a lot of suspects to rule out.

Declan's phone buzzed. "Stella," he said when he

glanced at the screen, and he put the call on speaker. "Is Kirby okay?"

Eden heard the worry in his voice. It was yet another layer of stress when they were already overloaded.

"Kirby's better," Stella answered. "In fact, the doc thinks he'll be able to go home today or tomorrow." She paused. "I asked him about the note. Tried to do it in a roundabout way, but he picked right up on the fact that I was trying to hide something."

Declan flexed his eyebrows, clearly not surprised by that. "Does he have any idea who wrote it?"

Another pause. A long one. "He said it's probably somebody from his past."

"Yeah," Declan agreed, but his eyes said something different. Did he doubt Kirby? "You mentioned the photos to him, especially the one from Germany?"

Even though Eden couldn't see Stella's expression, she could almost feel the hesitation in the woman. What the heck was going on? Was Stella trying to hide something at a time like this?

"Kirby wants to make some calls to ask about those pictures," Stella finally answered.

"No way," Declan snapped. "I don't want him doing anything to put his health at risk."

"Too late. You know how he is when he gets an idea in his hard head. I'm worried, Declan." And the woman's voice cracked. "There are secrets that could come back to haunt him. Haunt all of us," she added.

"What do you mean?" No snapping that time.

"I've said too much. Anything else needs to come from Kirby." And with that, Stella ended the call.

Declan groaned. Then cursed. Eden waited for him to tell her what he intended to do about the news Stella had just dropped on them, but he shot her a glance that let her know the subject was closed.

It wasn't.

Yes, the conversation had had a personal tone to it, but the threat that Declan received was connected to her. *They* were connected. And any secrets that Stella might want to keep couldn't be kept secret.

"You won't talk to Kirby about this," Declan warned her, and he pulled to a stop in the parking lot of the marshals' building.

Since it would have been a lie to agree to that, Eden kept quiet, but she would find a way to speak with Kirby. Or better yet, Stella. The woman obviously knew what was going on, and Eden would make sure she shared it. For now, however, they had a more immediate problem on their hands.

Well, two of them actually.

Declan and she made their way into the building, through the security checkpoint and up the stairs. She didn't even have to step into the sprawling office before she heard a familiar voice.

"You think I'd come here if I was guilty?" Leonard Kane's voice boomed, just short of a full-fledged shout, and Eden soon discovered he was talking to Wyatt, who didn't look at all pleased with their visitor.

The moment Eden appeared in the doorway, Leonard turned toward her and smiled an oily smile that only he and a charlatan could have managed.

She hadn't seen him in nearly three years, but he hadn't changed despite his brain-tumor diagnosis. Iron-gray hair that somehow made him look stronger rather than a man in his mid-fifties. He was wearing starched jeans, a leather jacket, expensive snakeskin boots and a shiny rodeo buckle the size of a grapefruit. Leonard was the opposite of a wallflower and clearly not show-ing any signs of his terminal illness.

"Well, look-y what the cat dragged in," Leonard greeted. Eden wasn't sure if she was the cat or what'd been dragged in. "I was just telling Marshal McCabe here that I'm an innocent man. And a dying one at that. I don't have time for false accusations from the marshals."

"I heard about your brain tumor," Eden said, but didn't offer any sympathy. And wouldn't. Unless she learned he had no part in this.

"Yeah. A kick in the teeth, right?" Leonard said. "The docs can't do a damn thing to cut it out without killing me on the spot. But I guess we all gotta go sometime. My boy, Corey, didn't get much of that time, though."

So they were already on to Kirby killing his son. Eden had figured it wouldn't take him long to bring that up, and maybe Leonard would say enough on the subject that it would give them a solid lead in this investigation.

"I gave the marshal my statement," Leonard went on, "telling him that I was nowhere near your place yester-day and that I ain't holding a grudge against anybody. Especially one of Kirby Granger's boys."

Declan looked past the man and met Wyatt's gaze. "Where's Jack?"

Wyatt hitched his thumb toward the hall. "First inter-rogation room. Best to keep these two apart. Leonard tried to take a swing at him."

"Because Jack's an idiot," Leonard volunteered, his smile turning to a smirk. "Jack's the one who got me in-volved with Zander Gray, and they're the reason I lost a whole boatload of money." The smirk was still in place when his attention came back to Eden. "When you cause a ruckus, you make it a Texas-size one, don't you, girl?"

"I didn't cause a ruckus." She had to get her teeth unclenched so she could finish. "But Marshal O'Malley and I were nearly killed. I'd like to know why."

"And you think I got the answers?" Leonard didn't wait for her to confirm that. "No, Jack's the one claiming to know something. Wish he'd claim to know how to get me back that money he and your daddy cost me. I'm just here to clear my name, give an official statement. And to find out where your daddy is. Because, you see, I figure he's behind all of this and is trying to frame me. I got some old scores to settle, and he's one I'm looking to settle with."

So, it was true. Leonard was cleaning house, but with all the bad he'd done, the world wouldn't miss him.

"Is Zander alive?" Declan asked the man.

Leonard lifted his shoulder. "You should be asking his daughter here, 'cause I don't know. Haven't heard a peep from him. But I'm thinking he's gotta want revenge against you for arresting him."

Declan went closer and got right in Leonard's face. "Why involve Eden?"

"Maybe that wasn't intentional." And though Leonard's voice dripped with sarcasm, Eden had to wonder if there was some truth behind what he'd said. Had her father tried to go after Declan and involved her instead? She didn't want to believe that, but she hadn't seen him in three years. If he was indeed alive, he could be a changed man hell-bent on getting revenge.

"That's it?" Declan's hands went on his hips. "That's all you came here to tell us—that Zander might not have intentionally involved his daughter? Well, that's not enough. Because as far as I'm concerned, you're just as much of a suspect as Zander is."

"Me?" Leonard howled. "I'm innocent. I already said, why would I be here if I was guilty?"

"You would if you didn't want to look guilty. Besides, we had probable cause to haul you in here whether you volunteered or not."

"Well, I didn't have any part in the shooting yesterday out at your place." His cocky look turned to a glare when it landed on the interrogation room where Jack was. "But I'm betting he'll say different. He'll try to pin this on me so it'll get the blame off himself."

Declan glanced at her to see if she knew what Leonard meant, but she had to shake her head. "Why would Jack want to kill Declan and me?" she came out and asked.

Leonard opened his mouth. Closed it. And the smile returned. "You really don't know?"

Declan took a step closer to the man. "Know what?"

His smile got wider. "Oh, you really need to talk to your foster daddy about this."

"I'd rather talk to you about it," Declan argued.

The door to the interrogation room flew open and the man stepped out. Unlike Leonard, Eden had never met Jack Vinson. Also unlike Leonard, he looked like a polished businessman in his navy suit and dark red tie.

"Marshal O'Malley," Jack greeted. "Declan." He said it as if they were old friends. But judging from the way Declan was eyeing him, he'd never met Jack, either.

"Here it comes," Leonard taunted. "He's gonna accuse me of something again. That's the real reason I came down here. This bozo called me and said he was coming in to rat me out. Hard to rat me out, though, when I done nothing wrong."

"Yeah, you're just a model citizen, aren't you?" Wyatt mumbled. Obviously, he'd had his fill of the men before Declan and she had arrived. He looked at his brother.

"Jack claims he has proof of Leonard's involvement in the shooting."

"He ain't got squat," Leonard said at the exact moment that Jack insisted, "I do have proof."

Jack waited until all eyes were on him before he continued. "Word on the street is that a man named Lonnie Reddick was out at Declan's place yesterday, and that he's the hired gun on the run that you've been looking for."

Declan glanced at Harlan, who was behind his desk. "Lonnie Reddick," Harlan repeated. "I'll see what I can find."

"You'll find that Reddick worked for Leonard," Jack supplied. "Still does. Follow the money trail and you'll have proof of the connection."

The profanity that left Leonard's mouth was fast and raw. He moved toward Jack, looking ready to punch him, but Declan stepped between them. "Is that true?" Declan asked Leonard.

"It's true that Reddick worked for me a while back, but I damn sure didn't hire him to kill you yesterday."

Eden stepped closer, as well. "Yes, but did he kill a gunman who could have confirmed who hired all three assassins?"

"No!" Leonard snarled. "I got no reason to hire anyone to come after you."

"No reason except a double motive—to get back at both Kirby and my father," Eden supplied.

Leonard's eyes narrowed to slits, but he aimed his glare at Jack. "You just had to put that in their heads, didn't you? Well, why don't you spill your motive, 'cause I know you got one."

While Leonard was practically spewing venom at the man, Jack remained cool. He eased his hands into his pockets. "It's not a motive. Just the opposite." His gaze returned to Declan. "Stella and I are old friends—"

"Old lovers," Leonard interrupted. "In fact, they were engaged, their wedding just days away when Stella called it off because of Kirby."

"Kirby?" Declan questioned, and judging from his tone, it was the first he was hearing of this. "But Stella and Kirby aren't involved like that."

"Probably because he's too sick to do anything about it." Leonard seemed happy to tell them, too. "But Kirby's always had a hot, dirty thing for Stella. And despite this whole butter-won't-melt-in-Jack's-mouth routine, he'd like nothing more than to get back at Kirby for stealing Stella away from him all those years ago."

"Water under the bridge," Jack said.

Eden looked at both men. Then at Declan to see if he was understanding this. The gunman possibly worked for Leonard. If it was true, that was the connection they'd been looking for.

But she couldn't see how Stella's old flame would play into this.

"There's more," Leonard happily added. "Jack's wife, Beatrice, isn't too happy about the way Kirby and Stella treated her hubby all those years ago. Yeah, Jack wouldn't have married Beatrice if Stella had stayed in his life. But Beatrice is dingbat crazy, so she could mean to get a little revenge of her own. Plus, I figure she's a whole lotta jealous when it comes to Stella, since Jack is still carrying a torch for her."

Jack's jaw muscles stirred a little. "My wife has no part in this." However, he didn't deny his feelings for Stella. He looked at Declan. "Beatrice has spent some time in therapy, but she's fine now."

"She was in a glorified nuthouse." Leonard laughed. "Right where a dingbat belongs."

Eden shook her head. "Okay, I'll bite. Why would Beatrice come after Declan and me because she was upset with Kirby and Stella?"

Leonard made a sound to indicate that the answer was obvious. "Dingbat logic ain't gotta make sense. Some people just carry a grudge for a long time, and when Beatrice married Jack, she married his money. Millions of it. No prenup. And she had to get that money by marrying a hubby who's in love with another woman. She probably figures if she's miserable and locked away in her own loony head, then she should spread that misery around like fertilizer."

"My wife has no part in this," Jack insisted.

Declan obviously didn't believe that. He looked at Harlan. "Do a background check on her."

"Running it now."

Jack mumbled something, shook his head. "I want Beatrice left out of this investigation. Stella, too. Whatever's going on here has nothing to do with them."

"Don't be so sure about that," Leonard continued. He was smiling again when he looked at Declan, and that smile put a knot in her stomach. "Good ol' Jack here helped Stella rig the paperwork that got you out of that Rocky Creek hellhole."

Declan's attention slashed to Jack, and the man didn't deny it. "You mean the paperwork that put me in Kirby's foster care?"

Some of Jack's cool exterior evaporated. "Yes. I admit it. I helped with the paperwork. That part's true. But what Leonard's going to claim is that I also helped murder Jonah Webb. I didn't."

Eden wasn't sure she believed him. Or that this mattered, but judging from the glance that Wyatt and Declan exchanged, maybe it did.

"Yeah, you're getting it now," Leonard said, obviously noticing that glance, too. "Jack's in the hot seat, maybe on the verge of being charged as an accessory to Webb's murder. No statute of limitations on that. His butt could land in jail for life. Or worse. So how far do you think Jack or his dingbat wife would go to stop Kirby from ratting him out?"

"Not *that far*," Jack insisted.

"Are you saying that Jack or Beatrice would try to kill Declan and me?" Eden pressed Leonard. "How would that keep him out of jail?"

"He's not trying to kill you. What happened yesterday was a message to Kirby. Bite the bullet and confess to the Webb murder, or there'll be hell to pay—with his all-grown-up foster kid."

Jack stared at the man who'd just accused him of attempted murder. "That's ridiculous. From what I heard, Declan and Eden were in grave danger. They could have been killed."

"We could have been," Eden verified.

But no one seemed to hear her.

"That's what Lonnie Reddick was all about," Leonard said. "The man hasn't worked for me for months, but Jack or his wife knew he could hire him to take out the gunmen firing those shots at you two. He knew Kirby would understand what was going on."

That created another shouting match between the two men, but Eden dropped back a step so she could take it all in.

Had Jack really set this up?

"If he did it, it's a stupid way to send a message," Declan said, as if reading her mind. "My brothers would have gone after him if I'd been killed. And if you'd been killed, *I* would have gone after him."

She tried not to be flattered about that last part. Especially since in that particular scenario she'd be dead. But she was grateful that Declan would find the culprit if something did indeed happen to her.

And that probably didn't have anything to do with the heat between them.

No. He was first and foremost a lawman.

"This meeting is over," Jack announced. For a moment Eden thought he was going to storm out, but he stopped right in front of Declan.

"If I find out you're behind this, I'm arresting you," Declan warned him.

"If I were behind this, I'd let you arrest me," Jack countered. There was no ripe anger in his voice, only the glare that he aimed at Leonard. "My advice? Don't believe a word he says and find an excuse—any excuse—to put him behind bars."

"I'll be looking to do the same to you," Declan assured him.

Jack stared at Declan a moment later, added something under his breath that Eden didn't catch and walked out.

"You should be arresting him," Leonard grumbled.

"No evidence. *Yet.* But I will be looking for some. Looking for something on you, too," Declan told Leonard.

Leonard glanced around, maybe trying to decide where to go with this. Obviously he hadn't gotten what he wanted. Jack hadn't been arrested. He looked down at his hands, and Eden saw that he was shaking.

"Damn tumor," Leonard grumbled. He shoved his hands in his pockets. "They say it'll get worse. The headaches, too. And then I'll just keel over." He stared at Eden. "Let's hope I can get my goodbyes finished before that happens."

"Is that some kind of threat?" she asked. And she didn't back down from him.

"The only people who should feel threatened are the ones with a reason to be. You got a reason to be threatened by me, Eden?"

Declan didn't give her a chance to answer. He stepped between them. "Can you finish interviewing him?" Declan asked Wyatt. "I need to talk to Kirby."

No doubt to ask him about Stella's cryptic comments. But Kirby would have to be questioned about this, too. All of the danger was starting to lead right back to him and maybe what had happened at Rocky Creek all those years ago.

Judging from Leonard's renewed scowl, he didn't appreciate being handed off to Wyatt or putting an end to his little word games, but Eden hoped that Declan's brother could get some usable information from the man.

"I'd like to go with you when you question Kirby," she said to Declan once Leonard was out of earshot.

"I'm not *questioning* him. He's too weak for that. I only want to talk to him for a few moments."

Eden didn't even try to stop herself from groaning. "You can't let your personal feelings play into this. Besides, I'm sure Kirby wants you to be safe, and if he knows anything that can make that happen, then he'll tell you."

She hoped.

Though Kirby might not be willing to share that information with her.

Declan's mouth tightened, but he didn't argue. "Let's go," he snarled.

"Someone's on the phone for you," Harlan called out before they could leave.

Declan and she turned back around, but it took her a moment to realize that Harlan was talking to her, not Declan.

Harlan had his hand over the receiver of the landline phone so that the caller wouldn't be able to hear. "He says it's important," he added.

Eden shook her head. No one would know to be calling her here at the marshals' office. Unless it was the bodyguard she'd hired to watch her sisters, and if he couldn't have reached her with just a call, then he might have contacted law enforcement.

Oh, God.

Maybe something bad had happened to them.

She hurried across the room and nearly ripped the phone from Harlan's hand. "Is everything all right?" And she couldn't ask it fast enough.

"No. Far from it."

Eden's stomach went to her knees. Not the bodyguard. But it was a voice she recognized.

Her father's.

He was alive.

The relief flooded through her. Quickly followed by the concern and the realization that she had both Harlan and Declan staring at her and waiting.

"Don't say anything," her father warned her. "And find out a way to ditch Marshal O'Malley. Because I need to see you *now*. And I need to see you alone."

Chapter Nine

Eden didn't say a word, and Declan couldn't hear what the caller was telling her. Whatever it was, it couldn't be good, and they already had enough bad news to deal with.

"I understand," she finally said and pressed the button to end the call. Eden eased the phone back onto Harlan's desk. She didn't look at him but instead kept her attention on the phone.

"What happened?" Declan asked, and he glanced at Harlan, who just shook his head.

"The caller was using a burner," Harlan let him know after he checked the laptop next to the phone.

No way to trace it, which meant this call might have been from the gunman. Whoever it was and whatever he'd said, it had caused the color to drain from Eden's face. She didn't say anything, and that told him loads about the call. If it'd been a threat or warning about immediate danger to her sisters, she would have blurted it out so they could spring into action.

Finally, her gaze came to his, and she took him by the arm. "We have to talk." With the others watching, she led Declan out into the hall. "Please don't make me regret telling you this." Her voice was a shaky whisper.

And Declan knew who'd just called. "Where's your father?"

"He didn't say." She swallowed hard.

"But he wants to meet with you."

She nodded. "*Alone*. He said he's not guilty, that he was framed for trying to kill the witness who was going to testify against him."

Of course, Zander would say that. It was rare for a criminal to admit guilt, but he wasn't likely to convince Eden of the possibility that her father could be a dangerous man. "Where's the meeting?"

Eden turned away from him. She would have avoided his gaze completely if Declan hadn't caught her chin and forced eye contact. "Where and when?" he demanded.

Still, she took her time answering, and it seemed as if she changed her mind several times about telling him this. "Half hour. A pond about ten miles out of town. It's on West Farm Road."

Declan knew the exact spot. It was a remote location with almost no traffic. Plenty of trees for cover. Plenty of places to hide a vehicle, too. Unfortunately, it also had escape routes, since there were several ranch trails that rimmed the pond.

"I own that land," Declan explained. And he doubted that was a coincidence. Zander had likely chosen it because he knew it would dig at Declan. Had Zander also known that Eden would tell him about the meeting location?

And he went a little further with that thought.

Was Eden telling him the whole truth?

She wouldn't lead him into a trap. But he rethought that and groaned. Apparently, this attraction had made him a complete idiot, because he shouldn't trust her.

But he did.

After everything they'd been through, he didn't think she'd put him in the path of more bullets. And he hoped like the devil that was true.

"I need you to stay here," Declan told her.

She didn't just shake her head. Eden took him by the shoulders. "If I'm not at the meeting, my father won't be, either."

"That's a chance I'll have to take."

"And it's a dumb chance." She huffed, and it seemed to take her a moment to rein in her temper. "If I don't step out near that pond, then my father will just disappear into the woods. I don't want that. I want to know the information he has about all of this."

Yeah, so did Declan, but he wasn't sure it was worth the risk.

"And I need to make sure he's okay. I'm going to that meeting," Eden insisted. "And if you leave me behind, I'll just figure out another way to get there. My being there is the best way to keep you safe."

Now he groaned. "It's not your job to keep me safe."

Her eyes narrowed a little. "I can say the same thing right back to you. I didn't ask for your protection." And then her eyes narrowed a lot. "I'm not backing down on this."

Nope. She wouldn't. Any fool could see the determination in her eyes, which weren't so darn bedroom at the moment. She'd find a way there all right, and nothing short of putting her in a jail cell would make her stay put. Declan considered doing just that—locking her up—but there was something else playing into this.

Without Eden, he wouldn't be able to get close to her father.

Zander had known exactly where she was. It meant he was watching them or had hired someone to do that.

And depending on how long he'd been watching them, Zander might indeed have information about the attack. Maybe even firsthand information that he'd volunteer or let slip when Declan talked to him.

Hoping he didn't regret this, he leaned back inside the squad room, caught Harlan's attention and motioned for him to join them.

"This meeting has to stay a secret," Eden insisted when she realized what was going on.

"Not a chance. We're not going out there without some kind of backup."

"I'm your backup," she protested.

But he ignored her and turned to Harlan. "I need you to follow us out to Old Saunder's pond. And if Zander Gray calls back, leave instructions to give him my cell number."

Harlan mumbled some profanity. "You're meeting with Eden's father?"

"Yeah. Right after I call the hospital."

Harlan didn't ask why he was doing that. His brother knew. Declan needed to ask Kirby about the things Leonard and Jack had said. It was probably nothing. He hoped. But it wouldn't feel like nothing until Kirby reassured him that he'd had no part in this.

Webb's murder was a different matter.

Even though there'd been no proof, before now anyway, as to who'd helped Sarah Webb murder her husband, Declan had always known that her accomplice could be a member of his foster family. Now he had another suspect to add to that list of possible accomplices.

Jack Vinson.

He had to figure out if Jack was trying to pressure Kirby into confessing to a crime he didn't commit. Or if Beatrice Vinson was so jealous of Stella that she was behind all of this.

Still mumbling, Harlan went back inside the squad room.

"I want my gun while we're at this meeting," Eden said.

Only then did he remember the sheriff had taken it from her since she'd fired it at the assassins who'd tried to kill them. It would have to be processed as part of the crime scene.

"My backup weapon's in the glove compartment. Come on." Declan grabbed their coats and they headed downstairs and to his truck. "But there are rules about this meeting. My rules. You'll follow them, or we'll drive right back to town and you won't see your father."

Her gaze slid to his. "What rules?"

"Easy ones." He hoped. "You stay behind me, and if anything goes wrong, you get on the ground. Agree to them or stay here. That's the only choice I'm giving you." He wasn't budging on this, either.

"Agreed," she finally said. "But if my father sees you with me, he won't show his face," Eden warned him right back.

Maybe. "I'm not letting you meet him alone. He could be behind these attempts to kill us."

"He won't hurt me."

Yeah, Declan was counting heavily on that. But he was also counting on backup in case his instincts were dead wrong.

Eden continued to argue, but the moment he unlocked the truck and she got inside, she took his gun from the glove compartment. Extra ammo, too, which she crammed into her pockets.

"Repeating myself here, but it's a bad idea for you to come with me," she grumbled.

"A lot of things happening between us fall into the bad-idea category." And with that obvious statement out of the way, he turned his attention to their surroundings.

Declan glanced around to see if they were being watched, then he eased out of the parking lot, making sure no one followed them. He didn't want to drive too fast because there might be ice on the roads, and he wanted to give Harlan a chance to catch up with them. Besides, he needed a little time to speak to Stella.

Declan tried her number and was a little surprised when she answered on the first ring—as if she'd been expecting him. He didn't want to put the call on speaker, though Eden no doubt wanted to hear every word. But this conversation was something he might need to keep in the family.

For now anyway.

Of course, Eden was trying to do the same with this meeting with her father. Still, a phone call wasn't dangerous. Well, not in a bullet-flying sort of way like a face-to-face encounter with Zander might be. But he could learn something from this call that Declan wasn't sure he wanted to learn.

"I just got off the phone with Jack Vinson," Stella immediately told him. "He said you had a meeting with Leonard Kane."

"We did." And Declan left it at that. If Jack and she had talked, then Stella already knew what he wanted from her.

Answers.

Or better yet, a denial of Kirby's involvement. But Stella didn't volunteer anything.

Eden mumbled something he didn't catch, but she was

clearly frustrated that she couldn't hear what Stella was saying, and she scooted across the seat closer to him. As far as her seat belt would allow, and until they were arm to arm. Not the best position, especially when she put her face next to his.

"Is Kirby up to seeing us?" Declan asked when Stella's silence continued.

"He's feeling better. And I'd like to keep it that way for a while longer." She paused, and even though he didn't hear her sniffling or anything, Declan could sense that this was not a conversation she wanted to have. "Maybe this can keep for a day or two."

"In a day or two, Eden and I could be dead." He hated just to toss that out there, but it was the truth. If the danger had been directed only at him, Declan would have gladly backed off for as long as Stella deemed necessary, but this had to stop.

"Look, I don't want to make Kirby any worse," Declan continued, "but you and I both know if he could do anything to prevent another attack, then he'd do it."

"Yes, he would." Another pause.

"You know you're going to have to tell me the truth?" Declan asked her.

"I know. But I'm not sure if the truth will help."

Declan didn't like the sound of that. He'd wanted Stella to deny there were any secrets. Especially secrets that had anything to do with Kirby's involvement not just in this situation but in Webb's murder.

"I need to hear it," Declan insisted.

The seconds crawled by. "Tonight then."

Declan had plenty to do between now and then. That included this little chat with Zander. But he suddenly wanted nothing more than to hurry to the hospital and demand the answers that Stella didn't want him to know.

Stella ended the call, and Declan put away his phone.

Eden backed away a little, but her stare stayed on him. "If Kirby knows anything about—"

"Then he'll tell me," Declan interrupted.

"Us," she corrected.

Declan wanted to insist that particular conversation be private, but this wasn't a privacy situation. There was indeed an *us* in this, and it wasn't based solely on the attraction. Eden's life was on the line, too.

"After we're finished with Zander, we'll deal with Kirby," he assured her, though he wasn't sure how to go about doing that.

"Finished," she repeated under her breath. "You do know that my father isn't just going to let you arrest him. And I don't want another shoot-out."

Neither did he, and that was why he had to take some basic precautions. He slowed to a crawl until he spotted Harlan's dark blue truck coming up behind them, and Declan turned onto one of the ranch trails.

He looked at the dirt and gravel surface to see if anyone had driven on it recently, but it was hard to tell since it was scabbed with ice.

Eden glanced around. "Where exactly are we going?"

"This trail takes us to the backside of the pond."

Of course, her father could have had someone hidden in the trees, watching them. He might know their every move, but this was just a basic precaution. Besides, the trees gave them much better cover than being out on the farm road itself.

Harlan stayed behind him, both vehicles bobbing across the uneven surface. Declan kept watch. So did Eden. Her gaze fired all around, and she had a death grip on the gun she was holding.

Declan followed the trail, moving deeper into the

trees. It was darker here since the tall live oaks choked out what little sun there was. They also choked the trail since some were so close that the branches scraped against the sides of his truck. Again, there were no signs that anyone had been here. At least not with a vehicle.

"The pond's just over there." Declan pointed to his right, but the water wasn't in sight yet. "We'll park and walk the rest of the way."

At least once they were outside he'd be able to hear footsteps or some other indication that they weren't alone in these woods. Of course, it'd be next to impossible to hear a shooter who was already in place.

Declan turned, intending to move off the trail and into a narrow clearing, but he spotted a pile of leaves just ahead. It didn't look like anything Mother Nature had formed, so he hit his brakes.

But it was too late.

The truck jolted. Eden and he did, too, and if they hadn't been wearing their seat belts, they would have slammed into the dash and steering wheel. Thankfully, Harlan was able to stop in time and didn't plow right into them.

Eden gasped, lifted her gun. "What happened?"

"I'm pretty sure someone put spikes or nails on the trail." Because whatever he'd hit had taken out both front tires. It'd also left them sitting ducks.

Hell. This was not the way he'd wanted things to play out.

Declan drew his gun. Looked around. Harlan's truck hadn't been disabled, so they'd need to use it to get the heck out of there.

"Move fast," Declan told Eden, and he opened his truck door. "Stay right with me." They started walking with her pressed against the truck and with him in front of her.

"See anyone?" Harlan asked, stepping from his truck, as well.

"No." But Declan had no sooner said it than he did see *something*. Movement behind one of the larger oaks. Whoever was there ducked back out of sight, and that couldn't be a good sign.

"Step away from the truck," someone shouted. "And keep your hands in the air so I can see them."

Declan saw the gun then. And not just one, but several, all pointed right at them.

The three of them were surrounded.

Chapter Ten

Eden didn't have time to react. But Declan sure did. He hooked his arm around her and dragged her to the ground.

Her heart slammed against her chest, and she braced herself for the gunshots. However, no shots came. Just the eerie silence and the sound of her own heartbeat crashing in her ears.

"Stand up," someone said. It was her father. "And remember that part about keeping your hands where I can see them."

Eden tried to get up, but Declan shoved her right back to the ground. He certainly didn't do as her father had ordered. He took aim at one of the shadowy figures behind a tree. Harlan pointed his gun at another one. Eden didn't do any pointing because one of those shadows was her father.

"O'Malley, if I wanted you dead, you already would be," her father said.

"Is that supposed to make me trust you?" Declan snapped.

"No, but this might."

She lifted her head just a fraction and saw her father step out from behind one of the trees. He was armed, a gun in his right hand and a large manila envelope in his left. He was dressed like a soldier going to combat, with camo and gear, and he had a black baseball cap slung low over his face.

The relief flooded through her—he was alive—but the relief was soon followed by the fear that he might not stay that way for long. This could easily turn into a gunfight if she didn't do something to defuse it.

"Declan saved my life," she volunteered, and despite the fact that he was trying to keep her on the ground, Eden managed to wiggle away from him and get to her feet. However, Declan did stop her from going closer to her father. "I don't want him or his brother hurt."

Declan cursed. Stood up. And stepped in front of her after he shot her a glare. "There are rules, and you just broke them."

"Admirable," her father said before she could respond to Declan. "You're trying to protect my daughter. Ironic, huh? Since you'd like nothing better than to see me dead."

"Not ironic. Your daughter didn't try to kill a witness and then escape from jail."

Her father shook his head. "I didn't try to kill a witness, either." He walked toward them and met her gaze. "I would give you a hug, but the marshal here wouldn't like that."

"I'm not sure I would, either," she answered. It hurt to say that, and it hurt to see the flash of surprise go through her father's eyes. "You should have let us know you were alive."

"Couldn't risk you telling the cops. Or the marshals. You always were a do-gooder, Eden."

His voice wasn't exactly cold, but the look he gave her was. There'd never been a lot of affection between them. Her father wasn't, well, fatherly. But she loved him as only a daughter could.

"I wouldn't have turned you in." She had to clear her throat and repeat it so that it was more than a whisper. "I would have tried to help you."

The corner of her father's mouth lifted. "And now you're sleeping with the enemy."

She was sure she blinked and then quickly shook her head.

"Eden's in my protective custody," Declan growled.

"And she spent the night with you," her father growled back.

"Not *with* me." Declan's jaw tightened. "Under the same roof, and she did that because she's in serious danger. Someone wants me and your daughter dead. I'm thinking that someone might be you."

Eden pulled in her breath and waited. Prayed, too. Her father couldn't be involved in this.

"Not me," her father insisted. "I wouldn't do anything to hurt Eden or any of my girls. The only reason I've stayed away is because it's safer for them."

"Safer for you, too," Declan reminded him. "After all, you're not in jail."

"Yes, but that doesn't mean there aren't people who want to silence me." Zander made a nervous glance around the woods. "More than once someone's tried to kill me, and damn if I know why. And before you ask, I don't know who's trying to kill you, either. Could be Leonard or Jack. Or Jack's crazy wife. Maybe Kirby."

"Not Kirby," Harlan and Declan said in unison.

"Someone from your past then," her father continued. "Maybe the same person who killed your family in Germany."

Because Declan's arm was touching hers, she felt

every muscle go stiff. That was probably the one connection he didn't want mentioned here. Because he had no leads, and the case had been cold for decades. Still, there'd been that photo included with the more recent ones, so this might indeed all be threaded together.

Her father took a step closer and dropped the thick envelope at Declan's feet. "There's the proof that I'm innocent."

Declan didn't reach down to retrieve the envelope. He kept his attention staked to her father. Beside him, Harlan was trying to keep an eye on the gunman. From what she could tell, there were two of them, at least, but they were both staying behind cover.

"What kind of so-called evidence do you claim to have?" Declan asked.

"The kind that I want you to investigate so I can clear my name. I can hire muscle, but I can't do this investigation on my own."

"I'm not interested in clearing your name. I have bigger fish to fry right now."

"Right." Not said sarcastically, but her father seemed to be in agreement. "I have something that might help speed things along."

He motioned toward one of the men lurking behind the tree, and someone stepped out. Not a gunman. This person was handcuffed, and he staggered forward when the gunman gave him a shove.

Eden didn't recognize the handcuffed man, but judging from Harlan's and Declan's reactions, they did.

"Lonnie Reddick," Declan mumbled.

The missing gunman. And possibly the same man who'd tried to murder them at Declan's house the day before. At a minimum, he'd murdered his wounded comrade before he could tell them who'd hired them to launch the attack.

"I figured you'd like the chance to talk to Reddick," her father went on, "and in turn, I want you to look into the papers in that envelope."

"I'll look at them, but I'm not making any promises," Declan insisted.

Her father gave a slight huff. "Find out who set me up. And keep my daughter safe. I'd do it myself, but I'm not exactly in the position for it." His gaze came to Eden. "I have to go, but as soon as I can, I'll come back to see you."

She nodded and felt the tears burn her eyes. Her father couldn't stay, she knew that, but Eden also knew that even if Declan proved his innocence, he'd still be arrested for breaking out of jail and becoming a fugitive. She doubted he'd just voluntarily go back to prison, and that meant he could still be killed while trying to evade the law.

And in this case, the law was Declan.

With his gun still aimed and ready, Harlan went forward, latched on to Reddick and hauled him toward his truck. "What should we do about him?" Harlan asked, tipping his head to her father.

Declan met her father's gaze head-on. "I can't just let you leave."

"And I can't let you arrest me," her father argued.

Her heart nearly stopped, because they were not the sort of men who backed down. She couldn't lose her father now that she'd just learned he was alive. But she couldn't lose Declan, either.

Eden silently cursed both of them. And the stalemate that followed. They stood there, the bitter cold wind whipping at them. Guns aimed.

"Please," Eden whispered. But she wasn't sure which one of them she wanted to give in.

"Boss?" one of the gunmen yelled.

But that was the only warning they got before the sound cracked though the air.

Someone had fired a shot.

DECLAN COULDN'T MOVE fast enough.

He threw himself against Eden and pulled her to the side of his truck and then onto the ground. Beside him, Harlan did the same with Reddick, and all of them cursed the bullets that started to slam around them. Harlan wedged both Reddick and himself in between the two trucks.

Zander cursed, too, and he dropped down just a few feet away from them. For just that split second of time, Declan had thought the shots might be coming from Zander's own hired guns, but judging from the man's fierce reaction, someone else was shooting.

Just what they didn't need.

Of course, this could be some kind of ploy set up by Zander to make it easier for him to escape, but if so, it was stupid. Because any one of those bullets could ricochet off something and hit Eden or the rest of them.

"He's to your right!" one of Zander's men behind the tree shouted.

Declan's attention was already aimed in that direction because it was where the shots were coming from. There was a cluster of trees, so thick that it would make a good hiding place. Of course, the question was how had this guy managed to sneak up on Zander's men? Or had he already been in place before Eden and he had even arrived?

"Stop the SOB!" Zander shouted.

A shot slapped into the ground right next to Eden and sent up a spray of dirt and pebbles. They had to move. But there weren't exactly a lot of options. Getting back into the truck would be a huge risk. Plus, Harlan was parked behind him, and going forward would mean moving closer to the shooter. With the front tires already out, that didn't seem like a good option. Of course, none of their options seemed good at this point.

"Can you see him?" Eden asked. Her breath was racing and every muscle in her body was tense.

Declan shook his head and tried to keep watch. And there was a lot to watch. Eden's father for one. Even though Zander was flat on the ground, he was still armed, and he could turn that weapon on Declan so he could try to escape.

To his left, he heard Harlan talking, and he realized he was calling for backup. Good. Maybe it'd arrive in time, but he cursed himself and their situation. Because once again, Eden was in danger.

Finally, Declan saw some movement in the tree cluster. So did Zander's men, because shots started to go in that direction. They were returning fire, and it might be enough to get the guy to stop. Declan figured there was a slim-to-none chance of keeping him alive so he could question him, but at least they had Reddick.

If they could keep him alive, that is.

He also had to consider that this attack was meant to kill Reddick, since he could likely spill a lot of details that a would-be killer would want to keep hidden. So there could be multiple targets here. Zander, Reddick, Eden or himself.

Or maybe all of them.

The more he learned about this investigation, the more he realized that everything was tangled together.

And they had to dodge these bullets if they ever hoped to untangle it.

More shots came. Seemingly from every direction. God knows how many people were actually shooting out there. In fact, their attacker could have plenty of backup of his own.

"Get Eden out of here now!" her father shouted, and Declan was pretty sure Zander was talking to him. "We'll settle our score later."

The shots continued, making it hard to think or hear, but Declan had to come up with some kind of plan, because this guy wasn't stopping. There had to be at least two of them, since the shots were coming nonstop.

"Crawl beneath my truck," Declan told her. So far, there'd been no shots fired there, but that didn't mean there wasn't another shooter out in the woods. One with a better shot at the other side of his truck.

Eden didn't move, and he could practically feel the hesitation in every part of her body. "I need that envelope," she said, and that was the only warning she gave Declan before she snaked out, grabbed it and then got back behind him.

Later, he'd chew her out for that, but for now, he just wanted to get her the heck out of there.

"Move under my truck," Declan ordered.

Thankfully, Eden didn't argue this time. She got on her belly and started crawling. Declan kept an eye on Zander, and he considered motioning for Harlan to get moving, too. But there was a problem. An escape would be next to impossible with a prisoner, and Declan had to consider that the complication was all part of Zander's plan.

Whatever plan that was.

If they all piled into Harlan's truck, Zander could escape, and Harlan, Eden and he could be left with Red-dick, who might try to fight his way out of the small space. With the gunmen firing shots, things could turn deadly fast. Still, it was riskier to stay put.

"Don't leave cover," Declan told Eden when she had reached the far side underneath his truck. He motioned for Harlan to get moving, as well. Not toward the shoot-ers, but toward what he hoped was the safe side of their vehicles.

"I'll be in touch," Declan warned Zander.

"Just read the papers in that envelope," Zander in-sisted.

He would. Once they were safely out of this, and he refused to believe that wouldn't happen. Declan scram-bled under the truck with Eden.

"What about my father?" she asked. She was breath-ing through her mouth now, the air gusting in and out, and she looked as terrified as she sounded.

"He wants you out of here," he reminded her. And, yeah, that wasn't the answer Eden wanted to hear, but Declan wanted her out of there, too.

In the distance he heard a welcome sound. Sirens. Probably one or more of his brothers responding. They wouldn't come in with guns blazing and bullets flying, but at least they were nearby in case things went from bad to worse.

Declan moved ahead of Eden so that he could look out. No sign of any shooters. Just Harlan, who had a meaty grip on Reddick's shirt collar. He and his brother made eye contact, and Declan motioned for Harlan to get in through the passenger's side.

The seconds slowed to a crawl, but Harlan finally stuffed both himself and Reddick into the truck. However, Reddick had barely managed to get in when there was another shot.

This one sent Declan's heart to his knees.

Because it hadn't been fired from the tree cluster. No. This one had slammed into the front of Harlan's truck.

Damn.

Either the shooter had moved or this was his backup. And it wasn't just one shot. They came crashing through his brother's truck.

Declan took aim, trying to pinpoint the shooter's location, and he fired. Judging from the sound of it, he hit a tree, but it must have been close enough because the shooter paused. It was just enough time for Harlan to dive onto the seat and get behind the wheel.

The shooter fired again. And this time, the bullet didn't go into a tree. Declan knew that sound. Bullet into flesh. Reddick snapped forward, his body twisting into an unnatural angle, before falling to the ground.

Someone had shot Reddick in the back of the head.

Declan didn't have to touch the man to know he was dead. It'd been a very accurate kill shot, and just like that, no more bullets came at them. Well, not from this angle anyway. The shots continued on the other side of the trucks.

"Get her out of here!" Zander yelled again.

Declan wanted nothing more, but he had to wait. And he didn't like what he heard. No more shots, but someone was running. The assassin, no doubt. Just as Reddick had done at his house, the gunman had been killed. And so had any link to the person who'd hired him.

"Let's move now," Declan insisted.

He gripped Eden's arm and they scurried out from beneath the truck. It was a short trek, but not an easy one, since they had to climb over Reddick's body. The moment they were inside, Harlan threw his truck into Reverse and gunned the engine.

Declan held his breath. Said a prayer, too, and that prayer was apparently answered because no other bullets came their way. The gunmen, however, continued to shoot, and the bullets pelted the ground near Declan's truck.

"Oh, God," Eden said on a gasp.

That snagged his attention, and Declan followed her gaze to her father. Zander was no longer on the ground but had gotten up to a crouching position. He aimed his gun in the direction of the trees where the shots were coming.

Declan couldn't tell if Zander managed to pull the trigger, but he saw the man's body jerk back. No doubt from a bullet slamming into his chest.

Eden screamed, the sound echoing over the bullet blasts and the roar of the engine. She would have bolted from the truck if Declan hadn't held on to her.

"My father's been shot," she said, and she kept repeating it.

Declan caught her face and forced her to look him in the eyes. "Stay in the truck with Harlan. He'll get you to safety."

Declan hoped.

"Slow down just for a second," he told Harlan.

Harlan cursed, called him a bad name mixed with some profanity, but he slowed just enough for Declan to jump from the truck. He hit the ground running.

Directly toward the shooters.

Chapter Eleven

Eden threw the envelope on the floor and tried to pull Declan back into the truck, but she wasn't fast enough. He ducked behind a tree, leaned out and fired. She couldn't see where his shot landed because Harlan kept going, the truck flying in Reverse.

"We have to help Declan," she insisted. "And my father."

Harlan didn't respond. He kept his eyes on the side mirror and maneuvered around a curve. Once he was on the other side, he stopped. Without the noise from the engine and the dirt and rocks slapping against the undercarriage, Eden could hear something surprising.

Silence.

However, she did hear something else. Sirens. They were getting closer, and it didn't take long before the blue lights were flashing all around them. The cruiser came to a stop behind them, and both Wyatt and the local sheriff, Rico Geary, cracked open their doors. Harlan did the same.

"Declan's out there," Harlan relayed to them. "Zander Gray, too, and at least three gunmen. There's also a dead body, Lonnie Reddick."

That brought Wyatt out of the cruiser, and with his gun drawn he walked toward them. "You two okay?"

Harlan looked at her. Nodded. "Don't know about Zander or Declan, though."

"My father was shot," Eden volunteered.

Wyatt spared them both a glance, but continued up the trail, using the trees and shrubs for cover. Sheriff Geary did the same on the other side, but when he reached the truck, Harlan got out.

"I need you to stay with Eden," he told the sheriff.

Geary didn't argue, but Harlan had only made it a few steps when she heard someone shout. "It's me. Don't shoot."

Declan.

Despite the sheriff's attempts to stop her, Eden bolted from the truck and started running. The relief was instant. So was the fear of how close he'd come to dying. Again.

She didn't think. Eden ran right to Declan and was surprised when he pulled her into his arms. He brushed a kiss on her cheek. Pulled back, examined her face. She did the same to him. No injuries, thank goodness. And she didn't kiss his cheek. She pressed her lips to his for several moments.

"What about my father?" she asked, hating to hear the answer.

Declan only shook his head. "He wasn't there when I got back. His men must have gotten him out. But I think he was wearing Kevlar because I didn't see any blood."

She replayed all those horrible images and realized he was right. Her father had fallen to the ground, clutching his chest, but there'd been no blood.

"You went back for my father," she said under her breath. Their eyes met, and whether he would admit it or not, he hadn't done that just so he could arrest him. Declan had done that for her. "Thank you."

"I didn't do it for him," Declan quickly let her know.

"We need to get out of here," Harlan reminded them before they could say anything else. "Those gunmen could come back."

"Yes," the sheriff agreed, "and I need to get the rangers out here to help with this crime scene." He looked at Declan. "Unless you want to do that yourself."

Declan shook his head, looped his arm around her waist and got them moving toward Harlan's truck. The sheriff had to move the cruiser, but Harlan was finally able to get turned around so they could drive out of there.

Eden glanced behind them one last time, both hoping to get a glimpse of her father and hoping she didn't. Because if any of the lawmen saw him, they'd arrest him. But at least she would know for certain that he was alive and unharmed.

"Either of you need to see a doctor?" Harlan asked. They both shook their heads. "Then I'm headed to the office. We've got a hell of a big mess to sort through."

They couldn't argue with that. Heaven knows how long it'd take to go through a crime scene that large.

Declan picked up the envelope that she'd tossed on the floor, but he didn't open it right away. He kept watch. So did Harlan.

No doubt in case there was another attack.

Her body was braced for one. Every nerve seemed to be right near the surface. And worse, this latest attack hadn't ended anything. They now had a dead gunman who couldn't give them any information. And her father was on the run again.

"You need to level your breathing," Declan told her.

Only then did she realize she wasn't just breathing fast, she was on the edge of hyperventilating. He slipped his arm around her, eased her to him, and Eden dropped her head on his shoulder.

It was wrong to take comfort from him this way, and Harlan obviously didn't approve of it, judging from the grunt he made. But Eden didn't pull away. She was afraid if she did, she might fall apart.

However, Declan didn't fall apart. With her still cradled against his arm, he opened the envelope and took out a handful of papers.

"They're bank records," Declan said, riffling through the pages. "Leonard Kane's."

That instantly got her attention, since Leonard was one of their suspects. "Do they show a huge payment at the time someone attempted to murder the witness?" Because it was that attempt that had ultimately sent her father to jail.

"There are a lot of big payments here." Declan continued to thumb through them but then stopped. "I'm betting your father didn't obtain these with Leonard's permission."

Even with the adrenaline still spiking through her, it didn't take Eden long to see where he was going with this. "So you wouldn't be able to use any of this to charge Leonard with a crime."

"Or even to get a court order," Harlan added. "Still, we'll give them to my brother, Clayton, and see what he can do with them."

Mercy. She didn't want Leonard or anyone else who was guilty to go free, but maybe the papers would still clear her father. Not officially. But in Declan's mind anyway. If that happened, he might dig harder to get to the truth about what had really happened.

Harlan pulled into the parking lot of the marshals' building, and as before, Declan rushed her inside. Unlike before, the office was practically deserted. Probably because the others had responded to the scene or were guarding Kirby and Stella. The only person in the room was one of Declan's brothers, Clayton.

"Any news about my father?" she immediately asked.

But Clayton shook his head and looked at Declan. "We do have a visitor though. Beatrice Vinson. I didn't call her in," he added. "She just showed up here about ten minutes ago and demanded to talk to Eden and you."

Declan groaned, scrubbed his hand over his face. "Is Jack with her?"

"She's alone. She didn't look like she'd be very comfortable in an interrogation room, so I had her wait in Saul's office. He's in a meeting and won't be back for a while."

Saul was the head marshal, and Eden hoped that his meeting involved something that would help them solve this case. He couldn't be pleased about several of his marshals being in the middle of a gunfight.

Harlan's phone buzzed, so he stepped away to his desk to take the call.

"I need you to see what you can do with these," Declan said, handing Clayton the envelope with the bank records.

Clayton glanced at them. Frowned. "Do I want to know where you got these?"

"From Eden's father, but I'm guessing he won't want to tell us his source."

"I'll get started on it," Clayton assured him. "You want me to tell Beatrice that your chat will have to wait? Neither of you look very steady on your feet right now."

"I'm not," Eden admitted. "But if she has information—"

"Not sure she does," Clayton interrupted. "She seems

a little off, if you ask me. Leonard might have been right about her being mentally unstable. The first thing she did when she got here was go into a rant about one of Kirby's lowlife brats causing her husband trouble."

Great. Just what they needed. Snobbish, jealous and perhaps crazy. As if they hadn't had enough of crazy for one day.

"What do we know about her?" Declan asked.

"She's fifty-eight and was first engaged to Jack over thirty years ago, but he broke off things to get engaged to Stella. Who then ended her engagement with Jack."

"For Kirby," Eden mumbled. "According to Leonard anyway. Is it true?"

"Still waiting for Stella to call back and confirm or deny it," Clayton explained. "But if it's true, Beatrice obviously made amends with Jack, and they've been married for going on thirty years. No kids. And they're rich. Very rich. It's his money, but she's half owner now. I'm still trying to get a handle on their net worth, but we're talking old money and plenty of it."

Eden glanced at the office where Beatrice was waiting. "I need a minute before we go in there and talk with her."

"You'll need more than a minute." Declan took her by the arm and led her down the hall to the break room. He shut the door and had her sit in one of the chairs. It wasn't exactly comfortable, more designed for someone having a quick bite or cup of coffee, but her legs were so wobbly that it was a relief just being off her feet.

"That call Harlan got could be about my father," she reminded him.

"And if it is, Harlan will come and tell us."

Since that was true, Eden stayed seated. Her thoughts were flying everywhere, probably because of the adrenaline pumping through her. But as bad as things were, and they were bad, she could only imagine how much worse it would be if she was going through it alone.

Declan took a bottle of water from the small fridge, opened it and had her take a sip. "Sorry that it's not something stronger." And it didn't sound as if he was joking.

Something stronger like a stiff drink was exactly what she needed. Or maybe not, she decided, when Declan dropped down next to her and eased his arm around her.

He definitely fell into the "something stronger" category.

"You can still see a doctor, you know," he offered.

"So can you. But I think we know a doctor won't have any fix for the shock of being shot at—again." She paused. "You'd think the second time would be easier. But it's not."

"If it got any easier, then it'd be time for me to turn in my badge. And for you to see a shrink. Nearly being killed should never feel *easier*."

Eden nodded. Groaned softly when she felt another slam of the fear. Her body was obviously still revved up for the fight that was over. Well, for now anyway. "My father—"

"Will be okay," Declan interrupted. "He had his men there, and if he's hurt, they'll get him the help he needs."

True. After all, they'd gotten him away from the scene, and there'd been no blood.

She looked at him, and even though there were dozens of things they could discuss about what had just happened, one of those whirlwind thoughts dropped from her head to her mouth. "My father thinks we're sleeping together."

"Yeah." He leaned in, brushed his lips over hers. Instant warmth. Or rather heat. Declan always seemed to know how to melt away the ice in her blood that the shooting had caused. "My brothers think that, too."

Eden groaned softly. "So we've been judged for something we haven't done."

"Yet," he added. The corner of his mouth lifted.

Ah, there it was. The killer smile to go along with those killer green eyes, rumpled black hair and perfect body. That helped, too. In fact, just being with him made things better. And that should have been a big red flag.

"Sleeping together won't help things," she reminded him. But then frowned because that didn't sound right. "Well, it might help with this ache, but it'll make our situation worse."

"There's an ache?" he asked.

She considered lying, but since the heat between them was past the sizzle stage, she'd only be wasting her breath. And speaking of breath, Declan pretty much robbed her of that when he leaned in and kissed her. Not one of those little lip touches he'd been giving her.

A real kiss.

She melted.

Like the rest of him, he was top-notch at that, too. His mouth moved over hers as if he wanted that ache to turn into something much more.

And it did.

The heat trickled through her. From her mouth to every inch of her. Especially the center of her body. A simple kiss had never been foreplay for her, but then a Declan kiss was far from simple.

With the water bottle still in her hand, Eden lifted her arms, first one and then the other, and she slipped them around his neck. The kiss deepened.

Everything did.

And they moved closer until they were touching breasts to chest. Until she wanted a whole lot more than she could have in the break room of the marshals' building.

"How's that ache now?" he said with his mouth still against hers.

Eden laughed. How that could happen, she didn't know. She could still hear the sound of those shots. Still see her father as he hit the ground. But somehow Declan had made her forget about it for a minute or two.

"I can't fall for you," she let him know.

He pulled back a little, pushed the hair from her face. "You already have."

Coming from any other man, that would have sounded cocky or even like a pick-up line, but Eden had to admit that it was true. She was falling for him. And that couldn't happen. She had to find a way to stop it, and she started by moving away from him.

It didn't help.

Even though they were no longer touching, she could still feel his hands on her. Could still taste him. And Eden knew she was well on her way to making what could turn out to be the biggest mistake of her life. Declan wasn't the sort of man she'd be able to just forget.

No.

He wasn't just inside her head now. He was edging his way into her heart. A far more dangerous place for him, considering in his eyes she'd always be her father's daughter.

"I'm tired of waiting," someone shouted from the hall. "I'll see Marshal O'Malley *now*."

That got Declan to his feet, and he moved Eden behind him. Protecting her again. But when he threw open the door, she wasn't so sure she needed his protection.

The woman coming toward them was tall but pencil thin. Hardly a physical threat.

Beatrice Vinson, no doubt.

She didn't look like a woman with mental problems, unless those problems included a serious high-end shopping addiction. She wore an expensive-looking creamy white cashmere skirt and matching sweater. No wrinkles anywhere on her face, and there wasn't any gray in her auburn hair. Her pale gray eyes went right to Declan.

"My husband came to see you." It sounded like an accusation of some kind.

Declan lifted his shoulder. "I questioned him about his possible involvement in a shooting. He's a suspect and, according to Leonard Kane, so are you."

The anger flashed through her eyes for just a second before she reined it in. "You're on a witch hunt. Probably on orders from Kirby Granger. Well, it won't do you any good. Neither my husband nor I had anything to do with these attacks."

"Then why are you here?" Eden asked.

Beatrice looked at her as if she were an insect to be swatted away. "You're Zander Gray's daughter, I assume."

Her icy gaze slid from Eden's head to her muddy shoes. She no doubt looked a wreck, felt like one, too, after Beatrice's scrutiny.

"The name says it all, doesn't it?" Beatrice added. "Your father's a criminal, and if Leonard didn't set all of this up, then Zander probably did." She paused. "I understand he's alive."

Declan jumped right on that. "How did you know?"

Beatrice dismissed that with the wave of her perfectly manicured hand. "I heard a rumor, but I'm not here to talk about Zander." Her gaze snapped to Declan. "I'm here to tell you to stop these ridiculous accusations about me and my husband. I don't care what the DNA test proves, you're not going to get one penny of my husband's money."

Eden had been following her. Until that last part. Declan was clearly confused, too, because he shook his head.

"Why would you think I'd want your money?" he demanded. "And what the hell does my DNA have to do with this?"

Now it was Beatrice's turn to look confused. Her fingers touched her parted lips.

"Stop!" someone called out.

Eden looked up the hall to see Stella frantically making her way toward Beatrice, Declan and her.

"Is something wrong with Kirby?" Declan immediately asked.

Stella was obviously too out of breath to answer right away, and she pressed her hand to her chest. However, her gaze went to Beatrice, and if looks could have killed, then Beatrice would be one dead woman.

"You had no right," Stella said to Beatrice.

Beatrice didn't back down. "Someone had to tell him the truth."

Declan went closer, nudging Beatrice aside, and he took Stella by the arm and led her into the break room. As he'd done earlier with Eden, he forced her to sit down.

"What's wrong?" Declan asked. "What's this all about?"

Stella and Beatrice looked at each other again. "If you don't tell him, I will," Beatrice threatened, her mouth in a tight red bud. "This ends right here, right now."

Eden glanced at Declan to see if he had any idea what was going on, but he didn't. He looked as dumbfounded as she did. Not Stella, though. The emotion was heavy in her eyes and face, but Eden couldn't tell what emotion it was exactly.

Stella looked up at Declan. "We have to talk. There are some things you need to know about your parents."

Chapter Twelve

A chill snaked down Declan's spine. He'd rarely seen Stella upset, but he was seeing it now. He was almost scared to guess what had put that look in her eyes.

Eden knew something was wrong, too, because she moved closer to him, taking his hand in hers.

"What about my parents?" Declan asked, and he tried to brace himself for an answer he was pretty sure he didn't want to hear.

Stella looked away from him. She kept her attention nailed to her hands in her lap, but he could have sworn she was blinking back tears.

"Tell him, Stella," Beatrice demanded.

Declan shot the woman a glare and was ready to toss her out of the building, but Stella finally looked up, met his gaze. He'd been right about those tears.

"I'm your birth mother," Stella whispered.

Declan shook his head, certain he'd misheard her. "You're *what?*"

"Your mother," Stella repeated.

Okay, so he hadn't misheard her after all, but it still took a moment to sink in. And when it did, those words came at him like a mountain being dropped on his head. The breath swooshed out of him, and because he had no choice, he leaned back against the doorjamb and let it support him.

"His mother?" Eden shook her head. "But his parents were killed in Germany when he was a boy."

"His adoptive parents were killed." Stella paused, blinked back more tears. "They were friends of friends with no link whatsoever to me. It had to be that way."

None of this made sense. "Why?" he managed to ask, and that one question could be about so many things. Declan didn't even know where to start.

"I'd just found out I was pregnant with you when someone tried to kill me," Stella continued. "I left the state. Tried to hide. But someone found me and attacked me again. That's when I left the country using a fake passport, and I gave birth to you in Germany."

Declan's head was pounding now. The thoughts flashing through them. The memories of his parents—meager memories, at that—were all lies. He wasn't the man he'd thought he was.

And Stella had spent decades lying to him.

He leaned down, still using the jamb for support, and he got right in her face. "Why didn't you tell me?"

"Because I was afraid someone would try to kill you." Despite the tears and shaky voice, she didn't hesitate. "The same person who tried to kill me."

"Someone killed my family," he reminded her, and he hated the anger in his voice. Stella was already on the verge of losing it. But he couldn't stop himself. Everything was crashing down on him.

Stella nodded. "I think they were murdered because someone was trying to get to you, because they found out you were my son. That's why you were sent to Ireland to be with Meg, a distant cousin of mine. But soon the threats started again, so I had you moved around from place to place."

"Until Meg dropped me off at Rocky Creek," Declan supplied.

"Yes." Stella paused again. "I arranged it after she couldn't handle the danger anymore. She was afraid she'd be murdered by the same person who'd killed your adoptive parents."

"Who killed them?" he shouted. Because he wanted them dead. That person had taken away everyone he'd loved, and had left him an orphan.

Or so he'd thought.

But his birth mother had been alive all along, and nearby the entire time he'd lived in Rocky Creek.

"Stella thinks I'm the one who tried to kill you," Beatrice volunteered.

Eden stepped between him and Beatrice, probably because she thought he might launch himself at the woman. "Why would she think that?"

But Beatrice didn't have to answer. Declan suddenly knew the reason why. "Because Jack Vinson is my biological father, and Beatrice was so insanely jealous that she wanted Stella and me dead."

That helped ease some of the, well, whatever the heck he was feeling for Stella. Anger, yes.

Maybe even rage.

And the feeling of being betrayed by someone he'd trusted. However, there was a bigger betrayal here, and she was standing right next to him wearing pricey clothes.

When Declan's glare landed on her, Beatrice actually dropped back a step, maybe because she saw that rage in him. She began to frantically shake her head.

"I didn't try to kill you. And I definitely didn't kill

your family. I wanted you out of my husband's life. Out of *my* life," she practically yelled. "You don't deserve to inherit anything *we* have."

"It's all about the money to her," Stella said in a whisper. "But until these attacks started and she showed up again, I had no idea she was behind them."

"I'm not!" Beatrice insisted.

Declan shut her out and motioned for Stella to continue. She was crying now, the tears streaking down her cheeks. "I thought the original attacks were from somebody that Kirby was investigating. He was dealing with some dangerous criminals in those days."

"Including Leonard Kane?" Eden asked.

Stella nodded. "This was about the same time that Kirby had to shoot and kill Leonard's son."

Declan's heart began to race even more than it already was, something he hadn't thought possible, since it felt as if his ribs were cracking. "Why would Leonard have gone after you?"

"Because he knew that Kirby loved her," Beatrice said before Stella could answer.

And Stella didn't deny it.

"I thought Jack Vinson could be behind the danger, too," Stella went on. "After all, I was engaged to him. And I cheated on him." That admission brought on more tears.

It also caused the room to go deadly silent.

Eden moved even closer to him. Slid her arm around his waist. Then they waited for Stella to finish. But that cheating confession was causing all sorts of thoughts to fly through his head.

"You cheated…with Kirby?" Declan asked.

"Who else?" Beatrice answered. "She never loved Jack. It was always about Kirby, and the moment she figured she could have him, she dropped Jack just like that." She snapped her fingers.

"You can leave now," Declan warned Beatrice, but he didn't take his attention off Stella. "Say it. I want to hear you say it."

Stella swallowed hard. "Kirby's your father."

Before he could stop it, a groan left his mouth, and even though Eden tried to hold on to him, he pushed her away.

Oh, man.

He hadn't seen this coming. Kirby was a good person. He'd saved him and his five foster brothers. But Stella and he had withheld the truth, and that cut Declan to the bone. To the very core of his soul.

"Kirby?" Beatrice looked at Stella as if she'd lost her mind. "You wish. You wanted your lover to be your baby's father, but we both know that Jack was."

"It was Kirby," Stella insisted. "I didn't tell him because I knew he'd probably end up getting killed trying to protect me and the baby. So after I gave birth to Declan in Germany, I left him with people I knew would give him a good, safe home. I thought I had covered my tracks." More tears came. "But obviously I hadn't."

"No, you hadn't." Declan wished he could cut her some slack. She was clearly hurting from all of this, but by God, the only family he'd known had been murdered.

"Does Kirby know now?" Eden asked.

Stella gave a shaky nod. "After Meg got sick, she called me to say she couldn't keep Declan any longer, so I arranged to have him brought to Rocky Creek. I told Kirby then."

Well, that explained why Kirby had taken such an interest in him. Except it hadn't felt like any more special treatment than he'd given the other boys who'd become his foster sons.

"Kirby wanted to tell you the truth," Stella went on, "but it was too dangerous. The threat was obviously still out there, and we didn't know who had killed your adoptive family. The safest thing for us to do was keep you close to us so we could watch out for you."

"So you changed his name?" Eden asked. "But he still had an Irish accent then. Didn't you think that'd make the killer suspicious?"

"The fear was always there, breathing down our necks," Stella verified. "But it wasn't as if we had a lot of choices. And besides, as far as the killer knew, Declan was in Germany somewhere, not Ireland. Then Kirby pointed out that the killer would think that Rocky Creek was the last place on earth we'd put our boy. Hiding him in plain sight, so to speak."

And it'd worked. He hadn't been free of Webb in those days, but a killer hadn't come after him.

There were so many questions that Declan wasn't sure where to start. "Someone left me a lot of money a while back, and I wasn't able to unravel where it came from."

"It was from me. It was my inheritance. I wanted you to have it, but I couldn't just give it to you, so I had it sent to you using a fake identity." She choked back a sob. "I swear, all these years, I was just trying to keep you safe."

"She's lying," Beatrice insisted. She pointed her finger at Declan. "I know you're Jack's son, and I know you want your hands on our money."

"My money," a man corrected.

Oh, man. It was Jack, and Declan didn't want to see him or anyone else right now.

Beatrice looked as if he'd slapped her, and she dropped back a step from him. "I didn't hear you come in."

"Obviously. Because you were too busy accusing Stella of lying." He walked closer, and his gaze connected with Stella's. "Is it true? Is Declan my son?"

Declan didn't realize he was holding his breath until his lungs started to ache.

Stella shook her head. "No. He's Kirby's. I got pregnant with him after you'd left on that business trip to Mexico."

Jack studied her. So did Declan. Beatrice just continued to mumble that Stella was lying.

"Why would I lie?" Stella challenged. "By admitting that Declan is Kirby's son, I'm not lessening the danger. I'm making it worse. And if I thought I had another choice, I'd take it. But despite everything I've done, I can't stop someone from trying to kill him."

Her voice broke, and she looked up at Declan. "I gave you up to save you."

He would have had to be an iceman not to react to that, and part of him wanted to pull her into his arms and say that he understood, but he couldn't do that. Not yet.

Maybe not ever.

Declan didn't say anything, couldn't, but Eden must have realized what he needed right now. She didn't waste any time moving both Jack and Beatrice aside. However, Eden did look back at Stella. "I'll call you later."

Maybe because she felt the pain that Stella was going through. Declan felt it, too, but he had to fight his way through all the other feelings first.

"Wait!" Jack called out. "I want to take a paternity test."

Declan didn't stop. He just kept moving. He had to get the hell out of there now.

"This isn't over," Jack added. "One way or another, I will learn the truth."

Yeah, so would Declan. After he came to grips with the world that'd just come crashing down hard around him.

Chapter Thirteen

Declan stormed out of the building so fast that Eden had a hard time keeping up with him. This had to be tearing him apart inside, yet he still gave their surroundings a lawman's glance before he got her into the parking lot and into his truck.

"I'm sorry," she said. The words were so useless, not nearly enough to help, but she wasn't sure anything would help right now.

Declan drove away fast, headed out of town and away from Stella. His mother. Even Eden was having trouble coming to terms with that, and she barely knew the woman. Or Kirby. But Kirby was also Declan's father.

If Stella had been telling the truth, that is.

Beatrice had been so adamant that she was lying, but as Stella had said—why would she lie about something that would ultimately only put Declan in more danger?

She wouldn't.

And that meant all these attempts on their lives were likely connected back to Kirby. It certainly made Leonard a stronger suspect. Of course, Beatrice had been very upset at the idea of sharing her husband's millions with a potential heir, so that gave her a serious motive to end Declan's life.

Without saying a word to her, Declan took out his

phone, and Eden saw from the name he pressed that he was calling Wyatt. His brother answered right away, and Declan pressed the speaker button and put the phone on the seat between them. Maybe because he had a white-knuckle grip on the steering wheel and didn't want to risk crushing the phone in his hand.

"I just talked to Stella," Wyatt said. "She's in pieces, Declan, and she's worried you'll do something reck-less. That was her word, not mine. I'm worried you'll do something stupid. Where are you?"

"With Eden. I need a favor." But he didn't continue for several long moments. "I need to know if Kirby's really my father."

"Already working on it. But even if it's true, you shouldn't be out there right now without backup. I don't have to remind you that someone wants you dead."

"No reminder needed. Let me know what you find out." And despite the fact that Wyatt was saying some-thing, Declan hit the end call button.

It didn't take long, just seconds, for Wyatt to call back, but Declan silenced the ringer and put his phone on vibrate before he shoved it into his pocket. "I can't turn it off," he mumbled.

No, because they were in the middle of a complex investigation. One they couldn't put on hold, because she doubted these attempts to kill them would just end. Updates would be coming in. And possibly the culprit's capture.

Or so she hoped.

"Are you going to talk to Kirby?" she asked.

"I can't."

She understood, but she also knew it wasn't a conver-sation that Declan could delay for long. Kirby might have the answers they needed to blow this case wide open.

Of course, that would mean talking to Kirby about this bombshell that'd just been dropped on him.

Declan drove toward the ranch, but when he reached the fork in the road he stopped, as if trying to decide if he should go to his own place or the family home.

"The ranch has a security system," he finally said as if reminding himself, and he headed that way. "Once we're inside, I can get started on some calls. I need to find out if either Beatrice or Jack had any contacts in Germany at the time my family was killed. I also need to check their bank records to see if there's been any money siphoned off to pay for those gunmen."

"It can wait." Even if it shouldn't.

Declan didn't answer her. He brought the truck to a stop near the back door of the ranch, caught her hand and hurried her inside. They'd barely made it to the kitchen when he locked the door, engaged the security system and started making one of those calls.

However, Eden put her hand over his phone to stop him. "Want to talk about it first?"

She was certain he'd say no, but he groaned and leaned against the door. "I'm not sure how I'm supposed to deal with this."

Eden had to shake her head. "I don't know, either." But she pulled him into her arms and hoped that just the small gesture would help.

His heart was racing. She could feel it beating against her own chest. Could feel the tight muscles in his back and arms, too. He didn't say anything, but he leaned in, brushed a kiss on her forehead. Eden wasn't even sure he was aware he was doing it.

"I have a lot of questions." His voice was a whisper now. "But I don't think I can ask them yet."

She eased back just enough to meet his gaze. "You're angry with Stella and Kirby."

He nodded. But then shook his head. "I think I'm pissed off about everything."

"Well, for an angry man, you're doing a good job keeping it together."

"Poker face," he mumbled and tried to smile.

Eden didn't even try to return the smile or make light of this. His pain went bone deep, and it was going to take more than a few hours at home for him to come to terms with it.

He stared at her, pushed a strand of hair off her face. "How are you holding up?"

"Fine. I didn't just have my life turned upside down."

"No, but you had bullets fired at you."

It was strange that she could push something like that aside. She certainly wasn't accustomed to having people try to kill her, or her father caught in the middle of an attack, and she prayed it never became routine. But it wasn't routine for her to see Declan hurting like this, either.

He leaned in again. Kissed her. It had no trace of the dark emotions that had to be boiling inside him. No trace of anything but a simple, sweet kiss.

And then it wasn't so sweet.

Declan made a sound. A groan of pain that came from deep within his chest. He eased his hand around the back of her neck, urged her closer and kissed her until Eden's legs felt wobbly. Until the heat seeped through every inch of her.

But this was wrong.

The kiss was past being good. Declan's always were, and she was getting maximum benefit from his mouth on hers. But it felt as if she was taking advantage of him.

He was in a very bad place, and the kisses he was using to shatter her into a thousand little pieces were kisses he was using to try to deal with the pain.

Better than punching something.

Not better, though, than trying to deal with it.

Still, he didn't stop and neither did she. Eden just let herself dissolve into his arms and let his mouth take her to the only place she wanted to go.

Eden heard the buzzing sound, and for a moment she thought it was part of the heat firing through her body. But then Declan cursed, took out his vibrating phone and she saw the screen lit up with a call from Unknown.

"Marshal O'Malley," Declan answered, caution in his voice, and he hit the speaker button.

"It's me, Zander. I need to speak to my daughter."

The relief was instant. But short-lived. "Are you all right? Were you shot?" she asked.

"I'm okay. I was wearing a bulletproof vest. It saved my life. Now, I need to know what the hell is going on. Who's trying to kill us?"

"We're not sure," Eden said.

Declan picked up where she left off. "We're still investigating it, but I haven't taken you off my suspect list."

"Well, you damn well should," her father insisted. "I was nearly killed today, and if that bullet had hit me in the head instead of the chest, I'd be a dead man. I'm not stupid, and I wouldn't have set up a fake attack that could have killed me and my daughter."

Declan only gave a heavy sigh, and she couldn't tell if he believed him or not. "Where are you? You need to turn yourself in."

"I will. I just need a little more time to prove my innocence. Did you find out anything useful with those bank records I gave you?"

"Nothing so far, except that they can't be used because they were illegally obtained. How'd you get them?"

"You wouldn't believe me if I told you." Her father mumbled something she couldn't understand. "Someone sent them to me. And I don't know who. The package didn't have a postmark and was left with a friend who knew how to get in touch with me in case of an emergency."

It hurt to know that he'd trusted someone else and not her in case of an emergency, but Eden wanted to give him the benefit of the doubt. Her father might have thought the marshals would have her phone tapped.

And they might have.

It would have been too risky for him to contact her.

"Keep looking for something. Anything," her father added. "And keep Eden locked inside wherever it's safe."

She wasn't sure such a place existed. Their attacker seemed to have a lot more information about them than they did him or her.

Her father hung up, but Declan didn't put his phone away. He scrolled through the numbers to call Clayton.

"People are worried about you," Clayton greeted. "Me included."

"I just need a little downtime," Declan said. He glanced at her mouth, and she wondered if the kiss had been just that. Downtime. An outlet for all that dangerous energy brewing inside him.

It'd be easier if it were.

But this attraction, for Eden, was the real deal. That didn't make it easier, but it did leave open the possibility that she'd walk away from this with a severely broken heart.

"Zander just called about those bank statements." Declan brushed a kiss on her cheek, stepped away from her.

Even from the other end of the line, she could hear Clayton take a deep breath. Maybe because he wanted to discuss his brother's well-being rather than the case. "The records seem to prove Leonard Kane took out a large sum of money from his offshore account around the same time someone tried to kill that witness who'd testified against Zander Gray."

The witness her father had been accused of trying to kill. But the problem was, this couldn't be used to prove anything. In fact, Leonard himself could have sent the records just as a way of adding some mental torture to this already torturous situation.

"The most recent records indicate that Leonard might be doing the same now," Clayton went on. "He transferred about a quarter of a million just a week ago."

"About the time someone was planning to hack into Eden's computer," Declan provided.

Oh, mercy. A quarter of a million could buy a lot of hired guns and bribe plenty of people to get whatever information he needed. But then, maybe someone was setting up Leonard.

Like Beatrice or Jack.

"Since we can't use the records, we'll have to try to find where the money was spent." Declan checked the clock on the wall. "I'll be there in about twenty minutes."

"No, you won't. Saul's orders. He told me to tell you to stay away from the office for the rest of the day."

Declan closed his eyes a moment. Not from relief. She could see the frustration all over his face. "I need to be there working."

"No, you need to be guarding Eden. Saul's put her in your protective custody."

Eden wasn't exactly surprised by that. She needed some kind of protection, and Declan was her best bet for that. But it did make her wonder if Declan's boss had heard rumors of the attraction simmering between them. Declan's brothers had certainly picked up on it.

"There's more," Clayton said a moment later. "Wyatt's working on your, well, paternity, but one of the first things that popped up was that Beatrice took a trip to Germany." He paused. "Declan, it was right around the time your family was killed."

"Hell." Declan added even more profanity and would have stormed back outside if Eden hadn't stepped in front of him.

"Any evidence that Beatrice hired someone to kill them?" Eden asked.

"None. In fact, Jack has her on a fairly tight personal budget because she tends to go through money like water. We're following the money trail she left when she was there, but her visit might have had nothing to do with the murders."

"Then why was she there, damn it?" Declan snapped.

"That's something I'll find out. And note that I said *I* and not *us*. That's because I've got to distance you from this. I don't want anything incriminating that we might find tossed out because the D.A. thinks we manufactured evidence."

The muscles in Declan's jaw stirred, and for a moment she thought he still might refuse, that he might head to the marshals' building anyway. However, he didn't reach to disarm the security system or open the door.

"Find something we can use," he told Clayton. "I'll

see what I can come up with without using official resources."

Declan hung up and started out of the room, probably
to work on something he wasn't ready to do. "I'll pour
you a drink," Eden offered.

The kitchen was huge, with over a dozen cabinets,
and she waited a moment, hoping that he'd point her in
the right direction for that drink. But he didn't. Declan
just stared at her.

"I'm sorry about this," he said. "But you're a better
fix than a drink."

And that was the only warning he gave her before
he snapped her to him and kissed her again. Not a gentle one this time. This was all heat and nerves. Mostly
nerves. But like his other kisses, it was still strong stuff.
The man knew how to light every fire in her body with
just his mouth.

He deepened the kiss. His grip on her got tighter. The
emotion upped a notch, something she hadn't thought
possible. So did the need that his kiss was building inside her.

But then he stopped, looked down at her. "I'm sorry
for this, too."

She shook her head, not understanding, but he came
right back to her for a kiss of a different kind. No nerves.

Just the heat.

Oh, she got it then. He was sorry that this was turning into something that neither of them seemed to be
emotionally ready for. Or able to stop.

Eden certainly couldn't.

She kissed him right back, and when he turned, pressing her against the counter, she pulled him right along
with her. Until his body was pressed against hers. Until
every inch of them was touching.

"You should say no," he reminded her, her mouth still against her.

"You should, too," she repeated to him.

But he kissed her again, and all reminders went right out the window.

"Whatever sympathy or pity you're feeling for me, it shouldn't play into this," he snarled.

Even though she had to break the kiss to do it, she looked him straight in the eye. "What I feel for you doesn't have anything to do with sympathy." She slid her hand over the front of his jeans, felt him hard and ready. "And apparently it doesn't for you, either."

He cursed again and looked as if he was in the middle of a serious mental debate. "I knew you were trouble when I first saw you. Too bad I really like this kind of trouble."

Well, good. Because it was all she could offer him now. Trouble and scalding-hot kisses. A bad combination, but it beat feeling the pressure from the danger and the investigation. Heck, this beat anything and everything she'd experienced.

His hand left her waist and slid beneath her shirt. He lit some little fires along the way as his fingers trailed up from her stomach to her breasts. His touch was like his kiss. Magic. And Eden knew this was going to lead them straight to the bed—or the floor—if she didn't stop it.

But she didn't want to stop.

And while Declan touched her and gave her another of those scalding kisses, she considered just how good this would be.

Bad, of course, too.

Because they didn't have time for sex and the aftermath it would create, and there would be an aftermath.

It would only deepen her feelings for a man who could ultimately destroy her father.

Or vice versa.

Besides, Declan would regret this. Maybe not today but eventually. And it was that reminder that gave her just enough strength to step back.

He let her slip from his arms, her top dropping back into place. But her breathing didn't level, and the burning need inside her didn't go away, either. Eden just stood there, waiting to see how long this puny dose of strength was going to last.

Probably not very long.

She wanted him more than all the rational reasons she could come up with for keeping out of his arms.

Declan's phone buzzed again, the soft sound shooting through the room. "Wyatt," he said, glancing at the screen. He looked at Eden as if debating if he should answer it and knowing he had no choice but to talk to his brother.

"No need to check up on me," Declan greeted him and put the call on speaker.

"Glad to hear it, 'cause I had plans to do that, but we got a problem. I'm leaving now to deal with a hostage situation over in Eagle Pass. But I just got a call from the deputy we have guarding Kirby's room."

"What happened?" Declan snapped.

Eden held her breath. Prayed. This had already been a hellish day without adding more.

"Leonard Kane just showed up and demanded to see Kirby," Wyatt explained. "And before Stella could call me to tell me what was going on, Kirby let Leonard into his room so they could *talk*. Little brother, you need to get over there fast."

Chapter Fourteen

Declan flew into the hospital parking lot, and as soon as he brought his truck to a stop, he barreled out. He did wait though for Eden to exit and hurry to his side. And he also glanced around to make sure this wasn't all some kind of setup for another attack.

Everything looked normal.

But it wouldn't stay that way. Not with Leonard and Kirby in the same room.

"If he hurts Kirby, Leonard's a dead man," Declan said under his breath.

Yeah, he was riled to the core that Kirby hadn't told him about being his father, but he owed Kirby a lot. His life, in fact, and there was no way he was going to let Leonard ride roughshod over a man too weak to fight back.

"The deputy wouldn't let Leonard do anything stupid," Eden reminded him.

It was a good reminder. The deputy was there. But Leonard was a man hell-bent on revenge because Kirby had shot and killed his son all those years ago. If Leonard had murder on his mind, he probably wouldn't let a deputy stop him.

Or Stella.

In fact, Leonard could kill all of them.

Declan hurried toward the side exit, and as on their previous visit, he maneuvered Eden through the halls to Kirby's room. The first sign of trouble he saw was the deputy standing outside Kirby's closed door. The deputy had his gun drawn, but he wasn't inside where he needed to be to protect Kirby and Stella.

"Why aren't you in there?" Declan shouted.

"Kirby's orders. He said he and his visitor needed to have a private discussion. Leonard agreed. He had his men go to the cafeteria to wait. Kirby sent Stella to Doc Landry's office and told her to stay there with the door locked. The hospital security guard's with her."

And that meant no one was with Kirby, protecting him.

Declan didn't even bother to hold back the profanity, but he did push Eden behind him and draw his gun. The deputy stepped aside so that Declan could throw open the door to Kirby's room.

He braced himself to see a fight, but Kirby was in his bed, sitting up and looking stronger than he had in weeks. Leonard was standing next to him and had no weapon. At least not a visible one.

"Get away from him," Declan insisted.

Leonard smiled, but there was no humor in it. "I'm here at Kirby's invitation."

Kirby nodded. "He is. I wanted to talk to him, to try to settle this old score between us."

"But it's a score that can't be settled," Leonard argued.

"You shouldn't be talking to this snake," Declan insisted. He tried to stay in front of Eden, but she stepped out and went closer to Kirby.

"Maybe this meeting can wait until you're stronger," Eden suggested softly to Kirby.

Kirby reached out, took her hand in his. "That's a kindness I don't deserve from you. Or you," he added, his gaze going to Declan. "Saying I'm sorry won't help, but I'm saying it anyway."

Declan glanced at Leonard to see if he knew anything about what this conversation meant. Judging from the smug look he got, he did.

"Yeah, I know he's your daddy," Leonard confirmed. "Some things started popping up a few weeks ago."

"Someone tried to run your DNA," Kirby explained. "I put a stop to it, but not before Leonard got his hands on it."

"Who ran his DNA?" Eden asked.

Declan wanted to know the same damn thing, but Kirby only shook his head. "I figured it was Leonard here, but he says no."

Leonard held up his hands, palms out. "Wasn't me. But Kirby thought that maybe it was the first step to me getting payment for what happened to my boy, Corey."

Kirby made a weary sigh, and he let go of Eden's hand. "I had no choice but to shoot Corey. Somewhere, deep down in your ice-cold heart, you know that. And you also know that trying to settle this score with Declan is just plain wrong. He had no part in Corey's death. No choice in fathers, either."

It was true. And ironic. Declan used to wish that Kirby was his real father. Now it was true, and he just couldn't get past the lies he'd been fed.

"Why didn't you tell me?" Declan came out and asked.

"I didn't know at first, not until Stella spilled everything after you'd arrived at Rocky Creek. Then, when I found out that someone might want you dead because of me, I couldn't risk telling you."

"You could have sent me away," Declan pointed out.

"Could have." Kirby paused after that agreement. "But I didn't figure that'd be any safer than having you in my sights. Of course, it meant you having to deal with that SOB, Jonah Webb."

Yeah, that'd been no picnic. Declan had gotten beatings from Webb, but now, looking back on it, he would have gotten a heck of a lot more if it hadn't been for Stella, and even Kirby, intervening.

"After I realized what Webb was doing and that I couldn't stop him, I tried just about everything I could to get you out of Rocky Creek," Kirby went on, "but I couldn't do it out in the open. Couldn't let anyone make the connection that you were my son."

And maybe that was why Kirby had fostered not just him but the boys who'd become his brothers. But Declan had to amend that. Whatever Kirby's reasons were for getting them out, there'd been no shortage of love and fatherly guidance before and after he'd taken them into foster care.

Kirby drew in a long breath, and he kept his gaze locked with Declan's. "But now the danger's back. Everything that Stella and I did to protect you wasn't enough. That's why I asked Leonard to come. If he feels the need for revenge, I want him to take it out on me. Not you."

"No." Declan charged forward, shoving Leonard aside. "You're not killing him."

Leonard stayed put and turned his glare on Declan. "Don't get your jeans in a twist. Killing Kirby is the last thing I want. It'll end his suffering too soon. It'll end this." He motioned first to Declan, then Kirby. "And as far as I can tell, I want *this*. Because it's clear that you and Kirby are at odds over his daddy lie."

Eden folded her arms over her chest. "Are you saying you don't want us dead?"

"No. I'm saying I don't want you dead *right now*." Leonard's gaze shifted to Declan. "And if you think you can use that to arrest me, think again, honey bun. Wishing you dead and doing something about it are two different things."

Declan couldn't argue with that. Still, he'd look for an excuse, any excuse, to slap this moron behind bars.

"The way I got it figured, Declan can put Kirby through a lot more pain and suffering than I can by putting a bullet in his blood kin," Leonard added. "Or a bullet in an old business partner's blood kin."

Eden's father. And since Leonard smiled when he said it, Declan figured Leonard still had a lot of ill will toward Zander. On this point, the feeling was mutual. At least it had been until today, but he was beginning to have serious doubts about Zander's guilt.

"So this feud is over?" Eden asked.

"Postponed," Leonard clarified. He winced a little, touched his fingers to his temple. "Of course, it can't be postponed for too long. I got my own deathbed to deal with."

Yeah, and Declan needed answers before that happened, because he had the sick feeling that Leonard had already made arrangements that would extend beyond his grave.

Arrangements to kill all of them.

"I know you hired someone to try to kill the witness scheduled to testify against Zander," Declan said. It wasn't exactly a bluff. He did know it, had the bank records that all but proved it, but he couldn't *prove* it in a court of law. Still, he wanted to see Leonard's reaction. "You did that to set Zander up for murder. A different kind of score to settle, huh?"

Leonard didn't respond other than to slide his fingers around the metal footboard on Kirby's bed. He certainly didn't deny it.

"Now you've hired more gunmen. More killers," Declan spelled out. "I want names so I can put a stop to this."

His demand undoubtedly would fall on deaf ears, but Declan had to try. And this time he did get a reaction. "I didn't hire anyone."

A lie, probably. But the look on Leonard's face seemed real. He went ashy pale, sweat popping out on his forehead, and his grip tightened on the footboard.

"Get a doctor in here now," Leonard said, his voice punctuated with his suddenly shallow breathing.

Eden obviously thought he wasn't faking it because she pressed the button on the wall next to Kirby's bed.

"Don't worry." Leonard's color was even worse now. So was his breathing. "I'm not ready to croak yet. Kirby and I still have some unfinished business."

With that threat still hanging in the air, the door opened and a nurse rushed in.

"I got a terminal, inoperable brain tumor," Leonard managed to say to her.

The nurse looked at Leonard, hurried to him and called for assistance. It didn't take long before the room was a flurry of activity. Another nurse and a medic came rushing in with a wheelchair, and the trio helped Leonard into it before they whisked him away.

Kirby still didn't lie down, but Eden adjusted his pillows and eased him back. "I can wait outside while you two talk," she offered.

Both Kirby and Declan shook their heads. "You need to stay here with me," Declan said, and it wasn't a suggestion. She wasn't leaving his sight because all of this could be a ploy by Leonard to separate them. Especially since Leonard would know that Kirby and Declan had to *talk*.

"I don't want pity playing into this," Kirby said, looking at Declan. "You need to go ahead and get it out. Blast me for what I did."

Declan wanted to do just that. He wanted this firestorm of feelings to go away and for things to go back to how they were. But that was impossible. He was looking at his birth father. A man who might be dying. So, yeah, pity would play into this. Worry and fear, too. There was no way he could blast Kirby while he was in this condition.

"I wish I'd known," Declan settled for saying. He reholstered his gun.

"I wish I'd been able to tell you. Just know I was always proud of you. Always loved you."

Declan hadn't doubted that, and he didn't doubt that Kirby loved his foster brothers equally.

"Don't put any of this on Stella," Kirby continued. "She was scared spitless for you, and she gave you up to make sure you'd live. That makes her a saint in my book."

"You still love her," Eden said under her breath.

But Kirby didn't have time to confirm or deny that. There were some voices in the hall, and a moment later someone appeared in the still-open doorway.

Declan drew his gun again.

As Beatrice stepped into the room.

She didn't step in easily. The deputy had hold of her arm, trying to haul her back, and despite the arctic glare she was giving him, he didn't let go.

"I have to speak to you." Her glare snapped to Declan. "Tell your Neanderthal to back off before I slap him with a lawsuit."

Declan didn't care if she sued or not, and he was about to tell the deputy to toss her out on her designer-clad butt.

"I have proof that Kirby's not your father," Beatrice snarled.

That stopped Declan from giving the toss-her-out order, and the moment the deputy's grip eased off her, Beatrice came storming toward him. She wasn't armed, but she did have a piece of paper in her hand. She thrust it toward him.

"It's the results of a DNA test I had run on you," she explained.

Declan didn't look at the paper yet. "How the hell did you get my DNA?"

Her chin came up. "I had someone take it from a cup you used at the diner across the street."

That seemed like a lot of trouble to go through, but then Beatrice was worried about his paternity.

"I had your DNA compared to Jack's, and it's a match," she continued. "That doesn't mean you have a right to our money. I checked, and since Kirby adopted you, that'll make it next to impossible for you to try to make any claims against Jack's estate."

Declan looked at the results. It was a standard lab test that he was used to reading, but he wasn't used to seeing his name associated with someone else who was supposed to be his biological father.

"The test results are fake," Kirby said. He met Beatrice's gaze. "I'm Declan's father, so there's no reason for Jack or you to come after him."

Beatrice shook her head. "I had the result tested at a reputable lab."

"BioMedical," Kirby provided. "I have a lot of friends in this field. Law enforcement, too. And I had flags put on Declan's name in case anyone tried to have his DNA tested. The lab called this morning and said there'd been a mix-up and the results had been released to you."

"The real results?" someone asked from the doorway. It was Jack.

Both Declan and Eden groaned. This meeting was already complicated enough without adding a paternity candidate to it.

"Beatrice got fake results," Kirby insisted. "I had a DNA test done years ago. One that I know wasn't tampered with, and Declan's my son."

Declan braced himself for Jack's denial, but the man only lifted a piece of paper that he was holding. "I heard Beatrice making arrangements for the DNA test, and I paid a lab tech to do a second test and give me the results." He walked closer, handed the paper to Declan.

"You what?" Beatrice snapped. "You went behind my back?"

Jack's eyes darkened. "You went behind mine."

That brought on an argument as to which one of them had done the right thing, but Declan tuned them out. Eden obviously did, too, because she looked at both the papers with him.

Hell.

What was this about?

"How can this be?" Eden asked, and her voice was loud enough to stop the Vinsons' argument. Both Jack and Beatrice turned to Declan and her.

Declan lifted the paper that Beatrice had given him. "This test claims that Jack is my biological father." He lifted the other one. "And the one that Jack gave me says that Kirby is."

Jack came closer, snatched the papers from Declan's hands and looked at them. He cursed. "Is this some kind of joke?"

"No joke," Kirby answered. "I didn't pay the tech to falsify the result, only to alert me that a DNA test had been ordered so I could do some damage control."

Beatrice had a look at the papers as well, and she looked as confused as her husband. "Who would have done this? And what's the truth?"

"I've already told you the truth," Kirby continued. "Declan is mine. Now, I know that makes him a target in Jack's eyes. He might want to eliminate him to get back at Stella and me—"

"I don't want to eliminate anyone," Jack snapped. "I just want the truth."

Kirby looked him straight in the eye. "He's my son, not yours." His gaze shifted to Beatrice. "And that gives you no motive for murder."

Beatrice gasped as if insulted that he would accuse her of such a thing, but she sure didn't deny it. She did, however, look at the papers again. "Who would have faked the DNA-test results?"

"Someone who wanted to incite you to kill Declan." Kirby's attention shifted to Jack. "And that's the same reason you got the real results. That gives both of you motives to try to kill him."

It was true. But the problem was, who had created the fakes? Either of them could have, whether to draw suspicion off themselves, or in Jack's case, maybe he wanted his wife to commit murder. Better than a divorce, where he'd have to split his assets with her. Of course, Beatrice could have faked the results to do the same to Jack. With Jack behind bars for murder, she'd have control of all the money.

So they were back to square one.

"I won't let either of you hurt him," Kirby said. And before Declan realized what he was doing, Kirby reached beneath his pillow and drew his gun.

He pointed it right at Jack.

Kirby's eyes narrowed, too. "I think it's time for you to confess everything you know about these attacks."

"I know nothing about them." Jack's hand moved toward his jacket, but Declan turned his own gun in the man's direction.

"I wouldn't do that if I were you," Declan warned him. "Nerves are a little bit raw right now." He glanced at Kirby. "Yours, too. Why don't you put that gun away and let me handle this."

But Kirby obviously didn't listen. He turned that frosty glare on Beatrice. "Start talking."

She frantically shook her head. "I don't know anything. I'm certainly not responsible for what's going on with your son." Beatrice made that particular label sound like a disease. "And I'm leaving. I won't stand here and be subjected to the likes of you."

Beatrice turned and walked out, practically knocking the deputy off balance. Declan was sure she'd actually left because he heard her heels clacking on the tile floor.

"You should go, too," Declan warned Jack.

Jack's mouth tightened, and he mumbled something Declan didn't catch before he, too, stormed out.

"You need to get Clayton on this," Kirby said the moment Jack was out of the room. He released a long, labored breath.

All of his foster brothers were already neck deep in this case and their regular investigations. Added to that, his sisters-in-law's lives were on hold because they couldn't return to the ranch until it was safe. At the rate they were going, that might never happen.

"More trouble?" Stella said from the doorway. She gave both Declan and Eden a concerned glance, but most of her concern was for Kirby. And he needed it. Kirby looked weaker than ever, and Stella went to him.

"Guess it won't do any good to say you shouldn't have had these meetings," she scolded him. Stella took the water glass from the stand and made Kirby take a sip.

Declan saw it then. The affection between the two. Maybe even the love.

Why hadn't he seen it earlier?

Maybe because he'd been too wrapped up in his own life and Kirby's illness. Now he was wrapped up in keeping Eden and himself alive. Kirby and Stella, too, because despite Kirby's warning, Declan figured Jack, Beatrice and even Leonard could all come back.

Declan walked closer to the deputy. "I need you to call the sheriff and have him beef up security here at the hospital. I don't want the Vinsons or Leonard Kane allowed back in the building, much less anywhere near Kirby."

The deputy nodded and took out his phone to make the call just as Declan's own cell buzzed. He glanced at the screen and saw the caller was Unknown again.

"I think it's your father," he relayed to Eden, and that sent her hurrying across the room toward him.

Declan answered the call and put it on speaker.

"O'Malley, I want you to take Eden someplace safe and keep her there until this is over."

Yeah, it was her father all right, and he sounded out of breath. As if he was running. Or chasing someone.

"What's wrong?" Declan asked.

"Something's finally right. I know who's trying to kill you, and I'm going to stop it. This ends *now*."

And with that, Zander hung up.

Chapter Fifteen

The waiting and not knowing were getting to her. By now, Eden figured she should be accustomed to both, but she obviously wasn't. She felt raw. Like one big giant nerve.

Nothing felt safe. Not even the ranch, though Declan had asked the hands to arm themselves and be on the lookout for anyone suspicious. It was only after those measures that Declan had brought her to wait for her father's call or any other update they could get on the case.

So far, they'd had zero in either department.

No more calls from her father. No breaks in the investigation. So they were in wait-and-worry mode. Well, she was anyway. Declan had disappeared into another part of the house just minutes earlier, so maybe he'd found something productive to do.

Not her, though. Unless pacing qualified as productive.

She was tired of pacing. Tired of the feeling of panic crawling over her. But she was afraid to sit for fear the exhaustion would take over and she'd collapse. That was the last thing Declan needed after everything he'd been through today.

And what they still had to face.

Maybe her father could fix this and put an end to the

danger. She prayed that was possible. But she didn't want that at the expense of his life. She had enough emotions to deal with without adding grief and guilt.

Speaking of guilt, she heard another sound of it coming her way. Declan. A guilty feeling of a different kind. Eden turned and spotted him making his way into the family room. He'd taken off his jacket, but still had on his holster over a great-fitting plain white T-shirt.

Mercy.

The man could make something that simple look good, along with helping some of the tension slide right from her body.

His walk was a swagger. Natural, no doubt, and his nondesigner jeans fit him like a glove. He had a drink in his left hand and was sipping from another in his right.

"You need this," he said, handing her the glass.

Even though Eden wasn't much of a drinker, she took a sip anyway, and the cool whiskey burned her throat all the way down.

Declan took another gulp of what appeared to be a quadruple shot. Apparently, he needed it, too. And he tipped his head to the stairs. "It's getting late. Why don't you get some rest and I'll keep watch."

The prospect was tempting, especially since the security system was on and there were a half dozen ranch hands guarding the place.

"Why don't we both rest," she suggested. The next sip of whiskey went straight to her head. Or maybe that was just Declan's doing. The man was potent stuff.

The corner of his mouth lifted. "If we rest together, it won't be restful."

True. And while that would complicate the heck out of both of their lives, it was tempting. Even more so when he leaned in and brushed one of those mind-numbing kisses on her lips. However, he didn't carry it any further. He just lit that particular fire, stepped away and leaned against the wall, facing her.

That didn't help, either.

He was drop-dead hot, and it didn't matter how bad their situation got. He was still drop-dead hot.

"Your father wouldn't approve anyway," Declan said, as if trying to talk himself out of whatever he was feeling.

And what was he feeling?

Eden realized they'd yet to talk about something so, well, normal. It'd all been criminal reports, interviews with suspects and dodging bullets. Hardly the right atmosphere for talking about what was going on inside their hearts. But there was a lot going on inside hers.

"My father definitely wouldn't approve," she agreed. "But he's never had a say in my personal life."

His eyebrow lifted. "With the way you defend him, I thought you were close."

"No. It's complicated." But then she laughed. "Something you know a little about."

"Yeah." He groaned and sank to the floor, his back still against the wall.

Even though it was a dangerous move, Eden went closer, stooped and sat down beside him. "Want to talk about Kirby and Stella?"

He stayed quiet for so long that Eden was certain he would say no. But he had another large sip of his whiskey. "I want to hate them, but I can't. Because I've thought of Kirby as my father for a long time now."

"And Stella?"

Declan lifted his shoulder and set his whiskey glass on the floor. "I remember her looking out for me at Rocky Creek. Once, Jonah Webb, the headmaster, was giving me a beating, and Stella stepped in and stopped it. She nearly got fired. After that, she always tried to keep herself between me and Webb. Sometimes, she succeeded."

It crushed her heart to hear what he'd been through at that horrible place. She'd read accounts of it, but nothing in those accounts told her of the physical abuse Declan had gone through.

"Don't." He leaned in, gave her another of those idle kisses. "No need to feel sorry for me. All of that happened a long time ago."

"It's the reason you became a marshal."

He nodded. "That and Kirby." He didn't kiss her, but he did run his thumb over her bottom lip and then brought it to his own mouth to taste.

Her stomach did a serious flip-flop.

He didn't make a move to turn that into a real kiss, so Eden did. She moved in on him, pressing her mouth to his and sliding her hand around the back of his neck.

Declan made a sound. Part groan, part grunt. But he didn't push her away. Nope. He hauled her to him and kissed her until all the nerves were gone. Well, the regular nerves. The heat and the sensations of pleasure were right there, urging her on.

But he didn't urge her for long. Declan eased back. Stared at her. "If I take you now, you'll regret it."

"You're sure? Because this doesn't feel like regret."

He chuckled. Like the rest of him, that was hot, too. Of course, in the state she was in, his breathing was a turn-on.

"Do you have any idea what you do to me?" she asked.

"Yeah. You do the same to me. That's why you'll take a shower alone. Clear your head. Then we can…talk if you're still feeling up to it."

He was giving her an out. An out Eden wasn't sure she wanted. But it was something he insisted on, because he got to his feet and helped her to hers.

Another kiss. Much too quick. And he put his hand on the small of her back to get her moving up the stairs. "I'll make some calls and see if anyone has any news."

That couldn't hurt, but she figured if there truly was news, someone would have already called. He led her to the guest room, where she'd stayed the night before. It was just up the hall from his. Two doors down.

But he didn't head there.

He waited in the doorway of her room, watching her. And she would have been blind not to see the heat in his eyes.

"You're sure I need some time?" she asked.

He smiled again. That slow, lazy smile that turned her to liquid fire. "I'm trying to be a gentleman here."

The seconds passed, slowly. His smile went south. And he pushed himself away from the doorjamb.

"But then we both know I'm not a gentleman," he drawled.

DECLAN CAME TOWARD her and hauled her into his arms.

He figured this was a few steps past stupid, but that didn't stop him. In fact, it'd take Eden telling him no to stop, and she definitely didn't say no. She pulled him closer and made a sound of what appeared to be relief. Declan totally got that. Eden and he had been skirting each other for two days now, and this blasted attraction had reached a boiling point.

One touch of his mouth to hers and the boiling point seemed cool compared to what he was feeling inside. It'd been a while since he'd wanted a woman this much, and in the back of his mind, he knew that was a lie. He'd *never* wanted anyone this much, even if she was the very woman he should be backing away from.

And maybe that was the bottom line here.

This was forbidden, and maybe that made it feel so damn necessary. And so much hotter.

He kissed her hard. Too hard. And while they fought to get closer, they off balanced themselves and darn near fell on their butts. All in all, the floor wouldn't have been a bad place to be, but he needed to get to his room, where he had some condoms. He didn't want to double his trouble by having unprotected sex. Protected sex was going to be memorable enough. And apparently inevitable.

Without breaking the kiss, Declan maneuvered Eden out of the guest room and in the direction of his room.

"You'd better not stop," she said against his mouth.

He wouldn't stop. Common sense was out the window now, and he was in take-her-now mode. Worse, Eden was in the same take-me frame of mind, so Declan figured he stood no chance of slowing this down. He got her inside his bedroom and kicked the door shut.

She went after his T-shirt, only to curse the holster that got in the way. Declan helped her with that, dropping the gun and holster on the nightstand, and they tumbled onto the bed. The feather mattress swelled up on both sides of them, cocooning them, and with one swift move, Eden was on top of him, straddling him.

Her eyes were wild and hot. Like the rest of her. And she finally got his T-shirt off and sent it sailing across the room. Now she slowed a little. Her gaze slid over his bare chest.

"No," she mumbled.

Declan glanced down to see what'd prompted that, and her attention was on the four-inch scar on the side of his chest. But only briefly. Her gaze went from the scar to the rest of him, including his stomach and lower, to the zipper of his jeans.

"No?" he asked.

"Not that kind of no," Eden quickly clarified. "No as in I was hoping your body wasn't as good as my imagination thought it'd be. But you're better than anything I could have imagined."

He was flattered. And confused. "So why the no?"

"Because with a body like yours, you're used to *wow,* and I don't have a wow kind of body."

Declan seriously doubted that. The woman burned him to ash, and he figured whatever was beneath those clothes would only make the burn faster and hotter.

So he did something to prove it.

Declan stripped off her top. And he gave her the same once-over she'd given him. She was wearing a bra, white and no frills, and he unclasped the front hook and rid her of that, too. Her breasts spilled into his hands.

Man, she was perfect.

But while he was gawking, he unzipped her jeans and shimmied them off her. The panties matched the bra. Nothing special, but when he removed those, the woman beneath still fell into that perfect category.

"You'll do just fine," he teased, and he pulled her down to him so he could kiss her the way he wanted.

First, her mouth.

Then he shifted their positions and went exploring. To the curve of her neck. He got a good response there. A nice little breathy moan. Then he went to her breasts and took her right nipple into his mouth.

Better-than-nice response.

The moan was louder, and she arched her back to give him more of her. He stayed there for several moments. Pleasuring her and pleasuring himself. Before he dropped some kisses on her stomach.

He took in her scent. Her sex. And coupled with the kissing, he was burning for her when she caught him and flipped their positions.

"I want these off now," Eden said, and she tackled the zipper on his jeans.

Yeah, he wanted that, too, but after she fumbled with the zipper, trying to get it down over the bulge of his erection, he wasn't sure what exactly she meant to *get off*.

So that he could prolong this past the foreplay stage, Declan reversed their positions again and helped her with the jeans and boots removal. Her hands were frantic now. Something he understood. Everything inside him was yelling for him to be inside her.

They were lying diagonally across the bed, and he groped behind him to open the nightstand drawer while Eden tackled his boxers. The need and urgency made them both a little sloppy, and her fingernails nicked his upper thigh. He didn't even feel the pain. The only thing he could feel was her beneath him.

Somehow he managed to grab a condom and get the darn thing on. And he could have sworn a lightning bolt hit him when he finally got inside her.

Yeah. Perfect.

This was special all right, and even though this fire made him stupid, he could still see that.

He forced himself to take a deep breath. Just so he could savor her and this for a few seconds before the breakneck pace started again. In those seconds, their gazes met. Declan saw the heat, of course. Saw Eden's amazing face. But he saw something else. Some emotion that he hadn't expected to see there.

This wasn't just sex for her.

Normally, that would have caused him to pull back, because he never wanted to lead a woman on. He'd never looked for anything permanent.

Still wasn't.

But there was something in the way Eden was looking at him that made him wish that he was doing that. That their situation wasn't what it was.

Then she lifted her hips, started moving and all thoughts of emotions and wishes went right out of his head. The need took over and dictated the speed. Dictated everything. Eden and he moved together with just one purpose.

To finish this.

It didn't take much. Probably because their foreplay had lasted two days, but Declan felt her climax ripple through her. It ripped through him, too, and brought him right to the edge.

However, before he went over, he leaned down and kissed her. Really kissed her.

It was Eden's taste in his mouth. The feel of her shattering around him. And the sight of the sight. He couldn't hold on any longer. So Declan took the plunge.

And landed right in Eden's waiting arms.

Chapter Sixteen

Eden's eyes flew open, and she bolted to a sitting position. Her heart was racing. Breath, too. She'd had a nightmare that had already faded, but it still caused the panic to rise inside her.

"It's okay," Declan murmured, and he pulled her back to him.

She glanced around. Then at him. It was dark, but she remembered she was in his bedroom. In his bed.

And they were both stark naked.

With the effects of the dream gone, her body relaxed. How, she didn't know. She'd never suspected she would be able to relax around a naked Declan. However, the thought had no sooner crossed her mind when Eden felt that trickle of heat.

A familiar one.

She let herself slide right back into that heat, and against Declan.

His eyes were closed, but he gathered her deeper into his arms and planted a lazy kiss on her forehead. "I'll get up in a minute."

Eden wanted to nix that idea right away. She wanted to stay like this, well, probably a lot longer than Declan did. He was a love-'em-and-leave-'em type. But she wasn't. It'd be hard when he walked away from her. And he would walk. Once this investigation was over, there'd be no reason for him to stay in her life.

Talk about a mixed bag.

The danger would be gone, but so would he. That put a pain in her chest as if someone had clamped a meaty fist around her heart.

Great.

Now she'd completely fallen for him.

The exact opposite of what she'd told herself to do.

Declan groaned softly, gave her another kiss. Not so soft and sweet this time. And he pulled away from her so he could sit up. He swung his feet off the bed, and she got a good view of his backside when he walked to the adjoining bathroom. He came back a few minutes later.

Still naked.

But this time she got a great view of the front of him.

He smiled, gave her another kiss and started to dress. Peep show was over, and Eden could only hope that they'd get to do this again.

"How soon will this be over?" Eden couldn't believe she'd blurted that out. And clearly she'd confused Declan because he just gave her an odd look.

He stood there, wearing just his boxers and that puzzled look. "I'm guessing we're not talking about the danger here?"

"No. Sadly, we aren't." She tried to wave him off, but Declan came closer, eased back on the edge of the bed. "Just so you know, I don't expect anything."

Mercy, she was babbling. And saying really stupid things.

"There's an old saying," she mumbled. "If you want to get out of a hole, the first thing you should stop doing is digging. I should stop digging."

The corner of his mouth lifted in one of his body-tingling half smiles. "You want to get out of that hole?" he asked.

And now she was the one puzzled. "I've done a thorough background check on you. I know you don't stay in relationships for long."

Now it made it sound as if long was what she wanted. And maybe she did. But that was a lot to dump on him after just having sex.

Incredible sex.

But it'd been just that once.

"Can we just forget everything I've said for the last five minutes?" she asked.

The smile returned, and he kissed her. All right. That made things better. The heat returned, too, washing away her blabbering.

"We'll talk soon," he promised. But then his forehead bunched up.

"You don't have a clue what you want to say to me," she guessed. It was apparently a good guess because he lifted his shoulder.

"I know I want to keep you safe." He glanced down at the scar on his chest. "And I know what happens when I lose focus. Not because I don't trust you," he quickly added. "I do. But I need to find this killer first. Then I'm thinking I'd like you back in my bed."

The next kiss he gave her left no doubts about that. Better yet, it cleared her own doubts. If sex was all that became of this, then it would still be some of the best memories of her life.

"You can stay in bed if you like," he offered, standing and continuing to dress. "You need the rest."

So did he, but he was obviously getting ready to work, and that meant she needed to work, as well. She got up and gathered her clothes, too, and was nearly dressed by the time Declan fished his phone from his pocket.

"No calls," he said under his breath.

So they hadn't missed anything. Again, a mixed bag. A good update on the case would have been a nice bonus.

Declan placed his phone on the nightstand while he strapped on his holster. Then he scrolled through the numbers on his phone and called Clayton. Because he put it on speaker, she could hear the ringing.

But Clayton didn't answer.

He tried Harlan next. But he got the same results. By the time he made it to Dallas's number, Declan was cursing.

"Something's wrong."

Eden moved closer and saw him try Stella next. Unlike the others, the woman answered on the first ring.

"Did you find him?" Stella immediately asked.

That question caused Eden to pull in her breath. Stella's tone was frantic, and it was obvious that something was wrong.

"Find who?" Declan asked.

"Kirby." Stella made a hoarse sob. "You don't know what happened, do you?" She didn't wait for him to answer. "I told Clayton you had your hands full guarding Eden. And besides, I thought you'd need some... distance."

"What the heck are you talking about, Stella!" No longer just a question but a demand. "What happened to Kirby?"

"Someone called him on his cell phone here at the hospital about an hour ago. I don't know who. Kirby said it was private and asked the guard to take me to the cafeteria for a while. When we came back, he was gone. His gun was missing, too."

"Gone?" Eden and Declan said in unison. Mercy, this couldn't be happening.

"How could he go anywhere?" Declan continued. "He's weak, going through chemo."

"Well, he somehow managed to get out. Or else someone took him. There was no sign of a struggle," she quickly added. "And he left me a note. He said he had to confront this killer once and for all."

Declan groaned. Then cursed. "Where'd he go?"

"I don't know, but Clayton and the others are looking for him."

"I'll call you back," Declan snapped. He hung up and fired off a text for Clayton to call him ASAP. He then sent the same text to the rest of his foster brothers.

The seconds crawled by, and Eden considered trying to reassure Declan that everything would be okay. But that would be a guess at best. A lie at worst. Because this sounded far from okay.

"I need to go look for him," Declan said. He glanced back at her. "And I don't want to leave you here."

She nodded. "I want to go with you."

Neither of them had to say that it might not be safe to do that. It didn't matter. Her father was out there, too, but he wasn't sick. He could fend for himself. It wasn't the same for Kirby, even though he'd apparently taken his gun with him.

The wait for a call from one of his brothers turned into what seemed an eternity, but Declan's phone finally buzzed, and she saw Wyatt's name on the screen.

"What happened?" Declan asked the moment he answered.

"We're still not sure. We don't think Kirby was kidnapped, but it's possible."

Declan's mouth tightened, his only visible reaction,

but she could feel the tension coming off him. "How did Kirby get past the deputy?"

"He got called away right before all of this happened. He said he thought the call was from dispatch, but it turns out it wasn't. It's possible Kirby was responsible for that, too."

It took Declan a moment to get his teeth unclenched. "But why the hell would Kirby do this?"

"We're not sure—yet. But we were able to put a tracer on his phone so we know where he's going." Wyatt paused. "Declan, Kirby's heading out to the abandoned Rocky Creek Children's Facility."

DECLAN COULDN'T GET Eden in the truck fast enough, and he gunned the engine so they could speed away. He had to get to Kirby, to stop whatever the hell was going on. But he had to be smart about this, too.

"This could be some kind of trap," he told her. "Keep watch around us." He'd do the same. But it might not be enough.

They were both armed, but it was getting dark, and their attacker could have set all of this up just to lure them out from the safety of the ranch. That nearly caused Declan to turn around and head back. He could leave Eden with the ranch hands.

But that could be a trap, too.

What if all of this was designed to get them apart? So that someone could pick them off one at a time? Besides, Eden wouldn't stay put while he went after Kirby. Declan was sure of that. She would try to help him, and in doing so, she could get herself killed.

Later, he'd curse himself for that. He shouldn't have slept with her. Should have kept this professional. But even now, with the unknown and the fear eating away at him, he knew that would have been impossible. From the moment he'd seen her on his back porch, he'd wanted her. And yeah, that didn't make sense, but then attraction rarely did.

"What would cause Kirby to go to Rocky Creek?" Eden asked.

Declan was still trying to work that out. "Maybe he didn't go voluntarily."

In fact, that was his first guess, because even if Kirby had learned the identity of the person who wanted them dead, he was too weak to go after him or her alone. He would have called one of his foster sons.

Unless he had believed his sons would refuse to let him go.

Which they all would have done.

They would have fought this fight for Kirby and forced him to stay at the hospital even if they'd had to cuff him to the blasted hospital bed.

"But why Rocky Creek?" Eden's gaze fired in all directions on the isolated country road. Keeping watch. "If he's doing this of his own free will, or even if someone took him, why go there?"

Declan had a theory about that. A bad one. "Maybe it's where Jack would have taken him to force Kirby to confess to Webb's murder."

Of course, that would only happen if Jack had been the one to kill Webb and now he wanted Kirby to take the blame.

But why do it this way?

A confession from his hospital bed would have accomplished the same darn thing. And why would Kirby have agreed to a confession anyway? Kirby was just as much of a suspect as Jack. Maybe more. And there was no physical evidence that Declan knew of to cause either of them to be arrested.

So what could Jack have on him that would make Kirby do this?

Eden made a sound to indicate she was thinking about his answer. "If Jack threatened to exchange your life for a confession, maybe Kirby's out here to meet him. And kill him."

Yeah. Declan's mind had already gone in that direction, and it wasn't a comforting direction to go. Kirby had been a good shot in his day, but this was no longer his day. Not with the cancer making him so weak. If he'd gone to Rocky Creek for a showdown, then it was a fight he could easily lose. With any of their suspects. Heck, even Beatrice would be able to outshoot him.

Declan's phone buzzed, and he put it on speaker as fast as he could. "It's me," Wyatt said. "Harlan, Dallas and I are at Rocky Creek. We had Clayton and Slade stay with Stella in case she's in danger. They're taking her back to the ranch."

Good idea, and Declan was glad his brothers were thinking more clearly than he was. That could be part of the trap, to divide and conquer, and if the killer managed to get Stella, it would give him or her a bargaining chip that could turn out to be a deadly one. All of them, including Kirby, would do whatever it took to protect Stella. Of course, Declan could say the same for Eden.

"We found Kirby's truck," Wyatt continued. "It's in a ditch about a quarter of a mile from Rocky Creek Facility. The engine's still running. The headlights are on."

Not good. That meant Kirby had exited in a hurry. Or had been forced from the vehicle.

"Any sign of footprints?" Or blood. But Declan didn't

have to ask that specifically. If it was there, Wyatt would let him know.

"No footprints. But there are drag marks."

Hell. That was not what Declan wanted to hear. Beside him, Eden pulled in her breath.

"The drag marks end just a few yards from the car," Wyatt added. "Looks like maybe someone picked him up and carried him, but the footprints have been brushed away."

"Kirby could be anywhere on the grounds," Declan grumbled.

"Yeah," Wyatt confirmed. "Dallas is headed to the main building. Harlan's taking the area near the creek. I'm going to the west side of the grounds."

"Eden and I will search the east side. We're just a couple of minutes out."

Declan shaved some time off those minutes by pushing even harder on the accelerator. He prayed there wasn't any ice on the roads, because he was taking the curves way too fast. He took the final turn on what had to be two wheels, but then had to slow on the uneven surface. It wouldn't do Kirby any good if they ended up in a ditch.

"Mercy, there are a lot of trees and shrubs," Eden said, looking out the window.

There were. Too many places for someone to hide. "When we get out, I need you to stay behind me, and if anything goes wrong, I want you to hit the ground. Agree, or it's the only way I'll let you out of this truck."

She nodded, but he didn't have time to push his point any further. Ahead, he saw Kirby's truck, and yeah, it was indeed in the ditch. The headlights cut through the dusk-gray winter landscape and created an eerie effect. Like stepping into a horror movie.

Wyatt was nowhere in sight, but Declan hadn't expected him to be. They were all out looking for Kirby, and he prayed that one of them would find the man alive and unharmed.

"Stay close," Declan reminded her. He grabbed the flashlight from the glove compartment in case the search went on longer than the twilight, and he shoved some extra magazines of ammo into his pockets. Eden did the same.

When he got out, the bitter wind nearly robbed him of his breath. Man, it was cold, and even though they were wearing coats, this still wouldn't be a pleasant search.

Declan made sure she was behind him, and they headed east. There were no buildings out there, but as Eden had noted, there were trees. Plus, there was a fence, and it, too, would make a good hiding place.

"Keep watch behind us," he whispered, and he got them moving fast. They had a lot of ground to cover. Acres. And with the wind howling, it would make it hard to hear if someone sneaked up on them.

He shoved aside a low-hanging branch, ducked underneath and saw the clearing just ahead. Declan stopped, tried to listen, because the clearing would be a good place for an attacker to gun them down. But there were no signs of anyone.

Declan turned on the flashlight and fanned it over the ground.

Footprints.

Definitely not drag marks, and they appeared to be fresh.

"Could they be Kirby's prints?" Eden whispered.

He shook his head. "Too big." And judging from the depth of the impressions, it was possible that this was someone who was carrying Kirby.

That sent his heart pounding against his ribs. Did that mean Kirby was hurt? Or worse? But Declan forced those questions aside. He couldn't help Kirby if he didn't focus solely on the search.

And on keeping Eden safe.

Because he darn sure didn't want her hurt because of some bad blood between Kirby, Jack or Leonard. Beatrice, either. Though if it was Jack's wife behind this, she'd obviously hired some muscle since she couldn't have carried Kirby from his truck.

"Move fast," Declan told her, and he turned off the flashlight.

He pulled in a hard breath and got them running toward a cluster of trees just on the other side of the clearing. Each step was a risk, and with each step he prayed that he didn't regret what he was doing.

Declan pulled Eden behind one of the larger oaks, and he took another second to try to hear anything that might be going on around him. Hard to hear, though, with his heartbeat crashing in his ears.

However, some movement caught his eye.

It must have caught Eden's, too, because she pivoted in the direction of another cluster of trees that was about twenty yards away. Even in the dim light, Declan could see the man.

Not an attacker.

Kirby.

Eden started to bolt toward the man, but Declan held her back so he could assess the situation. Hard to do with his foster father—correction, his father—so close.

Kirby was on his feet, leaning against a tree, and his arms were moving. His head was down with his chin practically touching his chest. No one was around him. At least no one that Declan could see.

Without taking his attention off Kirby and their surroundings, Declan eased his phone from his pocket and hit the first button. Wyatt's number. His brother answered almost immediately.

"We found Kirby," Declan whispered. "He's about a quarter of a mile from the road where I left my truck. Get here as fast as you can."

"Is he hurt?" Wyatt asked.

"I'm about to find that out now. Hurry," Declan repeated, and he ended the call so he could put his phone and the flashlight away. He wanted his hands free in case this turned into an attack.

Unfortunately, there was yet another clearing between Kirby and them. Not a wide one. But it was just enough to get them killed. Declan couldn't risk Eden's life like that, so he put her between him and a tree. That way he could take what he hoped would be a lesser risk.

"Kirby?" Declan softly called out.

He lifted his head. Not easily. "Declan." His voice sounded as weak as the man looked, and Declan wasn't sure how he was staying on his feet.

"Who did this?" Declan asked.

Kirby shook his head. "A lackey. All muscle and no talk. Don't know who he's working for because the guy didn't say a word."

Declan hoped they could soon remedy that. "Can you make your way to us?"

"Can't." It took him a moment and several labored breaths to continue. God knows what this cold and stress were doing to his body. "Someone tied me here."

Hell. This just kept getting worse.

"We have to go to him," Eden insisted. "We can get on the ground and crawl."

It wasn't a good plan, but it was better than darting

across the clearing. Besides, there wasn't much of an alternative. He couldn't leave Eden here alone because it might be part of the plan to grab her, too.

"Come on." Declan dropped to the ground and pulled her beside him. It wasn't easy. The ground was frozen and rocky, but they crawled toward Kirby.

Declan braced himself for an attack, but it didn't come. Thank God. They made it to Kirby, and Eden immediately started working to undo the rope that circled Kirby's chest and stomach.

"Are you hurt?" Declan asked, praying he wasn't.

"No. Just ready to fall flat on my face."

Yeah, he looked it. "What the hell happened? Why are you out here?"

"I got a call. Someone using a voice scrambler, but I think it was Jack. The person said I could end the danger to your life with a simple meeting. And a confession to Webb's murder."

Then the call must have been from Jack. But Declan rethought that. If it was Jack, why use a voice scrambler unless the man just wanted to throw them off his trail? However, there was someone else who could want that confession.

Beatrice.

Maybe so she could protect her husband from a murder rap. If she was so inclined.

Of course, Leonard could be the culprit, too. There were only two reasons for a suspect to use a voice scrambler. To muddy the waters or conceal their identity. But whoever was behind this, Declan intended to make them pay.

Eden finally got the rope undone, and Kirby practically dropped to the ground. Both Declan and she stopped that from happening by looping their arms around him. Even though Kirby had on a coat and his Stetson, he was freezing. That sent a new round of rage through Declan. This winter air could literally kill him.

"What now?" Eden asked.

Declan didn't want to go back through the two clearings with Kirby in tow, so he pulled them all as close to the tree as he could manage. "We'll wait for the others. They should be here soon."

He hoped.

That hope had barely had time to cross his mind when he heard the sounds. Footsteps, maybe. Maybe just the wind rattling the bare branches of the trees.

But the chill that went down his spine said it was something bad.

"Get down," Declan told them. And it wasn't a second too soon.

The shot blasted through the night air.

Chapter Seventeen

Eden tried to do what she could to protect Kirby, but despite his weakened condition, he'd have no part of that. He dragged her to him, shielding her with his body while Declan took aim in the direction of that shot.

Another bullet came their way, smacking into the tree. Then another. And it was that third shot that made Eden's heart go to her knees.

Because the angle had been different.

And that meant there wasn't just one shooter, but two. At least. All three of their suspects had enough money to hire plenty of assassins, so heaven knows how many had been paid to come here and kill them.

"Eden?" someone called out.

She hadn't thought it possible, but that got her heart racing even faster. It was her father.

What the devil was he doing here?

"Are you all right?" he shouted. He was somewhere to their left, in the direction of the fence. None of the shots had come from there, but he'd had men with him back in the woods near Maverick Springs.

Mercy, she hoped it wasn't them firing now.

"Don't answer," Declan warned her in a rough whisper. "I don't want anyone pinpointing our position."

It was a good argument, but she hated for her father

to think she'd been shot and therefore couldn't answer. Of course, that wasn't the worst of her fears. Her father couldn't be behind this attack. He just couldn't be. Whatever hatred he had for Declan, he wouldn't have gone this far with it.

She hoped.

But the little seed of doubt was there, and it tore away at her heart.

"Who's doing this?" her father asked.

But no one answered him. Well, no human anyway. Several thick blasts tore through the air. And this time they didn't come at Declan, Kirby and her—they went in her father's direction.

No. Someone was trying to kill him.

Kirby held on to her, maybe because he thought she might bolt from cover to help her dad. She couldn't. It'd be suicide, but she had to look for a way to end the danger now.

"My father's not behind this," she whispered. And she hated there was surprise mixed with the relief in her whisper.

"I got a call about an hour ago," her father continued. Judging from the sound of his voice, he'd moved. "The person said you were here at Rocky Creek and hurt and that you needed help."

And he'd come. Part of her was thankful for that, but another part of her wanted to throttle him for falling for such a thing. Declan and she had had no choice but to come after Kirby, but obviously someone had gotten her father here under false pretenses, since she hadn't been in need of help an hour ago.

She needed it now.

They'd need a miracle for all of them to get out of this alive.

But in a sick way it made sense that their attacker would want her father here. Both Leonard and Jack had a beef against him, and including her father and her in this dangerous mix would be a way to get total revenge.

The shots started up again. Mercy, did they. They came at them from both directions, and Declan, Kirby and she had no choice but to get flat on the ground. Maybe, just maybe, the gunmen wouldn't use that opportunity to close in on them.

"I can stop this," Kirby said. "It's me they want."

"You don't know that," Declan snapped. And when Kirby tried to get up, both Eden and Declan kept him on the ground. "You don't even know who's behind this."

"I know it's someone after me. Jack wants to kill me because of Stella. But not before he can get me to confess to Webb's murder. I can bargain with him to get you and Eden some time to escape."

"And if it's not Jack?" Declan didn't wait for him to answer. "Beatrice has several possible motives of her own. To get back at you for her husband's broken heart over Stella. Or to frame her husband for your murder. And then there's Leonard. Maybe he was lying about wanting to watch you suffer. He could have just waited until he had everything in place to come after you for killing his son, and if so, he's not the least bit interested in negotiation."

Kirby gave a weary sigh and quit struggling.

Good. At least Declan had put an end to that, but it didn't lessen the danger. For any of them. She prayed that her father would stay down and not try to do anything heroic to save her.

Even over the roar of the nonstop shots, she heard Declan's phone buzz. Because he had his focus on the gunmen, he handed her the phone.

"It's Wyatt," she relayed when she saw the name on the screen.

"Tell him and the others to stay back," Declan insisted. "I don't know how many shooters are involved or where they are."

Eden repeated that to Wyatt. "Best not to fire unless you have to," Wyatt answered. "I'm not exactly sure of Harlan's and Dallas's positions."

She ended the call, and even though Declan hadn't fired, she told him what Wyatt had said. It caused him to mumble some profanity, and she knew why. Not only were they pinned down in the freezing cold with a sick man, now they couldn't even return fire.

"I have to take out one of these guys," Declan said. "Use this if you have to. Just keep Eden safe." He reached in his boot and took out a small gun from the holster there. He handed it to Kirby.

But before Kirby could even take the weapon, Eden was shaking her head. "You can't go out there, Declan. You could be killed."

He leaned over, brushed a quick kiss on her mouth and levered himself up.

"You can't do this," she tried again.

But he got to a crouching position anyway. He did stay behind the cover of the tree, but he wouldn't have that meager protection for long.

"I'll sneak up behind one of them," Declan explained. And he got ready to move.

However, before he could go an inch, she heard a sound. Not the shouts and not a person's voice.

But a car engine.

The vehicle wasn't on the road, though. She could see the headlights slashing through the woods. And so was the vehicle. It was weaving in and out of the trees, the underbrush scraping against the sides like nails on a chalkboard.

"Maybe it's one of your brothers," Eden suggested.

If so, they were moving right into the line of fire.

The shots continued, and perhaps some of them were being fired into the approaching truck. It was hard to tell even after the vehicle came into view.

"Hell," Declan said. "That'd better not be who I think it is."

Kirby lifted his head and looked out. He cursed, too. "Stella."

Oh, God.

Had Stella really come or had she been brought here? Eden prayed not, but her prayers weren't answered. A moment later, the truck window inched down.

"I'm here to trade my life for theirs," Stella shouted.

The last word had barely had time to leave her mouth when the bullets began to tear through her truck.

"GET DOWN!" KIRBY yelled to Stella.

Once again, Declan had to stop the man from bolting into the clearing. But then Eden had to stop Declan. Every instinct inside him shouted for him to protect Stella. Maybe because she was a woman. Maybe because she was his mother. It didn't matter which—Declan had to force himself to stay put and try to figure out what to do.

He had to take out the shooter.

Why the devil was Stella here anyway? How could she have thought it would help to walk into this mess?

Of course, she might not have been thinking with her head but rather her heart. That particular organ was what had brought Declan out here. To save Kirby. Well, apparently Stella had the same notion. But there was one huge problem with that. She was now smack-dab in the middle of gunfire.

Eden still had his phone, and he glanced at it, then her. "Call Wyatt. Tell everyone to get down."

She did that immediately, but while he waited for his brothers to comply, the shots were continuing to slam into Stella's truck. Any one of those bullets could kill her.

If they hadn't already.

"Stay down," Declan warned Kirby and Eden.

He came up on one knee, took aim at the shooter to the right of the truck. And he fired. Declan couldn't actually see the guy, but he must have come close to hitting him because the shots stopped.

Well, on that side anyway.

They continued on the other, so Declan sent a bullet that way.

It worked. For a few seconds. Then the shots started again. His phone buzzed, too, and Eden answered it.

"Wyatt says he's dead center behind the truck," Eden relayed. "He's moving in closer to see if he can get a better shot."

Good. Declan kept his aim to the right and sent another two rounds that way. As before, the shots stopped, and when they started again, he realized the shooter had moved. Farther from the truck.

But closer to them.

Declan tried to keep himself positioned between Kirby and Eden, but then Eden lifted her head. "Dad, if you're still out there, get out of the way!" And she took aim at the left side of the truck and fired.

"What part of stay down didn't you understand?" Declan snarled.

But then Kirby fired, too, using the backup weapon

Declan had given him. He aimed at the same spot as Eden, and his shot smacked into one of the trees.

Hell's bells. He had a mutiny on his hands.

Declan was about to verbally blast them both, but he heard some profanity and didn't think it was coming from his brothers. Maybe one of the shooters had been hurt. Maybe either Eden or Kirby had managed to do one of them some harm.

"It's me!" Wyatt shouted, and he sounded close, probably right next to the rear of the truck.

And the next shot definitely came from Wyatt and went in the direction where Declan had been shooting. Eden and Kirby continued to fire, and soon the only shots were theirs. The footsteps confirmed they had the gunmen on the run.

"Cover me, Harlan!" Wyatt yelled.

Until then Declan hadn't realized Harlan was so close, but that was much-needed backup. Declan waited a few seconds. Then more. And when there were no shots fired, he got down on his belly so he could make it out to the truck.

Eden caught his arm to stop him, but Declan shook his head. "I have to make sure she's all right."

Her grip melted off him, and instead she held on to Kirby, probably because he had the same plan to check on Stella. Declan gave Eden one last look, thanking her, and he started to crawl across the clearing.

He didn't have to crawl far.

The truck door opened, and Stella stepped out. Or rather she staggered out. It was dark now, but thanks to a hunter's moon, Declan had no trouble seeing the blood on the right sleeve of her coat.

"I've been shot," she managed to say.

Declan jumped from the ground and raced to her.

He got to her just as she was collapsing, and she landed right in his arms. Cursing and praying, he scooped her up and ran back to cover.

"God, she's hurt," Kirby said, and he just kept repeating it.

Declan kept watch around them, knowing this would be the perfect time for an ambush, but he also kept glancing at Stella. She was pale. Her breathing was thin, and there was too much blood.

While Kirby cradled the woman in his arms, Eden called an ambulance. Of course, she had to tell the medics about the shots being fired, and that meant they wouldn't come close until the danger had passed. That couldn't happen soon enough or Stella might bleed out.

"Hold on," Declan told Stella, and he leaned out from the tree, trying to listen for any signs of those gunmen. He had to stop them, and that meant killing them.

"Go," Eden said to him, obviously figuring out what he had to do. "I'll protect them."

And she would. He had no doubt about that, but that didn't mean the gunmen couldn't get off some lucky shots. Still, it was an offer he'd have to take.

"Thanks." Declan brushed a quick kiss on her mouth and hoped he got the chance to give her a real thank-you later. She was putting herself in further danger to protect his family.

Declan stepped out of cover. Lifted his head. And he heard something. Not footsteps or voices. But some kind of crackling noise.

And then he smelled the smoke.

It seemed to come right at them in a thick wave.

"Fire!" Wyatt shouted. "Get the hell out of there now, Declan."

Declan saw the flames. Orangey red and thick in the

treed area to the right of them. It wasn't an ordinary fire. No. Not this. The flames shot up toward the sky.

Someone had set off a firebomb.

"This way." He helped Stella and Kirby to their feet and was about to head straight ahead to the truck.

But there was another of those bursting, crackling sounds, and the fire shot through that part of the woods. And worse, toward the truck. If the flames got to the gas tank, it'd explode.

No doubt what their attackers wanted.

"Change of plans," Declan said.

With Eden on one side of Stella and Kirby on the other, they started to the left. Toward the fence and the general area where they'd last heard Eden's father. If he was still out there, maybe he would decide it wasn't a good time to settle an old score with Declan.

However, they'd only made it a few steps when he heard a familiar sound that he damn sure didn't want to hear.

Another blaze roared up on their left.

And worse.

There was a fourth fire. The flames burst up behind them, and the smoke came at them from all sides.

They were trapped.

Chapter Eighteen

Eden looked all around them, and the terror rushed through her. The fire was everywhere. So was the smoke. And there was no visible escape route.

Sweet heaven.

Her father was out there somewhere, and he was no doubt in the middle of this, too. All of them could be killed, and they might never learn the reason for their deaths.

"Come on," Declan said. He hauled Stella into his arms and tried to help Kirby.

"I'll do it," Eden insisted. Declan had his hands full, and if they stood any chance of surviving, they had to move fast.

But in what direction?

There didn't seem to be a way out.

Worse, the smoke was rolling all around them. Smothering them. Eden choked back a cough, but Stella and Kirby weren't so lucky. Both of them started coughing.

Eden looped her arm around Kirby's waist. She couldn't carry him the way that Declan was carrying Stella, but she could help support his weight so he could move faster.

"This way," Declan ordered. "We have to get away from that truck before it explodes."

Oh, God. She hadn't considered that yet, but with her heart bashing in her chest and the adrenaline spiking through her, it was hard to think straight. Thank goodness Declan didn't seem to be having that trouble, even though she could see the terror on his face.

"Keep close," he added, "so we won't get separated."

The smoke would make it easy for that to happen. However, it wasn't so easy to keep up with him, either. Declan bolted toward the fence area. Where her father had been. There seemed to be just as much fire and smoke there as everywhere else, but maybe he'd seen some kind of opening.

Declan maneuvered them around a large tree. Then another. With each step the smoke thickened, making it harder to breathe. Kirby's coughing got worse, and he practically sagged against her.

"Leave me," Kirby insisted.

"Not a chance." If she couldn't save her own father, then she would save Declan's, though it broke her heart that she couldn't do both. Maybe, just maybe, her father had managed to get away before the firebombs had exploded.

Declan hurried, cutting through the seemingly endless line of trees. Did he know where he was going? Possibly. After all, he'd lived on these grounds when he was a kid, so maybe he knew a way out of all of this.

Stella moaned and dropped her head against Declan's shoulder. He mumbled something that Eden didn't catch, but she thought it might be a prayer.

"Declan?" someone shouted. It was Wyatt. He'd no sooner called out when there was another shot. Not a firebomb this time.

But a bullet.

And it'd been fired very near the sound of Wyatt's voice.

Now she prayed. Over half of Declan's family was in these woods, and heaven knew how many gunmen there were, ready to kill them if the fire didn't do that first.

Declan cursed but didn't answer his brother. No doubt because it would pinpoint their location and cause someone to fire at them, too. That was the last thing they needed.

Kirby stumbled, his legs giving way, but Eden caught him before he could hit the ground. She tried to get moving as fast as she could, but when she looked up, the thick smoke made it impossible to see Declan.

No!

She couldn't call out to him for fear of the gunmen. So she hurried. Or rather she tried to. But what remained of Kirby's strength was fading fast. Still, she didn't give up. Eden adjusted her arm around him, trying to keep her shooting hand free in case they were attacked, and she trudged forward.

With the smoke, she had no sense of direction, but she simply used the trees for cover and took it one frantic step at a time.

But that ended much too soon.

The flames shot up directly in front of them.

She pulled Kirby to the side, barely in time before the fire could burn him, and they ducked behind another tree.

"Gasoline," Kirby mumbled.

Yes, she smelled it, too, and she suspected it'd been poured on the ground. That would account for why the fire was moving in such a straight line. Of course, that line wouldn't last long because the fire would eventually burn through the dead leaves and limbs that littered the ground. It was freezing cold but dry, and that would only fuel the flames. The wind would, too.

They didn't have much time to get out of there.

She kept moving, though her lungs were burning, starved for air, and the muscles in her arms and legs were knotted.

"Eden?" she heard Declan say. Not in a shout but a rough whisper.

Despite their circumstances, the relief flooded through her, and she felt it even more when she spotted Declan just ahead. He caught her arm and pulled all of them behind an oak.

"You should save yourselves," Stella told them.

Kirby echoed that, but Declan obviously had no plans to listen. Good. Eden couldn't live with herself if she survived this ordeal at their expense.

Declan got them moving again, and they skirted along the lines of fire. Their attacker had obviously used a lot of gasoline, because she could smell it over the thickening smoke.

The sound blasted through the air, and even though Eden had tried to brace herself for pretty much anything, she hadn't braced herself nearly enough for that jolt that went through the entire woods.

"Stella's truck," Declan said.

It had obviously exploded, and she hoped no one was near it. Well, except for the gunmen. Maybe it had taken one or more of them out, but she doubted they would get that lucky. No, whoever was behind this attack had almost certainly planned an escape route.

Declan had to dodge another fire line, and they came out into a clearing. Except it wasn't very clear because of the smoke. He moved faster now but kept checking over his shoulder to make sure Kirby and she were keeping up.

They were.

Barely.

Her muscles were more than knotted now. They were cramping to the point of excrucation, and just when she thought she couldn't take another step, Eden saw some hope.

The white wooden fence.

She remembered it from their drive to the facility and thought it rimmed the entire property. But more important, it was next to the road. Maybe they could follow it back to Declan's truck and escape.

A howl of sirens cut through the other noises. The ambulance was already there. Nearby anyway. It couldn't approach until it was safe.

Whenever that would be.

Declan hurried to the fence and laid Stella on the ground. Eden did the same, and they both looked around to get their bearings. Not much to get, though. The smoke wasn't as thick here, and there was no sign of the fire. Good. It was a break they needed.

But then, Eden heard the sound.

Not the crackling flames. Not Stella's labored breathing. This was footsteps, and not just one set of them. Two or more.

Eden lifted her gun and tried to take aim. But it was already too late. The three men wearing dark clothes stepped out from the smoke. Like demons. Except those were real guns they were carrying. And they aimed those guns right at them.

"You can drop your weapons *now*," one of them said. "Or die right this second. Your choice."

DECLAN FROZE, BUT only because he couldn't get his weapon turned on all of the gunmen at once. He could take out one of them. Maybe even two. But that would leave a third one to start shooting.

That was a huge risk to take.

Of course, surrendering his weapon could be an even bigger risk, since he doubted these guys were just going to let them live.

So why hadn't the gunmen just opened fire?

Declan didn't know, but he figured that meant their boss had other plans that didn't involve a quick death. Maybe a slow, painful one so he or she could get the revenge they wanted.

He glanced around, looking for any way to escape. There were some more trees just to their left and near the fence. There was a ditch, too. Both might provide some cover if bullets started flying.

"My mother's hurt," Declan said to whoever could hear him. It was the first time he'd ever called her that, and the timing sure sucked, but maybe they'd be more receptive to what he was about to suggest if they thought of her as a mother and not their hostage.

Declan tipped his head to the end of the road. He couldn't see the ambulance, but judging from the sound of the sirens, it was there. "Let the medics come in and take both my father and her."

Again, it was the first time he'd called Kirby that, and he saw the tears in both Kirby's and Stella's eyes. Later, Declan would tell them that he no longer held a grudge for the secret they'd kept. Nearly dying put a lot of things in perspective.

Including Eden.

Here she was, her gun still aimed while she kept her

arm around Kirby. Protecting him. Just as she'd done on this entire nightmarish trek through the fiery woods.

And it could cost Eden her life.

Declan wasn't sure he'd get the chance to make that up to her, but he'd try. Yeah, he had things he needed to say to her, and somehow he had to create the chance for all of them to get out of this alive.

"Let the medics come and get my parents and Eden," he bargained. "Then we can talk and try to work this out."

Of course, letting the gunmen walk away from this was out of the question, since the trio could already be charged with multiple felonies. Also, none of them were wearing masks. Not a good sign. Because that meant they wouldn't want to leave any witnesses behind. Federal marshals and a P.I. would be huge loose ends.

"No way," the gunman in the middle said. "Just put down the guns."

"And then what?" Eden asked. "You shoot us all in cold blood?"

Declan didn't want her egging them on. Hell, he wished he could dig a hole and shove her in it. But he doubted Eden was going to let him do this by himself.

Nope.

She stood, slowly, and positioned herself arm to arm with him.

"Put down the guns now!" the man yelled. He took aim at Stella. "Or she gets another bullet. This one might not kill her, but she'll wish she was dead."

Declan had no doubt that the guy would shoot. Hell, maybe he'd been the one to shoot Stella in the first place. That didn't help quell the anger that rose hot and bitter in his throat.

"Go ahead," Kirby said. God, his voice was weak,

and this stress wasn't going to help matters. "Declan and Eden, do as they say. Put down your guns."

He glanced down at Kirby and saw the barrel of the backup weapon he'd given him. Kirby had it hidden under the edge of his coat.

Declan wanted to curse.

Normally, he would have liked having Kirby cover his back, but he doubted the man's hand was steady enough. Besides, if Kirby fired, those goons wouldn't waste a second shooting him.

"Do as they want and surrender your gun," Declan said to Eden. "But try to keep it close," he added in a whisper.

She gave a shaky nod, and she stooped to lay the gun on the ground just a few inches from her feet. Declan figured the guys would tell her to give it a good kick, but all three just looked at him.

"Your turn," one of them said to him.

Declan repeated Eden's movement, keeping his gun within stooping distance. Of course, that was way too far away if these guys started shooting.

"Anybody else got a gun?" someone called out, and it wasn't one of the goons.

It was Leonard Kane.

He stepped from the trees and drifts of smoke, and despite his earlier collapse at the hospital, he no longer looked weak and sickly.

Just the opposite.

He looked like a man pleased with himself.

And Leonard wasn't alone. He had another big, hulking gunman by his side. His, no doubt.

"You bastard," Stella said, and despite her injury, she tried to get to her feet, but thankfully Kirby kept her on the ground. At least that way they could scramble into the ditch if necessary.

And Declan figured it would become necessary.

He only prayed that Kirby, Stella and Eden could move fast enough when the bullets started flying again.

"Your lover there is the bastard," Leonard argued. "He killed my son."

"And hurting Declan won't bring him back," Eden snapped.

"No, but it'll make me feel a hell of a lot better." He sounded amused that Eden would give him an argument at a time like this. "Killing you will, too, because I know it'll get back at Zander for being such a jackass and trying to ruin my business. It's not enough for him to face attempted-murder charges for that witness."

"You set that up," Declan challenged.

"Yeah, I did. So what? Zander's still not behind bars, and that means he didn't get the payback he deserves."

Eden just shook her head. "You're dying. What good would revenge do now?"

"Well, for the short time I got left, it'll do a hell of a lot of good. Don't want to go to my grave without settling these last scores."

"And that score's with me," Kirby offered. He didn't get up, probably because he was still hiding the gun, but he did face Leonard head-on. "Let everybody go, and you and me will *settle* this. Here's your chance to finish me off."

"Too easy," Leonard answered. "Like I said, I want you to suffer. Besides, if I'd wanted you dead, I would have killed you a long time ago when I had Declan's parents killed. Oops. I guess that would be his adoptive parents, since he's your brat."

Stella cursed him again, and inside, Declan felt much

more than profanity. He'd spent a good deal of his life thinking about how he'd deal with the man who'd killed his adoptive parents.

And now he had the chance.

Except he couldn't take it without risking another set of parents and Eden. It cut him to the core that he couldn't just lash out at this SOB. But somehow, he would get that chance. Leonard was going to pay for all the misery he'd caused.

"I covered my tracks," Stella said. She was crying now. "There was no way you could trace his adoptive family to Kirby and me."

"Well, you sure didn't make it easy. I'd heard rumors that you'd had a kid, and I just kept digging. Didn't find anything for years, and then Beatrice stumbled onto the passport you thought had been destroyed. She did all the legwork for me."

"Beatrice was in on the murders?" Declan asked. Because if so, she'd pay, too.

"No. She's all talk, always whining about the money that she doesn't want to share. She found you, but all she'd planned to do was make sure Jack never located you. He was looking, too. So Beatrice set out to make sure no one ever found the passport or any link that would come back to Jack."

Declan wished that Beatrice had succeeded. But if she had, he would have never met Kirby. Never learned the truth about his parents.

And he would have never met Eden.

Of course, if he hadn't, Eden might not be on the verge of being killed by a revenge-seeking lunatic.

"And what about Jack?" Eden asked. "Did he help you with this plan?"

"Please." Leonard stretched that out a few syllables.

"I wouldn't trust that fool to take out my trash, much less put together something like this. A plan like this takes coordination. And hatred. A whole lot of hatred," he added through now-clenched teeth.

So according to Leonard, no one else was involved. That didn't make this situation less dangerous, not with those guns aimed at them. But Declan had to find a bargaining tool.

"If you kill me and leave Kirby alive to suffer," Declan said, "he and my brothers will track you down."

"They'll try," Leonard calmly. "But after this, I plan to leave the country and die in a quiet peaceful place, far from the long arm of the law." He paused. Lifted the gun he'd been holding by his side. "And now it's time for you to die."

"No!" Stella sobbed.

"Get them out of here first," Declan bargained. "Eden, too. No need for them to see you put a bullet in me." And that didn't mean he was surrendering.

No way.

If he had the others safely out of the way, then he could try to fight back.

"Everyone stays and watches," Leonard insisted. "And just so I can give you a little extra jab, Declan, I'll have Eden done first."

No. That couldn't happen. He couldn't lose her.

Leonard nodded. That was it, the order for her death. And the gunman in the middle, the one who'd issued those earlier threats, turned the gun on her so fast that Declan didn't have time to react.

The shot blasted through the air.

And Declan heard himself yell while he tried to push Eden out of the path of that bullet.

Chapter Nineteen

Eden braced herself for the pain. And for death.

The blast came. Loud and thick. Seconds before Declan knocked her to the ground. Even over the sound of the shot, she heard him shout her name.

But the bullet didn't go into her. The only pain she felt was from the impact of the fall.

Around her, everyone was scrambling. Declan, Kirby. Even Stella. They were all going for the guns, and it took her a moment to realize what was happening.

The man who'd tried to shoot her dropped face-first, his gun clattering away from him. Someone had shot him.

But who?

She didn't see anyone, but Eden didn't look that hard. She went after her gun instead. After all, Leonard was armed, and so were his three remaining goons.

The goons scrambled to the side behind some trees, and Leonard did, too, while he cursed a blue streak. Declan snatched up his gun, and in the same motion, he shoved Eden down into the ditch. Before she could get her own gun.

"Get Stella and Kirby," Declan told her, and she grabbed for them. Thankfully, they'd already started in her direction. Now she had to get Declan there, too, but he waited until they were all stashed behind the meager cover before he scrambled in with them.

One of the gunmen fired, but he missed Declan. That didn't stop him from trying again, though. But his weren't the only shots. There were others coming from the back part of the woods, where the smoke was still thick.

"Kirby, call off your boys," Leonard snarled. "Or they all die tonight."

"I'm not one of Kirby's boys," someone shouted back. Her father.

He was alive. But he was also close, right in the thick of this, and calling out to them meant Leonard's hired guns could pinpoint his position and kill him.

"I took out one of your men," her father added, "so why don't you come after me instead of my daughter?"

"No," Eden said. She didn't want this. She didn't want any of them to be in danger, but she was glad that her father had managed to take out one of them. Now hopefully it wouldn't make him a quick target for the gunmen.

"Maybe one of your brothers can take out the rest of Leonard's hired help," Kirby mumbled.

Eden wished the same thing. But it wouldn't be easy since they had to get through that fire.

"Put your hand on her shoulder to try to slow down the bleeding," Declan said to her. He tipped his head to Stella.

The bleeding was worse and Stella was shivering. Maybe going into shock. They needed to get her into an ambulance right away. Eden scooted closer to the woman and pressed her hand over the wound.

"Finish them," Leonard said to his men. "I'm gettin'

the heck out of here." And Leonard headed out with his bodyguard right by his worthless side.

Declan moved as if he might go after the man, but he glanced back at them. And instead of bolting, he took aim at the gunmen behind the trees.

The shots started.

Those gunmen began shooting at them, forcing Declan lower into the ditch so he couldn't return fire.

She heard Declan's phone buzz, and since he was busy watching to make sure those gunmen didn't come any closer, she took it from his pocket.

"Wyatt," she answered after she saw his name on the screen.

"Where are you?" Wyatt asked.

"Pinned down by the fence. Stella's hurt."

"How bad?"

Because Stella and Kirby were hanging on to every word, Eden would lie. "She'll be fine, but she needs a doctor." She ducked when a bullet tore up the chunk of the grassy ditch just above her head. "My father's here. Somewhere. And he took out one of the men, but Leonard's getting away. He's the one behind this."

Wyatt mumbled some profanity. "We're on the way. If possible, have Declan hold his fire so he doesn't hit one of us."

But before she could relay that to Declan, he fired. And for a good reason. One of the gunmen had run closer to them, ducking behind another tree. He was trying to move in for the kill.

"Just get here," she said to Wyatt, but he was no longer on the line.

More shots came. Closer than before. The gunman had obviously gotten into a better position. Eden's chest was tight from her pounding heart, and her breath was too fast. She tried to make herself settle down, but it was impossible.

It didn't help when Kirby levered himself up and returned fire with Declan's backup weapon. Both Declan and she pulled him back into the ditch, and that minimal effort seemed to exhaust him.

"Get down, Eden!" her father shouted.

That was the only warning they got before she saw him come out from the trees, and he started firing at the gunmen.

He took out the one nearest to them.

The other turned, took aim at her father. But Declan took care of him.

He double tapped the trigger, and the third gunman went down.

Eden said a prayer of thanks, but before she could even finish it, Declan was out of the ditch.

"You're not going after Leonard." And she tried not to make it sound like a question.

But that was exactly what he was doing.

"Wait with them," he said to her father. "And call the ambulance and tell the medics it's okay for them to come closer."

Good. The ambulance was nearby, waiting for the gunfire to end, so it shouldn't take long to arrive. But having her father stay with them meant Declan planned to do this alone. He wasn't going to wait for his brothers, probably because he knew every second counted. If Leonard managed to get away, they'd probably never catch him.

And a killer would go free.

God knows how long that would eat away at Declan. Probably for the rest of his life, and it wouldn't matter that the brain tumor would soon take care of Leonard.

Eden called the medic, relayed Declan's message and then got to her feet.

"I have to go," she told her father. She took the gun from Kirby's hand. "Stay with Stella and Kirby until the ambulance gets here."

Of course, if Declan's brothers got there first, they'd have to arrest Zander, but that wasn't something she could worry about right now. Declan was about to face down his own personal demon.

Her father tried to grab her arm to stop her, but Eden got away from him and hurried after Declan, who already had a good head start on her. Leonard had backup, and Declan would need it, too. Of course, he wouldn't want it. Not from her anyway. Still, she caught up with him just on the other side of the clearing.

"Go back," he ordered.

"Only if you will," she argued.

He kept walking, but he also looked all around them. Until then, she hadn't considered that Leonard might try to ambush them. She figured he'd get out of there fast.

But the sound had her rethinking that.

More footsteps just ahead.

Declan yanked her behind a tree and peered out.

"Looking for me?" someone said. Not ahead of them. But behind her. And it wasn't Leonard or any of Declan's brothers. This must be the bodyguard Leonard had with him.

Eden was between Declan and the man, so she snapped toward him, and she gave him a split second glance to make sure it wasn't someone they knew. It wasn't.

She fired.

So did he.

But Eden dropped down and fired again. The man

dropped, too, but before he even hit the ground, there was another shot. Not the gunman's. This one came from in front of them and smacked into the tree. It missed Declan's head by what had to be a fraction of an inch.

Declan cursed, shoved her all the way down and returned fire.

There was little smoke here. The wind had carried it in the other direction. So she had no trouble seeing Leonard in the moonlight.

"I won!" Leonard shouted. And he fired a second shot at Declan. "You and Kirby will have nightmares about me for the rest of your life."

Leonard took aim at Declan again. Declan aimed, too. He was the first to fire.

And Declan didn't miss.

She saw the look of startled surprise on Leonard Kane's face, as if he hadn't expected to die. Not ever. And a single word of profanity left his mouth as he slumped forward.

Declan didn't even wait a second. He hurried first to the bodyguard and touched his fingers to his throat.

"Dead," Declan mumbled. And he raced to the clearing to do the same to Leonard. Eden kept her gun aimed just in case the bullet hadn't killed him.

But it had.

As she'd done with Leonard, she looked at Declan's face but saw no relief there. No sign of victory.

"Stella," Declan said, catching onto her arm. They started to run. "We have to get Kirby and her to the hospital now."

Chapter Twenty

Declan sucked at waiting, but he wasn't the only one. Like him, Eden was pacing in the hospital waiting room.

Dallas was on his umpteenth call with his wife. Clayton, too. Both had plenty of nervous energy coming off them. Slade wasn't pacing or chatting on the phone, but he had his wife, Maya, wrapped in his arms as if a hug could bring them some peace.

Maybe it could.

Because the pacing and the nonstop phone conversations sure weren't working.

Only Harlan and Wyatt were seated. Wyatt had his legs stretched out in front of him, his Stetson over his eyes, but Declan figured he wasn't getting much rest. Neither was Harlan, and it was likely to stay that way until they got some news about Stella and Kirby. They both had to be all right, and even though Declan didn't want his mind to go in that direction, he couldn't help but think the worst. Stella had lost a lot of blood, and Kirby was weak from the cancer. God knows what this ordeal had done to him.

"How the heck did Stella get away from you?" Declan asked Clayton once he was off the phone. He extended that question to Slade. After all, both of them had been at the hospital guarding her.

"She's sneakier than she looks," Clayton grumbled.

"And faster," Slade supplied, not sounding at all pleased that he'd been outsmarted by a woman twenty years older than he was. "Once we got her back to the ranch, she slipped out through the kitchen and jumped in her truck. She drove away before we could stop her."

"We had no idea she'd try something that stupid," Clayton added.

Yeah, it was stupid all right, but Declan looked at his brothers' faces. Both Slade and Clayton were parents now, their sons tucked safely at the ranch with their nannies. And Declan was betting that his brothers would do anything to save their children.

Even something stupid.

"At least now we know why Declan's so hardheaded," Harlan added.

Declan appreciated the insult. Coming from a brother, it was practically mandatory in situations like these. However, it didn't help cut through the worry that any of them were feeling.

"Both Kirby and Stella will be okay," Eden tried to assure Declan. She maneuvered her pacing closer to him and brushed her hand over his arm. It helped. But not enough.

There was worry all over her face, too, and like Leonard had said, this would give them enough nightmares for a lifetime. Thankfully, Eden's sisters were okay. Declan and she had confirmed that with a phone call on the drive to the hospital.

"I should have been able to protect everyone better," he told her. "Including you."

She lifted her shoulder. Gave a weak smile. "We're in one piece. I'd say you did a pretty good job."

Now, that gave him some comfort. She didn't hate

him for the mess he hadn't been able to prevent. Because he thought they both could use it, he leaned in and kissed her. If that garnered anyone's attention, they didn't say anything.

Harlan, however, grunted. "Maybe no one will shoot at us today."

Wyatt put his thumb to the brim of his Stetson and eased it back a bit. "I get shot at all the time."

"A lot of things happen to you that don't happen to normal people," Harlan grumbled. "It's that pretty face of yours. Too pretty to be a lawman. Just makes people want to shoot you."

Declan was thankful for the brotherly ribbing. It was an attempt at normal when the situation was anything but.

"The cold weather slowed the bleeding," Eden added in a whisper. She put her arms around him. "Plus, Stella's otherwise strong and healthy."

Both true. But it crushed his heart to think of her in surgery to remove a bullet put there because a man believed he needed to avenge an old wrong.

Declan heard the footsteps in the hall, and everyone turned in that direction. Hoping for news. But it wasn't the news they were expecting.

It was Sheriff Geary and Zander Gray.

Eden went to her father, hugged him and some of the worry faded from her expression. "I didn't know if I'd get to see you before they took you to jail."

Declan hadn't been sure of it, either, but if the sheriff hadn't brought Zander by the hospital, then Declan would have taken Eden to the jail as soon as they had word about Stella and Kirby. It didn't matter what differences Zander and he had had. Eden loved him, and she deserved to see him before he was whisked away.

"The murder charges will be dropped," Declan explained to Zander. "Leonard confessed to hiring someone to kill the witness, and he did that to set you up so that you'd look guilty."

Zander nodded. "Thanks."

"Don't thank me yet. You'll still have to serve time for the original charges." But maybe it wouldn't be much. He no longer had a burning desire to see justice served when it came to Zander.

Because he was Eden's father.

And it would hurt her to see him behind bars.

Still, she seemed to accept that jail time was inevitable, and she left her father's side to return to Declan's. She slipped her arm around his waist again.

"I'll talk to the D.A.," Declan continued, talking to her father, "and tell him you helped us stop Leonard and his hired guns." He paused. "Thank you for protecting my parents during the gunfight."

"Thank you for protecting my daughter."

Declan hadn't expected Zander's thanks to mean that much. But it did. "It wasn't a chore."

"Yeah, I can see that." His gaze turned to Eden. "Come and see me when you can."

She nodded, but anything she was about to say was cut off by more footsteps. This time, it was Dr. Cheryl Landry, and she no doubt had an update about Stella and Kirby. Declan couldn't tell if the news was good or bad from the look on her face.

"Stella's asking to see you," the doctor said. "All of you." And she included Eden in the glance.

The sheriff took hold of Zander's arm. "We need to head out."

Eden mouthed a goodbye and *I love you* to her father, and then hurried down the hall with the rest of them. Declan braced himself for what he might see in the post-op room. He hated that this might be Stella's deathbed farewell.

But it wasn't.

She wasn't exactly sitting up and looking fit, but she was awake and smiling as much as she could, considering she'd recently come out of the operating room.

"The surgery went well," the doctor explained. "I was able to remove the bullet, and I don't think there'll be any permanent damage. She'll be here a day or two." She hitched her thumb to the corner of the room. "Him, too."

Only then did Declan see Kirby in a wheelchair.

"He insisted on being here." Dr. Landry frowned. "But now that he's sure Stella's going to be okay, I need to get him back in his own room. He'll need to stay overnight. He's fine. No injuries. It's just a precaution."

"I wasn't going anywhere until I knew she was okay," Kirby grumbled.

Stella's weak smile returned, and even though her eyelids were already drifting down, she motioned for Declan to come closer. When he did, she took his hand and gave it a gentle squeeze. "You called me your mother tonight. That's the first time."

He kissed her forehead. "Won't be the last."

And that was true. Nearly losing her had brought it all crashing down. In a good way, this time. He'd always loved Stella. Always thought of her as his protector and caregiver. Now he wanted some time to get to know her as his mother. The woman who'd made a lot of sacrifices to keep him alive.

And she had.

"Does this mean Declan will get special treatment now?" Wyatt asked, kissing Stella's cheek, too.

"All you boys are mine. He's just the only one who got my blood."

Clayton, Harlan and Dallas came forward to give her the same cheek kiss, and even though Stella was clearly enjoying the attention, at the moment she couldn't keep her eyes open.

"I need all of you out," the doctor insisted. "A recovery room means there's some recovering to do, and Stella needs that right now. But you can come back in the morning."

They would. Declan needed to have a long chat with Stella, but it could wait. For now, he leaned down and whispered in her ear, "I love you."

Despite her half-shut eyes, he saw the tears, but he thought they were of the happy variety. He made a mental note to tell her that more often.

When the doctor gave them another get-out order, his brothers began to trickle out, each of them stopping by Kirby first. No hugs. Kirby wasn't the hugging type, but Declan figured the man knew how they felt about him.

"You speaking to me?" Kirby asked when Declan stopped in front of him. "Because I could see why you wouldn't want to."

"I'm speaking to you all right, and I'm warning you to never again pull that sneaking-out stunt. You fought enough of my battles when I was a kid. You don't need to go fighting more."

Kirby nodded. Maybe thanking him. But probably not agreeing. If it came down to it, Kirby would fight for any of his sons, and Declan knew if their situations were reversed, he'd do the same thing.

"Well, I do have one battle left," Kirby said. "Webb's murder. The rangers aren't just going to drop this.

They'll keep looking for his killer, and they'll keep looking at all of us."

"We'll handle it when and if the time comes." Declan gave Kirby's shoulder a gentle squeeze. Not a hug, but close enough.

"I'm proud of you, boy. Proud of all of you."

Declan felt his own eyes burn. It wasn't that Kirby had withheld praise. He'd been plenty generous with it over the years. But it never got old hearing it from his father.

Eden gave both Stella and Kirby a kiss on the cheeks, and they left before Dr. Landry pushed them out of the room. Declan didn't feel the actual relief until he got into the hall where his brothers were waiting. And it hit him then.

They'd survived.

All of them.

"You okay?" Eden asked, and she took his arm, maneuvered him so that his back was against the wall. Probably because he didn't look too steady on his feet.

He managed a nod. He was more than okay. "I'm thinking we should start dating," Declan told her.

Dallas grumbled something he didn't catch. "I'm out of here. See you back at the ranch." Slade left behind him. Then Clayton.

But Wyatt stayed, as if amused by this.

Eden put her mouth directly to his ear. "Dating? But we've already had sex. Great sex," she amended in a whisper.

"Yeah, but we can still date, and then maybe you'll consider moving in with me. Of course, since I live in the sticks, you might not want—"

She stopped him with a kiss. A good one, too. "I'd love to move in with you."

All right. This was going pretty well. "Then maybe you'll fall in love with me. Hope so anyway. Because I'm sure as hell in love with you."

"You cursed when you said I love you," Wyatt pointed out. "Women don't like that."

Declan shot him a glare. "Don't you have someplace else to be, maybe some other shooting to get mixed up with?"

"Nope. Besides, I like watching my kid brother trip over his tongue." But he chuckled and looked at Eden. "Make him suffer a little. Wait a month or two before you let him know you're in love with him, too." He met Declan's gaze. "Because she *is* in love with you, you know. Or maybe you're just too dense to see what the rest of us already know."

With that, Wyatt strolled away.

"Are you in love with me?" Declan asked her.

"Yes." And she didn't hesitate, either. She even added another of those mind-numbing kisses.

Oh, man. This day had started like a nightmare, but the ending was getting better and better.

He'd never be thankful to Leonard for what he'd done, but it had brought them to this point. Of course, they would have gotten here anyway. He'd been crazy about Eden since he'd seen her on his porch.

Declan moved closer to her, put his mouth to her ear. "After you move in, I figure I'll give it a month or two, and then I'll ask you to marry me."

She smiled. "Then I figure I'll say yes. You're not getting away, Declan. I want you for life."

Life sounded pretty darn good.

Declan contributed one of those mind-numbing kisses, as well. Then another. Because she tasted so good and felt so right in his arms.

In fact, everything about this felt right, and that was the first time in his life he'd been able to say that. Declan pulled Eden to him and didn't let go.

* * * * *

"If someone gets too pushy or personal for you, call me about that, too. Anything. I'm not taking any chances with our star witness."

So the warmth of his hand on her arm and the patient, adult conversation was about protecting the outcome of his task force investigation. "You're not taking any chances?"

"No."

With a wry smile, Bailey shook her head. Spencer Montgomery had KCPD running through his veins. Any shivers of awareness she might feel at his warm hands or masculine smells or polite attention were misguided responses to a man who was simply doing his job.

She was the surviving victim who could put away the Rose Red Rapist forever.

"I'll call," Bailey promised. "If I suspect anything's not right, I'll call."

"Don't go shopping by yourself. Make sure someone knows where you are at all times. You do whatever you have to to stay safe."

She'd had younger, more charming men hit on her with sweet words and shower her with gifts. But she'd never responded so easily, so basically, to any one of them the way she was reacting to Spencer Montgomery today.

"I'll try not to let you down, Mr Montgomery."

"You won't."

You won't.

Did those last two words mean Detective Montgomery had faith in her ability to get the job done?

Or were they a warning that he intended to make sure she didn't screw this up?

"If someone gets too pushy or personal for you, call me about that too. Anything I'm not taking any chances with our star witness."

YULETIDE PROTECTOR

BY
JULIE MILLER

© Julie Miller 2012

MILLS & BOON

All the characters in this book have no existence outside the imagination of the author, and have no relation whatsoever to anyone bearing the same name or names. They are not even distantly inspired by any individual known or unknown to the author, and all the incidents are pure invention.

All Rights Reserved including the right of reproduction in whole or in part in any form. This edition is published by arrangement with Harlequin Enterprises II B.V./S.à.r.l. The text of this publication or any part thereof may not be reproduced or transmitted in any form or by any means, electronic or mechanical, including photocopying, recording, storage in an information retrieval system, or otherwise, without the written permission of the publisher.

This book is sold subject to the condition that it shall not, by way of trade or otherwise, be lent, resold, hired out or otherwise circulated without the prior consent of the publisher in any form of binding or cover other than that in which it is published and without a similar condition including this condition being imposed on the subsequent purchaser.

® and ™ are trademarks owned and used by the trademark owner and/or its licensee. Trademarks marked with ® are registered with the United Kingdom Patent Office and/or the Office for Harmonisation in the Internal Market and in other countries.

First published in Great Britain 2013
by Mills & Boon, an imprint of Harlequin (UK) Limited,
Eton House, 18-24 Paradise Road, Richmond, Surrey TW9 1SR

© Julie Miller 2013

ISBN: 978 0 263 90385 0

46-1213

Harlequin (UK) policy is to use papers that are natural, renewable and recyclable products and made from wood grown in sustainable forests. The logging and manufacturing processes conform to the legal environmental regulations of the country of origin.

Printed and bound in Spain
by Blackprint CPI, Barcelona

USA TODAY bestselling author **Julie Miller** attributes her passion for writing romance to all those books she read growing up. When shyness and asthma kept her from becoming the action-adventure heroine she longed to be, Julie created stories in her head to keep herself entertained. Encouragement from her family to write down the feelings and ideas she couldn't express became a love for the written word. She gets continued support from her fellow members of the Prairieland Romance Writers, where this teacher serves as the resident "grammar goddess." Inspired by the likes of Agatha Christie and Encyclopedia Brown, Julie believes the only thing better than a good mystery is a good romance.

Born and raised in Missouri, this award-winning author now lives in Nebraska with her husband, son and an assortment of spoiled pets. To contact Julie or to learn more about her books, write to PO Box 5162, Grand Island, NE 68802-5162, USA, or check out her website and monthly newsletter at www.juliemiller.org.

For Clarice Metz and Rhonda Glasford Metz, two of my Fulton fans. Mom loves it when you talk about my books with her. ;) Thanks for reading them!

Prologue

September

"I'll save you," she whispered into the phone.

Brian Elliott looked at her through glass that separated them. The lines of strain around his blue eyes and handsome mouth were more pronounced. And the orange jumpsuit certainly didn't flatter.

After all she'd done for him, he still doubted her? "You don't think they're screening all my visitors? You're tempting fate by coming here."

If he wasn't looking so haggard, so in need of the comfort he normally sought from her, she would have been irritated by his doubt. Instead, she smoothed a smile on her face—for his benefit as well as the guards who might be watching. "It makes perfect, logical sense for me to come see you. Besides, you've had a lot of visitors, haven't you? Too many for the authorities to focus solely on me."

"You arranged all those visits?"

"Not many people can benefit from being associated with an alleged serial rapist." She'd gone to work as soon as she learned the news of his arrest. "Some of your friends and business associates probably are truly concerned for your welfare. And I might have suggested to some of them how staying in your good graces would prove most beneficial once you're acquitted."

He tipped his mouth closer to the phone that connected them and rubbed at his temple, as though the stress of the past couple of days had given him a headache. "How can you be sure that will happen? The police have eyewitness testimony. Experts from the crime lab to talk about trace evidence and DNA."

"The only thing their evidence proves is that you once fathered a child with a woman who's now in a mental institution. The D.A. will never put her on the stand to argue that it wasn't consensual sex. Everything else is circumstantial. A good lawyer will make that go away—and you've got the best attorney in town on your payroll. Any other charges are minor, and I expect you'll get probation and time served."

Her heart twisted with sympathy when he rubbed at the cuts and scratches on his forearm, painful wounds inflicted during his arrest just days earlier. "All it takes is one woman to stand up and identify me as the man who raped her."

"An eyewitness?" Despite his pain, she had to laugh. "How can any victim swear it was you? They were all unconscious, and you wore a mask."

"There's Hope Lockhart."

"You didn't rape her."

He cupped the receiver with his hand and revealed

a hushed admission. "I wanted to. I wanted to hurt her so badly—"

"Shh." She leaned toward the glass and splayed her fingers there, wishing she could physically touch him and reassure him. "A jury can't convict you for being angry and having these revenge fantasies. But it won't help public perception if word gets out that you…enjoy the violence."

"I'm sitting in a jail cell. My bail hearing isn't until tomorrow. Public opinion doesn't matter in here."

"You talk as though you don't believe you're getting out."

She was pleased when he flattened his larger hand close to his side of the reinforced glass, touching her in the only way he could. For now. As long as he needed her, as long as he loved her, she'd find a way to make it work so they could both get what they wanted. "Do you really think we can fix this and make it go away?"

"Yes. But you have to trust me." She pulled her hand away, getting down to business. Brian had always appreciated her practical sense about how to get things done. It was one of the things that had drawn them together in the first place, even though the arguments often drove them apart. "I would have taken care of that issue with Miss Lockhart, too, if I had known how upset you were. If you had listened to me before, if you had let me handle the situation, you wouldn't be sitting where you are now."

"Let *you* handle it? I can't tolerate a betrayal like that. She needed to understand that I—"

"Hush." She quieted him before his agitation drew

the guard's attention to their conversation. "Your emotions are your Achilles heel, Brian. I can think rationally, for the both of us. Let me do this for you. I've saved your gorgeous hide more than once. That was our agreement, remember? I take care of you. I know you're sick. I can live with that. As long as you love me. But you have to trust—"

"Sick?" He shook his head and leaned back, the boardroom glare that had intimidated many an adversary directed squarely at her. "Trusting a woman is what got me into this mess in the first place."

She smiled. Poor thing. Didn't he know by now she couldn't be intimidated? "Trusting a woman is what will get you out of it, too."

She waited, displaying far more patience than he had ever shown her. At last, his broad shoulders lifted with a heavy breath and he nodded, accepting her promise. Accepting her.

"I love you." Pursing her lips together, she blew him a kiss. "Oh, and Brian, darling?" There were rules to this relationship, and he needed to understand them. "I'm willing to do whatever is necessary to save you. But if you betray who I am to anyone—a cell mate, a police officer or even a fly on the wall—I will destroy you." She smiled again. "Now, say you love me."

She held the defiant challenge in his dark eyes until, with a nod of understanding, he lowered his gaze. "I love you."

She hung up the phone and walked away.

Chapter One

December

"That's him. I recognize his voice. The build's right and the eyes are the same. He's the man who raped me."

Bailey Austin braced her hand against the chilly window that separated her from the suspect and decoys lined up in the adjoining room at KCPD's Fourth Precinct headquarters and closed her eyes. They all wore black clothes and surgical masks over the lower half of their faces. But she didn't need a visual to relive the sounds and smells and every violent, humiliating touch that had changed her life more than a year ago.

"Shut up!" A fist smashed across her cheekbone when she'd dared to beg him to stop. Pain pulsed through her fractured skull, swirling her plastic-covered surroundings into a dizzying vertigo that made her nauseous. Her stomach was already churning from the stingingly bitter smell of vinegar and soap on the washcloth he was bathing her with. As if he could simply wash away the pain and shock and violation of what he had done to her. Bound and battered, helpless

to struggle against him, she tried to blank her mind against the unspeakable things he was doing to her. "I'm the one in charge here, you filthy thing," he needlessly reminded her.

Dark eyes swam in and out of focus from the grotesque black-and-white mask he wore. "Please..."

"Close your eyes and that mouth, or I'll put the hood on you again." She squeezed her eyes shut, dutifully doing what she could to save herself more punishment. "Do exactly what I tell you," he warned her, scrubbing away any evidentiary trace of himself or the crime scene from her body, "and maybe I'll let you live."

Bailey had been one of the lucky ones. She'd survived.

But she hadn't been able to erase the memory that night, and she couldn't now. Even with a simple recitation from a Kansas City travel brochure, she recognized his voice—so bitter and devoid of caring. "That's him," she repeated, opening her eyes to see a uniformed officer stop and cuff the black-haired man she'd identified. When he peeled off his mask, she recognized his face from the business and society pages of the Kansas City papers. "Brian Elliott is the man who... He's the Rose Red Rapist."

District Attorney Dwight Powers stood beside her at the one-way window. "You'll testify to that in court? You'll point him out to the jury?"

She swallowed the emotions that rose in her throat. Despite all logic that told her she was invisible to him here in the look-at room, Bailey hugged her orange wool coat tighter in her arms and backed away from the glass when her attacker turned and looked in her direction. She nodded, transfixed by the cruel eyes, warm with color and yet so cold. There was something wrong with that man, something sick or disconnected inside his head. A brilliantly successful businessman, charming on the surface, yet twisted, damaged, inside. And he'd taken all that rage, all that self-loathing out on her. As if she'd been the cause of his pain. Even through the glass she felt his hatred aimed squarely at her.

She could feel his hands on her all over again, her arms pinned above her head, his body on top of hers, and she shuddered.

"This is a dubious identification at best, Powers, and you know it." Shaking off the nightmare crawling over her skin, Bailey turned away from the glass as Kenna Parker, Brian Elliott's articulate defense attorney, started earning her expensive fee. The taller woman clutched her leather attaché in her fist and looked down with sympathy. "I'm sorry for what you've gone through, Miss Austin. But if the district attorney here puts you on the stand, I can promise you that my cross-examination won't be pleasant. If you're certain my client is your attacker, then why didn't you identify him sooner? He's a known figure in Kansas City society."

"I didn't know him. Not personally." Bailey's gaze darted up to meet the blond woman's faintly accusatory question. "I identified him by voice. And I did recognize his eyes as soon as I saw them again. Once he was arrested, I picked out his mug shot from a group of several suspects."

"You had a head injury, didn't you? Perhaps your memory isn't as clear as you'd like it to be."

Before Bailey could form the appropriate words to defend her competence as the prosecution's star witness, Harper Pierce, the family attorney her parents had insisted accompany them down to Precinct headquarters this morning, interrupted.

"Is that a threat, Kenna?" he challenged.

The woman smiled up at the attorney in the three-piece suit. "Of course not. I'm good enough I don't need to make threats." With a polite nod to everyone in the room, she turned on her Italian leather pumps and headed out the door. "Now if you'll excuse me, I need to go talk to my client. Chief Taylor?"

Mitch Taylor, the Precinct commander who blocked the door, folded his arms across his barrel-chest. "My people made a good arrest, Ms. Parker. They pulled a dangerous man off the streets."

"Did they?" She waited until he stepped aside to let her pass. "Or did they just find a convenient scapegoat so you could close your investigation and get the press off your back?"

Everyone in the tiny room turned their heads at the onslaught of voices and bright lights that greeted the lady attorney as soon as she stepped into the hallway. Reporters.

"Ms. Parker. Is your client a free man?"

"Will he still be out on bail?"

"Did the witness identify him as the Rose Red Rapist?"

"Who is the witness?"

Bailey clutched her stomach as a wave of nausea churned inside her. They were closing in like vultures. "Oh, my."

Dwight Powers braced his hand beneath her elbow. "Mitch," he warned.

"I'm on it." With a curt nod, Mitch stepped into the hallway. With a booming voice that made Bailey tremble, he took charge of the surging crowd. "This is a police station, not gossip central. Kate Kilpatrick, our task force liaison to the press, will answer your questions downstairs."

"Is that Brian Elliot?" a woman asked. "Could we talk to him?"

"My client is being released on bail, and we'll be making a formal statement later," Kenna promised.

"Joe! Sarge!" Bailey ducked behind the D.A.'s broad back as Chief Taylor called for backup. "Get them out of here. I'm not putting on a press conference for that scum. The reporters can talk to Elliott outside, once we get his ankle bracelet back on him."

"Yes, sir." A dutiful voice from the hallway hastened to do his chief's bidding. "Ms. Owen. Mr. Knight. This way, people. I'll escort you down to the front door."

As soon as Chief Taylor closed the door behind him, Bailey's mother, Loretta Austin-Mayweather, spoke from the back of the room. "I don't like that woman. Do you think Kenna Parker staged that harangue of reporters to frighten Bailey?"

With the reporters' protesting voices reduced to a murmur, the D.A. released his grip on Bailey. "It's a possibility. She'll use every weapon in her arsenal to prove reasonable doubt to the jury. And since a lot of our case rests on your daughter…"

Bailey's chin popped up when he turned his eyes on her. Forcing herself to take easy, calming breaths, Bailey nodded. She had to do this. "Don't worry, Mr. Powers. You can count on me."

Loretta glanced up at the distinguished gentleman standing beside her. Her beautiful features were drawn with worry and fatigue. "Jackson, isn't there something you can do about Ms. Parker to protect Bailey? I've already lost Kyle. I don't think I could stand to see another child get hurt."

Too late for that, Bailey thought as a less-than-kind impulse bubbled up. But her sarcasm quickly turned to sympathy. They'd all been devastated by Kyle's death, her mother to the point that when Bailey had needed her most, Loretta had been incapable of empathizing with her daughter's pain. Her mother had lost weight from the stress and turned to a nightly glass or two of wine in order to sleep. For months now, Loretta had deflected any conversation more serious than the weather or the family's social calendar.

They all had their ways of coping. Bailey just hoped her efforts to take charge of her own life and to confront her attacker would lead to her own healing.

"We won't let that happen," Harper Pierce assured Loretta. "Will we." Bailey had to look away from the solicitous expression on the attorney's handsome face.

He used to look at her that way—before the assault, when they'd been engaged to be married—when she'd been able to tolerate a flirtatious wink or intimate touch, when she would have been satisfied to become his trophy wife and take her place at his side in Kansas City society. Once, that look would have bolstered her courage. Now, that sly wink was just something else she had to deal with.

"You can't talk me out of this, Harper," Bailey stated firmly. She was no longer the wide-eyed Pollyanna who'd doted on his needs and shared so many interests with him. Understandably, she had to put herself—and now her mother—first. She crossed the room to give her mother a gentle hug, then pulled away, smiling into the blue eyes that matched her own. "But I promise I'll be as careful as I can, Mother. Mr. Powers has assured my anonymity for as long as possible. And you know my counseling sessions with Dr. Kilpatrick have included lots of advice on ways a woman can keep herself safe. I've been listening. I won't take any unnecessary chances."

"I wish you hadn't cut your hair, dear." Without even acknowledging her daughter's attempt to reassure her, Loretta reached up to smooth Bailey's bangs back into the short wisps at her temple. "Those long, blonde waves were so beautiful."

Yes, but the short haircut was all about being safe, not making the pages of a fashion magazine. Having a man grab her by the hair and sling her to the floor or into the back of a van had a tendency to make a woman want to remove any "handles" that made it easy for an attacker to latch on. "Mother—"

"Jackson?" Loretta clung to her husband's arm, turning to Bailey's stepfather for the answers she wanted. "Can't you make this whole mess go away?"

Bailey's stepfather wasn't oblivious to the emotional undercurrents in the room. But his typical response was to try to fix whatever the problem might be. He slid a supportive arm around his wife's waist. "I'll do whatever's necessary to protect this family, dear." He turned to the D.A. "Do you think Ms. Parker will bring that ugly business with my stepson into the trial?"

"I had nothing to do with that," Bailey protested. She wasn't sure when or where her brother had gotten so caught up with greed that his reckless business dealings had made him desperate enough to kidnap and attempt to murder their half sister, Charlotte. But she knew the devious, violent man who'd been arrested, and subsequently murdered in prison, had no resemblance to the brother she'd once loved and admired. A different sort of character ran through her veins. Something smarter. Stronger. She hoped. "What Kyle did has nothing to do with what happened to me."

But Jackson was looking to the men in the room for a solution, not her. The D.A. understood his concern. "It's possible she could bring your family history into the courtroom, use it to taint the veracity of Bailey's testimony. If there's one liar in the family, why not two? I'd argue irrelevancy, of course."

"I'm not lying," Bailey insisted. "And my head wasn't so scrambled that I've forgotten what I heard and saw and went through that night."

The burly D.A. nodded. "I'm counting on it. The KCPD task force has given me plenty of forensic and circumstantial evidence to make a case. But science and legal jargon can overwhelm a jury. I need you to be the face of all his victims. The jury will sympathize with you and with your eyewitness testimony. They'll convict him, and the judge will put Elliott away for the rest of his life. Kenna Parker, however, is going to do everything she can to discredit you on the witness stand."

Chief Taylor, who put together the task force that had finally brought in the Rose Red Rapist, muttered a choice word beneath his breath. "Leave it to Elliott to buy the best. Parker's already got him out on bail. From what I hear, he got his ex-wife, Mara Boyd-Elliott who runs the *Journal*, to post it."

"Sounds like Elliott's got all kinds of friends we'll be up against."

Chief Taylor agreed. "I have somebody watching him around the clock, but he's running his business and buying Christmas presents, acting like he's facing traffic court instead of twenty or more years in prison. Kenna's only been in Kansas City for a year, and she's already earned a cutthroat reputation by winning cases." The senior cop pointed a warning finger at the D.A. "My task force worked for more than a year putting this case together and finally bringing him in. It'll demoralize my team, if not this entire city, if Elliott wins in court. Can you beat her, Dwight?"

"I win cases, too. Against tougher odds than this." To his credit, Dwight Powers didn't seem the least bit intimidated by either the reputation of his opposing counsel, pressure from the police department, or the wealth and influence Jackson Mayweather commanded.

Top attorneys. Top cop. Top society movers and shakers. Ex-fiancé. A nervous city. Her own fragile sense of confidence. They were all formidable opponents to stand up against in order to make herself heard. But Bailey finally shut down the memories and fear, and hastened to reassure Dwight Powers that he could rely on her to help send Brian Elliott to prison. "I can talk about the rose he left with me, the van he transported me in, how he dumped me in that alley, and what happened during the assault. Once I came to in that horrible room, I remember everything. He bathed me afterward and *disinfected* me with vinegar." She ignored her mother's pained gasp. "I'm not confused about any of it."

The burly D.A. pulled a pen from his suit jacket and jotted a note onto the yellow legal pad he held. "You'll confirm the surgical mask and stocking cap he wore, as well as a description of the construction site where he took you?"

Bailey nodded. She could do this. She *had* to stand up and face her attacker in the courtroom or she'd never be able to stand up for herself and feel any sense of strength or self-worth again. "I'll tell everything."

"Oh, sweetie. Surely not everything." Loretta crossed the room to squeeze her daughter's hand. "You were always such a sensitive child. And after this nightmare—"

"Mother." Just because she'd never been called on to deal with something like this before didn't mean she couldn't. Bailey pulled her hand away. "I'm twenty-six years old, not a child. I can do this. I need your support, not a lecture to talk me out of doing it." She thumbed over her shoulder toward the empty lineup room. "If

I don't stand up against that man now, then I'll be his victim all over again—and for the rest of my life." Her hand turned into a fist as angry tears stung her eyes. "And he doesn't get to win."

Jackson came up beside Loretta, draping an arm around her as he squeezed Bailey's shoulder. "We understand that this is part of your recovery, dear. But one of the hardest things in the world is for a parent to see her child suffer. Be patient with us. We'll support whatever you decide. Just know we love you and that we'll be here for you."

As the tears welled up in her mother's eyes, Bailey sniffed back her own. She nodded her thanks and turned to Dwight. "Anything you ask," she vowed. "Anything Ms. Parker asks, I'll answer it. It can't be any harder than knowing he could go free to do the same thing to another woman. I want to feel safe again. I want him rotting in prison."

With a curt nod, Dwight packed his briefcase. "So do I." He latched it shut before shaking Bailey's hand. "I'll see you Monday morning at the courthouse when the trial begins, then. With your testimony, I'll have a guilty verdict by Christmas. And Brian Elliott will never celebrate another New Year's with his family and friends. Chief Taylor?"

"Thank you, Miss Austin, for being so courageous." The police chief shook her hand, too, before reaching behind him to open the door. "I've got a roll-call meeting to get to. I'll have an officer walk you out."

"I've got it, sir." A tall detective with crisp, golden-red hair straightened from the wall across the hallway where he'd been leaning. Without a wasted motion, he buttoned the front of his steel-gray suit jacket over the badge and gun belted at his trim waist. "Miss Austin."

Bailey halted in the doorway as her eyes locked on to Spencer Montgomery's cool granite gaze. He was a decade her senior, with nothing boyish about him to soften his chiseled, unreadable face. He was an old family foe who'd investigated her brother's illegal activities—meaning that most of their past conversations had put one or the other of them on the defensive, as he grilled her with questions or she did what she could to protect her family. But, as leader of the KCPD task force, he'd turned those same dogged, calculating investigative skills to solving the string of crimes committed by the Rose Red Rapist. That made him the one man most responsible for Brian Elliott's arrest. And for that, he would always be her hero.

Still, Spencer Montgomery was probably here to make sure she hadn't made a mistake in identifying his suspect, that she hadn't screwed up his year-long investigation. Despite an innate appreciation for his mature intelligence and faintly military bearing, Bailey's pulse rate went on wary alert. "Detective Montgomery."

"If you have a moment, I'd like to talk to you."

Judging by the grim line of his mouth, she had a feeling she wasn't going to like whatever he had to say.

Chapter Two

She'd cut her hair.

Spencer noted the change in Bailey Austin's appearance—noted that the short, sun-kissed waves made her look a lot more grown-up than he remembered. She'd always been pretty, but the changes he noticed today made her…interesting. But just as quickly as he decided he liked the new look, he dismissed the revelation.

Any latent attraction he had to the woman was irrelevant. The last time he'd seen Bailey, she'd been in a hospital bed, beaten within an inch of her life—the victim of a violent rape by the man his task force had eventually identified and arrested, entrepreneur and real estate developer Brian Elliott. He should be content to see the bruises gone and the vibrancy back in her azure-blue eyes instead of noticing the leaner curves beneath the wool slacks and cashmere sweater she wore and the way those sculpted wisps of hair gleamed like spun gold, even under the fluorescent lights of the precinct hallway.

No, he couldn't notice those things at all. He was here to do his job. Period. And if that job included babysitting a fragile debutante-in-distress from Kansas City society, then so be it.

Besides, Chief Taylor was clapping him on the shoulder, demanding his attention. "You're going to see this job through to the bitter end, aren't you, Spence."

"Yes, sir."

"I knew there was a reason I made you point man on the task force." Mitch Taylor might be graying at the temples, but the man was still the powerhouse of the Fourth Precinct. He was the boss whose recommendation could make or break a promotion. Spencer respected the dedicated cop who'd worked his way up the ranks at KCPD. And since his goal was to do the same, getting asked to do a favor for the boss was an opportunity he didn't intend to squander.

"I appreciate the faith you had in us, sir."

"Your work isn't done yet," the chief reminded him, referring either to the outcome of Brian Elliott's trial or the task force's ongoing search for the Rose Red Rapist's accomplice—a woman they'd dubbed The Cleaner because of her efforts to destroy evidence and take out witnesses to Elliott's crimes. "You remember our chat yesterday?"

I want you to check in on Miss Austin from time to time. Make yourself available to her in case anything comes up that could spook her out of testifying against Elliott.

"I do."

Spencer had walked out of Chief Taylor's office understanding his mission. The Cleaner hadn't shown up on their radar since they'd made the arrest and the rapes had stopped. But then Elliott had been under KCPD's watch 24/7 from the moment his ex-wife had posted bail. Their vigilance might have driven the accomplice underground or out of town—or maybe whatever sick relationship the woman shared with a serial rapist had failed now that he was no longer able to commit the crimes that had terrorized Kansas City for several years. Or, as both Mitch Taylor and Spencer suspected, the woman could be biding her time, waiting to make some big move to *save her man* again.

Until The Cleaner was identified and put out of commission, Spencer intended to keep his task force on full alert. Scoring a few points with the boss along the way couldn't hurt, either.

The chief gestured to the group filing out of the look-at room behind Bailey. "I take it you know everyone here?"

Spencer nodded. While he couldn't claim to be friends with anyone in Bailey's entourage, they were certainly well acquainted. "We've met several times. On this investigation and the Rich Girl Killer case."

"You closed that one for me, too." Mitch Taylor praised him before winking a brown eye at Bailey. "I leave you in good hands, Miss Austin." The chief turned and hurried down the hallway after D.A. Powers. "Dwight, wait up."

While Bailey hugged her purse and coat to her waist, waiting expectantly for him to explain why Chief Taylor had asked him to chat with her, a protective force of allies circled behind her.

Loretta Austin-Mayweather's disgusted snort was

audible, her blue eyes unforgiving. "Jackson, please. I'd like to go home. I have nothing to say to this man. Bailey, come."

Yes, he'd brought the Rich Girl Killer murder investigation to their home, and had been obligated to interrogate each and every one of them. And though Bailey's brother, Kyle Austin, hadn't ultimately been the murderer Spencer had sought, he *had* been guilty of other crimes, including embezzlement, stalking his own stepsister and kidnapping. And the real killer, who hadn't appreciated a copycat using his M.O., had ultimately murdered the Austin heir while he'd been in prison.

Since Spencer had no children—no family at all, to speak of—he supposed he couldn't truly understand a parent's loss of a child. He could only play whipping boy and hold back the reminder that without KCPD's intervention, the entire Mayweather family might have fallen victim to Kyle Austin's desperate actions and the killer who'd threatened them.

"Detective." Jackson Mayweather's acknowledgment was more civil, but clearly the man had a meeting to get to, or an eagerness to defuse his wife's displeasure, because he looped his arm around Loretta's shoulder and started down the hallway. "Come along, dear. I'll have the driver meet us at the front door."

"Bailey." Loretta practically clicked her tongue, calling her daughter to join them.

Despite a deep sigh that indicated she was schooling her patience, Bailey simply smiled and turned her head. "Detective Montgomery is the leader of the Rose

Red Rapist investigation. He probably needs to discuss something with me."

Harper Pierce, a tall, blond piece-of-work who'd stonewalled more than one KCPD investigation with his legal acrobatics, placed his hand at the small of Bailey's back. "Then he can make an appointment. Let's go."

Before Spencer could evaluate the way his own body braced at the proprietary touch, Bailey arched her back away from the other man's hand and sent Pierce on his way. "Would you mind looking after Jackson and Mother? I know she'd appreciate the extra arm to lean on."

"I'm not leaving you with—"

"Please, Harper. Go." Her melodic voice lost its sweet tone and her body seemed to hug itself around the orange coat she clutched. So she didn't like to be touched? Was that an aftereffect of the rape? Or was it that she just didn't want her ex-fiancé putting his hands on her?

Flashing a suspicious eye toward Spencer, as if *he* was somehow to blame for the dismissal, Harper relented. "I'll hold the elevator for you."

"That won't be necessary."

"Bails—"

"I'll walk her to her car," Spencer volunteered, eager to send the others on their way. That'd give him a few minutes of private time with Bailey to have the conversation Chief Taylor wanted him to have with her. Then he could get back to some real work.

"How did you know I drove myself?" Bailey arched a golden eyebrow as she turned her attention back to him.

Spencer dropped his gaze down to the keys dangling from her fist and grinned. Easy deduction. "I *am* a detective."

A responding grin eased the strain on her mouth and relaxed some of the tension from her posture. "So you are." The gentleness returned to her voice as she spoke to her parents and ex-fiancé again. "You all go ahead. I need to get back to my apartment and organize my portfolio for the job interview I have tomorrow, anyway. It'll save you a stop."

"Can't you put that off until another day?" Loretta sounded more irritated than hurt by her daughter's excuse to leave them. "The Butler-Smythes are coming to dinner tonight, remember? Their son Cameron is just home from his trip to China. You know he was sweet on you back in school, and I thought—"

"I can't, Mother." A rosy hue tinted Bailey's cheeks, indicating the level of impatience or distress she was keeping in check at her mother's efforts to plan her evening and her life. "I have errands to run before I go home. And I'm still fixing up my apartment. I want to finish painting the trim around the windows tonight." Spencer would have stopped with a solid *no,* but Bailey threw in a bit of logic to salvage her mother's feelings. "Besides, you know I'm not feeling terribly social right now. If you want me to make an appearance at your holiday gala this weekend, I need to save up my social energy to face all those people. Deal?"

Loretta's dramatic sigh indicated her daughter had finally come up with an excuse she could accept. "I suppose it's a fair tradeoff. I do want you at the Christmas ball. I can guarantee yeses to every invitation if our guests know you'll be there."

Spencer felt himself bristling on Bailey's behalf. The young woman was gearing up to testify against her rapist—to face the man who'd nearly killed her—across the short distance of a courtroom. And her mother was worried about matchmaking and society fund-raisers?

Although the tension crept back into her posture, Bailey continued to smile when her mother came to give her a hug. "Please give Cam and his parents my regards, but I won't be there."

Loretta's cutting gaze swept over Spencer as she pulled away. Then she brushed Bailey's bangs off her forehead and straightened the angel pendant hanging around her neck. "Very well then. I'll call you tomorrow about the Christmas Ball."

Bailey nodded. "I'll talk to you then."

"Call me if you need an escort to the ball." Bailey stiffened when Harper leaned in to press a kiss to her temple and Spencer felt a protective urge make him stand straighter. And even though she managed a smile before Pierce followed Loretta and Jackson Mayweather down the hallway, it didn't last.

"I apologize for my family and…" she thumbed over her shoulder "…my attorney."

"They're understandably protective of you."

"Smothering is more like it." She unfolded the coat she carried and flipped it around her shoulders. "Happy holidays, Detective. I hope you're well."

"What?"

Her mouth relaxed with a soft giggle, probably at

catching him off guard with the friendly chitchat. "It's customary when someone issues you a greeting like that for you say something similar in return."

"Oh. Right." When she juggled her keys and purse to shrug into her coat, Spencer decided to test his no-touch theory. He pointed, alerting her to his intent before moving behind her to hold her coat. She paused for a moment before thanking him and sliding her arms into the sleeves. After settling the collar up around her neck, he smoothed his hands across her shoulders and patted her arms. It was Pierce's touch she hadn't liked. Or maybe being touched without being asked first. She wasn't skittish with him standing behind her. She hadn't frozen up. Maybe she was going to make a calmer, more reliable witness than Chief Taylor thought. "Happy holidays, Bailey."

What the heck? Spencer popped his grip open and stepped back when he realized he was still holding her shoulders, still breathing in the faint citrusy scent of her hair, still feeling her warmth.

And did she just shiver when he pulled away? Was that a soft gasp he heard? She'd liked his touch. Or, at the very least, she hadn't minded his hands lingering on her.

There were times when possessing his finely honed eye for detail sucked. *Think job, Montgomery. Forget the woman. Forget the attraction.*

You know what hell that will lead you to.

"How are you holding up?" he asked, his tone more brusque than he'd intended.

"Are you worried I'm going to screw up all your hard

work?" Bailey slipped her purse onto her shoulder, inhaling a deep breath before turning to face him. They stood close enough now that she had to tilt her face up to see his. Good grief, her eyes were blue.

A pair of pretty brown eyes, buried deep within his memory, suddenly surfaced in his mind, blurring his vision. Spencer blinked away the vision before the pain could follow. He slipped his hands into the pockets of his slacks and strolled a few steps toward the main room at the end of the hall, pretending he was still on his game. "Chief Taylor wanted me to run through some safety precautions with you—make sure you're all ready to go for Monday, or whenever you get called to the stand."

"So you *are* worried. You don't think I'll go through with this, either, do you?"

The accusation stopped him in his tracks and Spencer turned. "This is an important case, Bailey."

"It's important to me, too." She shoved her keys into her pocket and faced off against him. "Everyone thinks I'm going to freak out on the stand or run away and hide somewhere. But I have to do this. There has to be a reason why this happened to me."

Spencer's eyes narrowed at the emotion staining her cheeks. If she got worked up arguing with him, how was she going to handle it if Kenna Parker tried to rattle her on the witness stand? "That's a lot of pressure to put on yourself."

"Yes. But I can handle it."

He pulled his hand from his pocket and tapped the fingers fisted around the strap of her purse, silently arguing her cool-under-fire argument. "Have you ever done anything like this before? Have you ever bared your fears and soul and worst nightmare in front of the man who made you afraid?"

"No. Of course not, but…"

He let the reality of what they were asking of her set in, and watched her cheeks pale and her gaze drop to the center of his chest. "This is going to get messy before it gets done. Are you sure you're up for this?"

"You'd think I'd have at least one person cheering me on and bucking up my confidence instead of telling me all the reasons why I can't or shouldn't do it." She tilted her chin up, venting a mixture of temper and frustration. "Since you've been so obsessed with catching this guy, I would have thought you'd be in my corner. But you're as much of a doubting Thomas as anybody else."

"I'm not the kind of man to give pep talks, Bailey." As Bailey's voice grew louder and more animated, Spencer's hushed, articulating every word as he dipped his head closer to hers. "There's a lot that can happen between now and when you're called up to that witness stand. Besides you 'freaking out' and deciding not to testify, there's a possibility Brian Elliott's accomplice may do something to try to stop you."

"You're talking about The Cleaner, aren't you?"

"Yes, I'm talking about The Cleaner—and she's nobody you want to mess with. You need to lock your doors and windows. Don't go out by yourself at night. Have someone walk you to your car. Hang with people you know and trust. And if something does happen, call me or 911 before it's too late to do anything about it."

With every sentence, her eyes widened and her skin cooled to a pale porcelain color. "Too late…?"

"I'm not here to sugarcoat anything. I'm just stating the facts."

After an endless moment of silence she tore her gaze from his and focused her attention on buttoning her coat. "Don't worry, detective. No one would ever mistake you for a warm and fuzzy kind of guy." She tied her orange belt with equal fervor. "Now, was that the lecture you were supposed to give me? Watch my back and don't be stupid? Or do you have some more doom and gloom you'd like to share? Let's get it over with because I really do need to get home and hide away in my little ivory tower of naïveté and incompetence."

"I didn't call you stupid."

"No, you're just intimating that I can't take care of myself."

Really? This defiant little show of sarcasm was supposed to convince him to trust her to close his case? Was this an attempt to show her strength? By butting heads with him? And since when did he get in anyone's face and argue back?

Spencer's blood was still pumping hard through his veins when he heard a door open in the hallway behind him. He saw the shock register on Bailey's face and instinctively went on guard against the unseen threat as he spun around.

Two uniformed officers led Brian Elliott out of the nearby interview room. He'd changed into an expensively tailored suit and a smug untouchability that made him look more like a Forbes 500 mogul than the prisoner wearing a pair of handcuffs and ankle-band tracking device he truly was. An entourage of his attorney, Kenna Parker, and Elliott's ex-wife, Mara Boyd-Elliott, followed behind. One a dark blonde, the other, platinum, both women wore business suits and carried winter coats and attaché cases, looking like they'd all just finished a business meeting instead of a legal debriefing.

Spencer's arm went out to push Bailey behind him as the group came closer. He felt her fingers curling into the back of his jacket and something inside him shifted, grew wary. When Elliott spotted Spencer, the bastard grinned in recognition. The other man slowed his stride and the soft gasp at Spencer's back made him reach down to fold his hand around Bailey's wrist beside him.

"Keep walking, Elliott," Spencer ordered.

"Now, now, detective. I've missed our little chats in the interrogation room" the man taunted. "Arrest any other innocent people lately?"

"Brian." That was the ex, laying a hand on his shoulder. "Don't make me regret my investment. I'm willing to support you to a point, but antagonizing the police won't help your case."

Elliott shrugged off her touch. "You only posted bail so your paper could report on the trial without it looking like a personal vendetta against me."

Mara eased a calming sigh behind his back. "Unbiased reporting isn't the only reason. There's still a place in my heart for you. And I believe in…your innocence."

Innocence? The newspaper publisher could barely choke out the word. Spencer wondered how the woman could live with herself, putting Elliott out on the street just so she could sell more papers.

Did he need to remind them about blood matching Elliott's type being found at the scene of one of the assaults? Had they forgotten his DNA matching the child of a woman who claimed to have been raped by the Rose Red Rapist? Did any of them think Elliott could deny kidnapping a woman and being captured by the K-9 cop and his German Shepherd partner on Spencer's task force?

Spencer could easily imagine the arguments Elliott's attorney would bring up. The blood sample had been corrupted and could match any number of suspects. The child's birth mother, who'd never reported being raped, had had a nervous breakdown and been committed to a mental hospital, so her version of events was suspect. The abduction could be pled down to a lesser crime and argued that it was a solo occurrence, not the culmination of a reign of serial terror through the city.

But there was no arguing away the eyewitness testimony of the courageous woman digging her fingers into his shoulder blade right now. Or Spencer's driving need to protect the truth she represented.

"Get him out of here, Ms. Parker." Spencer repeated the command to move the handcuffed man.

But when the uniformed guards urged the prisoner forward, Brian Elliott planted his feet and turned. "Wait. Do I know you, miss?"

Bailey released her death grip on Spencer's jacket and slid her right hand down his arm. At the brush of her chilled skin against his, he turned his palm into hers, lacing their fingers together, offering his protection and support against the man who'd terrorized her a year earlier. When she latched on to him with both hands, Spencer tightened his hold.

Be tough, Bailey, he wanted to say. He could feel her trembling beside him. *Be just as strong as you claim to be.*

Kenna Parker nudged aside one of the uniformed officers and moved in front of her client. "You shouldn't have any contact with the opposing witnesses."

Damn straight.

But Elliott ignored his attorney's plea. "You're Jackson Mayweather's daughter, er, stepdaughter. I've had a few business dealings with Jackson, and I've given a lot of money to your mother's charities. She does good work for local hospitals and children's groups." He was making small talk with Bailey? Was he hoping she'd recant her statement because he knew her parents or could pour on the charm? "You're the woman who thinks I hurt you."

"Thinks?" The trembling stopped. Was some steel creeping into that delicate backbone of hers? Or was she on the verge of passing out?

"Brian," Kenna Parker warned. "Don't say another word."

Mara Elliott tried to get him moving, too. "Darling, we need to go."

"Don't *darling* me—!" The cuffs that linked Elliott's wrist jangled as he jerked against them.

Bailey's hand jerked in Spencer's grip. Good. Not passing out.

He snapped an order to the two unis. "Get him out of here."

The brief show of anger quickly passed, and, with the officers grabbing hold of Brian Elliott, the perp raised his hands in calm surrender. "I'm all right, dear," he apologized to his ex. "I've got this, Kenna." Then he turned his attention back to Spencer. "I'm sorry for what happened to your friend there. Yes, I've made some mistakes, but I'm not the monster you think I am. The man you want is still out there, Montgomery, lying in wait to hurt some other helpless woman." He gestured to the women there to support him, as if their presence was proof of his innocence. "I'm no serial rapist."

Maybe Spencer's command hadn't been clear. "Go. Now."

A brunette woman, wearing a coat over her suit, and holding a cell phone to her ear, came around the corner and stopped. Her dark eyes widened as she took in the confrontation in the hallway. "Mr. Elliott?" Regina Hollister, Brian Elliott's executive assistant, paused for a moment, then asked the party on her call to wait while she joined the group. "I have your car waiting for us out front. Is everything all right?"

"Get him out of here." Or Spencer would do the job himself.

The two officers pulled Elliott into step between them. Kenna Parker hurried ahead to consult with Elliott's assistant. "Out front where the reporters are?"

Regina nodded and put her cell phone back to her ear. "I'll ask the driver to meet us someplace else."

"No." Kenna stopped her and turned to face her client, walking backward as they continued down the hallway. "Let's use the press to our advantage. The officers will uncuff you before you leave the building. I don't want you to make any comment, but let's show Kansas City that you're a free man."

"For now," Spencer called after them. "Don't let that ankle bracelet pinch too tight, Elliott."

When Brian Elliott began a retort, Kenna Parker pressed her finger against his lips to shush him until he smiled and nodded his acquiescence. Spencer didn't move or look away until Brian Elliott and the others had turned the corner toward the bank of public elevators and disappeared from sight.

Easing out a tense breath as the threat left, Spencer quickly became aware of other sorts of tension humming through his body. Bailey had her left hand curled around his arm now. Her whole body was hugged up against his side, seeking shelter or maybe just something stronger than she was to hold her upright. Several more seconds passed before Spencer acknowledged that he wasn't moving away from the warmth of her curves pressed against his arm. And that was his thumb stroking across the back of her knuckles, soothing the crushing grip of her hand.

It was happening again. This was getting personal. This was how it had started with Ellen, and he couldn't go through that again. *Move away, Montgomery.* Cop. Witness. Keep her safe. Don't let any feelings get involved with this.

"Do your job," he mouthed to himself.

"What?" Bailey whispered beside him.

Even worse than feeling the damn emotions was someone else knowing they were there, providing a weapon they could use against him.

So he emptied his lungs on a forceful breath of air and pulled his body away from Bailey's to face her. "You okay?" he asked.

"Yes." Her nod wasn't all that convincing. She squeezed her eyes shut for second and shook her head, as if clearing some graphic image from her mind. But when they opened again, that azure gaze tilted up and locked on to his. "I smelled that vile cologne he had on. I'm sure it's something expensive, but…" The strength of her gaze faltered. "He had it on that night, too. I *know* he's the man who raped me."

"I have no doubt," Spencer agreed. "That's exactly the kind of detail that will make the D.A.'s case for us." When the taut line of her mouth softened into a smile, he ignored that little kick of awareness that made him smile in return.

"Thank you for saying that. And thank you for being here when…" She visibly shuddered. "He was close enough he could have touched me."

"Brian Elliott will never touch you again." When he heard how vehemently he'd spoken those words, as if he'd just made some kind of promise to Bailey Austin, Spencer released her hand and broke contact entirely. It wasn't his job to care about the awful turmoil she must go through each time she had to revisit the violence that had been done to her. Maybe she was okay with being touched, or maybe she'd been too scared to realize how hard she'd been holding on to him. Either way was a head game he wasn't comfortable playing. She needed a sensitive kind of guy or her therapist to walk her through the emotional minefield of taking down the Rose Red Rapist. And he wasn't that guy.

He needed some distance. This situation was getting inside his head—the woman was getting under his skin. Setting up a safe house and guarding a witness weren't part of his job description anymore. He was *not* this woman's protector. He was seeing his investigation through to the very end, like any good detective would. He was doing a favor for Chief Taylor.

He was *not* putting himself in a position to lose anyone else who mattered to him.

Ignoring the questioning look in Bailey's eyes, Spencer inclined his head toward the bullpen—the maze of desks and cubicles in the main room where he and dozens of other detectives worked. "Come on. Let me get my coat and then I'll walk you to your car." He moved out without a backward glance, lengthening his stride to put some impersonal space between them. "I'll give you my card and my partner's, and, of course, you can call the precinct if you need anything else."

Her heels clicked on the marble tiles behind him as she hurried to catch up.

All of Bailey's brave talk about testifying had flown out the window when she'd come face to face with Brian Elliott…right along with Spencer's resolve not to let things get personal with her.

He wouldn't let either one happen again.

Chapter Three

Starch.

That was the subtle, clean scent filling the elevator. Bailey clutched the strap of her purse to her stomach, almost smiling beside the jut of Spencer Montgomery's shoulder as he watched the third-level light come on above the doors of the parking garage elevator.

After traveling down through the bowels of the Fourth Precinct building and out a side entrance, they'd hurried through the bracing air and blowing snow to enter the parking garage a block away from the bright lights and electronic noise of the impromptu press conference on the front steps of the tall granite building across the street. The multistory parking garage might be filled with cars, but with the cold wind blowing through the open levels, chasing the patrons indoors, there'd been no one around when Spencer had bustled her onto the elevator and punched the button. This silent ride up the elevator gave Bailey a calming reprieve from the emotional battles she'd fought all morning with her family, Brian Elliott and within herself.

Not that she'd call her time spent with Spencer Montgomery relaxing, exactly.

Since his promise to walk her to her car, everything had been a rush. Papers neatly stacked on his desk. Chair pushed in. A quick introduction to his partner, Nick Fensom. She'd hurried to keep up with his long strides, been relegated to quick nods in response to his clipped requests and commands. The damp chill in the air outside had nipped at her ears and nose. But now that she had a few moments alone in the elevator with him to catch her breath and thaw out, she had the strangest urge to turn her nose into the nubby wool of his charcoal-gray coat.

Nothing more than starch and soap and cold, crisp air. Emanating from the charcoal-gray coat and crisp white shirt he wore, and maybe from the man himself, Spencer's scent was as straightforward and masculine as every other detail she'd noticed about the steely-eyed detective.

Unlike the overpowering smell of Brian Elliott's cologne that triggered nightmares, Spencer's undoctored scent elicited something feminine and long forgotten inside her. Its simplicity soothed her overwrought senses, yet awakened warm frissons of awareness that she hadn't been sure she'd ever be able to feel again for a man. It was a gentler, although no less impactful response than what she'd felt outside the look-at room when she'd anchored herself to the unwavering strength of his hand holding hers. Spencer's unexpected touch had centered her, strengthened her, allowed her to push aside her gut reaction of panicked fear and handle Brian

Elliott's attempt to strike up a conversation and deny what he'd done to her.

Yes, they'd argued. Yes, he'd pushed her to keep up with his long strides. Yes, it irritated her that Detective Montgomery pictured her as some sort of naive girl who couldn't think or do for herself, and had no idea what she was getting into. But it had felt invigorating for a few moments to have someone actually let her speak her mind and vent her emotions without trying to quickly apologize or change the subject. He hadn't slowed down and lowered his expectations because he thought she was too fragile to handle any kind of stress. And she definitely wasn't feeling anything girlish around the man.

Not when he smelled so good.

Not when he'd stood between her and her rapist.

Not when he made her feel, period.

After all this time, sheltered by her family, sheltered by the protective mental and emotional barriers she'd put up around herself since the rape, it was just as unsettling as it was intriguing to realize that the tall, no-nonsense detective could make her feel normal, womanly things again.

The elevator slowed; the signal dinged.

"Straight to your car, then straight home, right?"

Her secret grin faded at Spencer's brusque reminder. Clearly, whatever crush was forming inside her head wasn't mutual. She was just another piece of evidence in his case against the Rose Red Rapist he wanted to protect. She'd be wise to remember that, and keep the relationship between them as businesslike as he did.

"Yes. I have plenty to do to keep me busy at my apartment tonight."

The doors slid open and he wound his hand around her upper arm like he had before, pulling her into step beside him as soon as she pointed out her white Lexus. "You'll check the parking lot before you get out of your car. Lock the—"

"—doors. Have my key card ready to go into the building. Check the doors and windows. Call someone to let them know I'm home."

"I see you were listening." For the first time in the last thirty minutes, Spencer shortened his stride to let her walk naturally beside him. Was that a grin?

Bailey wondered what would happen to that stern, angular face if he loosened up enough to smile or laugh. "After hearing the same speech upstairs at your office, on the hike across the street and in the elevator coming up here, I started to pick up on what you were trying to say."

That snort might be as close to a laugh as she was going to get out of him. And his warm breath formed a cloud in the cold air, masking a glimpse of what, if any, changes might have softened the strong line of his mouth or add warmth to the granite in his eyes.

But the grip on her arm eased as they crossed the concrete platform, heading toward the thick pillar where she'd parked. "Bailey, I don't think you're a dumb blonde. If anything, I think you're a courageous woman. You may have pushed a few of my buttons earlier and I said some things that didn't come out the way I meant them. I don't normally lose my cool like that."

Um, when exactly had he lost his cool? Brian Elliott's temper had flared briefly in that hallway, throwing Bailey back to that night when he'd ranted at her and punished her for daring to speak her mind or beg for mercy. If Spencer thought he'd come anywhere close to a hotheaded reaction, he was apologizing for nothing. "You were just being a cop. You don't have to explain yourself."

"Yeah, I do. Logically, I think you feel you're doing the right thing—God knows I and half of Kansas City are glad you're testifying. But I worry that you may not fully understand the dangers and challenges you'll have to face when this trial starts. Elliott won't be in handcuffs in that courtroom. And if The Cleaner shows up—"

Bailey pulled his business card from her pocket and waved it in front of his face. "Then I'll call you or your partner or 911."

Another deep breath obscured his reaction. But she might have glimpsed a wry smile. "I guess I need to stop warning you, hmm?"

"You mean treat me like a grown-up?"

"Message received. Got your keys out?"

Bailey swapped the card for the keys in her pocket and pressed the remote, unlocking the car and starting the ignition. "Yes, sir."

"Bailey—" The grip on her arm suddenly tightened and Spencer pulled her to a stop. "Ah, hell."

A dark-haired woman climbed out of the car parked across from Bailey's. The spiky heels of her black leather boots didn't slow her at all as she crossed to the trunk of Bailey's car. The striking brunette pulled a microphone from the folds of her coat. "Are you the star witness Dwight Powers keeps bragging about?"

"Bragging?" Hadn't they escaped the onslaught of reporters?

A second door opened and the reporter waved her camera man forward. "I'm Vanessa Owen, Channel Ten News. Do you mind if I ask you a few questions, Miss Austin?"

Was the dark-haired woman giving her a choice? Vanessa was pushing for confirmation of her suspicions. But Bailey wasn't going to give her what she wanted. When the camera pointed her way and the light came on, nearly blinding her in the dimness of the garage, Bailey kept her expression placid despite the clench of her fist. "I'm *a* witness. I'm sure the D.A. is talking to as many of the Rose Red Rapist's victims that he can."

"Don't you mean alleged victims?" Vanessa Owen's dark gaze flitted over Bailey's shoulder to include Spencer in the interrogation. "Has he really been committing these crimes undetected for as many years as the D.A. claims?"

"Your questions are done, Ms. Owen." Spencer reached around Bailey to push the camera lens toward the ground and warn the camera man to kill the light and stop recording. In a subtle move that wasn't lost on either woman, he went into detective mode, sliding his shoulder in front of Bailey and blocking her from any attempt to question her again. Then *he* went on the offensive. "From what I hear, you and Brian Elliott have been pretty chummy. If you want to talk allegations,

I have it on good intel that you and Elliott are having an affair."

"Past tense, Detective…Montgomery, is it? Leader of KCPD's illustrious task force? Brian and I may have attended a few social events together, but we're no longer an item. Get your facts straight." Vanessa's ruby-tinted lips widened into a smile that never reached her eyes. "That's all I'm trying to do."

But Spencer didn't back down from the taunt. "Either way, I'd think your viewers would be alarmed to learn just how biased your reporting on this case has been." If anything, he leaned in. "Or did you get involved with a rapist just to get the inside scoop on his crimes? If that's the case, I'd like to talk to you about withholding evidence from the police and abetting a suspected felon."

With an amused laugh, Vanessa waved her cameraman back to their car. "Nicely played, Detective. I get your message. I'll back off from Miss Austin. For now." She tilted her head to acknowledge Bailey with a nod, then took a step closer to Spencer. "But this is the biggest story to hit Kansas City in years. I have a feeling there's more to it than what KCPD or the D.A.'s office is sharing. And when her testimony becomes public record? Trust me, I'll get the story. And I'll take it all the way to the national market. Neither the D.A.'s stone-walling nor your task force are going to stop me from telling the biggest story of my career."

"Just make sure you tell the truth." Spencer turned his face to the side and Bailey gasped when she saw a black-haired man she hadn't noticed leaning against a concrete pillar. "That goes for you, too, Knight. Whatever gripe you've got against KCPD, you're not going to use Miss Austin to malign us in your editorials again."

The second reporter, who'd been jotting something on a notepad, straightened. "They're not editorials. They're facts." Even though his blue eyes were focused squarely on the detective, Bailey couldn't help reaching for the sleeve of Spencer's coat as the black-haired reporter approached. "How many months did it take your task force to capture Brian Elliott?" He stuffed his notebook and pen into the pockets of his insulated jacket. "And what kind of progress are you making on capturing his accomplice, The Cleaner?"

"Gabriel Knight, *Kansas City Journal.* I assume you already know Miss Austin, or you wouldn't be here." Spencer's arm eased back against Bailey's hand as he made the introduction, almost inviting her to hang on to his unflappable strength if she needed to.

Bailey curled her fingers into the wool but fought for a bit of independence by stepping up beside him. "Why aren't you two with the other reporters?" she asked.

Vanessa Owen answered. "Because the story's here."

Gabriel Knight agreed. "I've heard all of Elliott's claims of innocence. I'm more interested in knowing who's going to finally shut him up."

"Eloquent as always, Gabe," Vanessa sneered.

Tension bunched in the muscles beneath Bailey's hand, but Spencer's authoritative tone never changed. "If you two want to talk KCPD business, you contact me or the task force press liaison, Kate Kilpatrick. If you want specifics on how Dwight Powers is going to prosecute Elliott, talk to him. Victims have a right to privacy. Leave Bailey Austin out of it."

Gabriel Knight shook his head. "You're betting all your cards on the story of a poor little rich girl, Detective?"

"Excuse me?" A story? Did he think for one minute that her words would be any less true than what he wrote in his paper?

"I'm not a gambler, Mr. Knight." Spencer cut Bailey off before she could organize her thoughts into a protest. He laid his gloved hand over hers where it clung to his arm. "I'm putting all my faith in the truth."

Spencer's adamant defense was just as surprising as the insult to her character and reliability had been, catching Bailey off guard. She looked up to gauge the sincerity of his words, the meaning behind his touch. But the profile of his clenched jaw revealed nothing.

The reporter lifted the camera that hung from his neck and snapped a picture. "Can I quote you on that?"

When Spencer refused to answer the taunt, Gabriel Knight nodded, lowering his camera and accepting détente, for now. "I wish you the best of luck next week, Miss Austin. The department could use it."

Apparently, Vanessa Owen needed to have a last word, too. "We'll be at the courthouse next week, Detective. You can't keep your girlfriend away from us forever."

Girlfriend?

Vanessa's gaze dropped to the spot where Bailey's hand nestled beneath Spencer's, daring him to deny the gossipy enticement. But he didn't say another word.

"She's right." Breaking the tense silence, Gabriel Knight offered Bailey a wink. "I'll see you at the Christmas Ball this weekend. I get to escort my boss to the event to help cover a feel-good story for the holidays."

"You're coming…?" Bailey felt the winter chill seep through her coat.

Of course there'd be reporters at the event. Her mother counted on the publicity to generate more donations after the fact, while the big donors at the ball appreciated the positive press. But she'd foolishly expected them to focus on the needs of the children's hospital wing or the award-winning holiday decor, evening gowns and tuxedoes. She hadn't counted on a hard news man like Gabriel Knight to be there.

"See you then." Knight nodded to his competition. "Vanessa."

"Gabe."

Both reporters walked to their cars and drove away before Spencer abruptly released her. Bailey tried to smooth the wrinkles she'd left on his sleeve, but he moved away to open the car door for her. Wondering if she should apologize for clinging to him again, yet worried he'd tell her the needy grabs were proof that she wasn't emotionally ready to testify, Bailey chose to address the two reporters. "Gabe Knight is an antagonistic, unpleasant man. It almost sounds as if he's got some beef against the police department."

"I don't know what Knight's problem is. He's always been critical of the department. And Vanessa Owen's an ambitious, opportunistic—"

"She's not a lady?"

"Something like that." He gestured to the seat behind the wheel and Bailey dutifully climbed inside. "Don't let him corner you at that ball, all right? You don't have to talk to him."

Bailey buckled her seat belt and turned on the heat. "What about the other reporters? At the very least, Mother will want them to take a family picture."

"Pictures are fine. And you can talk to the other guests. Just don't say more than 'Merry Christmas' or 'Where's your checkbook?' to anyone." He reached into his jacket and pulled out his cell phone as he stepped back. "You've got my card, right?"

She flashed it from her coat pocket before tucking it back inside. "Wait a minute." She could talk to the other guests? Bailey tilted her head up to the detective who was punching a number into his phone. "Mr. Knight's boss is the editor of the *Kansas City Journal*. She'll be there Saturday night. The editor is Brian Elliott's ex-wife, Mara Boyd."

"And she posted Elliott's bail." Spencer waved his phone, letting her know he'd already made the connection. "If she's willing to post a half-million-dollar bond for the man she divorced, then she may be willing to do a lot more."

Was Brian Elliott's ex-wife The Cleaner? Or was she being blackmailed into helping her ex like so many of The Cleaner's accomplices had done? And if Mara Boyd-Elliott showed up at her mother's fund-raiser this weekend, should Bailey avoid the woman or ask what the hell she was thinking by helping such a vile, violent man? Or maybe she could find out if Mara needed some kind of help to get away from him?

"Bailey." Granite eyes demanded her attention. "Leave the detective work to me," he warned, as if reading her thoughts. "You just show up at the courthouse Monday morning. Remember the rules and stay safe." He grabbed the car door as he put the phone to his ear. "Hey, Nick. I need you to run a check on—"

He pushed the door shut and waited for her to lock it before he strode away, turning his attention to his partner on the phone. But when he stopped at the elevator, he faced her again, pulling back his coat to prop a hand at his waist, continuing his conversation—completely impervious to the winter air or sneaky reporters or eyewitnesses who wouldn't go away.

Do what you're told. Let someone else handle the tough stuff.

Understanding the unspoken message in his watchful gaze better than she wanted to, Bailey shifted the car into Reverse and backed out of her parking space. Reluctantly, she drove around the pillar and down the ramp to the garage's lower level, losing sight of that beacon of red-gold hair and the man who'd taken over her life for the past hour or so.

The weather looked far more drab, her world felt far more lonesome, than it had just a few minutes earlier. Spencer Montgomery irritated her with his cool, emotionless obsession with duty. But it was that same undeniable strength and grace under pressure that she had clung to when she'd been afraid or unsure of herself this morning.

Bailey braked at the garage's exit and waited for traffic to pass. She couldn't help glancing at the stairwell and elevator, wondering if she'd catch another glimpse of the man she found so compelling. But the street cleared and Bailey pulled out, leaving the fireworks of her time spent with Spencer Montgomery behind.

She shook her head at the irony of being attracted to a man who held himself in such control. During the time she'd spent in Spencer's company, she'd felt anger, security, frustration, strength, uncertainty, excitement and fear. In short, everything a normal woman should feel.

But that was the curse of her life, wasn't it? Until the trial was finished and Brian Elliott was behind bars permanently, she had no real chance at *normal*.

Chapter Four

Bailey shoved open the front door of the restored 1910 brick office building that had looked so charming an hour ago and hurried away from the suffocating atmosphere inside.

Not even the blast of cold through her coat or the swirling snowflakes that stuck to her hair and melted against her cheeks could temper the frustration brewing inside her. The heels of her leather boots clicked a quick staccato down the salted concrete steps until she crunched into the pristine layer of new snow masking the half-frozen slush and grimy cinders in the parking lot.

Her face ached with the smile she'd glued on her face, and for what? The executive she'd just met with was probably trading blonde jokes with his assistant right now. Imagine, thinking heiress Bailey Austin really wanted to get down in the trenches and work like any other young woman eager to launch a meaningful career.

Bailey pulled her sunglasses from her purse to protect her eyes from the brightness reflecting off the white landscape of cars and concrete. She trudged toward the row of denuded dogwood trees, their branches brushed with snow and decorated with clear Christmas lights. The decorations had made her festive and hopeful an hour ago. Now they were simply a bunch of trees that separated the parking lot from the street, reminding her how far away from the building she'd had to park—and how the long walk and the anxious nerves had all been a waste of time and emotional energy. The end result of her job interview was the same as it had been last week, and two weeks before that.

No experience? No chance.

Apparently, she had only one thing going for her. And that was only because her mother had married a wealthy man.

Bailey punched the remote engine start on her key fob and grumbled against the wrap of her navy wool scarf, mimicking the foundation chairman she'd left upstairs. "We're so pleased the Mayweathers are interested in our museum." Bailey unlocked her car as she approached, dropping her voice to its regular pitch. "But you're not interested in *me,* are you?"

She opened the door to drop her purse on the front seat and retrieve the windshield brush and scraper. When she slammed the door, a glob of snow and slush plopped onto the pointy toes of her boots. Feeling the ultimate indignity, she turned her face to the upper window of the office where she'd interviewed. "All you're interested in, Mr. Stern, is Jackson's checkbook."

The accusation traveled up into the air on a warm cloud of breath, dissipating far more quickly than the

emotions simmering inside her. Turning her attention
to the necessities at hand, Bailey brushed the snow off
the windshield and lifted the wiper to scrape away the
icy bits that had frozen underneath. The physical exertion stretched her muscles and deepened her breathing, giving her an idea of where she'd head to next
instead of finishing up some Christmas shopping as
she'd planned. Her trauma counselor had recommended
regular physical activity to combat any signs of depression or post-traumatic stress. These bursts of frustrated
anger certainly qualified as a symptom of PTSD. Bailey
could tell a good workout would go a lot further than a
shopping expedition toward dispelling the self doubts
and helplessness that were crushing her today.

Circling the hood of her car, Bailey tackled the other
half of the windshield, anxious now to get to the gym to
find the catharsis she needed—to reclaim some control
of her life. She felt trapped somewhere between use-
lessness and a mockery of the woman she wanted to be.
She had to be good for something in this world besides
having money and being a gracious hostess. That re-
sumé hadn't done her a bit of good the night of the rape.

Maybe if she'd been smarter. Braver. Wiser about
the world. In control of her own life. Maybe if she'd
been independent enough to stand up for herself that
night, Brian Elliott never would have pegged her as an
easy victim.

That was the reason she had agreed to testify at his
trial. The walls of helplessness and frustration that had
been building up around her since the assault had grown
so tall that they were collapsing in on her, burying any

spirit, any self-confidence she had left. She needed to take care of herself, not be taken care of. She needed to be necessary to someone else—vital to some cause.

She'd survived that night for a reason. But beyond testifying, she'd yet to find what that reason might be. She desperately needed to find some purpose, and soon. Or she was going to go stark, raving, absolutely stinking crazy.

A bright flash of light darted across the lenses of her sunglasses, startling her like a gunshot.

"What the...?" Instinctively, she spun her back against the solid protection of the car.

A second flash turned her attention to the far end of the parking lot. She glimpsed a small circle of glass reflecting the brightness of the sun and realized it was a camera's zoom lens.

Pointed at her.

"Hey!" she called out. Seriously? Some reporter had tracked her to a job interview? Probably Vanessa Owen or Gabriel Knight trying to scoop their competition again.

It could be some version of publicity for this weekend's Christmas Ball. It wouldn't the first time a paparazzo had snapped a picture of the Mayweather heiress. But she plain old wasn't in the mood to be rich or famous or somebody else's ticket to success right now. "What do you want...?"

The dark figure, more like the blur of a shadow, ducked down behind the row of cars, pulling the camera with him. She heard a car door slam and Bailey instinctively ran to the trunk of her car and stretched up on tiptoe, trying to get another glimpse of the photographer. But there was no one to see. She couldn't even be sure which car or truck he'd gotten into.

She sank back onto her heels and glanced up and down the lane of parked vehicles. There was no movement anywhere except for the lines of traffic on the street behind her.

"Where did you go?" she whispered, backing her hip against the cold, wet fender of her Lexus. Since when did the paparazzi want a picture of her at anything other than a high-profile social event? And how did this particular photographer know who she was, all bundled up like this, or where she'd be?

"Call me if anything makes you feel nervous or you sense any kind of threat."

Spencer Montgomery's terse warning from the day before echoed in her head. She slipped her fingers into her coat pocket, closing them around his business card.

Was this a threat? Should she call the detective?

She'd been an assignment for him yesterday—and an annoying one at that. He'd delivered Chief Taylor's warning about keeping herself safe. He'd drilled it into her head more than once that she was woefully unprepared for the challenges of the trial. Spencer Montgomery didn't think she could take care of herself. But she could. She had to.

Bailey's gaze darted to the sound of an engine turning over in the distance. She had no doubt the photographer's attention had been on her. That he'd taken one or more pictures of her.

She heard wheels squealing against the pavement,

burning away the snow and slush until they found traction. The noise drew her attention to the smoky exhaust
rising from a black car some thirty yards away.

She watched the black roof of the sedan backing out
of its parking space and turning, not toward the exit at
that end of the parking lot to make a quick getaway,
but down through the long lines of cars between Bailey and the building. He might be one row over, but the
driver was creeping closer. He was coming toward her.

"Idiot." The air whooshed out of her lungs as sense
returned. She didn't waste a moment trying to figure
out the driver's identity, whether he might be someone
with the legitimate press or more gossipy tabloids, or
even if he was something much more sinister. Bailey
dashed around the car and climbed inside, locking the
doors behind her.

Take care of yourself, Bailey.

Swearing at her own foolishness, she tossed the
scraper to the floor boards and squeezed her hands
around the steering wheel. Counting her breaths so
she wouldn't hyperventilate, she flipped on the lights
and wipers and shifted her car into Reverse, repeatedly
checking her side- and rear-view mirrors to track the
position of the black car.

The driver hadn't reached the end yet, hadn't turned
the corner to either take the south exit or come up the
lane where she was parked.

Sensing some sort of short reprieve, Bailey quickly
backed out of her parking space and shifted into drive,
heading in the opposite direction without giving any

thought to her destination. *Away* was all she had in mind. *Get away.*

Her pulse rate quickened when she spotted the car in her rearview mirror. Bright lights. Dark windows. No chance to see the driver inside.

Bailey pressed harder on the accelerator as the car behind her picked up speed. The driver hadn't exited the parking lot. He was following her. He wanted something more.

She turned a quick left toward the north exit but had to pump her brakes and slide to a stop at the beginnings of rush-hour traffic clogging the street. She needed to go left to get to her gym and apartment, and turned on her signal. But until the stoplights switched at the nearby intersection, there wasn't going to be a break in traffic.

And the black car was coming closer.

"Come on, red light." Bailey's fingers drummed against the steering wheel. She didn't even have an opportunity to turn right if she'd wanted to. All the people who weren't heading home to the suburbs were apparently eager to get to the shopping and nightlife districts near downtown K.C.

Five lanes of traffic, all blocking her escape.

"Come on." Unless she was willing to cause a wreck, she was trapped.

How long had the man in the car been spying on her? He must have been lying in wait, biding his time until she emerged from the building. How could he have known she was even coming here at all unless he'd followed her from her lunch date with her mother at the Mayweather estate to the interview? Or even longer than that? Had he been at her apartment? Did he know where she lived? Why hadn't she sensed his presence earlier?

Maybe *she* was the only thing that was off today. She'd been so angry, so unsettled by another argument with her mother and the outcome of the interview, that she'd forgotten the cardinal rule of personal safety—be aware of your surroundings. Know where you are and who's there with you. Detective Montgomery would be saying *"I told you so"* right now. She knew better. She'd let this happen.

Could there be a longer red light anywhere in the city? "Come on!"

She pounded her fist on the steering wheel. She'd been angry *that* night, too. Angry that her mother and Harper were taking over the plans for her wedding, that her future was spinning out of her control. She'd stormed away from the Fairy Tale Bridal Shop, wanting fresh air, needing time alone. She hadn't been aware of the danger stalking her until it was too late.

Maybe she *did* need someone to take care of her.

The black car was close enough that she could make out the shape of the driver, if not his face. His window was sliding down. She spotted the narrow camera lens again. Just the flash of reflected sunshine on glass. Aimed her way.

That *was* a camera, wasn't it?

Could that be the scope of a rifle instead?

With a desperate sound that was half groan, half scream, Bailey stomped on the accelerator and fishtailed out into the nearest lane of traffic. Horns honked, cars skidded. But she managed to put three vehicles between her and the black car before the light finally turned red and she was forced to stop.

She checked her rearview mirror, then turned all the way around in her seat to verify that the black car had leisurely pulled out of the parking lot and turned left, merging into traffic and heading in the opposite direction.

Not following. Not interested. Not a gun. Not threatening her in any way.

Sinking back into her seat, Bailey closed her eyes. The relief coursing through her was so intense that it made her lightheaded.

It took another blast of honking horns to open her eyes and pull forward at the green light. Remembering the relaxation techniques Dr. Kilpatrick had taught her, Bailey breathed in deeply, in through her nose and out through her mouth. She organized her thoughts as she settled into the normal flow of traffic. Had she ever been in any danger at all? Had the only threat been inside her head? She'd been in the papers before, and probably would be again.

Perhaps her mother had even leaked Bailey's name to the press. Just like the Blue & Gold Ball a decade earlier, where she'd been presented as a debutante, Loretta's Christmas Ball would be Bailey's reintroduction to Kansas City society—and a huge publicity coup in the name of charity. The press's interest in her might be annoying, but it wasn't dangerous.

The photographer's appearance probably merited a heart-to-heart with her mother about avoiding the spotlight, not a phone call to Detective Montgomery about imminent danger. Thank God she hadn't called him. He'd probably shake his head at her paranoid imagination, blowing the perceived danger all out of proportion. If she overreacted like this any time someone showed the least bit of curiosity about her, then he was right to worry that she wouldn't make a credible witness on the stand.

And she didn't want Spencer Montgomery to worry about her competence. Tempting as it might be to surrender herself to the detective's protection, it wasn't Spencer Montgomery's job to drop everything and come to her rescue anytime something spooked her. Besides, she'd probably only look more like a child in his eyes, like that *poor little rich girl* who couldn't fend for herself Gabe Knight had accused her of being. And she definitely wanted Spencer Montgomery to think of her as a competent, capable *woman*.

Because she was thinking far too often about him— even when she didn't need a cop.

A smile curved her lips as panic dissipated and calmer, more intimate thoughts replaced her fear. Despite the difference in their ages, Bailey had felt that subtle spark of interest from the red-haired detective, just as surely as she'd felt those ribbons of heat warming her skin when he'd touched her, waking something feral and feminine inside her.

What the man lacked in warm fuzziness, he made up for in rock-solid dependability. Spencer Montgomery was a steely-eyed warrior in a suit and badge. He was all male. All mature. All the time.

He was definitely a man she could lean on. What would her life have been like if she'd been engaged to Spencer a year ago? Would she have stormed away from planning a wedding with him? Would he have allowed her to get hurt?

But even as she remembered how the detective had seen to her safety and taken care of her yesterday, Bailey was reconsidering this attraction to a man who surely only saw her as the means to finally closing his task force investigation. After all she'd been through, she got the logic of falling for a man who was such a no-nonsense protector, a man she could trust.

But what happened to taking care of herself? To asserting her own independence as part of the healing process? She didn't have time for romance right now. She wasn't sure she was ready to fall in love and be the strong, self-sufficient woman that a man like Spencer Montgomery deserved. She had so much growing yet to accomplish, so much healing left to do.

Whatever she was feeling for Detective Montgomery needed to be buried away as a schoolgirl crush on a heroic man, or her hormones finally getting over the shock of the rape and latching on to the first available male to stir her interest in more than a year.

"How'd I do, doctor?" she chided herself in the rearview mirror as if she'd been discussing her thoughts aloud with her therapist. "You tell me, Bailey," she answered, imagining Dr. Kilpatrick's kind yet challenging response.

Bailey nodded her understanding as if she were in the middle of a counseling session. "Get a grip on those emotions," she advised. "Find something mean-ingful, practical and tangible to do to rebuild your self-confidence and keep you too busy to second-guess every thought or action."

Winking at her reflection, Bailey took the therapist's advice to heart. "Yes, ma'am."

She was learning to trust her instincts again, to allow herself to feel emotions like fear and anger without them crippling her. Now she needed to put those rusty skills into practice.

"Meaningful." Making a decision would be a good place to start.

"I'm going to do something practical." A workout would provide both a mental and physical health benefit.

"Now, make it tangible." She shook her head at the obvious solution. How about figuring out how she was going to get to her gym for a workout now that she was driving in the opposite direction?

Her pulse settled into a normal beat as her thoughts centered and her fears calmed. She pulled into the turn lane at the next stoplight to get off the main traffic way and circle back to the tony neighborhood where her apartment and the nearby gym were located.

Bailey sat there for a couple of minutes, waiting for the light to change. She watched car after car drive past in front of her—silver cars, white cars, dirty cars, black cars. A shiver of unease rippled down her spine, despite the self-talk that had shored up her confidence.

Was that the same black car driving across the inter-section? Had the photographer changed directions and tracked her down again?

Turning after the light changed, Bailey tried to block those suspicions from burrowing back into her imagination. She went on to the next through street and turned right again, heading back in the right direction, at least.

But her gaze kept sliding to her mirrors. Had the man with the camera slipped back into traffic behind her when she wasn't looking? There was another black sedan following the pickup truck behind her. And another even farther back.

One black car—no problem. Two? A silly coincidence. Three? Four? Suddenly, it was hard to tell the black cars apart. Was that driver peeking around the truck to check on her or the heavy traffic? Had that one darted into the lane behind her to avoid detection or to stay on her tail? Maybe one of the oncoming cars was the photographer searching for her again—signaling to someone else that she'd been spotted.

"Stop it." Bailey slowed at the next light and turned. "The threat isn't real," she told herself. "This is all in your head."

The truck zipped straight through the intersection and the black car turned and pulled right up behind her. But with the lights and the snow flurries, she couldn't make out the driver. Was it a man? A woman? The Cleaner was a woman. The Cleaner wouldn't want her to testify.

Bailey muttered an unladylike curse, hating the automatic turn of her thoughts. "Really? You're going make yourself scared of everything?"

To prove she was creating a problem out of nothing,

she made two more random turns. But the black car stayed with her.

Was that still a coincidence?

Pressing on the accelerator, she raced through a yellow light.

The black car picked up speed and followed.

With her breath catching in her throat, Bailey glanced into the rearview mirror. "*That's* not my imagination."

Forget her craving for independence. Forget risking embarrassment with the first man to awaken anything inside her since the rape. She had a responsibility to the D.A.'s office, the women of Kansas City and herself to fulfill. There was paranoid, and then there was stupid.

After turning onto the interstate, the busiest road she could find, Bailey pulled Spencer's card out of her pocket and reached for her phone.

Chapter Five

Spencer leaned back in his chair. "Detective Montgomery."

"I don't want you to think I'm crazy."

Odd way to begin a conversation. But he'd recognize that soft, sweetly articulate voice anywhere. He turned his mouth closer to the phone. "Bailey?"

"Yes. I know you're a busy man. But, you said if I felt… If I…" Her long pause lingered in his ear long enough for him to identify the traffic noise in the background. "I'm not sure what to do."

"Where are you?" Her gasp triggered something urgent and wary that he'd rather not feel. He sat up straight when she didn't immediately answer. "What's wrong? Bailey?"

Spencer's dark-haired partner, Nick Fensom, looked up from the desk across from him. "Problem?"

Possibly. But the woman wasn't making much sense. "What's going on?"

"My mistake," she announced abruptly. "I'm sorry I bothered you."

"Hold on." When she started to hang up, Spencer

tossed the file he'd been updating onto his desk and turned his full attention to his phone. "Why did you call?"

The next pause transformed his concern into a vague irritation rising beneath his skin. Either she was searching for a good lie to tell, or the woman was addled. And he didn't believe there was a thing wrong with that brain of hers. Just as he opened his mouth to prompt an answer, her words spilled out. "There was a black car. I swear it was following me. But it just pulled off onto four thirty-five south, and I'm still headed east on seventy. And now I'm counting up exactly how many black cars are on the road. There are hundreds of them, aren't there? I probably imagined it."

To her credit, she didn't lie. But the tremulous quality in her voice told him something about the black car had spooked her. And that fear didn't sit well with him, either.

Spencer rose from his desk. "Did you see the driver?"

"Not clearly."

"Get a plate number?"

"Missouri?" That wasn't much to go on. "The angle was wrong or I was going too fast."

"And you're safe now?"

"Yes." Her laugh wasn't very convincing. "Other than surviving the perils of rush-hour traffic."

"Why did you think he was following you?" Spencer waved off Nick's sotto voce offer to call in backup.

"He wasn't. Look, I'm sorry I bothered you. It's just that there was a reporter earlier who took a picture, and I thought…" Her deliberate pause to breathe in deeply and slow her words only made him more suspicious. In his experience, there were very few random acts—sometimes, people did things without conscious thought, but there was always a reason behind the choices they made.

Bailey Austin had chosen to call him. No way was this a random mistake. "Was it Gabe Knight? Vanessa Owen?"

"I don't know. I couldn't see."

"Where are you now?"

"On my way to the gym. I figured I'd be safe with a bunch of people around, and there's always a big crowd after work." At least she had some self-preservation instincts in her. "Look, I really am trying to follow your rules, detective. But I suppose I'm still off-kilter after seeing Brian Elliott yesterday, and was projecting…"

What? Whether the cause was legit or not, there was no mistaking the fear in her voice. A fearful witness might change her mind about testifying. And Chief Taylor had charged him with making sure the woman showed up in court. "Bailey?"

"I should have thought it through before I called. My apologies. Goodbye."

"Don't—"

She'd hung up before he recognized there was something more than professional concern fueling his questions. Yeah, he was a busy man. He stayed that way for a reason. But he was also a cop, and when someone was scared, his instinct was to respond to the threat. To find the source of that fear and negate it. He didn't need Chief Taylor to give him that order.

Even if Bailey Austin hadn't intended to call him, Spencer was the man who'd answered.

And now he was the man walking through the front doors of a popular workout franchise to see with his own eyes that the witness who could put the Rose Red Rapist away forever wasn't in any real danger.

After identifying himself at the front desk, Spencer clipped his badge to the top pocket of his wool coat and pushed through a second set of doors to locate Bailey. It hadn't taken much detective work to track down the gym where she was registered, but she'd been right about the crowd. Judging by the size and popularity of the place, it'd take a stroke of luck to find her here.

He scanned the rows of men and women walking or jogging on treadmills and stair-climbers, searching for the chin-high blonde with stylishly short layers of sunny-gold hair. He swept through the weight room, taking note of anyone more interested in a cop strolling through than he should be.

No reporters. No TV cameras. No one who looked out of place.

He found Bailey in the back of the workout center, wearing gray yoga pants, a pink tank top and fingerless gloves as she pummeled a heavy punching bag. Spencer's concern eased considerably, seeing her in one piece. But then he got close enough to hear how hard she was breathing, and see the vee of perspiration that darkened the back of her top. Every punch, every muttered word, told him she was working through some visceral emotions that he rarely indulged.

"Stupid." Smack. "Curator." Punch. "Wouldn't even give me—" Left, right, left, right.

"So how was that interview?"

Bailey gasped when he announced his quiet approach. She slipped halfway behind the heavy bag, holding it between them, hiding from the thing that had startled her. Her big blue eyes locked on to his, then narrowed as her initial fear dissipated and her flushed skin cooled to its natural color.

"Why don't you wear a bell around your neck?" Bailey chided him, wiping at her parted lips with the back of her wrist.

Her small, firm breasts rose and fell as she calmed the deep breaths of exertion and surprise. Her porcelain skin glistened, and even in those modest workout clothes, he could see she was built slim and sleek like a racehorse. She looked at lot different than the demure sweater-and-pearls lady who'd clung to his hand at Precinct HQ yesterday. How could a skinny, sweaty society debutante like Bailey Austin be so hot?

Oh, hell no. As soon as the electricity humming through his body registered, Spencer glanced away, burying his primal reaction to an unexpectedly sexy woman beneath a cool sweep of their surroundings. As oblivious as she'd been to his arrival, was she equally unaware of the curious weightlifters watching to see what the cop wanted with her? Or the wannabe boxer with the straying eyes sparring with a punching bag just a few feet away? A pointed look from Spencer earned an apologetic wave and turned the younger man's interest away from the curve of Bailey's backside.

Seriously? Now he was making some kind of proprietary claim? Although he'd like to think he was simply acting like a cop, defending an innocent woman from a sneaky leer, Spencer was honest enough to identify the latent attraction simmering between him and Bailey—and smart enough to know nothing should ever come of it.

Pulling back the front of his coat and jacket, Spencer slid his hands into his pockets and offered her a nonchalant shrug. "Instead of me wearing a bell, why don't you be more aware of what's going on around you?" he countered. "You need to know when people are approaching you. Or following you through traffic."

"That was a mistake." A delicate fist against the leather bag punctuated her irritation. She pointed a warning finger at him before going to task with the bag again. "I told you that on the phone."

"You did." *Take note, Montgomery.* Bailey's emotions, bubbling so close to the surface, were all the evidence he needed to remind himself that she was not relationship material for him. Not only was she younger than the women he usually dated, she was the prime witness in the case that could make his career and put him on the fast track to making captain—if not chief or commissioner one day. But most importantly, as the survivor of a violent crime, she needed the kind of sensitivity and empathy that a man so distanced from his own emotions could never offer.

"So why are you here?" she asked.

He let the cop in him do the talking. "Because you *did* call. I'd like to know why."

The rhythm of her dancing hips stuttered and she dropped her fists to her sides. "Your card was right there, in my pocket. I punched the number in before I thought it through. Everything turned out to be just fine. I got here safely. I hope I didn't take you away from anything important."

"I'm off the clock."

"Oh, so now I'm intruding on your personal life, too. Sorry."

Considering he didn't have a personal life, it wasn't much of an inconvenience. "Why do you assume that you made a mistake? Maybe that reporter *was* following you, and simply turned off when he reached his exit or once he realized you were on to him."

"Is that supposed to make me feel better? No, I'm not crazy, but yes, someone *is* after me?"

Watching the fire drain from her posture shouldn't be nudging at that locked up door inside him that wanted to care about someone again. Ignoring the impulse, Spencer easily fell back on the skills that made him such a successful investigator. Instead of offering her some meaningless reassurance, or asking her directly about the car she'd mentioned, he invited her to talk about something else. Just to get her talking. Because he didn't believe for one minute that she'd contacted him by mistake. Despite her assertion that everything had turned out "just fine," something had spooked her. And he wasn't about to risk the successful outcome of his task force investigation on the chance that a man taking her picture was a perfectly innocent coincidence. "Tell me about your interview today."

She made a decidedly unladylike scoffing noise. "It was a joke."

"So you didn't get the job?"

"No." Spencer stepped onto the mat when she turned to the bag again to vent her frustration. "Mr. Stern asked how much Jackson would donate if I took the PR position. As if my stepfather has to buy me a job. I think that was the only reason the foundation would even consider hiring me." Breathless from the exertion, she stopped punching and tilted those azure eyes up to his, frowning. "He didn't even ask about my work experience. Not that I have much except for some retail jobs when I was in college. He barely looked at the portfolio of campaign projects I created during my senior internship. The only qualification he was interested in was Jackson's money. I love my stepfather dearly, but…"

One more punch punctuated her wounded self-esteem. And though the petulant action reminded Spencer of the pampered society princess he'd once pegged her to be, there was something about the trembling line of her jaw tilting upward that spoke of depth and determination, something about the squaring of her shoulders that spoke of a fatigue that went beyond the physical exertion of an intense workout. This wasn't the same woman he'd known before her assault. That woman had been beautiful, sharp-witted, oh-so-young and off-limits. This Bailey was layered, mysterious, all grown-up…interesting.

Sexy and complex—a dangerous one-two punch for a man who didn't do relationships. He inhaled a steadying breath to cool the desire firing through his blood.

He should turn around and walk away. The last time Spencer had gotten involved with a witness, the results had been disastrous. But his will was stronger than the libidinous urges sparking inside him. His obsession with seeing the Rose Red Rapist case through to the very end didn't mean he was involved with Bailey Austin. Instead, he rationalized that he was a dedicated professional who was still working the investigation. He hadn't gotten the answers he'd come looking for yet. "Why'd you take up boxing?"

Her eyebrows arched as if she suspected his random questions might have a more specific purpose. But she played along. "My trauma counselor suggested I take up some kind of exercise that would build up my strength and give me a physical outlet for my…temper." She shrugged, curving her finely sculpted lips into a wry smile. "I never even knew I had a temper. I've always been the peacemaker in my family."

That meant she'd probably downplayed her emotions for years. But a traumatic event like a rape—*or the murder of someone you loved and swore to protect,* a cruel little voice inside him taunted—changed a person. Spencer had locked up tight, subjugated his emotions beneath logic and levelheaded thinking so that he'd never make that kind of mistake or feel that kind of pain again. But with Bailey, everything she was feeling, everything she'd once schooled beneath a ladylike facade, was rising to the surface.

Very complex. And more vulnerable to the dangers she'd face with this trial than the brave tilt of that chin let on.

Spencer shrugged out of his coat and jacket, dropping them both to the mat before unbuttoning his cuffs and rolling up his sleeves.

This was not why he'd answered Bailey's call.

Bailey backed away a step when he approached the opposite side of the heavy bag. "What are you doing?"

He needed the D.A.'s star witness to show up in court and give the testimony that would lock Elliott away in his cell forever. He needed Bailey to be safe. If she suspected a threat, he needed her to trust that instinct and take the proper action to protect herself. Time to change this catharsis of a workout to a more focused lesson in self-defense. He steadied the swinging bag between his hands. "Where's your opponent?"

Her blue eyes narrowed with confusion, but didn't look away.

Spencer leaned in closer to her. "If this bag is the schmuck who interviewed you, how tall is he?"

"Schmuck?"

"Clearly, he missed your…passion…for the job. If he didn't recognize your hunger for making an impact on his organization, then he's clearly a schmuck." When she grinned at his sardonically worded support, he felt like some kind of hero. Spencer quickly squelched the warming sensation that made him smile in return, and got down to business. "Now, where would he stand if this bag was him?"

"You really think that man was following me today, don't you?" she challenged. "That it wasn't just some paparazzo getting the scoop on Mother's Christmas Ball. The D.A. promised that I'd remain an anonymous witness until the trial begins. No one outside that look-at room yesterday knows I'm testifying."

"Brian Elliott knows. At least two members of the press do."

What color was left in her porcelain skin drained away. "You really do suck at pep talks, don't you?"

Spencer dipped his head closer to hers, dropping his voice to a whisper. "I'm a cop, not you're therapist. I don't see any point in sugarcoating the truth. If you felt there was a threat, then there probably was. Vanessa Owen is notorious for sensationalist reporting. Elliott or his attorney could have leaked your name to the press. He might have contacted The Cleaner to throw a scare into you. There are any number of possible scenarios to explain that man following you. Trust your instincts. Don't take chances."

"Take care of myself," she whispered.

"Yes." Once he realized he was close enough to count the shades of blue in Bailey's upturned eyes, Spencer abruptly pulled back and braced the heavy bag against his shoulder. "Let's start by learning a few rules of self-defense. Now, how tall was Mr. Stern?"

"I guess about there." With a nod, she shook off the hushed stupor that seemed to have temporarily claimed her, too, and pointed to the bag. "Taller than me. Shorter than you."

"Let's focus that temper so it does you some good." He gave her a quick lesson in hand-to-hand combat. "You need to punch higher or lower than where you've been aiming. Go for the throat or up his nose, or the soft gut or between his legs. You'll only hurt your hand if you punch him in the jaw or sternum like that."

"I thought I was working out my frustration." She slid back into a boxer's stance with her fists raised.

"Nothing wrong with that. But let's make every punch or kick count." He pointed to her targets and steadied the bag for her. "Try it. Nose, neck, gut or groin."

She followed his instructions with soft punches to get the placement of the blows right. He encouraged her to do it again, harder, faster, until he could feel the impact of each blow stinging him through the bag.

"Now kick him where it counts." She gritted her teeth and lifted her knee, slamming the bag against him with a feral grunt and knocking Spencer back a step. He released the bag and raised his hands in surrender, grinning. "You're a quick study. Trust me, I'm down. Or at least disabled enough that you can run away."

The admission made her smile between her panting breaths. "You made that seem easy, like I could really do it if I had to."

He pulled down his sleeves and buttoned his cuffs. "I suppose in real life the bag would fight back."

She laughed at the lame joke. "Next time a punching bag attacks me, I'll feel better prepared. Thanks." She picked up her towel from the corner of the mat, giving him a view of a sweetly rounded backside that warmed a lot more than his ego.

But when she straightened, the pensive vulnerability shadowed her eyes again, reminding him that his hormones had no business noticing anything about the fragile beauty. Bailey Austin was a job. A witness to be protected. A means to an end. Period.

"There are very few people who expect me to be able to do anything meaningful on my own, detective. That's one reason I agreed to testify. I led a charmed, sheltered life before the attack. And afterward…" She dabbed at the perspiration on her forehead and neck. "I feel like a useless bit of fluff most days. My family treats me with kid gloves. My ex tries to fix everything for me. I make my friends uncomfortable, and they never share any of their problems with me because they think I can't handle anything negative or difficult anymore. If I lose my temper, people put up with it—if I cry, they try to appease me. If I panic over a reporter stealing a picture of me…" Her gaze dropped to the middle of his chest as her voice trailed away.

"Then the cops come calling."

"Something like that. I want to stand on my own two feet. I want to make a difference. I want…" She looped the towel around her neck and reached for him. Spencer's breath caught as her fingers settled at the front of his shirt. "Your tie's crooked." As rare as it was to catch him off guard, her firm touch surprised him. Spencer held himself still while she straightened the knot of his tie and smoothed his collar. "See? This is what I'm good for. A useless bit of fluff."

He surprised himself by catching her hands when she would have pulled away. At her startled gasp, he splayed her fingers against his chest and held them there, waiting for her questioning gaze to meet his.

"What you're doing is incredibly brave. A lot of people won't understand what facing your attacker can cost you. You may not even fully understand the repercussions of standing up against Elliott." He understood the emotional turmoil of all she was dealing with far better than she could imagine. "Post-Traumatic Stress Disorder is a lot like grief. It manifests itself in different ways for different people. Some get angry. Some fall into a depression. It robs some people of their self-confidence and ability to make a decision while others grit their teeth and plow through life as though…" Ah, hell. Like a blind-side sucker punch, anger and despair roiled up inside him. "…as though nothing ever happened."

Bailey frowned at the tightness creeping into his voice. "You?"

Ellen Vartran's chocolate-brown eyes suddenly filled his vision, and his fingers burned with the memory of her blood seeping between them. He'd forgotten the job for a few hours and followed his heart. He'd been outgunned and outmanned, but still, the mistake had been his. And Ellen had paid the price.

"Detective Montgomery? Spencer?"

The brand of ten gentle fingertips dug into the skin beneath his shirt, chasing the horrific memory from his thoughts.

He willfully squeezed the heart-wrenching guilt from his mind and met Bailey's compassionate gaze. "I've dealt with PTSD, too."

"What happened?"

The tenderness he hadn't asked for broke a chunk off the emotional armor that kept him sane. Ah, hell. Lusting after Bailey Austin was one thing. But feeling something for her? Drinking in her caring like some kind of antidote for the guilt he carried inside him? Before anymore of his strength crumbled into dust, Spencer pulled her hands from his chest and moved away to pick up his jacket. "I'm a cop. I see a lot of stuff."

"I thought you meant something personal…" Way too personal. She'd zeroed right in on his Achilles' heel. He shrugged into his jacket, making sure she got the full view of his back while he erased whatever had tipped her off from his expression. "See what I mean?" Sarcasm seeped into her sweet voice. "No one thinks I can handle anything."

Jerk. Now he could add regret to the things he felt around this woman. Time to dial it back a notch with Bailey Austin and remind himself he was a cop on a call here, not a man who cared about a woman or who needed one to care about him. He spun around to face her again. "Tell me about the car that followed you."

Really big jerk. It was no use apologizing, either. The damage had already been done. With a stiffness to her posture that hadn't been there before, she circled behind the bag to retrieve her water bottle.

"Right. Forgot you were the relentless detective there for a minute." She peeled off her gloves and took a long drink, struggling to rein in her feelings as neatly as he'd boxed up his. "Give me a chance to shower and change first."

"I'll wait."

BAILEY WALKED AWAY from Spencer Montgomery feeling all kinds of hot and bothered. He'd seemed so solid, unflappable, patient—that it had felt natural opening up to him and sharing what she was really thinking. And then his eyes had darkened and grown distant and pain had radiated off him in waves. She'd been as drawn to that surprising revelation of humanity as she'd been to the hard warmth of his chest.

But the moment she'd dared to act on the personal connection humming between them, he'd shut her down and pushed her away. Bailey had run a gamut of emotions from surprise to wounded fury, from self-doubt to invigorating confidence, from caution to concern, from suspicion to that inevitable awareness she felt whenever the stoic detective turned those steel-gray eyes on her.

The tepid shower beating down on her skin helped cool the embarrassment of mistakenly thinking he cared about her on some personal level. Although the raw memory she'd read in his shadowed eyes and taut voice indicated that they at least shared a familiarity with personal tragedy. The hurt she'd felt at his abrupt dismissal of her concern for him eased with the reviving scent of the citrus shampoo she massaged through her hair. And by the time she was stepping out of the locker room shower and wrapping a fluffy white towel around her body, she was breathing normally again.

Detective Montgomery had come here as a courtesy in response to her frantic phone call. His concern for her safety might only be professional, but it was genuine. And she couldn't fault the man for wanting to keep their relationship strictly business when he'd just spent more time listening to her troubles and offering a constructive way to deal with her emotions than her fawning ex-fiancé or her drama queen of a mother had.

After sliding into her flip-flops, Bailey cinched the towel together over her breasts and hurried back to her locker. The first thing on her agenda was to apologize for wigging out on the red-haired detective. The second thing was to answer whatever questions he needed her to.

Bailey set her shower caddy down on the bench beside her workout clothes and twisted the combination to open up the locker's metal door. With a quick glance at the mirror inside, she finger-combed her short hair into place, then reached for the bag of clean clothes she stored on the bottom shelf.

Her fingers froze before touching the quilted strap. She curled them into a fist, she drew back to her stomach as she tried to make sense of the three photos resting on top of her bag. The black-and-white prints were small enough to be stuffed through the air vents of the locked door, she thought obliquely, studying the images scattered over her things.

Images of her. Brushing snow off the windshield of her car. Staring daggers up at the window of the CEO who'd interviewed her. Clinging to the steering wheel of her Lexus, looking afraid.

These pictures had been taken just a couple of hours ago.

That man *had* followed her.

And he wasn't any reporter.

Her face had been crossed out in two of the photos. And on the third, scrawled in thick ink across the black-

and-white image, she'd been sent a message that was frighteningly clear.

Your family will be sending out funeral notices instead of Christmas cards if you testify.

Bailey huddled inside her towel. Her blood ran as cold as the weather outside. She wasn't safe at all. Not in her car. Not here at the gym. Not anywhere.

"Detective Montgomery?" she murmured, waiting for her brain to shove aside that sense of violation so she could connect the dots. The Cleaner had found her. The woman protecting the man who'd raped Bailey had followed her, watched her, touched her things. The Cleaner had been right here, standing where Bailey now stood. She shuffled away from the ugly threat. The back of her bare knees hit the bench, startling her past the fear. She turned and shouted, "Detective? Spencer! Spence!"

She heard the startled yelps and high-pitched protests before she heard the running footsteps. A woman's voice reprimanded the locker-room intruder. "You can't bring that in—"

"Bailey?" The tall, red-haired detective swung around the end of the row of lockers. Spencer's gun was drawn and down at his side, his gray eyes fixed on her as his long strides carried him straight to her. "What happened?" he ordered, closing his free hand around her bare arm and turning her to face him.

Bailey angled her head toward her locker and he followed her gaze. "I didn't imagine anything."

"Son of a bitch." He loosened his grip and smoothed his hand up and down her arm, chasing away the chill on her skin. His sharp gaze took in everything around them before coming back to her. "You're all right?"

She nodded.

"Say it. I need to know you're not in shock."

Bailey nodded again. "I'm okay."

"Stay put." In a rapid efficiency of movement, he released her entirely, ordered the curious crowd of half-dressed women to vacate the locker room, pulled a cell phone from his jacket and punched in a number. She could hear him talking to his partner, interrupting some kind of family event, while he stalked up and down the rows of lockers, sinks and showers, making sure no physical threat remained.

Bailey was still standing there in her towel, shivering from the inside out, when he finally returned. His gaze zeroed in on hers, reassuring her, assessing her, as he holstered his weapon and spoke into the phone. "Yeah, Nick. It had to be within the past two hours. Probably not even that long. Elliott's accomplice was here—or someone she hired or blackmailed, at any rate."

Spencer held out his hand as he approached, and for one dumbfounded moment, Bailey didn't understand what the gesture meant. But when he folded his long arm around her and pulled her into his chest, she released her death grip on the towel and willingly aligned her body to his. She didn't mind the scratchy wool of his lapel beneath her cheek, or the rasp of his sleeve pricking goose bumps across her bare shoulders. He was warm. He was solid. He was safe.

"Just to secure the perimeter. I've cleared the room and I've got eyes on Miss Austin." His chin brushed against the crown of her damp hair as he glanced up. "There are no security cameras in here to monitor comings and goings, but I'll get a list of names from the check-in sheet at the front desk. You get Annie and her CSI team here pronto." He leaned back at the waist and Bailey lifted her head to meet that handsome gray gaze that searched her face. "She's safe." His fingers splayed and settled at the small of her back, keeping her close when she would have backed away. "Yes, I'm okay with that," he grumbled. Then, in a more normal, clipped tone, "Thanks, Nick."

After hanging up, that same hand tugged against her towel, pulling her away as if he'd just now discovered that he wanted to distance himself from her. "The task force is en route," he stated matter-of-factly. "I'll stay with you until backup arrives." He nodded to the goose bumps dotting her skin, and then shrugged out of his suit jacket. "You're cold."

Cold and scared. "It's her, isn't it. The Cleaner?" Spencer draped the lined gray wool around her shoulders, surrounding her in the warmth and starchy scent that lingered from his body, wrapping her up in a hug that reminded her of the strength of his body surrounding and shielding hers. It wasn't the full body contact they'd just shared, but she'd take it. At that moment, she needed whatever strength he was willing to offer to shore up her own. "I wasn't being paranoid. She *was* following me this afternoon."

"Someone was." He clutched the lapels together at the base of her throat, hesitating for one uncharacteristic moment. "I know they're not fresh, but can you put your workout clothes back on? I want the lab to check everything in your locker for fingerprints or trace before you disturb any of it."

Calmed by both his consideration and straightforward explanation, Bailey dutifully took over holding the jacket, allowing him to free his hands and regain the professional distance he seemed to prefer. "I can do that." She picked up her sweaty things off the bench. "And don't worry. I still intend to testify."

"I'm learning that about you. There's some backbone to you." He surprised her by reaching out to cup the side of her neck and jaw. Tiny muscles jumped beneath her skin at the gentle contact. "You're someone different every time we meet."

His fingertips tunneled into the damp tendrils at her nape, and suddenly, she was plenty warm again. Could it be that Spencer Montgomery wasn't as detached from his emotions as he'd like to be? "Is that a good thing?" she asked.

"I don't know yet." As soon as Bailey turned her cheek into the caress, he pulled away. Some sort of inner battle he was waging etched a few extra lines into his face. "But I do know I won't let her get to you again."

Then he nodded to her clothes and the cop was back. "Get dressed."

Chapter Six

The colorful holiday lights outlining every rooftop and spire of the Country Club Plaza reflected in Spencer's rearview mirror as he pulled into a parking space near Bailey's Lexus outside her brownstone apartment building.

Leaving his coat open to have easy access to his gun and badge, he climbed out of his SUV and locked it. The wintry dampness of the night air bit into the tips of his nose and ears, sharpening his senses as he turned a slow 360. The security here was decent enough, he supposed. Good neighborhood, home to young professionals and wealthy retirees. Well-lit street with private parking. A key pad and card-swipe lock on the front and side doors.

He wasn't thrilled with the high mountains of snow piled beside the walkways and parking lot where the pavement had been cleared. Both impeded sight lines and offered anyone who covered his or her tracks several easy places to hide. And the snowflakes, hanging like dust motes in the air, the last gasp of this afternoon's storm, would need to be scraped from the sidewalks and drive before it glazed over into icy patches that could hinder traction should Bailey need to run or drive away quickly.

"Are you going to stand out here and freeze?" Bailey's remote beeped twice, signaling that her car was locked. "Or did you see something?" Her head swiveled around toward the street. "Is someone following us?"

"No. We're good."

A cloud of warm breath obscured her face for a moment when she turned back to face him. When the frosty cloud cleared, Spencer could see the fatigue that shadowed her eyes and the soft lines that bracketed her rosy pink lips. Part of him wanted to keep seeing the woman who was too young and ingenuous for his sensibilities. But despite the earmuffs and orange coat, Bailey's expression hinted at a knowledge of the darker side of life that could only be learned through fear and loss. "So what's the problem?" she asked.

She had a woman's mouth, Spencer observed idly. Full, soft, articulate. Like the lean curves of her body, there was little that was girlish about Bailey Austin anymore. He'd have to find some other excuse to keep her at arm's length and convince his libido that he wasn't interested in her.

He met her expectant gaze over the roof of her car, proving to himself that he could look into those changeable blue eyes and not react. "I'll walk you in."

She moved to meet him at the front of her car. "You didn't answer my question."

He settled his hand at the small of her back, urging her into a brisk walk to the front door. He took note of the number of windows lit up in the building. "Do you know all your neighbors?"

"Most of them." She pulled her key from her purse. "You didn't answer my question. Did you see something that alarmed you?"

"What floor are you on?"

"Second."

"Good. First floor apartments are easier to break into."

"Interesting fact. Not very comforting, and still not an answer to my question." They stopped at the front door and she glanced up.

Spencer avoided making eye contact this time and nodded toward the lock. He had nothing to prove to himself. He was just a cop escorting a frightened woman home. He wasn't involved. "I want to have a look around inside your apartment, too. Double-check that everything's secure."

With a sigh of frustration, she slid her card through the lock and pushed open the door. "Spencer. If there's one thing I can count on you to do is to give me a straight answer. Even if I don't like what you have to say."

He relented once they were standing on the lobby's beige-and-gold carpet, waiting for the wrought-iron elevator to make its way downstairs. "So far, everything's fine. Since we left the gym, I haven't seen any indication of anyone showing more interest in you than they should."

Except for himself.

Spencer wisely pulled his hand away from Bailey's

back and unbuttoned his coat. He'd made the mistake of reaching for her more than once at the gym—making sure she was unharmed, reassuring her…reassuring himself she was okay. Touching her was a habit he could too easily fall into if he didn't keep his fingers busy with other important things, like tucking his gloves into his pockets or brushing the snow from his hair.

"That's good, right?" She wanted an explanation for his heightened sense of vigilance. "Do you think there'll be more threats?"

With only the muffled sounds of a television behind the building's thick walls to indicate that there was anyone else about, and the doors locked behind him, he had no reason to be standing this close to her. Since the antique elevator seemed to be taking its time, he headed for the stairs, and Bailey followed.

"The Cleaner will probably wait to see how you react to the first warning." He shortened his stride to take the stairs one at a time, allowing her to pass him and lead the way to her apartment. "But I don't want to take the chance that the threats escalate into something more serious."

She stopped at the door marked with a black number 10 on it. "Thank you for talking to me like I'm an adult." She inserted one key into the dead bolt lock and turned it. "It still scares me, but at least I can be prepared. I have an idea of what to expect."

"No, you don't." She wanted straight answers? "If the pictures don't scare you away from Elliott's trial, then she's going to look for other ways to intimidate you. Or save herself the trouble of a drawn-out stalking campaign and eliminate you as a witness altogether."

She paused with her key in the door knob and her face went pale. "Eliminate...?"

"Bailey?" The door to number 12 swung open and Bailey jumped. Spencer pushed aside his jacket and had his fingers on the snap of his holster before a barefoot dynamo with an oversize Park University sweatshirt and a blond ponytail stepped out, flashing a big smile and a friendly "hey" to him before turning to Bailey. "I thought I heard voices out here. I'm glad I caught you. You're home late. How'd the job interview go? And who's the tall Scotsman?"

"Scotsman...?" The color returned to Bailey's cheeks and Spencer let his jacket slide back into place over his gun. "Oh, the red hair. Hi, Corie." Bailey's wry smile met a matching one in return. "This afternoon wasn't great."

"Sorry to hear that. Next time, right?" The girl next door was a shorter, slightly younger version of Bailey, reminding him of the Bailey he'd first met a couple of years earlier. The woman nudged Bailey's elbow. "I didn't know this was date night. And all I'm doing is sittin' at home, painting my toenails. So...do I get an introduction?"

"Sorry to disappoint you, but it's not a date. Corie Rudolf, this is Spencer Montgomery."

Chatty, yes, but not unobservant. The petite blonde extended her hand, glancing at Spencer's badge. "Cop?"

"Yes, ma'am. KCPD."

Corie tapped her chest. "Accountant. Eckhardt and Galloway. Taken?"

Wow. The woman was certainly direct. But Spencer had neither the time nor the inclination to flirt. "Nice to meet you." He made a quick assessment of her natural coloring and last name. "German?"

The young blonde laughed. "Oh, you're good. And was I right about your heritage?"

Spencer nodded. "Guilty as charged."

"He's a charmer, Bails." The frown Bailey tilted his way indicated she might disagree. Good. He didn't need any more of whatever this magnetic pull was zinging between them, anyway.

"Were you looking for me?" Bailey asked, putting the kibosh on the other woman's flirty chitchat.

"Right." Corie snapped her fingers before reaching inside her front door. She returned with a small, cube-shaped package wrapped in brown paper and a shipping label. "The delivery man dropped this off at my place since you were gone."

"Hold on." Spencer grabbed the package before Corie could hand it off. "Did you order anything?"

"I've done lots of online Christmas shopping." Bailey pointed to the logo on the box. "That was one company I used."

"All right." Spencer scanned the box for a quick verification of the return address. Recognizing the online store instead of an anonymous package, he relaxed his suspicion a fraction, even if the timing of the gift bothered him. "Here."

He handed off the package and Bailey thanked her

friend before turning to him. "Am I supposed to sec-ond guess everything that comes into my world now?"

"It's better to err on the side of caution." Straight talk, as promised. No charm needed for that.

"Is something going on?" Corie asked, the wattage of her smile finally dimming. "The delivery man said someone had to sign for it, so I did. I hope that was okay."

"Of course," Bailey assured her. "That's the stand-ing agreement between us, right? Water each other's plants, pick up each other's packages. I appreciate you having my back."

"For a minute there, I thought I was in trouble." Co-rie's sigh of relief was audible. Did she not know about Bailey's rape? He didn't suppose that was something that came up in casual conversation with the next door neighbor. And he had a feeling Corie Rudolf spent a lot more time socializing than keeping up with current events. "Because I'm half tempted to order some more Christmas presents so that guy has to deliver them. He was a cutie. And no wedding ring. I checked when he took his gloves off. Shameless, aren't I?"

Seizing the opportunity to keep Bailey in one safe space for a few moments, Spencer pulled the ring of keys from her hand. "Let me go in and check your place out first, while you two catch up." He spared one more look for Corie. "Keep your apartment locked in the fu-ture. And don't open the door unless you know who's on the other side."

"Yes, Officer." Corie giggled nervously at the practical advice. Then the tenor of her voice changed. "Are you sure everything's all right?"

"Detective Montgomery worked the Rose Red Rapist case," Bailey explained, keeping her far-too-personal familiarity with the investigation out of the conversation. "He's a stickler for personal safety."

"Did you know that guy's trial starts Monday? I saw a preliminary report on the news tonight. Vanessa Owen said she's got the inside…"

Spencer pushed open the door and the conversation faded. Well, Corie's monologue faded. He shook his head as the door closed behind him. Bailey definitely didn't seem too young, anymore.

But that still didn't make her the right woman for him.

After setting Bailey's keys on the table beside the front door, Spencer swept his gaze around the remodeled apartment's open floor plan, taking note of the formal dining room with a dark red poinsettia centerpiece, and the galley-style kitchen with a trio of carved wooden Santas sitting on the counter. Breathing in the fresh scent of pine, he moved into the living area. A Christmas tree, standing taller than him and four times as wide, stood in front of the two main windows. Although the lights weren't turned on, he counted several rows of clear bulbs and gold ribbon circling the pine branches. There was a white angel at the top and a dozen wrapped presents on the floor below.

"How'd you get that in here, woman?" he muttered, half admiring her determination to celebrate the season, despite all that had happened, and half worried about what kind of help she'd recruited to bring that behemoth up to the second floor.

Hopefully, she'd asked a close friend. Or someone who worked for her father. Not a stranger she'd paid and invited into her home. "Where you could plant a bug or camera, get the lay of the place, or gerry-rig one of the locks so you can come back later."

The possibilities of how easily an unseen threat could infiltrate Bailey's world got Spencer moving. He checked the locks on the windows behind the tree. The snow was undisturbed and drifting on the fire escape outside. Spencer verified that the fire escape ladder was up and locked into place and that the outside stairs only went to the floor above hers. An intruder would have to rappel if he wanted to get in from the roof.

The bathroom was tiny and windowless, and could make a passable safe room if she could find something to reinforce the flimsy lock. He checked the walk-in closet in her bedroom, glanced underneath the dust ruffle on the white mission-style bed and moved the blinds aside to secure the lock on the window there.

Spencer came out of Bailey's bedroom to find her draping her coat over the back of a chair and pulling a stool up to the kitchen's long, granite-top island. "Do I pass inspection?"

He glanced over at the dead bolt to make sure she'd locked it behind her. "A little heavy-handed with the holiday decor, but I like the steel-framed windows and that you have curtains or blinds covering all of them. No one can sneak a photograph of you here. And they're all secure. No signs of unwanted entry or that anyone's been peeking in."

"That's good." She set the earmuffs beside her purse and fluffed her sunny hair into a tousled disarray. "Not into Christmas?"

He shrugged, crossing through the apartment to join her. "Don't have the time for it."

"That's sad. Do you have parents or someone special you're at least going to spend the day with?" She sat on the stool to unzip her boots and pull them off.

"Now you're sounding like your friend Corie." When she bent over, Spencer reached out to smooth down a spike of golden hair, but drew his fingers back when she straightened. "No parents. No siblings. No…" An image of Ellen stepping out of the shower and shaking her long wet hair down her back tried to surface, but he quickly slammed the door on that memory. "No one special."

He turned to the counter and gripped the edge of the cold granite, willing the emotions that stirred up around Bailey Austin to settle back into place.

"I hit that same nerve again, didn't I." Her hand slid across the counter toward his. The muscles beneath his skin pulsed when her fingers brushed across his knuckles. When he fisted his hand, she pulled away. "Sorry."

She jumped down from her stool so abruptly that Spencer knew he'd hurt her feelings. While she set her boots on the tile by the front door, Spencer inhaled a cleansing breath. She couldn't get to him. He wouldn't let her. But he needed to make sure she wasn't so upset or ticked off at him that she'd get distracted from the things she needed to do to stay safe.

"I am invited to my partner Nick's house for Christmas dinner. They're a big family and they always make room for one more. I complimented his grandma Connie's cherry pie one time, and I've been an adopted son ever since."

Continuing the conversation was enough of an olive branch for her to come back to the counter, although he could see her purposely keeping some distance between them. "The cherry pie got through the infamous Montgomery armor, hmm?"

That armor didn't seem to be so tough today. And he placed the blame directly on those shadowed blue eyes and determined chin. "I've been known to indulge in a homemade dessert on occasion."

"You're lucky to have friends like that." Bailey pulled a pair of scissors from a jar on the counter and sat to open her package. "I apologize for Corie. I hope she didn't make you uncomfortable. She can talk the ears off a basset hound, and she's a little man-crazy—"

"You think?"

"—but she's got a good heart." Spencer slipped onto the stool beside her for a closer look as she sliced through the package's sealing tape. "It's been nice to have a friend who doesn't walk on eggshells around me. We share normal conversations about nothing and everything."

"You didn't tell her about the rape or the trial?"

"It hasn't come up. If she knows, she hasn't said anything. Maybe she's worried that the topic would make me uncomfortable. A lot of people don't mention it."

Spencer raised a skeptical eyebrow. "I have a feel-

ing there's very little that makes that woman uncomfortable."

Finally, the shadows receded and her lips softened
with a smile. "Corie's right about one thing."

"What's that?"

She set down the scissors and lifted a red envelope
and a squarish jewelry case from the box. "You can
be charming when you're not trying to be all relentless cop."

"Charming?" The idea of Corie Rudolf turning all
that man-hungry energy on him made Spencer a little
sick to his stomach. "I was going for businesslike and
authoritative. Remind me to do gruff and tough next
time I see her."

The answering laugh died in Bailey's throat when
she flipped open the jewelry case. Spencer rose to see
what had changed her expression.

It was a man's watch. Expensive, shiny and new.
And in pieces.

She set the box down and shuffled through the paperwork again. Something was off.

"Is that for your dad?" he asked. He hoped it was
some careless shipping and handling that upset her.

"I didn't order a watch." She handed him the paper,
then slipped her thumb beneath the flap of the envelope
to pull out a Christmas card. "It says 'gift.' It's clearly
addressed to me, but the sender's name isn't filled in.
Who would give me a man's watch? A broken one at
that. Maybe the card will explain the mix-up."

Bailey recoiled from the holiday card, and Spencer

was behind her shoulder in an instant to read the message scrawled inside.

You'd better watch out
You'd better not cry wolf…
Or you'll be in pieces.

"Set the card down. Don't touch anything else." Spencer punched his partner's number on his cell.

She set the card on the counter as if it might detonate in her hand and stood. "This scares me."

"I think that's the idea."

"I mean, how long has this person been watching me? I only noticed someone this afternoon. But they couldn't have sent this today. Look at the date."

When she reached over to point out last Friday's date, Spencer pulled her away from the counter. "Do you make coffee?"

"What?"

"Do you have coffee in your pantry?"

"Of course, I—"

"Make it a full pot." He eased the urgency from his grip on her arm. He needed to only think about being a detective right now. He shouldn't be concerned with the frustration and fear flaring into her cheeks, or feel guilty about putting them there. He dropped his gaze down to her bare toes beneath the hem of her yoga pants, opting for something in the neutral zone between cop and caring. "Get something warm on your feet. Stay busy. I need to work."

With a surprising understanding, or maybe just resignation, Bailey nodded and prepped the coffee maker before disappearing into her bedroom.

While the phone rang, Spencer pulled off his coat and scarf and tossed them over the back of one of the dining room chairs. This was going to be a much longer night than he'd planned.

Nick finally picked up. The breathless laughter on the other end of the line told Spencer he'd interrupted something more than the dinner date his partner had mentioned at work. "Your timing sucks, buddy. What do you need?"

Not that he begrudged his best friend some private time with the woman he was going to marry, but business was business. "Put your fiancée on the phone."

Nick's tone instantly changed. "There's been another threat?"

Spencer glared at the mysterious package and cryptically worded message. If it wasn't for that Christmas card, he'd have excused it as a retail mistake at this busiest time of year. "It came through a delivery service. I need it processed for any trace."

"Miss Austin's apartment?" Spencer heard whispers in the background, shuffling sounds that meant Annie and his partner were already gearing up to leave.

"Yes."

"We'll be there in twenty minutes."

Two hours later, Spencer lifted his gaze from the fuzzy brown slipper boots Bailey wore to watch her rinse out the empty coffeepot and load the four dirty mugs into the dishwasher. Heeding his advice in a head-down kind of way that brought to mind her vulnerable admission that she sometimes considered herself a *useless bit of fluff*, Bailey had worked in the kitchen the entire time. She'd emptied the dishwasher, wiped down counters, swept the floor and refilled coffee nonstop while he and Nick canvassed neighbors in the building and made phone calls and CSI Hermann processed the watch, card and packaging with her lab kit.

How could a woman with the guts to ignore her over-protective family's advice and stand up to her rapist in court ever think of herself as useless?

But now Annie was stowing evidence bags and packing her kit, and Nick was reporting that the delivery man who'd brought the package into the building was someone new. While it wasn't unusual to add extra drivers to the regular routes to make deliveries this time of year, no one in the building seemed to recognize the description of the man Corie Rudolf had given them. *Brown hair. Brown eyes. Super cute.* Nick had already put a call in to the company's local office to confirm an ID and get a picture of the man.

Spencer heard enough of Nick's report to know he wasn't going to get any conclusive answers tonight. He might as well listen to Annie's analysis and get out of here before he strayed from the neutral zone and went over to the kitchen sink to take Bailey in his arms again and tell her how much he admired someone with her courage and work ethic. He could confirm that the crown of that silky gold hair really did fit just under his chin, and that the lean muscle of that fit body curved in all the right places.

And he could completely screw up Bailey's life and this case if he gave in to the temptation to touch her again.

So he blinked her from his sight and thoughts, and turned his attention to Annie's dark brown eyes. "What can you tell me?"

"Good news?" Annie picked up the sealed bag that held the watch. "It's an expensive brand with a manufacturer's mark on the back that'll make it easier to trace to the source. We'll know if it was bought locally and repackaged, or where the retail order originated."

Spencer nodded. "So we can confirm a location. Maybe we can get a description of the sender. And the bad news?"

Annie placed the bag inside her kit and peeled off her sterile gloves. "The card is generic, from a set of boxed cards that are sold in shops across the country. Pretty impossible to track down. Preliminary handwriting analysis says it matches the photographs from this afternoon, but we've got nothing to compare the samples to. As for the rest? There are no fingerprints besides Miss Austin's and the neighbor's anywhere on the watch, case, card or packaging. No stray hairs in the tape, nothing that can identify the sender."

"So even if we get an address or phone number, which will probably turn out to be P.O. box or business, we can't prove who at that address sent it."

Nick crossed his arms and muttered a curse. "I can tell you who it's from."

The water stopped running in the sink and Bailey came to the opposite side of the kitchen island from where the rest of them stood. "What's the significance of the broken watch? Other than it *is* broken. The message would have been just as clear with something from a discount store. Does that mean The Cleaner is some-one who has a lot of money?"

"I think I know the answer to that." Annie's dark eyes looked from Bailey to Nick, then up to Spencer. "But my idea's a little outside the box."

Spencer didn't need hesitation. He needed answers. "I didn't choose you for my team because you think like other people do."

Nick moved beside her to offer his encouragement. "Whatcha got, slugger?"

After a squeeze from Nick's hand, Annie answered, "It's what's not here that worries me."

"What's that?" Nick urged.

"Unless you just like to show off that you can afford an expensive watch, or you're a serious runner who's timing sprints or laps, there's not much call for a watch like this. Even if it's in perfect condition."

Bailey wrung the dish towel in her fists. "What would you use a watch like that for? What piece is missing?"

Spencer nodded an okay for Annie to answer, even though Bailey's face was already growing pale.

"The timer. I'd use it to build a bomb."

Chapter Seven

Spencer tapped his fingers on the polished walnut counter at the Shamrock Bar, and waved the muscle-bound bartender with the scarred-up face over to refill his glass with bourbon.

The neighborhood cop bar was quiet tonight—partly because of the late hour, partly because of the weather that slicked the streets and made it too cold for all but the hardiest of souls to venture outside, and partly because of the holiday season. Most people had parties with friends to go to or family gatherings to attend. At the very least, they were home watching TV specials and wrapping presents.

Spencer just had his thoughts, a criminologist's printout about what other elements besides watch parts would be necessary to complete a bomb, and a really, really bad feeling that something deadly was closing in on Bailey Austin.

Jake Lonergan, the silver-haired bruiser who was tending bar, pulled the good stuff from the top shelf, but set the bottle on the bar top without pouring. "This will be your third one, Spence. You on duty tonight?"

"No."

"Driving?"

He didn't answer that one. He'd never been a heavy drinker—well, there'd been a spell there after losing Ellen where he'd indulged more than he should. He and Nick used to trade off driving responsibilities so that the other could have a few. But Spencer and his partner didn't go out for drinks after a particularly tough shift or closing a case the way they used to. Nick spent most of his evenings with Annie now, remodeling and repainting an old house they planned to move into following their spring wedding on the baseball field at Kaufmann Stadium.

Spencer spent his nights at home catching up on reading reports, working late at the precinct office or hanging out here at the Shamrock, reflecting on the events of one day and organizing his plan for the next. It was a sane, solid routine that had kept him moving forward toward his career goals for the past five years.

But tonight, that dedication to duty just felt lonesome. Wrong. Like he was somehow wasting his time.

"You got a case that's weighing on your mind?" Jake asked, flipping around the wrinkled diagram Spencer had spread on top of the bar. "So now you're researching explosives. Thinking of going postal on me?"

Spencer folded up the paper and tucked it inside his suit jacket. "You know, one of the things I like best about you, Jake, is that you don't stick your nose into other people's business."

Jake laughed. "You can't dent my hide, Montgomery.

I can handle whatever sarcasm you dish out." He lifted the bottle in his beefy hand. "Still want the drink?"

After a nod, Jake poured him another shot. Jake Lonergan was a good man, even if there was a lot about him that remained a mystery. The man walked and talked like a cop, but didn't wear a badge, although he knew him to carry a knife in his boot. The two had become friends earlier in the Rose Red Rapist case when Jake rescued a woman from an assault Spencer's team had investigated. The fact Jake had identified the drawing as the specs for a bomb told him the big man had a lot of expertise in weaponry, despite gaps in other parts of his memory.

Spencer picked up his glass and set it back down without taking a sip. He pulled the drawing back out and handed it to Jake. "Did you ever run across a device like that?"

Jake's icy eyes skimmed over the printout. "I'd like to say I don't remember, but yeah. It's a homemade bomb. You can get the parts online or in the right store easily enough without the purchases registering on any federal watch-group radar." He handed the paper back. "The actual explosive is the hard thing to get, but doable if you have access to demolition or construction."

"And you'd definitely need a watch like that to pull it off?"

"If you want to control when and where it goes off with any precision. Most bombers don't want to be around when the thing goes boom."

Brian Elliott had earned his millions in property development and renovation. Certainly, his construction crews and anyone who worked for them would have access to those materials. With KCPD monitoring Elliott 24/7, he wouldn't be able to put together a bomb. But who else in the circle of employees or friends around him would be willing to at least make it look like a serious enough threat to send Bailey into hiding or do something on a bigger scale to derail Elliott's trial? Could one of them be The Cleaner?

Of course, there were dozens of construction companies, big and small, in Kansas City. Another explosives source could be the munitions storage facilities and manufacturing plants dotting the area, or maybe even one of the National Guard posts or nearby military base.

There were too many possibilities, too few facts for Spencer to reach any logical conclusions and come up with a direction to steer his investigation into who had threatened Bailey—or even confirm that the anonymous gift was indeed another threat.

"I could talk to my friend Charlie Nash at the DEA," Jake interrupted Spencer's thoughts. "Maybe he could tell us if the Feds have any word on something like that going down here in the Midwest."

Spencer shook his head. "This isn't about terrorism. It's about intimidation." He returned the paper to his pocket, needing some time to fine tune a list of suspects. "I'll make some calls in the morning." Since the bartender had brought up one of the mysteries of his past, Spencer asked, "Have you given anymore thought to going back to the DEA or some other law enforcement agency?"

Jake pulled the towel from his apron and wiped down

the bar in front of Spencer. "Not until this trial is over
and the people who are a threat to my wife and daughter have been put away." Right. Jake had married the
woman he'd rescued and adopted her baby, all in the
span of a few months. "Until then, my most important
job is playing bodyguard-slash-babysitter to Robin and
Emma."

Bodyguard. Not a role Spencer could stomach anymore. That's why he'd left a black-and-white unit parked
outside Bailey's building tonight, and was maxing out
his favors to keep someone with eyes on her around
the clock until there were no more threats and the trial
was over. He'd focus on the investigation, on unmask-
ing The Cleaner and the thugs she liked to hire, not the
D.A.'s star witness.

"Where are Robin and Emma now?" Spencer asked,
wondering how Jake could step away from guard duty if
he really believed there was still a threat to his family.

He replaced the bottle behind the bar. "With Hope
Lockhart and your buddy Pike Taylor."

"Wedding plans?" Pike was a K-9 officer on the task
force. Was every man he knew building a home life
outside of work?

Jake nodded. "Robin agreed to be Hope's matron
of honor. I'm guessing Pike is out with the dog while
the ladies discuss invitations or whatever's next on the
list. It's turning into the biggest production I've ever
been privy to. I swear to God, if they make me put on
a tux…"

Spencer picked up his glass, swirling the golden-
brown liquid around the bottom while his thoughts

drifted back to the night he'd lost Ellen Vartran. He'd impulsively proposed to her that night, not sure if he was feeling love or lust, and not caring. They'd made love in the shower and the words had popped out.

He'd had one job—protect the witness in the safe house. And he'd failed. When his shift changed, he'd gone out to buy a ring. When he came back…he'd had no chance to save any of them.

He'd been an empty man and a useless cop for months afterward.

A useless bit of fluff.

Spencer knew exactly what Bailey was feeling right now—that driving need to do something meaningful to atone for the sins and shortcomings that ate away at a person's soul, to make a difference that might just assuage the fear and pain and guilt that tore a person apart inside.

Finding the mole who'd betrayed the safe house had been Spencer's first step toward redemption. Arresting the Rich Girl Killer had been the second. Putting Brian Elliott away for the Rose Red rapes might finally put a staunch on the emotional wound that still bled inside him.

He raised his glass to his lips, maybe sending up a prayer for inner peace at the same time.

But the image on the television screen above the bar stopped him. "Hey, Jake. Will you turn that up?"

Spencer set his drink down and leaned in to catch Vanessa Owen's pretrial update on the ten o'clock news. Although the beautiful brunette's face filled up the center of the screen, it was the still photo in the bottom right corner that drew his attention.

It was a picture of a younger Bailey at some fancy-shmancy society event on the arm of her ex, Harper Pierce. She wore long hair swept up on top of her head. The look was innocent. Disinterested. Pageantlike. Not as sexy or compelling or touchable as the Bailey he'd spent time with today was.

"Dwight Powers has made it no secret that Mayweather heiress Bailey Austin is scheduled to testify in the trial of alleged Rose Red Rapist, Brian Elliott. As many viewers may recall, Jackson Mayweather's step-daughter was brutally beaten and raped, just over a year ago in downtown Kansas City." Vanessa Owen's voice hushed for a moment, as if tears of compassion or out-rage clogged her throat. But Spencer wasn't buying the act of a woman who'd lain in wait to corner Bailey in the parking garage yesterday morning. "This reporter has the inside scoop that Miss Austin is extremely fragile right now. She has received anonymous threats indicat-ing she may come to some harm if she agrees to testify. While KCPD and the D.A.'s office have no official com-ment, the information was confirmed by Miss Austin's mother, Loretta Austin-Mayweather. As many of you know, Mrs. Mayweather's annual Christmas Ball, which has raised millions of dollars for children's charities—"

Spencer pushed to his feet and pulled out his wallet.

Bailey Austin fragile? In looks, perhaps. Maybe even in demeanor. But the woman could be made of steel if her mother, the damned reporters and the rest of the world gave her the chance she needed to succeed.

Jake muted the television. "There's not much to like about that woman, is there."

"No." Spencer threw some bills on the bar to pay his tab without touching his drink. He already wasn't thinking with a clear head if he was listening to his gut. And though he knew that could get him into trouble, it wasn't stopping him. He grabbed his coat off the bar stool beside him.

"You heading out?" Jake asked, clearing his glass.

"Yeah. I've got work to do."

A half hour later, Spencer was setting up camp on the street outside Bailey's apartment building. He'd dismissed the uniformed officer, who was glad enough to report back to HQ for a refill of hot coffee. Sipping on his own to-go cup of java, Spencer settled behind the wheel of his SUV. He unbuttoned his collar, loosened his tie and tucked his wool scarf more tightly around his neck.

The snow had stopped falling except for a few flakes dancing through the cones of light from the street lamps along the sidewalk. All the windows that had been lit up earlier in Bailey's building were now dark, including hers. Hopefully, exhaustion, at least, would allow her a good night's sleep.

Tomorrow, he'd have answers. The delivery man could be ID'd. He'd have a list of Elliott's employees and other companies in the area with access to explosives. He'd know more from the lab regarding the origin of the watch.

Tonight, he'd sit, wait, watch and make sure Bailey Austin got that good night's sleep.

Spencer squared himself in the seat so he had a clear view of both exterior doors and Bailey's bedroom window. He was cold, tired, wearing the same clothes he'd put on that morning and his legs were too damn long for this kind of stakeout.

But it was the only way he would find any peace.

SPENCER CRACKED ONE eye open as the hazy white ball of sunrise cleared the horizon and transformed the world outside his car into a glistening crystal wonderland.

He briefly considered polishing off the dregs of the ice-cold coffee in the Suburban's cup holder, then decided he wasn't quite that miserable. Instead, he stretched the kinks out of his neck and shoulders and checked his watch. He had to report for his shift in a couple of hours, so the twenty minutes he'd lost dozing in the SUV were going to have to suffice for a night's sleep. Nodding off on a stakeout also provided more evidence that he wasn't cut out for security work anymore, either.

He'd driven over here on a whim last night, trying to make amends for a past mistake he could never truly rectify. And this is what he had to show for it—nasty coffee, bleary eyes and a cramp in his right calf that just wouldn't quit.

A quick glance across the street showed a light shining behind the blinds in Bailey's bedroom window. He'd missed when that had come on. She was probably eager to get an early start on whatever meaningful activities she had planned. He wondered how she intended to make a difference in the world today—another job interview? Helping her mother with the fund-raiser?

Spencer pulled off his glove and rubbed his hand over his stubbled face and jaw, wiping off the grin forming there. Maybe Bailey's fears about the threats she'd received or a nightmare with Brian Elliott's face in it had kept her from sleeping through the night. She might be in there pacing, worrying, wondering who she could call at this time of morning.

"Ah, sweetheart," he murmured on a heavy sigh that fogged up the side window.

It took him a second to realize he'd placed his hand over his heart, above the chest pocket where he'd stowed his cell phone. "Smooth, Montgomery," he chided himself. Boy, did he need some real shut-eye—his thoughts weren't making any sense. Wishing for a call from Bailey was asking for trouble. Spencer sat up as straight as he could and flexed his leg while he wiped the frosty moisture of his breath from the cold glass.

That's when he saw the man jiggling the handle on the building's side door. Black pants, black parka, black stocking cap on top of his head—built on the heavy side and stuck without a key to get in, judging by the way he tugged on the latch and peeked through the windows on either side of the door.

Spencer slid his hand inside his jacket to retrieve his phone to call it in. But what would he report? A resident locked himself out of the building? Maybe that was the maintenance guy who'd come out to shovel sidewalks and had forgotten his key card.

He needed to wait. Observe. Make the right decision.

After a furtive look to his right and left and the parking lot behind him, the man trudged through the knee-deep snow to the front sidewalk. He tried the same routine on the front door, twisting the handle and peeking in.

Suspicion fueled the heat traveling through Spencer's veins. He unbuttoned his coat and clipped his badge onto his outside pocket while he watched. He pulled back the edge of his jacket to have clear access to his gun and snugged his gloves into place around his fingers while his gaze trailed the man's movements around the building.

When the man gave up on easy entry at the front door, he lifted the hem of his parka. Spencer's left fingers curled around the door handle when he spotted the tan leather case attached to the man's belt. Could be a carrier for a cell phone, could be the bottom edge of a holster or sheath for a knife.

Spencer pulled the handle and inched the SUV's door open, acclimating himself to the bracing temperature outside. A quick scan up and down the street revealed no traffic, no one moving in the parking lot, no one even out to snow-blow their driveways or throw down some sidewalk salt yet. Just a lone man in a parka, possibly armed, his face half-obscured by a pair of wraparound sunglasses, prowling outside Bailey's apartment building.

The man pulled down his jacket without retrieving anything from his belt. Had he sensed Spencer's presence? Did he know he was being watched?

He was scanning the sidewalks and street now, too.

But Spencer held himself still enough that the man's attention never settled on the black Suburban and the cop watching him. As if deciding the coast was clear, the man suddenly jumped off the front steps into the snow and jogged past the first window. When he moved, Spencer moved. Spencer dashed across the street and crouched down beside a parked car, pulling his gun to cradle it between his hands, controlling his breath so a big cloud wouldn't give away his location in the frigid morning air. He peered through the windows to keep an eye on Mr. Suspicious.

The guy with the sunglasses stopped at the bottom of the fire escape and kicked aside several layers of snow, clearing a space before jumping up to capture the bottom rung of the fire-escape ladder. After one more quick look around him, he pulled the ladder down and put his boot on the first rung.

Spencer was around the car in a flash. He leaped over the slush piled at the curb and broke through the top crust of frozen snow as he crossed the yard, impervious to the cold seeping into his feet and legs as he ran straight for the intruder.

"KCPD! Put your hands on top of your head!"

"What?" The man hopped to the ground and turned.

Spencer braced his feet and aimed his Glock. "Hands up!"

"Put the gun down, man." Instead of obeying the command, the man lifted the hem of his coat.

"Hands!" Spencer didn't give him a second chance. Time to move. "Face the wall."

"There's been a mistake, Officer." The guy raised

one arm, but the other was moving toward his parka again. "I'm reaching for my ID."

"Yeah?" The man was younger and bulkier than Spencer, but not as tall or quick. Spencer spun him and shoved him against the brown bricks, pressing his Glock at the base of the perp's neck to keep him in place while Spencer quickly patted him down. Cell phone. Belt buckle. Ah, hell. *Mistake, my ass.* Spencer unsnapped the holster he'd spotted earlier and pulled a gun from the guy's belt. "You sure you're not reaching for this?"

Although the man was smart enough to keep his hands on the wall, he didn't give up the fight. "I've got a permit for that Sig Sauer. I'm a security guard. ID's in my front right pocket. I'm familiarizing myself with the building, making sure it's locked up tight."

After tucking the Sig Sauer into his own belt, Spencer pulled the intruder's hands behind his back and cuffed him. Only then did he holster his own weapon and pull his prisoner from the wall. "A guard who carries an FBI-grade weapon and doesn't know his own building? Is that why you were climbing up to the second floor to break in?"

"I wasn't breaking— Hey!"

The so-called security guard swore when Spencer took off his sunglasses and pushed up the edge of his stocking cap. Brown eyes. Brown hair. He fit the vague description of the man who'd delivered Bailey's package yesterday. "Is this your first time here—" he read the name on the ID he pulled from his pocket "—Mr. Duncan?"

"You can read what it says, can't you? Zeiss Security? Max Duncan?" The dark-haired man tried a taunting glare that might have worked on someone else. Spencer wasn't in the mood. "I'm legit. Now unlock these things."

"You didn't answer my question." Spencer stuck the ID back into Duncan's parka. If Duncan *was* his name. Annie Hermann had nearly been killed by a man working for The Cleaner, a man who'd been impersonating a police officer to gain access to one of the Rose Red Rapist's crime scenes. He wasn't taking a chance on being fooled twice by the same M.O. He pushed the alleged Max Duncan through the snow to the front door. "I don't know you, pal. Until I get some answers I like, I don't care who that billfold says you are."

Max jerked his arm from Spencer's grip and climbed the front steps himself. "Buzz apartment ten. She'll vouch for me."

Bailey's apartment? Not likely. Spencer pushed the button to number twelve, instead.

"Yes?" a sleepy voice answered after the third buzz.

Spencer grabbed Duncan's wrists behind his back and twisted just enough to remind the man who was in charge here. "Miss Rudolf? This is Detective Montgomery from KCPD. We met last night?"

"Ooh, yes. The ruddy Scotsman who *isn't* dating Bailey." Her drowsy voice perked up and the door unlocked. "Come on up."

Gritting his teeth against the flirty subtext of her invitation, Spencer pushed Duncan inside and followed him up the stairs.

"I tell you my name's Duncan," Spencer's prisoner protested. "Call my boss, Mr. Zeiss. I'm running security here. That ID is legit."

"One question first."

Corie Rudolf opened her door as they crossed the landing, foolishly forgetting his warning to identify any guest before unlocking her door. "Hey, Detective. You're here bright and early." Her friendly greeting chilled and she pulled her pink flannel robe together at the neck as she looked up at Max. "And you brought company."

Was that a glimmer of recognition in her eyes?

"Is this the man who delivered Bailey's package to your apartment yesterday?" Spencer asked. "Have you seen him before?"

"Maybe?" she answered after a moment's hesitation. Her eyes darted to Spencer, making him wonder if he should trust her answer. Was she just saying what she thought he wanted to hear? But suddenly she was chatty again. "Yes. Yes, he is. Where's your uniform? That kind of threw me off. Did you have another package for me?" She thrust out her hand and smiled. "We didn't get a chance to officially meet before. I'm Corie."

Duncan eyed her extended hand, rattled his handcuffs and shook his head. "Lady, you and I—"

The dead bolt turned in the door to apartment ten and Spencer shifted to put himself between Bailey and his prisoner.

"Spencer?" She appeared in the crack of the open door, wearing a pair of black pants and a lime-green jacket, with a towel wrapped around her head. Fresh out of the shower and in the middle of dressing, he guessed, judging by the towel on top and her bare feet below. She peeked over the chain at the dark-haired man beside him and frowned. "Max?" She closed the door to quickly unhook the chain and then swung it open. "What are you doing here? Are those handcuffs?"

"Miss Austin. Your stepdad sent me over to keep an eye on you." Max pushed against Spencer's hand, but he wasn't budging. "You want to tell this butthead cop that I'm on your side?"

Bailey's mouth opened, then closed. Then she inhaled a quick breath. "It's okay, Spence. Max works for Zeiss Security. They work for Jackson."

"You're not the delivery guy?" Corie reached across the gap between the doors to squeeze Bailey's hand. "Are we in some kind of danger? Bails, what's going on?"

"Read the news sometime, Corie." Spencer's redhaired temper rarely surfaced, but he was too tired to keep from snapping.

"Excuse me?"

"Spencer." The gentle reprimand from Bailey surprised him.

Those blue eyes searching his for some kind of explanation quickly defused his raw impatience. "My apologies."

Several silent seconds passed while she took in his disheveled state, wet shoes and sour mood. Then she patted Corie's hand and smiled. "Sorry if we woke you. You're perfectly safe. I've…been working with the D.A.'s office on a project and…Detective Montgomery is helping me. Max is…an old friend. Go back to bed. I promise I won't let these two argue anymore."

"Well, I didn't really mind. I'm just glad everything's okay." The two women traded a hug before Corie retreated into her apartment with a winsome smile. "Nice to meet you, Max."

After the door locked on apartment twelve, Bailey led the two men into her apartment and closed the door behind them. She walked straight past them to the kitchen, pausing to nod toward the cuffs on Duncan's wrists. "Unless you're arresting Max, those aren't necessary."

Spencer pulled out his keys to unlock the handcuffs.

"Thanks." Max nodded to her and pushed his wrists toward Spencer.

"You didn't know Duncan was coming?" When she shook her head, Spencer closed the key in his fist and pointed to her phone. "Call your stepdad to confirm his assignment."

Max swore.

Bailey pulled the towel off her head and combed her fingers through her hair. "Are you going to tell me what's wrong?"

Spencer stood firm. "I'm a stickler for details. Make the call."

Five minutes later, Spencer had his answer, along with a throbbing headache behind his eyes and a nagging skepticism that there was still something wrong with this whole scenario. Either Max Duncan wasn't who he said he was or Corie Rudolf was lying. They couldn't both be right. And both of them were too close to Bailey for him to feel comfortable about any of this.

"Did you deliver a package to Corie Rudolf yesterday?" Spencer asked, unhooking the handcuffs.

Once he was free, Duncan faced Spencer, rubbing his wrists and looking like he wanted to punch him. "My gun?"

"My question?"

Understanding who had the upper hand here, the stocky man pulled off his cap and waved it toward the adjoining wall between apartments. "I have no idea what that crazy woman was talking about. If I look like somebody she's supposed to know, that's on her. My boss told me to provide some extra security for Jackson Mayweather's stepdaughter. I'm supposed to shadow Miss Austin and keep an eye on her place today. I was familiarizing myself with the layout of the building and testing its access points when you went all Dirty Harry on me."

What he said made sense. But Spencer wasn't willing to ignore his suspicions. "You say there have been others from Zeiss watching Miss Austin?"

"Yeah. For about a week now. Ever since she started talking to the D.A."

"A week?" Bailey set her towel on the island and circled around to stand beside Spencer. He didn't think it was the cool air or the shower that made her so pale. "You've been following me that long? In a black car?"

Max glanced at her in confusion. "I drive a pickup."

She glanced up, worried. "Spence? The watch?"

"I know." It had been mailed during the same week-long time frame. Spencer pulled out his business card and handed it to Duncan. "I want to know the names of every man assigned to her detail, with photo IDs and license numbers for personal vehicles as well as company cars. If you've got activity logs on those days she was being watched, I want those, too. You can email them to my computer at work."

"I'll have to ask my supervisor."

"No, you'll do it. Or I'll call Jackson Mayweather and tell him what a piss-poor job your team has done thus far. Bailey's received threats and she's been followed. Either your company hasn't been sharp enough to recognize the danger, or you're the ones spooking her."

Duncan unzipped his parka and held it open so Spencer could see him pull out his cell phone. "Sorry, ma'am. We'll make this right."

With a nod, Spencer pulled the Sig Sauer from his belt and handed it back. "Make sure you keep the safety on that gun when you're around Miss Austin."

Duncan growled a response. "I know how to do my damn job."

"Well, you'd better start doing it better than you have been." He slipped his hand beneath Bailey's elbow while Duncan made his call. "Can I talk to you?" he whispered, pulling her out into the hallway.

Spencer released Bailey and turned to face her while she closed the door behind them. "Do you really think Mr. Zeiss's security team have been in the cars I thought were following me?"

Pulling back his coat and jacket, Spencer propped

his hands at his waist and shrugged. "It's a possibility. I'll look into it more when I get to the precinct office."

"What if The Cleaner is blackmailing one of them? Or paid one of their staff a lot of money to betray me?" She curled her toes into the beige carpet and hugged her arms around her middle, clearly unsettled by the potential threat. "You said that's how she works, isn't it?"

"Yeah." Spencer couldn't keep looking at the hopeful trust in those blue eyes without feeling the need to pull her into his arms and make promises he couldn't keep. He turned his face to the ceiling and exhaled a deep breath before zeroing in on the loose tendrils of hair that clung to her cheeks and forehead. Still damp from the shower, her hair was a darker shade of wheat than its usual color, and added to Bailey's touchably soft and vulnerable look.

Damn his eye for detail.

It had to be fatigue that weakened his will like this. He took another deep breath to ease the raw need inside, and forced himself to look her straight in the eye. "I'll check out Zeiss backwards and forwards—make sure none of the employees have done something that can be used against them. I'll also run their bank accounts."

"I know you'll find The Cleaner."

"Let's just hope it's before she finds you." Spencer groaned at how that must sound. "I won't stop looking until I have her in my sights."

"I believe you. You're a mess," she gently teased, changing the subject. She reached up to straighten his collar while he was trying to be tough and professional and get through what he needed to say. She fastened the top two buttons of his shirt and adjusted the knot of his day-old tie, her fingers lightly brushing across his chest and neck. Nerve endings danced beneath his skin, chasing every firm, yet delicate touch. Spencer wasn't even strong enough to back away when she cupped the side of his jaw and rubbed her fingertips against the beard stubble there. "Looks like you've had a long night. Do you want some coffee? Breakfast?"

"No." He shouldn't want this, either.

"What are you doing here?" she asked, stroking her fingers along his jaw, as if she could feel the tension there.

He nodded toward the door. "Kincaid looked like he was breaking into the building. You're sure you trust him?"

"Yes. I've known him for a couple of years. His supervisor has worked for Jackson's company since I was a teenager. They provide security for Mother and Jackson's house, or when visiting dignitaries fly into town to do business with Jackson. I'm sure they'll be at the Ball on Saturday." Her fingers stopped their sensuous petting and she dropped her hands back to the middle of his chest. "I meant, why are you here in the first place? Or should I say the last place? Have you been watching over me, all night?"

He couldn't answer that. It would mean admitting more than he should. Still, his hands weren't getting the message from his brain, and they came up to settle over hers. "Why wouldn't your stepfather tell you he was assigning men to keep an eye on you?"

"Maybe he didn't want to infringe on my quest for

independence. More likely, he didn't want to alarm my mother. She isn't dealing well with the risk I'm taking."

"*She* can't deal with it? You're the one who was assaulted."

"She doesn't understand my need to…fight back." Bailey pulled away and shoved her fingers through her hair, leaving a rumpled mess in their wake. "I think she wants it to all just go away so that she doesn't have to worry about me anymore. So she doesn't have to worry about anything but her parties and giving Jackson a beautiful home. Try to find some sympathy for her, Spencer. She's not a strong person."

"She leaked the threats you received to the press."

"I saw the news last night. Mother called to say Vanessa Owen had spoken to her." She shivered visibly before hugging her arms around herself again. "Vanessa told my mother it would be good PR for the Christmas Ball to mention my name."

That stupid ball. Such a public event. Although The Cleaner liked to work in the shadows, and catch her victims when they were vulnerable and alone, he still didn't like the idea of such a bright spotlight being focused on Bailey. Even if Zeiss Security proved to be a topnotch protection service, there'd be too many people to watch, too many opportunities to lose track of the D.A.'s star witness, too many ways she could get hurt.

"Are your parents going to make sure someone's with you around the clock?"

"I suppose."

"They better. Because I can't be here for you."

Her cheeks blanched to an unnatural shade of pale

at his sharp tone. "But you were here all night…" Then she smiled, misunderstanding the meaning of his words. "That's okay. Do you work today? Will you have a chance to sleep?"

The emotions bubbled up, and his voice grew harsh as he tried to control them. "I'm talking long-term, Bailey. I want you to be safe. That's my top priority right now. I'll solve the damn case. But I can't be your bodyguard."

"I didn't ask—"

"If that bruiser loses track of you, or locks himself out again, and you're in trouble, remember the lesson I gave you. Nose, throat, gut and groin." Spencer caught her hands and pulled them to his face, neck and stomach. They lingered at his waist, then slid beneath his coat and jacket to his flanks. Her brave touch humbled him, branded him. "You're not like your mother. You're strong. You can take care of yourself."

"I understand. I'm responsible for my own safety. I'll talk to Jackson again. I'll make sure the security team introduces themselves to me so there are no more misunderstandings." Her eyes grew bright with tears she tried to blink away. "Thank you, anyway, for… being there for me when I needed you. I won't bother you again."

"That's not what I meant." His fingers locked on to her wrists, keeping her hands from pulling away. "If you need a cop, of course, I'll be here for you. You can always call. I just can't—"

"It's okay." She shushed him as one of the tears spilled over onto her cheek. "I know I'm an inconvenience. You have important work to do. I'm not the type of woman you need. You have a life of your own. Whatever the reason is, I can sense you don't want things to get personal between us. Even though…"

She didn't have to finish the sentence. It had been like this between them from day one. They were meant to be. But they couldn't be. The timing had never been right. He'd been grieving Ellen. She'd been engaged. Completing the task force's work was his sole mission. She needed a patience and sensitivity to recover from the rape he couldn't provide. And the situation now was as far from right as it could get.

Another tear left a shiny trail across her cheek and Spencer moved his thumb there to wipe it away from her cool skin. "I'm sorry." He tunneled his fingers into the damp silk of her hair and framed her head in his hands, tilting her face up to his as he drifted closer. "Work and relationships don't mix well for me. I've lost so much and you need more than I can give. You're something special, and I'm tempted, but…"

Her tears shimmered against the shadows of pain in her eyes, and a tight knot twisted deep in his gut at knowing he was any part of the hurt she felt. Spencer pressed a kiss to her forehead and lingered there, committing to memory the softness of her skin, the sunny warm scent of her hair, the sheer perfection of her brave spirit and gentle, compassionate soul.

"Thank you for understanding."

And when she should have nodded her head, when he should have pulled away, Bailey stretched up to kiss the corner of his mouth and whispered, "Thank *you*. For everything."

Ah, hell. She had a beautiful *woman's* mouth—as soft and sleek and sexy as the rest of her. Spencer felt the strain in his muscles, all the way down to his toes, as he fought the urge to move his lips over hers. He hovered. She waited. He wanted. Her breathy sigh was a tickle of warmth against his skin.

Spencer lost the battle and closed his mouth over hers. His fingertips tightened against her scalp. Hers dug into the sides of his waist. The tips of her breasts beaded against his chest as she leaned into the kiss, sending shards of longing south of his belt buckle and deeper inside. He stroked his tongue over the supple seam of her lips and they parted for him. With a stuttering hum of surrender she slid her tongue against his, tasting him as he plundered her mouth.

He pressed a kiss to the tip of her nose, to the corner of each eye where he sipped away the salty residue of her tears. When her arms slid around his waist and her sweet curves molded to his harder frame, he claimed her mouth again. He crowded his hips and thighs into hers, wanting to feel every exquisite inch of her against his body.

He was hungry for this woman, starving. She was holding on with both fists, giving everything he asked for, demanding he hold nothing back.

The kiss should have released the tension inside him, but it only coiled tighter and tighter.

Maybe that was the lesson to be learned from giving in to this kiss. What his heart and body wanted didn't matter.

Bailey Austin mattered.

And he couldn't do this *and* be the man she needed him to be.

It took all the strength he possessed to tear his mouth from hers and ease the tangle of his fingers in her hair. She leaned back against the wall, pulling her arms from his waist and resting them against the rapid rise and fall of his chest. Her deep breaths matched his own and the stunned look in her eyes matched what he was feeling inside.

"I haven't…," she began. Then her fingers curled around his tie as if she was reluctant to pull away entirely.

Spencer rested his forehead against hers and looked down to meet her upturned gaze. "You haven't what?"

"I haven't kissed a man since…before…" The rape. Ah, hell. He'd come on like a crazy man, practically driving her against the wall. He could have hurt her, scared her, reminded her— She tugged on his tie, as if reading his mind and reprimanding him for his regrets. "I haven't thought about anyone that way until you. I've never been so ready for a man to kiss me."

There were words to say—*thank-you's* and *you deserve better* and *I've been waiting for that kiss, too.*

But Spencer said none of those things. He thought of Ellen Vartran and just how much he could lose. He imagined Bailey dying in his arms, making promises she could never hope to keep.

He stroked her swollen lips with the pad of his thumb.

Walk away. Now.

Or he never would.

He took a step back, and retreated a lot farther inside. "You'll be fine. My people are going to track down the watch and whoever took those photos of you. I'll verify each of the men your stepfather has watching you. We'll get The Cleaner. You'll be just fine. I promise."

Bailey's eyes widened, then shuttered. She'd given him the finest compliment a man could ask for and he'd answered as if he were making a report to the chief. She pulled her hands from his tie, breaking their last contact. "I'll see you at the courthouse on Monday."

"Goodbye, B. Lock the door behind you."

She nodded and reached behind her to turn the door knob and slip back inside. "Goodbye."

Chapter Eight

"Stop that." She swatted Brian's hand away when he reached down to rub the raw skin beneath the ankle bracelet that allowed KCPD to keep track of his movements.

"Here." Sitting on the edge of the bed, the woman dabbed a cotton ball soaked with hydrogen peroxide against the wounds where he'd scratched it. His breath hissed as she pushed aside his pajama pant leg to cleanse the self-inflicted wounds. "Poor thing," she sympathized, glancing at the clock on the bedside table as she reached for the ointment. Her colleague had better call soon. The police weren't the only ones with the ability to monitor their prey. She smiled as she straightened and opened the tube. "It must sting."

His hands fisted in the covers as he fought to control his illness. "I want it off. Now."

"You can't do that, darling." She rubbed the soothing gel beneath the ring on his leg. "We have to show the judge how well you're cooperating with his mandate. You must be patient if we're going to win this case."

"At least if I go to prison I won't have to wear this damn thing anymore."

There he'd be living with mice and bugs and most likely a cell mate, with a stainless-steel toilet right there near the cot where he'd sleep. Brian couldn't survive a situation like that with his obsessive-compulsive disorder.

But she wasn't worried. "You aren't going to prison." He belonged in this hotel's penthouse suite with her, even if there was a black-and-white police car parked on the street below them. "Soon, everything will be taken care of."

His deep blue eyes demanded she see reason. "If Bailey Austin testifies—"

"She won't." *She* had always been the voice of reason in this relationship. He was the brilliant designer, the innovative business tycoon with a vision for restoring this city to its architectural splendor. Let him be the castle-builder whom so many people admired. She was the clever workhorse who did the unpleasant jobs, who smoothed over the rough patches of an illustrious career, who loved him despite his mood swings and obsessions. She wiped her fingers on a towel before gently touching his lips. "I promised I'd take care of you. And I always will."

He grabbed her wrist and pulled her hand from his mouth. "I am not some babe to be taken care of."

He swiped the towel from her hand and wiped his lips.

No. He was certainly a man. A great man in her eyes. Their relationship had to remain secret, but for years—

longer than anyone might suspect—it had remained strong. They shared a stormy history of love and hate and lots of taking. They both had benefitted from this affair. But no one had ever needed her the way this man did. And for that need, for him, she would do anything.

The telephone rang and she got up, tying her robe securely around her waist. "There's the call I'm waiting for." She pointed a warning finger at him as he swung his feet to the floor. "Try not to scratch." When she reached the desk in the adjoining office, she picked up the phone. "Yes?"

"That red-haired cop—Montgomery—he was at her place again."

"I see." She kept her voice pleasant, and her smile in place so as not to alarm Brian. She'd just gotten him settled down. He'd surveyed his newest warehouse renovation project, and signed all the office papers and checks for the day. It was her time now. The time when he'd show just how much he still loved her, and why all her hard work on his behalf was worth it. "And now?"

"He drove off. He didn't look happy. Neither did she."

Good. Distance between Bailey Austin and the crusading detective would work to her advantage. The woman crossed her arms beneath her breasts and turned away. "Where is Bailey now?"

"Still in her apartment. You don't need me to keep doing this, do you? Spying on her?" Her colleague was wavering, questioning her instructions. "I mean, the trial starts in three days. If you haven't scared her off yet, then you're not going to. Maybe she's got more backbone than you think, and your plan won't work."

Her plans always worked. "Not only will you keep eyes on her and report anything you find out, you will take the next step. This afternoon, I think."

"I don't know. This doesn't feel right."

Now this just wouldn't do. Her colleagues could be easily replaced—but timing was crucial, and this one was in the perfect position to carry out her orders. Recruiting someone new would take time Brian didn't have. "Would you rather I leak the name of the strip club where you worked to the tabloids? Let's see, that particular establishment had connections to organized crime, didn't it? Wouldn't that make a juicy story on the evening news?" She paused to let the seriousness of the threat set in. "I have several reporters' numbers on speed dial."

"That would cost me my job and my license."

"And?" The long pause at the other end of the line meant cooperation was now guaranteed. Oh, how it paid to know other people's secrets.

"What do you need me to do?"

THE WIND WHIPPED across the hilltop at Mt. Washington Cemetery, stinging his cheeks and ruffling his hair, but Spencer didn't feel it.

The yellow rose he'd laid on the ground in front of the red marble marker had blown across the snow and caught in one of the foot prints he'd made when he'd dug down to uncover Ellen Vartran's grave. Twenty-seven years. Not nearly a long enough life. Only one year older than Bailey Austin.

He couldn't bury someone else at so young an age.

He couldn't lose another… Spencer couldn't bring himself to even think the word *love*. It just wasn't a part of his vocabulary anymore.

So why did he kiss Bailey?

Because he hadn't been thinking. He'd only been feeling.

That was a mistake he could never repeat. Or else he'd end up here on another dreary day with another flower.

Alive was the only outcome he wanted for Bailey Austin. The best way to ensure that was to keep a clear head, track down and erase The Cleaner and finish Brian Elliott's trial.

Love wasn't anywhere in that picture.

Okay, so maybe he was feeling the wintry chill a little. Inside, where a wool coat and knitted scarf didn't do him any good.

"Why'd you do it, El?" Spencer shoved his hands deep into the pockets of his coat, still wondering how that last night at the safe house had gone so wrong. Why hadn't he seen her looking for a way out of testifying against the men her brother had worked for? A better cop would have seen the darting looks, would have noticed his phone sitting on top of his clothes instead of inside the pocket of his jeans where he'd dropped them on the way into the shower with her. She hadn't trusted him enough to keep her safe, and she'd been right. He'd been focused on her, on them—he hadn't been paying close enough attention. "Why'd you make that phone call?"

His answer was the sound of an engine shifting into

4-wheel drive. Spencer turned his face into the north wind to see Nick Fensom's Jeep slowly climbing the hairpin turns and pulling to a stop on the road behind his Suburban. Nick had Annie with him, and the two were arguing about something until Nick leaned across the seat and kissed her. With a smile and a shake of her head, she nudged him toward the door and gave Spencer a small wave.

Spencer nodded in return as Nick left the motor running and climbed out. He tightened the gray scarf around his neck and clapped his gloved hands together against the cold. "Thought I'd find you here. Annie's worried you'll get frostbite. She says I need to talk you into coming over to the new house tonight for some takeout and friendly company."

"You just want to put me to work painting the new kitchen." This teasing give and take had always been easy with Nick. Sometimes, they were the only conversations he had all day that had nothing to do with work.

"Isn't that part of the best man's responsibilities? Helping his buddy remodel the old house the bride and groom are going to be moving into?"

Spencer glanced down at his partner's wise-ass expression. "That's what your brothers and sisters and contractor father are far. All I have to do is show up with the ring. And make sure you show up at the wedding."

Nick grinned and looked toward his Jeep. "Nothing's keeping me from spending the rest of my life with that woman."

"Good. We all chipped in so Annie would get you out of our hair."

Nick's laugh echoed off the trees surrounding the cemetery, and Spencer felt the constriction in his chest easing a little bit.

When the laughter stopped, the two men stood in silence for several seconds, paying their respects and simply being. But the reprieve couldn't last. "You know, Bailey Austin and Ellen Vartran aren't the same person."

Spencer stood half a head taller than Nick, was a better shot and had seniority over him. But the stocky, streetwise detective didn't back away from anything.

Even forbidden topics between friends.

"Stay out of my love life," Spencer warned.

A warning, which Nick duly ignored. "You don't have a love life, buddy." Even a well-practiced glare couldn't deter him. "Are you still not over Ellen? Is that what's holding you back?"

"Whatever Ellen and I had was brief and fiery and done. It was a younger man's love."

"Oh, yeah, because you are so over the hill at thirty-six."

Inhaling a deep breath that chilled his lungs and cleared his head, Spencer tried to explain. "Maybe it's the guilt you never get over. She used my phone that night in the safe house. Called her brother while I was in the shower, then joined me. Either she was distracting me from seeing the outgoing call or she was saying goodbye. When I came back the next morning, the safe house was already under attack. Her brother and the guard were dead. She was bleeding out." He stared at the rose carved beside Ellen's name. "I screwed up."

"As I recall, you got shot trying to save her—and you took out one of the hit men. KCPD rounded up the rest of the hit squad and Dwight Powers put them away."

"But it took us a lot longer to bring down the rest of the organization. Ellen died and I blew our investigation."

"Bailey will testify." Nick said it like he believed it. Like there was no way she could be intimidated into changing her mind. Like she couldn't be harmed or killed. "Even if you screw up whatever you two should have going, she's still going to take down Brian Elliott for us. I can feel it in my gut. She's good for this."

As much as he trusted Nick's instincts about people, Spencer nodded toward the gravestone. "Even your gut can't guarantee that."

Nick propped his hands at his waist and challenged Spencer. "So what are you going to do about it?"

Spencer's logical brain warred with the rusty armor guarding his heart. But he knew where his strength lay. "You got a report for me?"

Nick muttered a curse before pulling a notepad from inside his leather jacket and flipping it open. "I looked into Zeiss Security. Zeiss is retired German military and his employees are all bonded and look legit. I left Sarge doing her computer magic at the office—she'll let us know if any of her in-depth research pops up anything suspicious."

"What's their connection to Bailey?"

"Zeiss subcontracts with Gallagher Security Systems and does most of the bodyguard and security work for

GSS. They've been providing service for the Mayweathers for at least ten years."

"So they check out. What about Max Duncan?"

"Former Army—did most of his stint as an MP at Fort Leonard Wood." Nick snapped his notepad shut and put it away. "He's not your delivery man. I showed Duncan's picture to some of the other residents in Bailey's building. No one recognized him."

"I thought Corie Rudolf might be lying. She was just trying to score points with me. Like she's my type."

"Your type is a little classier. A little taller, a little blonder."

"Nick—"

"Why can't you just admit Bailey means something to you? I've never known you to lie to me, Spence. Don't lie to yourself, either." Nick puffed up like a fierce banty rooster beside him, daring him to deny the truth. "From the night we answered that rape call outside the Fairy Tale Bridal Shop, and you saw that the victim was Bailey Austin, this case has been personal for you."

"Chief Taylor put me in charge of this task force. I'm not going to blow the D.A.'s case or our investigation. I'm not going to let Elliott get away with rape or The Cleaner get away with murder." It was a valiant, solid argument.

But Nick wasn't buying it. "Remember which of us is the more stubborn partner."

"I thought you claimed to be the better-lookin' one."

Nick grinned. "That, too." But he quickly got serious. "It's okay to be happy, Spence. You saw what Annie and I could have long before I did." He reached over and squeezed Spencer's shoulder before giving it a smack and pulling away. "I'm trying to return the favor."

Spencer tucked his chin against the wind and pointed toward Ellen's marker. Damn it if Nick didn't make sense. Or was he only wanting him to make sense? "What if it happens again? I can't go through this twice."

"You didn't have me for a partner last time."

Spencer arched an eyebrow. "*That's* the argument you're going with?"

"You know I've got your back. Look, I don't know a more thorough cop than you. Don't know one who's smarter. You set 'em up and I finish the fight. Together, we get the job done. That's always worked for us." Nick patted Spencer's shoulder and started up the hill. "Come on. I'm freezing my yum-yums off out here."

"Tracking Bailey might be the best way to get a lead on The Cleaner," Spencer pondered out loud. If the stalker was targeting anyone but Bailey, that'd be the logical step he'd take.

"Told you you were the smart one." Nick had reached the side of the road. "Are you coming with us or heading back to Bailey's?"

As he worked out the viable scenarios, Spencer followed Nick's path through the snow. "I don't know yet."

Nick opened his door and a wave of warm air rushed out. "Just give me a call when you need that backup."

Spencer waited in his SUV behind Nick and Annie at the cemetery gate. When the light changed, Nick pulled out to the right.

Spencer turned left.

"I'M SURE SHOPPING isn't your favorite thing, Max." Bailey heard herself apologizing for the second time as they stepped off the tall curb and hurried across the street with the rest of the crowd on Kansas City's Country Club Plaza.

"Not a problem, Miss Austin." He took her elbow and helped her over the next curb, pausing to get his bearings at the five-way intersection. "You said it's up this way?"

She pointed to the tall sign outlined with white lights. "It's a couple of storefronts beyond the coffee shop."

He hurried her past a volunteer ringing a bell in front of a model train store. "I wish we could have parked closer. I don't like being out in the open like this."

Bailey gestured to the bumper-to-bumper cars lining the sidewalks. "Your only other option was to drop me off and find a parking space. And I know you didn't want to leave me alone."

"No," he agreed, pulling her into step beside him again. "Mr. Zeiss said I was to stay with you until my replacement comes this evening. And I sure as hell don't want that detective friend of yours breathing down my neck again."

"No. We certainly don't want that."

Thoughts of Spencer Montgomery made her steps stutter, and Max automatically shortened his stride to stay beside her.

She thought she'd been happily content, working around her apartment today, baking cookies and wrapping more presents. But when Max had reminded her that she needed to get down to the Plaza, and he'd rather do that while there was still some daylight out, Bailey realized she'd been hiding out. Maybe even feeling sorry for herself.

Wasn't that the same thing as being a prisoner? She wouldn't let difficult circumstances make her a victim again. Maybe Spencer hadn't stayed. She understood that his work was more important than babysitting her until Monday.

But that kiss this morning had felt so right that she thought he was feeling the same irresistible draw she was. She didn't have a crush on the man. It wasn't gratitude. It was a bone-deep attraction to his strength, his intelligence, that protective nature, his unquestionable code of honor. And it had meant so much more.

That desperate, feverish embrace against the hallway wall was the first thing in a long time that she'd been sure of. She wasn't a poor little rich girl who needed to be taken care of. She wasn't a victim. She was a woman—real, strong, necessary.

It was as if all the jumbled pieces of her life this past year had finally fallen into place. Holding Spencer, tasting him, absorbing his strength—knowing he wanted her gave her confidence, made her feel stronger.

But the kiss had been a mistake.

Spencer didn't want her in that way. There was some mutual lust there—she wasn't so naive to pretend there wasn't—but it hadn't meant the same thing to him. He'd just gotten caught up in the moment and had been too exhausted to fight it. All he really wanted was a witness to close his case.

The crushing blow to her heart had nearly sent her to bed. And that's when Bailey knew she had to get out of her well-appointed prison and do something with her day—do something with her life. She wouldn't sit there and pine over a man who'd made it clear he didn't want to want her.

It might not be much, but she could help her mother with the Christmas Ball. She could show up, be a gracious hostess and help raise lots of money for a good cause. She could reassure her mother's fractured nerves that her daughter was safe and happy and okay. Well, two of the three. Maybe then her mother wouldn't worry quite so much when Bailey took the witness stand.

Alleviating her mother's fears. That was something useful she could do.

So she'd put on warm slacks, a sweater and boots, convinced Max that she had only one stop to make at the Plaza shops and braved the holiday crowds to pick up her dress for tomorrow night.

It was nice to have Max's muscle clear a space for her through the tourists lined up to watch the animated window displays and the shoppers hurrying up and down the wide sidewalks to get to their next destination. Max didn't have to touch anyone to literally clear a path. But something about the big shoulders and unsmiling face made people walk a wide berth around him, and since she was connected to him by his hand on her elbow, they walked a wide berth around her, as well.

Until the coffee shop door swung open and Corie Rudolf dashed out. "Bailey?"

"Corie?"

"Look out." They would have collided with each other if Max hadn't grabbed the door and pulled Bailey to a stop. "Everybody okay?" he asked, pushing the door closed and pulling Bailey into the vestibule in front of the shop.

Corie beamed a smile up at Max. "No harm done."

But the shorter woman was juggling her purse, her cell phone and a tall cup of coffee. Bailey reached out to take the coffee for a moment before Corie spilled it down the front of her short coat and long, cream-colored scarf. "Oops. Not in the clear yet."

"Thanks." Corie tucked her phone into her purse and straightened the matching cream knit cap she wore before taking her coffee back. "That was a close one."

"What are you doing here?" Bailey asked.

Max eyed the couple coming out of the coffee shop while Corie dodged the passersby on the sidewalk. "My date canceled on me. I remembered you said you were coming down to the Plaza, and I thought we could grab a coffee or maybe take in a movie?" She patted the side of her purse where she'd tucked her cell. "I was just calling your number to see if I could track you down in this crowd."

Bailey glanced up at her bodyguard, and he was already shaking his head. "The movie's out," she explained to Corie. "We were on our way to the formal shop. You're welcome to join us if you'd like."

"Sure. Maybe I could try on one of those fancy

dresses, too." A gap formed in the stream of pedestrians on the sidewalk as the lights at the intersection changed. Corie backed up and started walking with them. She pointed to her tiny compact car as they approached. "I'm parked right here. Maybe I'd better put my coffee inside."

Bailey agreed. "I'm sure the store manager won't want that around his merchandise."

"I'm glad I found you." Whatever awkwardness Corie had displayed earlier was gone as she quickened her pace to get a few steps ahead. She looked around Bailey to Max. "I owe you an apology. I hope I didn't get you into trouble with Detective Montgomery. I'm not very good with faces. But I do remember backsides, and yours…"

"Corie," Bailey chided her with a smile. The woman was shameless.

All was forgiven, apparently, because Max grinned, flattered. "Mine's better, right?"

Corie pulled out her keys to press the remote. "Let's just say I certainly would have remembered—"

Bailey saw a flash of light beneath the hood of the car an instant before Corie flew into the air and the deafening shock wave of the exploding car knocked Bailey to the ground.

Fiery embers took a bite out of her cheek and arm. Her head rang with the concussive noise. Glass shattered and fell down like snow. The ball of fire burning in the street hurt her eyes and she looked away to see people running away, mouths open, screaming without making a sound.

She turned her head the other direction to see Max rolling on the sidewalk, clutching his leg. He had scrape marks along the sleeve of his coat and a hole at the elbow where the insulated material had been completely torn away.

Max was saying something to her, pointing toward the street. He repeated himself, maybe shouting this time because she could hear his words like a muffled whisper through the fog of her brain. "Are you okay? Is she okay?"

Bailey nodded. Other than the ringing in her ears and the burning on her cheek and wrist, she couldn't feel any broken bones. Bracing her hands against the concrete, she pushed herself to a sitting position. She touched her fingers to her aching cheek and came away with blood on her glove. Her coat was grimy and torn, with more red drops staining the chest and sleeve. "I'm okay," she repeated with more force, wondering if Max could hear her. "I'm okay."

"What about Blondie?" She heard Max again, more clearly this time, and turned her head.

"Corie!"

The decorative shrubs near Corie's shell of a car were burning. Corie lay at the base of the hedge, her chest panting with fast shallow breaths. There was blood in her ear, at the corner of her mouth. Her cream-colored scarf and hat were both turning red with the blood.

"Oh, my God." Heedless of the aches and bruises of her own body, Bailey crawled across the ice-cold sidewalk to her friend. "Corie?"

She dragged her friend's body away from the fire,

apologizing for every shriek of pain she caused. When the heat from the burning wreckage felt less intense, Bailey unwound her scarf and wadded it up to place it beneath Corie's neck. But then what? She needed to help, but didn't know where to start. The head wound? The glazed eyes? The twisted shard of metal in her chest?

"Oh, Corie, I'm sorry." Memories of broken watches and complicated devices of her own imagination filled her head. Annie Hermann had warned her of the possibility of a bomb—that the threats against her could have very real consequences. But Bailey hadn't completely understood—Spencer had been right—she had no idea of the scope of the danger she was facing, no idea that anyone else could get hurt. Because of her. Her fault.

Suddenly, Bailey couldn't catch her breath. Someone else was controlling her life again. Her eyes filled with tears at the enormity of what was happening here. Corie wasn't the only one hurt. Max was, too. Maybe others. Someone else had a vicious, violent power over her. Over them all. She was helpless. Useless. Afraid.

"Stop it!" Corie's unfocused eyes opened at her shout.

"You're strong. You can take care of yourself."

Spencer's encouraging words, even as he'd been saying goodbye, echoed through her. Someone did believe in her. Someone thought she was strong enough to get through adversity.

She *was* strong enough. Bailey swiped the tears from her eyes and urged her shivering friend to look at her. "Corie?" She untied her coat and eased it off over the cut on her wrist. She could hear sirens in the distance now, horns honking, people shouting. "Corie? Can you hear me?" Bailey spread her coat over her friend, carefully avoiding the shrapnel on the left side of her chest. Then she scooped up Corie's hand. There was no answering response, but she squeezed it anyway. "I need to go check on Max. Okay, sweetie? Don't close your eyes."

The wintry air seeping into her skin, and floating debris landing on her clothes barely registered. There was so much blood on the sidewalk beneath Corie. Her pupils were dilated, her skin so pale.

"KCPD! Clear the area. Get back! Bailey?" There was one voice in the crowd, shouting above the others—more intense, more authoritative than any other.

Spencer.

"Spence!" Bailey lurched to her feet. She spotted the red hair first.

"B!" He tucked his badge into his pocket as he pushed through the crowd. His long coat billowed out when he opened his arms and Bailey threw herself against his chest. His arms cinched around her, lifting her onto her toes as he pressed a kiss to her temple and surrounded her with his warmth and strength. "Are you okay?"

"I thought you weren't coming back." She locked her arms around him and turned her face into his neck, inhaling his clean, familiar scent. "Thank God, you did."

"Are you hurt?" There was another quick kiss before he set her down and framed her face between his hands. Those cool gray eyes scowled like fury as they took in the cut on her face. "Ah, hell." With his sharp gaze darting from one compass point to the next, he released her entirely and shrugged out of his coat. He swung it over her shoulders and buttoned it together at her neck. "You're freezing."

The weight and warmth was pure comfort, but Bailey knew she wasn't the one who needed his attention. "I'm okay. Max's leg is broken and Corie…" Clutching his coat around her, she pushed away and dropped to her knees beside her friend. "Her car exploded. Just as we were walking past. We have to help her."

Spencer peeled off one glove and knelt beside Bailey to check Corie's neck for a pulse. He wrapped an arm around Bailey's shoulders. "I don't know, sweetheart."

"I have to call for help."

"Already done." He glanced up and Bailey followed his gaze to the cars that had rear-ended each other on the street, to the drivers on their cell phones. To the curious onlookers in the windows of the shops across the street, and on the sidewalk below—so many of them on their phones or taking pictures. There were red and blue flashing lights farther away, uniformed cops clearing traffic to get a fire engine to the scene.

"Bailey Austin?" She heard whispers from the crowd. "Is that Bailey Austin?"

She ignored the curious pointing fingers and flashing telephones and looked down to her friend. "Her eyes are closed again. We have to help her."

"I don't think we can." She felt Spencer's hands pinching around her shoulders, pulling her to her feet. "I need to get you out of here."

"But Corie—"

"I'll stay with her," Max volunteered, sliding over on his hip and uninjured arm. "My knee's shattered. I'm not going anywhere." He looked up at Bailey, then to Spencer. "Take care of her."

"I'm so sorry," Bailey repeated over and over to her fallen friends as Spencer dropped his arm behind her waist and turned her away.

"We have to go, B."

Bailey pushed against his hand and twisted from his grasp. "This is my fault. I have to help."

"Sweetheart, you need medical attention." He caught her hand and pulled her back beside him. "I need to get you out of here."

Bailey planted her feet and shoved against his chest. "Spencer, stop! I can help."

But he didn't budge. His hands were anchored to her shoulders again. "There are too many people. I can't control this crime scene. Someone just tried to kill you and they may try again." He hunched down to look her straight in the eye. "Do you want anyone else to get hurt?"

The harsh reminder drained the anger, the desperation, right out of her. She shook her head. "That was supposed to be me. They were after me."

He wrapped his arms around her, coat and all, and she burrowed against him. He walked her toward the parting crowd. "I know, B. I know."

That's when the first shot rang out.

Chapter Nine

"Get down!"

Spencer pulled Bailey to the ground and bent his chest over her as he pulled his gun and craned his neck to see where the shot had come from.

A second shot shattered the storefront window above their heads. Bailey screamed.

"Move!" he shouted to the curious onlookers still gathered around, trying to steal a picture or standing there in shock. "Get out of here!"

A third shot clipped the branch off a landscaping tree and he dragged Bailey into the snowbank, closer to the curb where the parked cars offered some protection. The gunfire was coming from a higher vantage point from someplace across the street.

"Go!" At last the people were running, saving themselves. He glanced back to see Max Duncan taking cover behind the dying fire of Corie Rudolf's shell of a car. He caught glimpses of uniformed officers hurrying in, guiding people to safety.

Spencer caught the eye of one uni and waved him over, but a shot chipped the bricks above his head and he was forced to duck behind a concrete pillar at the entrance to a nearby parking garage. If they couldn't get reinforcements to him, then they needed to go after the shooter. "Get someone on that roof! Now!"

With a nod, the young man pulled out his radio and darted back the way he'd come.

After the fifth shot, Bailey fisted her hands in Spencer's jacket and he glanced down to see the despair looking up from those deep blue eyes, asking if she was the cause of this chaos, too.

But she already knew the answer. He cupped his hand beside her undamaged cheek. "We need to make a run for it, sweetheart. Can you do that for me?"

He saw no other wounds than that bloody gash on her pale cheek and the cut at her wrist. She startled when a sixth shot blew out a string of lights on a nearby awning, dropping the bulbs to the pavement, where they exploded like mini ricochets off the concrete. Ellen's dark eyes were just a flash of memory. Bailey was pulling him down to her, pulling herself up. Her blue eyes were clear. And she was nodding. "I can run."

The seventh shot meant an automatic weapon or more than one gun or magazine of bullets. The explosion had been a distraction. Using Bailey for target practice was the goal. If the bomb hadn't killed her, the sniper on top of the roof was here to finish the job.

The parking garage offered better protection than the open sidewalk. But twenty, twenty-five feet to the entrance? Or a closer leap over the divider wall to get inside? Either way, that was several feet of open ground, and his spare Kevlar was in the trunk of his car.

"What are we waiting for?" Bailey asked, pushing to sit up before he was ready for her to expose even the curls on top of her head.

He pushed her back into the snow, crazily aware of the warmth of her body buried beneath his, and shouted over his shoulder. "Duncan! You got eyes on the shooter?"

"Not yet. But he's on the roof of the Mercantile Building." The muscle man's every other word was a curse, but he had his gun at the ready and his aim fixed upward. "Go! Get her out of here. I'll lay down cover fire."

Shots eight and nine answered when Duncan fired his first round.

Time was precious, and that sidewalk was way too open for his liking. And he was all that stood between Bailey and the next bullet. "Ah, hell." Propping himself up on his elbows. Spencer holstered his gun and untucked his shirt from his belt, ripping at the buttons.

When he reached inside to tear apart the straps on his own vest, Bailey's hands were there to stop him. "Don't you dare. I don't want anyone else to get hurt."

"B—"

"If he shoots you, who'll take care of me? How will I get out of here and get to that trial?"

Of all the crazy times to have a logical, smarter-than-he-was thought…

Groaning, cursing, he grabbed her hand and pulled her to her feet. "You'll take care of yourself, damn it. Now, Duncan!"

With the rapid shots from Max's Sig Sauer keeping

the shooter at bay for a few seconds, Spencer shielded his body around Bailey's and ran for the parking garage wall.

"Hold on!"

Bailey latched on tight when he dove over the wall. Another shot whizzed over their heads before they hit the concrete hard and rolled. Spencer twisted to take the brunt of the fall, but he was going to feel the impact in his hip and shoulder tomorrow.

Just as vividly as he felt Bailey's legs tangled between his now. Though they lurched to a stop against the wheel of a car and rebounded a few inches across the floor, her arms held on as though she never intended to let go. She was fighting to get through this. Fighting to live. Her cheek was cool against his, her hair was a citrusy balm that eased some of the concern out of him with each rapid breath.

"We're okay, sweetheart." He wound his arm behind her back, absorbing the aftershocks trembling through her body, keeping her close as he turned onto his side to get a glimpse over the top edge of the wall. Good. No direct sight line from the Mercantile's roof. He wound the other arm around her and kissed the silky hair at her temple. "We're okay, B."

She loosened her grip on his neck and framed his jaw between her hands. Even though she was nodding, her eyes were looking to him for reassurance. "Okay." She tugged on his face and pressed a sweet kiss against his lips. "Okay."

His entire body spasmed in an ill-timed response to those gentle lips pillowing against his. Her warm breath against his cold skin made him want to consume her as much as he wanted to comfort her. But he understood his priorities, even if the long thigh wedged precariously between both of his and the thundering response of his pulse tried to tell him something different.

But Bailey's eyes looked away before he could say something distancing and appropriate. "I don't hear any more shooting."

Do your job.

Exhaling a cloudy breath of air, Spencer pulled away, glad for the chilly temps and lack of a coat to keep his head clear. Keeping them both low to the floor, he helped Bailey sit up with her back against the divider wall. He knelt down beside her, quickly checking for any new injuries, batting away her hands as they tried to do the same for him.

"You're right." He nodded at the ongoing silence. Well, people were still shouting, horns were honking and sirens were blaring. But there was no gunfire.

He counted sixty seconds of silence before he risked peering over the top of the wall. No movement on the roof, no flash of a reflection that would indicate a weapon. "Duncan! Duncan, can you hear me? Report!"

"Max?" He let Bailey get up to her knees, but kept her beside him.

"I'm okay," the bodyguard finally answered. "Shooting's stopped. Lousy shot. Doesn't look like he hit anybody. Did your men get him?"

Spencer pulled his radio from his belt and called in. "This is Detective Spencer Montgomery. Senior officer on the scene. Did we get the shooter?" There was a long pause of static and chatter on the line. "Did we get him?"

The line cleared and Spencer got the answer he needed—but didn't want to hear. "Negative, sir," an officer answered. "I've got footprints in the snow up here, but there's no one but us."

"Shell casings?"

"Negative. We've got nothing. He must have gone down the fire escape and disappeared into the crowd."

All right. So The Cleaner or her latest thug had gotten away. She could have her victory. For now. But priorities shifted when the threat went underground. That meant moving on to canvassing the neighborhood. Taking care of injured people and a safe, orderly evacuation of this part of the city before anyone else got hurt. Although Spencer preferred to get his hands around the bastard's neck in an interrogation room, he knew what he had to do.

"Get a bus here ASAP. We've got a DB at the explosion site and a wounded man." The Plaza was a maze of pricey shops and entertainment venues with multiple entrances, several parking garages and crisscrossing streets. No way could they stop every person to search for a weapon. But they had to try. "Get Chief Taylor on this. Call it in to top brass. Deputy Commissioner Madigan is a friend of mine—my partner's uncle. Ask him free up any men we can spare. I want every vehicle stopped before it leaves the Plaza district. I want a patrol in every shop. I want eyes in the crowd. Call Pike Taylor and tell him we need K-9 units here. We need to find this shooter."

"Yes, sir."

Spencer put the radio back on his belt, made sure it was safe to stand, and helped Bailey to her feet. She was battered and bleeding. There was snow in her hair and a smear on his coat. But she was gorgeous. And alive. "You okay?"

"Not a hundred percent," she answered honestly. "But okay enough. You?"

"I'm okay." Bumps and bruises, frustration and nagging fears didn't count.

She could see his thoughts were distracting him as he leaned over the concrete divider and looked back toward the burning car and potential kill zone. Bailey peeked out, too. "No one else was hurt, were they?"

Spencer pulled her back inside the relative security of the parking garage and moved her behind this first row of cars toward the exit gate. He sealed his hand around hers and kept her beside him. "No one was supposed to get hurt."

Her fingers tightened around his. "How do you explain my dead friend?"

Spencer flipped his collar up against the cold. "With ten bullets, even a lousy shot would get lucky and hit somebody. Those shots were all aimed over our heads. Warning shots."

"To scare us?" Bailey stopped. "To scare me?"

"Did it work?" He turned and threaded his fingers through her tousled hair, gently freeing them from the wound on her cheek. He didn't want Bailey to be scared. Seeing her brave spirit cowed in any way bothered him as much as seeing her hurt. Nick had been right—he was lying to himself if he thought he didn't have feelings for this woman.

"Miss Austin?" Spencer pulled his gun and whirled around at the male voice behind him. "Whoa! I'm innocent!"

A young man, maybe twenty, with curling dark hair and a bright red Chiefs parka, flattened his back against the pillar at the front gate and raised his hands in surrender. "Take off your coat."

"What?"

"Take off your coat," Spencer repeated, keeping the business end of his gun pointed straight at the kid. "Are you carrying any weapons?"

"No, sir. No, officer." He unzipped the parka and dropped it at his feet, thrusting his hands back into the air and turning around, giving Spencer a better view of any hidden gun. "All I have is this."

"Spencer." He saw the green envelope in the kid's hand at the same time Bailey touched his arm, urging him to lower his weapon. "Where did you get that?"

Keeping a nervous eye on the man with the gun, the kid inched forward, holding the envelope out to Bailey. But Spencer snatched it from his hand before she could touch it. They both recognized the same green stationery that had come in the package with the watch. The young man hugged his arms around his middle, shivering in his baggy jeans. "A lady in the crowd said I should give it to Miss Austin. I know who you are from the newspapers, ma'am." He smiled at Bailey but frowned at Spencer. "Can I put my coat back on now?"

"Can you give me a description of that woman?" Spencer prompted.

Once he'd holstered his gun and nodded permission to bundle up again, the kid answered, "No. We were getting jostled around—my buddy and me—with all the people running away from the explosion. She slipped the card and a hundred-dollar bill in my hand and said not to look."

"What about your buddy—did he get a look?"

"I don't know. We got separated." The young man shrugged into his coat and zipped it up. "The lady said if I didn't turn around, there was another hundred in it for me." He brushed the dust and snow from his parka and shrugged. "I'm a college student. I didn't look."

A uniformed officer had arrived on the scene. Spencer raised his hand to tell the startled young man to relax, and to tell the officer to keep his service weapon holstered. This kid was a witness, not a threat. "I need you to go over to that officer there and describe anything you can remember about the woman. Her height, what she smelled like, what she was wearing."

"Yes, sir."

"And I need those two bills."

"Oh, man," the kid whined. "I knew this was too good to be true. Do you know how much gas that'll put in my car?"

Bailey tilted her face up to him. "Do you think you can get trace off those bills?"

"Probably not. But I'm going to try."

Huddled inside his oversize coat, Bailey probably looked as nonthreatening as he looked like an armed menace. She took a couple of steps closer to the boy. "Give the police officer your name and address, and I'll write you a check for *three* hundred dollars."

The young man glanced from Bailey up to Spencer and back.

Spencer helped him decide. "We're not giving you a choice, son. Three hundred or nothing. I'd take the deal."

"Yes, sir." He quickly pulled the money from his pocket and handed it to Spencer who stowed it in a plastic evidence bag from his pocket while the kid walked out with the officer.

Once they were alone again, and Spencer had called Nick to alert the rest of the task force, Bailey nodded to the card he was holding in his gloved hand. "I believe that's for me."

As soon as he got to his SUV and a second evidence bag, he was putting it away. "Do you even need to open it?"

Fragile and feminine to look at, but made of pretty stern stuff. "Corie's dead, isn't she."

He knew she counted on him to be honest and up front with her, but he hated saying anything that would add to the sadness in her eyes. "I wasn't getting a pulse."

Spencer slipped his arm around her as he handed her the card. She leaned against him and slipped her thumb beneath the flap of the envelope. "Then let's see what that murdering witch has to say for herself."

I see you when you're sleeping.
I know when you're awake.

I can find you anytime, anywhere.

It's your choice—say Brian Elliott raped you...or live to see Christmas.

SPENCER WAS STILL on the phone. He sat at the big walnut desk in the alcove beneath the stairs leading to the second floor of his suburban condo, jotting notes and asking concise questions. When she'd gone into the kitchen to retrieve the scissors she'd spotted after dinner, he'd been pacing through the living room. As soon as they'd walked in to the modern condominium, with its tall windows, dark wood and gray walls, he'd locked the door, shown her where the bathroom and towels were, and picked up the phone.

She was guessing the man wasn't used to having company. And that her nightmarish afternoon on the Plaza had put almost all of Kansas City's finest on some kind of duty tonight.

Bailey hitched up the black KCPD sweatpants Spencer had lent her and padded across the polished wood floor in the white athletic socks she'd borrowed from him. The shower and clean clothes, even if the sweats were several sizes too large for her, had been a refreshing, comforting welcome after her trip through the E.R., a lengthy interview with Detective Nick Fensom and a quick meeting with her trauma counselor, Kate Kilpatrick.

She was fine. She was safe. She'd shared a heart-wrenching phone call with her mother and stepfather. Her mother had cried the entire time and Jackson had promised to give her a sedative and make sure she got a decent night's sleep.

Bailey sat on the black leather couch and curled her legs beneath her, trying to concentrate on cutting shapes out of the white paper she'd borrowed from Spencer's computer printer. She was doing her best not to eavesdrop on his investigation. But it was hard not to pick up on the gist of the conversations he'd had these past few hours.

He'd had several calls from his partner, Nick Fensom, talking *plan B* and *perimeter security*. Annie Hermann had called with results from the lab—no usable trace on the cash The Cleaner had paid the college student to deliver that last threat, but she was following up on several calls to and from Corie Rudolf's cell phone before she'd died. Someone named Pike Taylor and a police dog had reported on tracking the shooter from the roof of the Plaza Mercantile Building. But that trail had gone cold with time and snow and some type of chemical on the sidewalk.

Spencer could be talking to the deputy commissioner or Mitch Taylor or any of a hundred other police officers, lab techs and who knew what kind of experts right now.

And she…was cutting snowflakes.

Spencer leaned back in his leather desk chair, smoothing his hand over his damp red-gold hair. "No, Kate. Tell the press Miss Austin isn't giving any interviews before the trial. And if I see any more photographs from today's attack on the television or in a newspaper or online, you can inform them that I'll be charging them with witness tampering."

Bailey unfolded her grade-school creations and carried them to the tall silk fern by the living room window. She'd already raided Spencer's desk for a box of colored paper clips that she'd hooked together and draped like garland through the fern's long leaves.

Although she could see the lights of the downtown skyline from the seventh-story window, Spencer lived far enough from the main highways and thoroughfares that the sky was nearly black when she looked outside. The moon wasn't even bright enough to pierce the low-hanging clouds or lighten her mood.

Still, she anchored the paper snowflakes to the clips, determined not to slip into one of those desperate funks that could be even more dangerous to her recovery than those anger episodes she sometimes had to deal with since the rape.

"It's close enough." Spencer rose from his chair to pace again. "The judge is already threatening to sequester the jury before the trial even starts. Endangering Bailey and jeopardizing the fairness of this trial sounds like tampering to me." She watched his reflection in the window, and saw when his attention shifted from the phone call to her. "I'd better let you get to bed. Is Sheriff Harrison in town with you? He's a good man. Thanks, Kate."

Spencer set the phone on the coffee table as he crossed the room to join her at the window. He scrubbed his hand over his jaw before splaying his fingers at the waist of his jeans. "What are you doing now?"

Bailey stood back from her handiwork. "Pretty pathetic, isn't it?"

"You're hanging paper clips on my fern."

"It's a Christmas tree." She caught the long sleeves of the sweatshirt she wore in her fists and hugged her arms around her waist. Right. Like that didn't sound lame.

"You've already fixed us an omelet and washed the dishes. My kitchen has never been that clean." Spencer propped his hip on the ledge of the window and sat back to face her. "I didn't bring you to my place to cure my Scrooge-ish spirit. I brought you here so I can keep you safe. Away from all that craziness out there today. This way I can keep an eye on you while I work on tracking down the shooter and who might have put that bomb together."

He'd missed a button on the collar of the striped oxford shirt he wore. Bailey curled her fingers into the soft cotton shirt, fighting the urge to button it for him. "I know you have to work. I don't begrudge you that for a minute. But there's nothing for me to do here except think. I don't have any clothes to unpack until Sergeant Murdock brings the suitcase from my place. I don't have a job with work I can bring home. I have to do something to stay busy." She spun away from the window, gesturing to both floors. "And you weren't kidding when you said you didn't celebrate Christmas. There's not a stitch of decoration or a present to be seen anywhere around here."

She heard him stand and felt his hands close around her shoulders. "B, you don't have to take care of me. I'm used to working late and fending for myself."

Bailey turned. "Maybe you don't need anything, but I…" She reached up and fastened the tiny button before smoothing the open placket of his shirt. "I need…to take care of you. I can do little jobs while you're working. I want to help."

He captured her hands as they moved across the crisp material and pulled her to the couch to sit beside him. "You're not useless."

"You remember me saying that?" Bailey's cheeks flooded with heat and she pulled away. The man never forgot a detail, did he?

Spencer perched on the edge of the couch, taking her hands and rubbing them between his bigger, warmer ones. "You don't think putting Brian Elliott away in prison is the bravest, most helpful thing you can do? Think of all the women you're protecting by getting him off the streets. Think of families you're saving from heartbreak and tragedy."

He'd hunched down to her level and those handsome gray eyes were right there in front of her. The sincerity she read there was fiercely sweet. Bailey smiled her thanks, but pulled her fingers free to hold his in her lap. "I know that's important. And trust me, I'm not forgetting what a challenge it will be to talk about that night again in front of Brian and all those other people, strangers I don't even know, who'll be in that courtroom."

He waited patiently for her to continue, and Bailey discovered that having Spencer Montgomery focused solely on her—listening, watching, caring—could be as empowering as it was intimidating.

Her grasp tightened around his. "But the only reason I'm any help to you or the police department or Kansas City is because that man beat me until I was unconscious and did…unspeakable things to me."

"B—"

"No." She pulled away when he reached for her, trying to make things right, trying to take care of her and make the pain go away. She would have moved away, but his hand settled lightly on her knee, silently asking her to stay close and finish what she had to say. "What else do I have to offer the world, Spencer? When this trial is done, I don't want to be that poor little rich girl again. I want to do something meaningful with my life. I need to be something more than what I was…before. And if all I can do is wash your dishes and bring a lame little bit of Christmas into this sterile home, then that's what I'm going to do."

He studied her for several long seconds, taking in the butterfly bandage on her cheek, her vehement words, her frustration. Then his hand tightened around her knee and he leaned in to kiss her. His left hand tunneled into her hair to hold her at the nape and anchor her lips to his until she surrendered to his gentle persuasion and parted for him. She caught his jaw with her hand, holding on as he deepened the kiss.

It was tender, leisurely, giving, sweet. She tasted the coffee from dinner on his tongue and felt a languid heat curling inside her belly and seeping out into every extremity until she was far too warm for a winter's evening, and far too bewitched to recall the unsettling emotions that had left her feeling raw and second-rate just a few minutes earlier.

"I don't understand," she whispered on a husky voice when he finally broke away.

Spencer's fingers lingered in her hair and he rested his forehead against hers. His deep, uneven breaths made her think he'd gotten lost for a few moments in that kiss, too. But he was smiling when he straightened and looked into her eyes. "You're ambitious, Bailey Austin." His fingers stroked the hair at her nape. "As horrible as that night must have been for you—and as angry as it makes me to think a man would ever put his hands on you like that—I think the attack awakened a fighting spirit in you. You're no longer content to accept the status quo. You want to make your own decisions, make your own mistakes, create your own victories. You'll never settle for having them handed to you again."

A year's worth of therapy sessions with her counselor, and she'd never heard her internal struggle verbalized for her so perfectly.

"Yes."

Spencer understood. As twisted and complicated as her life had become, as volatile and bewildering as her emotions could be, he understood. She just wanted to be a normal woman again. Maybe for the first time in her life. With all his logic and acrimony and deductive genius, he got that.

No wonder she'd fallen in love with the man.

Even as the revelation blossomed in her heart and filled her with an anticipation and apprehension that were too new and unfamiliar to fully understand, he was pulling her to her feet and leading her across the living room to the foyer closet.

"I guess I have to ask you to be patient and not try to conquer all those battles tonight. Here." He pulled a box off the top shelf and handed it to her. "These are a few things I kept from my parents' estate." He lifted the lid to reveal a tray of glass ornaments, thinning silver garland and a pair of clumsily painted angels made out of popsicle sticks and cupcake wrappers—one red, one green.

Bailey lifted the green angel from its tissue wrapping and held it up. "Did you make these?"

"Yeah. A couple or thirty years ago." Spencer closed the box of decorations and carried it to the coffee table. "I think my mom kept everything I made in school."

"They're precious."

"I'm not leaving you alone to go get a real tree, but—" he pointed to the window where the silk plants are "—the ferns are all yours."

Laughing, she impulsively threw her arms around his neck and hugged him. "Who'd have that the stoic detective had a sentimental streak?"

"Don't let that get around the precinct, okay?" For a few moments, he hugged her back. Then his hands slipped to her waist and he was pushing some space between them. The stoic detective truly had returned. "I've got two more calls to make. We're trying to get some more background on Corie Rudolf. We dumped the numbers on her phone and discovered she'd made and received several calls from the same disposable cell number—almost all of them after the D.A. announced you'd be testifying at Elliott's trial. The last one came right before that bomb went off today."

Corie had been on the phone when she'd come out of the coffee shop. Maybe she hadn't been trying to call Bailey at all. Maybe her neighbor had followed her to the Plaza. "Do you think Corie was working for The Cleaner?"

"It's a possibility," Spencer admitted. "But not a fact yet. I need to run down a few more leads." He reached around her to pick up his phone. "Will transforming this bachelor pad into something more festive be meaningful enough work for now?"

Bailey nodded, sobered by the possible treachery of a friend who'd been murdered. "Thank you. You do your job. I'll be fine."

The rest of the evening passed by in relative silence between Bailey and Spencer. He worked until about midnight while she created a unique, silly display in the window that brought some childish fun and holiday colors to the otherwise austere condo. Bailey took her thoughts to bed with her and was sound asleep in the guest bedroom by the time Spencer came up the stairs.

Chapter Ten

It was 2:00 a.m. when Bailey rolled over in the dark, tangled in the covers of an unfamiliar bed, and the panic hit.

"Don't hurt me!" She fought against the tape that bound her wrists.

He was here.

"I told you not to look at me, you filthy witch!" Her captor pulled the hood over her face, plunging her into darkness. "You're like every other woman who doesn't know her place. I'm the man here." Her body jerked as he ripped her skirt off her hips. She screamed as he cut through her slip and pantyhose. The spicy, musky assault of his cologne burned into her memory as his weight crushed her into the mattress and plastic underneath her.

"Bailey?"

Lights flashed behind her eyelids. He was pouring something all over her, washing her body with a pungent liquid, inside and out. "No!"

Her nightmare exploded in a blast of fire and pain,

throwing her to the ground. She fought to escape. Fought to live.

"Bailey!"

She woke up swinging, blindly smacking her attacker. "Let me go!"

"Easy. Easy, B." She wasn't trapped in the dark. There was no hood on her head. No man in a surgical mask hovering above her. She was in a bed. There was a lamp on beside her. Granite-colored eyes blazed in the light. "It's me, Spencer. Do you know me now?"

She took several more seconds to comprehend when and where she was. Not in the past. Not in a windowless construction site draped with plastic tarps. She was in Spencer Montgomery's home. On a winter's night. She saw the scratches she'd raked across his chest and felt his strong hands pinning her wrists into her pillow.

"B?"

When she nodded, he released her and sat up on the side of her bed.

"Sorry I had to hold you down," he apologized as she sat up and pushed her hair off her face. "You were wailing pretty good on me. I had to protect myself. I can tell you've been working out." He winked. But she didn't see the humor. "I didn't hurt you, did I?"

He rubbed at his bare right shoulder. She'd done worse than scratch him? She climbed onto her knees beneath the sheet and blanket, and pushed the long sleeves of the black sweatshirt up past her elbows to free her hands before reaching out to brush her fingertips across the rusty-gold hair above his heart. "Did I hurt *you?*"

His muscle flinched as she neared the mark she'd

made and he sucked in his breath, pulling away from her touch. "I can imagine who you were really fighting, and I hope you did hit him that hard." But he shook his head and pointed to the bruise on his tricep. "I jarred this pretty good diving into the parking garage this afternoon. But I heard you crying out, and…"

Now she saw the gun sitting on the table beside the lamp. He thought there'd been an intruder, that one of The Cleaner's hired thugs had gotten to her. Was that why she saw concern still lining his face?

"I'm okay. I'm safe. The nightmare woke me and I was disoriented, and it all got mixed together. I'm sorry I woke you." She looked up at the ceiling, knowing there were condos above and below them. "Do you think I woke anyone else?"

"We're pretty soundproofed here. Don't worry."

Bailey was breathing normally now and was fully able to distinguish memory from reality now. Her gaze was drawn back to his long, lean torso and she realized he'd charged to her rescue with nothing more than his gun and a pair of flannel pajama pants that rode temptingly low beneath his belly button.

And though her blood heated with a different kind of tension, it wasn't only longing that made her reach out to touch the puckered white scar that formed a jagged circle on his right flank. She'd seen something like that on a TV show—the scar from a bullet.

"What happened?" His flat stomach quivered when she touched his skin and Spencer shot to his feet.

"It's an old war wound." He picked up his gun and

headed toward the door. "If you're okay, I'll go back and get some sleep now."

"Spencer." *Don't brush away my concern. Don't think I can't handle it.* Bailey swung her legs off the side of the bed, not bothering to pull the sweat pants back on over her panties as she hurried into the hallway after him. The shirt hit low enough on her thighs to make a modest nightgown. "I may not carry a badge or have a therapist's license, but I know how to listen."

She followed him straight into his bedroom, a carbon copy of the gray walls and dark wood downstairs.

"Don't come in here unless you intend to stay the night."

Bailey took another step in, stopping at the foot of his king-size bed while he circled around it. "Is that supposed to scare me away?"

"You make me feel things I haven't felt in a long time, Bailey. I don't know that I want to feel them."

"Because it hurts?" She was trying to piece together what he was admitting to her. "Something about the nightmare, about me crying out, bothered you."

"Let's see." He holstered his gun and set it on the bedside table before picking up the dove-gray comforter and shaking out the messy folds from his hasty dash to her room. "Someone tried to kill you today. She threatened to finish the job if you won't crawl into a hole and forget about the trial."

"Don't." Bailey snatched the cover from his hand and folded it back, out of his reach. "This isn't that relentless cop thing you do. That scar means something.

Tell me about it. Tell me what makes you so afraid to feel something for me."

When he turned around, there was a look of such pain and anguish on his chiseled face that Bailey immediately reached out.

He caught her hand, laced his fingers together with hers and pulled her half a step closer so that he could touch her, instead. One fingertip touched the bandage that closed the cut on her cheekbone, and then all five fingers sifted through her sleep-tossed hair to cup the side of her head.

"Can I keep you close tonight?" he asked. "Will it frighten you to have a man in your bed?"

Bailey leaned her cheek into the caress. "Not if it's you. And…" Her heart might be quick to answer, but she knew her limitations. "Not if we keep a light on."

Spencer turned off the overhead light, but left the lamp beside his bed on to cast a glow across the room as Bailey crawled in between the cool sheets. "Brr."

"Cold?" He gathered her into his arms without asking permission, and Bailey didn't mind a bit when she tumbled against a mile of skin and he rolled onto his side to face her. "Better?"

"Much." She rested her head on the pillow of his shoulder and quickly stopped shivering as the thick comforter and his tall, strong body cocooned her in a haven of warmth. But he was mistaken if he thought she was going to drift off to sleep. "Were you shot in the line of duty?"

He chuckled against her hair. "You go straight to the heart of things, don't you."

Bailey hadn't been intimate with a man since long before the rape, and she seemed to have forgotten where to rest her hands. But Spencer gently stopped them from dancing across his shoulders and waist, and held them against his chest where she could feel the strong beat of his heart beneath the ticklish dusting of hair.

"Back when I first made detective," he started, "I was assigned to an investigation. Money laundering through a restaurant. They were a front for organized crime."

"Sounds dangerous."

His heart beat a little faster. "The investigation was the easy part. It was pretty clear the owner was doctoring his books whenever he made a big wholesale foods purchase or catered a large event."

Bailey started tracing delicate circles across his skin, feeling antsy at how his story would end. "Did you have to deal with any of the mobsters?"

His chest expanded with a deep sigh, pushing Bailey slightly away. But he slid his hand beneath the sweatshirt and flattened his palm at the small of her back to keep her close. "That part comes later. I suppose the short version is that we convinced the owner's sister to testify against the men who were using her brother. Ellen was an accountant. She put two and two together when she paid the monthly bills. She knew the kind of men who came to the restaurant. She was afraid her brother would get hurt."

A woman. This was about a woman. Bailey's heart squeezed in her chest. Was this accountant the reason

Spencer worked so hard to detach himself from his emotions?

"Who was Ellen to you?"

"I loved her." A painful gasp stuck in Bailey's throat. Spencer's hand moved beneath her shirt, trailing slowly up and down her back in a long, frictive caress. "Past tense, B. I loved her."

Once she'd moved past that jealous moment, or maybe once Spencer had calmed the thumping beat of his heart, he continued. "The D.A.'s office talked her into testifying against the men her brother worked for."

"Testify?" This time Bailey pushed away. But Spencer threw his top leg over both of hers to keep her close. And suddenly she understood that he needed her here. He needed the reassurance of her warmth. He needed the patience in her heart to open up this painful chapter of his past.

She stretched her left arm around his waist and nestled in beneath his chin.

"See any similarities?" His lips brushed against the crown of her hair.

"What happened to Ellen?" Bailey could already guess. But he needed to say it.

"We put her in a safe house right before the trial. I was one of the men assigned to protect her."

"Oh, Spencer. And I—"

"Shh."

He slipped a finger beneath her chin and tilted her face up to his. He pressed a soothing kiss to her lips. And though the stubble of his beard made it slightly rougher than he intended, the friction of it reminded

Bailey of the contrasts between them—a man, a woman, lying close in bed in the heart of the night, sharing a hushed, private conversation. He kissed her again, stirring a response deep inside her.

"I lost my focus, B." The minimalist nickname was his alone for her. She felt uniquely linked to Spencer every time he said it.

There *was* a link between them. She couldn't care this deeply or trust this openly with a man she didn't share a special connection with. "Did Ellen die?"

His arms convulsed almost painfully tight around her and Bailey wanted to weep at the depth of what Spencer Montgomery could really feel. "She was afraid her brother would get if she testified. She'd changed her mind, but I don't think she knew how to tell me."

Changed her mind? "No wonder you didn't believe I'd stand up to Brian Elliott."

"Don't mention his name here. Not in this room. Ever."

Bailey pressed her lips against the pulse in Spencer's neck, and tasted salty, delicious heat.

"Ellen used my phone to call her brother. She thought he'd help her escape. But he came to the safe house with a bunch of thugs. They shot Ellen, her brother, a guard."

"You." She moved her lips to the taut underside of his chin, offering comfort, offering whatever he needed from her.

"She died in my arms because I didn't know how to love her *and* be a cop."

She kissed the marks she'd accidentally scratched on his chest, wishing she could heal his fractured image of himself as easily as these would heal. "Spencer, you can't put that kind of burden on yourself."

He crushed her tight against his chest. "I should have saved her. What if something happens and I can't save you?"

Bailey squiggled some space between them and tipped her chin to look into those guilt-stricken eyes. "Life isn't easy, Spencer." She knew this secret far better than she ever would have liked. "Sometimes, stuff happens that isn't your fault, that you can't control. It doesn't mean you've failed or that you won't fail again. It just means that you have to fight harder. You have to be stronger. You can't let the bad stuff win. You have to keep getting up and moving forward even when you're afraid to or you don't think you can."

"B, don't say—"

"Something may happen to me."

"No."

"But it won't be your fault."

"I don't want to lose you!"

The words were so raw, so filled with an emotion that even Spencer himself didn't understand, that Bailey knew of only one thing to say.

"Then love me."

THAT WAS ONE order Spencer was willing to obey.

When Bailey lifted her lips to give him a kiss, he crushed his mouth over hers, accepting what she so generously offered, giving back all he could. He rolled her partly beneath him, running one hand beneath that sack of a sweatshirt she wore to touch the soft skin of her back, tangling the other hand in her even softer hair. He plunged his tongue into the silky warmth of her mouth and tasted her tongue sliding against his. He could get drunk on this woman's kisses—her dewy lips, their supple strength, their bold curiosity and unselfish welcome.

Her arms wound around his neck. Her fingers tunneled through his hair. She whimpered a seductive little hum in her throat that drew his lips to the tiny vibration of sound beneath her cool skin. His right hand roamed at will, dipping beneath the elastic of her panties to squeeze that roundly delicious bottom, sliding up the plane of her stomach to cup a taut, plump mound of flesh.

Bailey was at once a burning fire and a soothing balm. A classy lady and an irresistible siren. A gentle spirit and a passionate heart.

He knew Nick was in the lobby downstairs, keeping watch over the building, allowing Spencer the respite he needed to sleep. But even more than rest, he needed to make love to the brave woman who'd set her own fears aside to listen to his. To share his pain. To understand his guilt. To heal his broken soul.

When he caught the turgid pearl at the tip of her breast and rolled it between his thumb and forefinger, she gasped aloud and buried her face against his chest. "Spencer…"

He instantly moved his hand to the more neutral territory of her back and pulled the heavy erection between his thighs away from the curve of her hip. "Did

I hurt you?" he rasped, tilting her face up to read the truth in her eyes.

"No. It was…overwhelming. I'd forgotten."

Forgotten how good this could feel? Or forgotten how another man's hands had made her feel? "Did I frighten you? I don't want to do anything to remind you of him."

She silenced his apology with a finger over his lips. Then quickly replaced it with a soft, healing kiss. "He doesn't come into this room, remember?"

"That wasn't fair of me to say. I know you live with those memories every day. Have you even been with a man since then?"

She shook her head.

Spencer was hard with desire, but he'd take a cold shower before he'd do anything to hurt her. "Can you do this? Are you ready to be with a man?"

"I'm ready to be loved, not forced."

"Ah, hell, sweetheart." His lips went to hers again, reassuring her with everything in him that there was no other way he'd have her. "Tell me what you like. Tell me what you don't. Tell me to stop. Anytime. I'm not the most sensitive guy, but I can—"

"Could I be on top?" She whispered the request, the sweetest yes a man could know. "Is that okay?"

Rising up on one elbow, Spencer shucked the sweatshirt off over her head, removed her panties. She threw the covers back when he rolled away to pull a condom from the nightstand and sheathe himself. Then he lay back on the pillows, and pulled her over to straddle him, making himself as vulnerable to her as he knew how.

When she shyly covered her breasts from uncertainty

or the chilled air, Spencer gently pried her hands away and brought them down to rest on the dancing, eager skin of his chest. She was porcelain and perfect from head to toe except for the rosy pink tips of her breasts, and the golden thatch of hair at her thighs.

Her beauty and trust were humbling things. "You mean you want me to be able to watch all this beautiful skin and touch these beautiful breasts and…"

Her breathing quickened as he did what he described. She rubbed her bottom against his shaft and he groaned with need.

"Do you want me?" she asked.

There were no other words. "Yes."

"That's what I need, Spencer. I need someone who wants me just because it's me."

"I need you." He pulled down to his chest for a kiss. With her breasts branding his chest, he lifted her bottom and slowly entered her tight, moist heat. "Ah, B," he growled, growing hard again as her body gripped him. "Ah, sweetheart."

She pushed herself up and he thrust inside her. "Spencer? That's good. I like that. I—"

When she closed her eyes and the tremors clutched him inside her, he was done talking. He thrust deeper, faster. He reached for her breasts and she covered his hands, linking their fingers together, squeezing them tight.

Bailey gasped his name as thrust himself up one last time and shook with the power of his own release.

Afterward, she collapsed on top of him and Spencer gathered her in his arms and pulled the comforter up to cover them both. They slept like that, with her spent body draped over his and his arms wrapped around her. And, for a few hours, Spencer Montgomery wasn't a cop.

For a few hours, at least, he was only a man in love.

Chapter Eleven

"I knew you'd look smashing in a tuxedo."

The compliment was genuine, but seemed to fall on deaf ears.

Bailey took Spencer's hand and stepped out of the SUV onto the cleared bricks leading up to the front steps of the Mayweather estate. Twin Christmas trees, festooned with white lights and crystal ornaments, framed the front door, with layers of snow filling the branches in such a way that it looked as if it had been placed there for a holiday magazine ad. A red carpet led the way past a grandstand of reporters into the wide marble foyer where she could see glimpses of white roses and evergreen garlands hanging with more lights inside. The music of a small chamber orchestra, playing both classical pieces and holiday tunes, danced softly on the chilling breeze.

It was everything a Christmas ball should be. With lines of cars circling the driveway, dignitaries and wealthy guests pausing for pictures and sound bites before joining the party, it was everything her mother could want. It was probably everything Spencer loathed and it was an opportunity for Bailey.

Spencer handed his keys off to a parking valet she recognized as his partner, Nick Fensom. With a wink to Bailey and an "Everyone's in place" to Spence, he hurried around the hood to climb behind the wheel and drive away.

Bailey inhaled a deep breath through her nose and released the steaming air out through her carefully made-up lips. She hadn't expected tonight to be anything like a real date, but it might be reassuring to see at least a glimpse of the lover who'd bared his soul to her, and held her, skin to skin, in the warmth of his arms throughout the night.

It was important for her to be here—to calm her mother's fears that explosions and gunfire weren't any more of a threat than a Christmas card with an unpleasant message inside. She'd gotten the idea early this morning, as she'd lain in bed, snugged to Spencer's side, thinking. If she could manage her nightmares, overcome her fears of intimacy, and be the woman that a strong, confident man like Spencer Montgomery needed, then she could face the reporters, face her family, face the possibility of The Cleaner or one of his hired thugs showing up tonight to try to silence her one last time.

Without any usable leads panning out, it might be the only way the police could ferret out the Rose Red Rapist's accomplice and ensure the safety and success of his trial.

Spencer hated the idea. But he didn't have a better one.

Spencer tapped the bud in his ear and dipped his chin toward the lapel microphone that could have passed for a fraternity pin. "Montgomery here. I've got Bailey with me. We need eyes on her every minute tonight. If anyone senses anything out of place, I'm the first to know." She knew an unsettling thrill to be hanging on the arm of a man who conveyed such authority and generated such respect. She figured with Spencer was the safest place to be. Even if he doubted his ability to protect her now that things had gotten personal between them, she had no doubts. "Remember. Bailey and the guests are our first priority. If we can get this perp, do it. But we neutralize any threats to the civilians first. Understood?" A litany of responses buzzed in his ear. "Apprise Zeiss's men of our status. Montgomery out."

Bailey waited beside him, shivering beneath her midnight-blue wrap, fighting the cold air as much as her own trepidation about tonight. And about them.

Maybe Spencer could only allow a *them* for one night. Maybe he considered being with her a weakness he didn't want to repeat. Maybe he truly couldn't be both a cop and a man who cared.

The relentless cop had shown up to escort her to the ball tonight. The man she loved was buried somewhere deep under the starched white collar and gun and badge hidden beneath the trim fit of his suit.

If he wouldn't tell her that things would be okay, that the massive security and crowd of cameras and guests would keep her safe enough tonight, then maybe she should reassure him.

While he looked from side to side, taking note of the

cars that had pulled up behind him and eyeing anyone who strayed too close, Bailey reached up to straighten his collar where the curling wire that connected his radio to the members of his task force had caught. "You said I could do anything I set my mind to."

He pulled her hand through the crook of his elbow and led her onto the red carpet. "Setting yourself up as bait and getting yourself killed for the trouble weren't what I had in mind."

"Spencer—"

"I know. You need to do this." His grip tightened and he pulled her aside, dropping his lips to her ear to whisper, "If anything happens tonight—if I'm not there for you—you fight. That's what you do, Bailey Austin. You get up and you fight."

Bailey reached up and brushed her fingertips along the cool line of his jaw. Maybe the man she loved *had* shown up tonight. "I will, Spencer," she promised. "Nose, throat, gut or groin. Keep moving. Keep fighting. I won't be the victim again."

He leaned in to press a kiss to her temple and Bailey tilted her head, savoring the tender touch.

Then the moment was over and he tugged her closer to his side as the cameras flashed. The cop was back. "Brace yourself. The fun's about to begin."

"Miss Austin?"

"Look this way!"

"Who are you with tonight?"

"How are you feeling?"

"Who are you wearing?"

"Any lasting effects from yesterday's attack?"

The rapid-fire barrage of snapshots and questions caught her off guard for a moment. But then she found her smile and the gracious genes she'd inherited from her mother, and paused for pictures and answered questions. She introduced Spencer, raved about her mother's decorations and reminded readers and viewers to donate as generously as they could afford.

When they reached the edge of the grandstand at the bottom of the stairs, a large television camera swung her way, capturing her in its spotlight. Vanessa Owen stepped forward with her microphone and Bailey dug her fingers into the fine wool of Spencer's sleeve, as wary of this encounter as she'd been the night the reporter had ambushed her in the KCPD parking garage.

"Happy Holidays, Miss Austin." The striking brunette wore a toasty-looking black coat with a fur-trimmed collar, and smiled into the camera as if she had no care about the frosty temps or her provocative questions. "How does it feel to know that an innocent woman was killed because of you? Maybe even killed because she was mistaken for you?"

"You're out of line, Miss Owen." Spencer tried to push past the reporter and camera, but Bailey was dragging her feet.

The shock and sadness of her neighbor's death washed over her anew. "Corie Rudolf was a friend of mine. I deeply mourn her passing and send my prayers to her family over their tragic loss."

But another emotion was growing inside her, too. The same emotion that had motivated her to say yes to the D.A.'s request to have the Rose Red Rapist's most prominent victim agree to testify, the same emotion that drove her to come here in the first place, the same emotion that made her want to shove Vanessa Owen's microwave right down the opportunistic brunette's throat.

Bailey smiled serenely, holding up her hand and interrupting before Vanessa could ask some other sensationalist question that was meant to get beneath her skin. "I am not to blame for Corie's murder. There's a woman called The Cleaner who has covered up crimes and destroyed people's lives and killed them...to help out a rapist. The same rapist who assaulted me."

"B—"

"*They* are the ones to blame. Not the victims." The anger, the helplessness and frustration, the stark, cold fear she hated to feel all rose to the surface and oozed out in succinct, daring words. "I blame The Cleaner for Corie's murder. And I think she ought to know that killing my friend only makes me more determined than ever to see that justice is done."

"Brave words for a person who's received how many threats? And you're still going to testify?"

"Yes."

Vanessa's predatory eyes narrowed. "Aren't you afraid The Cleaner will come after you again? Aren't you terrified?" The dark-haired woman leaned in. "Shouldn't we all be terrified that you're here with us tonight? Haven't you put all of us in danger?"

"We're all safe here," Spencer announced, even though he hadn't said those words to Bailey. "This interview is done."

Vanessa's phone rang as Spencer pushed Bailey past

the last of the cameras. When she glanced back, she saw the look of irritation on the reporter's face as she read the incoming number.

"Yes?" she answered. "What? I can't. I'm on a live feed right now. Are you sure? Tonight?" She lifted her gaze to meet Bailey's at the top of the stairs. And held it. "That *would* be a fabulous story to tell." She repeated herself when the caller must have argued. "I'll take care of it." Then she disconnected the call and made a cutting gesture across her throat to tell her cameraman to turn off the feed.

"Spencer?" Bailey tugged on his sleeve when the reporter slipped through the cadre of reporters and disappeared from sight. "Where is she going?"

He pulled her inside to the marble foyer before answering. "Way to bait the trap, B. Challenging The Cleaner to come find you here?"

"Are you making a joke?"

"I'm on the job. I don't joke." His gray eyes were more probing than Vanessa's had been. "If she's not already here, she or her henchmen will be soon." He tapped the radio in his ear again. "Nick. Tell Zeiss's men to go on full alert. I think we're going to have a real party tonight. And somebody find me Vanessa Owen."

Bailey slipped off her wrap and moved on to the check-in table while Spencer relayed orders to his team. There were so many people here. The estate was huge, and nearly every room on the first floor was being used. Waitstaff moved through the guests, carrying trays of champagne and hors d'oeuvres. The musicians sat at one end of the open ballroom and dancers waltzed in a circle. There was a giant Christmas tree at the foot of the winding staircase where a professional photographer was snapping souvenir photos of the donors attending.

If The Cleaner was here, finding her wouldn't be easy. Bailey idly wondered if it would be just as difficult for The Cleaner to find her. She glanced back out at the reporters' stand. What if she already had? Vanessa Owen had once dated Brian Elliott. Would she still be loyal to him? Was she so hungry for a career-making story that she'd set up the very crimes she wanted to cover?

"Miss Austin?" A friendly voice diverted her attention away from the missing newswoman. Max Duncan, the bodyguard who'd nearly gotten arrested and had helped save her life, sat behind the table, wearing a suit and tie, an earbud like Spencer's, and those same reflective sunglasses he'd worn out in the snowy sunshine wrapped around the back of his neck. "How are you this evening?"

"Good, Max." She stretched up on tiptoe to look over the edge of the table and saw he was sitting on a stool with his leg out straight in a brace. A metal cane leaned against the table beside him. "How are you feeling?"

"Beat up and embarrassed. Dislocated my kneecap and cracked my shin bone." He read through the list of guests on his clipboard and checked off her name. "But it's all hands on deck with a party this big. I figured I could at least watch the door for Mr. Zeiss tonight. I need to get back on his nice list."

Bailey smiled. "It's good to see you in one piece."

"Yes, ma'am. You, too." Max's gaze strayed up to

greet the red-haired man brushing his hand against Bailey's back. She startled at the faintly possessive touch, and was disappointed when Spencer pulled away just as quickly. "Detective." Max picked up his clipboard again and found Spencer's name. "You carrying?"

"Yes." Spencer nodded and pulled back his jacket to reveal the gun holstered there before buttoning it shut again. "You've got a registration of everyone else here who's carrying a weapon?"

Max made another check on his list. "Your people. And all the Zeiss personnel. We're the ones in the gray uniforms." He patted the brace on his thigh. "I, personally, won't get there very fast. But we'll come running if you need us."

Spencer thanked him. "Good to know."

"Bailey!"

Bailey groaned as her mother called to her from the photographer's station and swept across the foyer in a sashay of wine-red taffeta. "Now it's my turn to say, 'Brace yourself.'"

Linking her arm through Spencer's, Bailey crossed to the foot of the staircase to meet Loretta Austin-Mayweather halfway. Her mother hugged her, carefully turning her cheek so as not to smudge either of their makeup. "I'm so glad you came. This color is divine on you. Darling, let me look at you."

Loretta caught Bailey's hands and leaned back, zeroing in on the bandage on her cheek. "Oh, dear. I knew you'd been hurt." She touched her fingers to the bruising cut and frowned. "Will that leave a scar?" Before Bailey could answer, she pulled her over to the photographer, who snapped a candid photo of them both. By the time the afterimage of the flash had cleared Bailey's retinas, Loretta was already pointing to her injury. "This can be edited out of the pictures, can't it?"

"Yes, ma'am."

Loretta had her by the hand again, pulling her toward the ballroom. "I want you to come say hello to the mayor."

"Mother?" Bailey planted her feet. She didn't care about scars in pictures or scoring points with local politicians. But she did care that her mother acknowledge the danger her daughter was facing, and maybe, just maybe, find the strength to show a little compassion. "You remember my friend Spencer."

"Your friend?" Loretta's tone was decidedly less welcoming than her eagerness to see Bailey had been. "Detective Montgomery."

"Mrs. Mayweather."

"Mother. I dressed up and came to your party for you. Be nice."

Something like despair put instant lines on Loretta's delicate features. She reached out to squeeze Spencer's hand. "Thank you for saving my daughter's life." Then the lines vanished and she pointed a stern finger at him. "But if your people do anything to ruin this fund-raiser, you're not going to be in tonight's family portrait."

SPENCER WOULD BE happy to dance every dance with Bailey for the rest of the evening. While it was pure torture to hold her in his arms and concentrate on something besides the way the color of her dress deepened the blue of her eyes or how the summery scent of her hair followed him with every twirl around the floor, at least she was in his arms. Locked down tight, her location secure.

But he'd spent as many dances standing on the sidelines, watching her chat up the deputy commissioner, a retired real estate developer and a player from the chief's football team. He'd catch his breath when he lost sight of her behind a taller dancer, breathe easier once those sunny-gold curls reappeared.

She'd make a fine wife for any man who wanted to move up the corporate ladder or make chief or commissioner one day. She'd be a finer wife for any man who wanted a true partner—a woman whose strengths and talents complemented his own, whose gentle heart and tenacious spirit could ease a man's troubled spirit or ignite the fires of passion inside him.

Spencer squeezed his eyes shut as the longing hit him again. He just had to get her through tonight. He had to get her through tomorrow. He had to get her to that trial on Monday, and then maybe he could decide if he could get through a life with Bailey at his side. But as long as she was in danger, as long as The Cleaner was out there, could he really risk…

Spencer opened his eyes and felt his heart skip a beat when he didn't see her. "B?"

He quickly scanned the dance floor. Couples spun by him in a Viennese waltz. But no dark blue gown. No golden hair.

He was crossing the room to the corner where he'd last seen her. His fingertip was at his ear to call for backup when he spotted her dancing out the door into the foyer with a black-haired man.

Oh, no, no, no, no, no. Spencer crossed straight out the ballroom's second door to cut off Gabriel Knight before he could corner Bailey and grill her with the same accusatory questions Vanessa Owen had, or throw out another of those *poor little rich girl* cracks. But as he excused his way through a group of laughing, chatting guests, Spencer saw that Gabe Knight wasn't questioning Bailey at all.

Knight was introducing Bailey to his date, his boss, Mara Boyd-Elliott. The platinum blonde was sitting behind one of the dozens of Christmas trees decorating the house. Her head was bent toward a sheaf of papers in her lap. She signed her name to one and pushed the documents off to the brunette sitting beside her, standing as Bailey approached. "Miss Austin."

Seriously? That was one screwed-up ex-family dynamic. What was Regina Hollister doing here? Judging by the business jacket and slacks she wore, she hadn't received an invitation.

But she did seem eager to reclaim Mara's attention. "Ms. Boyd, if you could finishing signing—"

"Regina, please," the blonde woman snapped. "This isn't my office. This is a social event. We're celebrating the holidays."

Regina exhaled a weary sigh that puffed the dark bangs off her forehead. "I understand that, ma'am, and I'm sorry to intrude. But I'm trying to help Brian take care of things before the…" Her gaze darted to Bailey and she rephrased her explanation with a bit of a sneer. "Before Monday." She held out the pen and documents one more time. "He needs your signature on these shared asset forms so we can get the property liquidated before the end of the year. Please."

"Oh, very well." With a flourish that was more style than business, Mara grabbed the papers and signed each copy before dropping them back in Regina's hands.

"Thank you, Ms. Boyd. I know he'll appreciate it." She included Bailey and Knight, as well, as she picked up her coat and briefcase and hurried toward the front door. "Enjoy your evening."

So what did Mara have to say to Bailey? Apologize for ever helping her scumbag of an ex get out of jail? Ask if she'd do an interview for her newspaper?

Or maybe this meeting was Bailey's idea. "Do you still do business with your ex-husband?"

"It was an amicable divorce, Miss Austin. We've continued a mutually beneficial working relationship ever since."

"I said to leave the detective work to me," Spencer grumbled. But as long as he had eyes on Bailey…and the suspect was talking.

Spencer hung back at the fringe of the other group and listened to the snippets of hushed, urgent conversation he could hear.

Good girl. Bailey hugged her arms around her middle, keeping her distance from both Knight and Mrs. Elliott. "Why are you telling me this?" she asked.

Mara Boyd was pleading her case with Bailey, it sounded like. "Because you don't know Brian the way I do."

"I'm certain we don't." Bailey shook her head. "How could you ever help someone like that?"

"He's not well. That's one reason we still own properties jointly—" she gestured toward the front door "—one reason Regina is working weekends to take care of his paperwork. We're trying to protect his best interests." The older woman reached for Bailey's hand, but she cringed away. Rebuffed, Mara tucked her arm through Gabe Knight's and leaned against him, instead. "When I inherited the paper and my father's fortune, something changed with Brian. He was a self-made man. Suddenly, I eclipsed him. I wasn't the helpmate he wanted any longer. I think he saw me as competition. I know he resented my success."

"That's a sad story," Bailey said. "But it doesn't change what he did to me."

"No, but..." Mara sat back down and Spencer inched up to the tree to hear what she had to say. "I'm a smart woman, Miss Austin. I can do the math. The rapes started right after I divorced Brian. I'm the reason he hates women. Everything that he's done is my fault."

What she was sharing with Bailey was merely circumstantial, not any kind of conclusive evidence. Spencer had heard enough. The woman was trying to assuage her own guilt. And she didn't need to be dumping that on Bailey. "Then that makes you another victim, Mrs. Elliott." He circled around Knight and slid his arm behind Bailey's waist. "Or an accomplice. Is there some information about your ex that you've been withholding from the police throughout this whole investigation? For example, did he ever display any of those violent rages when he was with you? Did he hurt you?"

"My ex-husband is a sick man," she reiterated. "I'm trying to protect him. I owe him that." She stood and linked her arm through Knight's. "Gabriel, I think I'd like to leave now."

Once they'd gone, Spencer released Bailey and turned to face her. "What part of don't go off by yourself don't you understand? Let me talk to Mara Elliott, Regina Hollister and Gabe Knight. You don't need to get that close to those people."

"I thought she could be The Cleaner. You heard her. She wants to protect her ex. She's probably paying his attorney's fees for him, too. I bet that's why she's liquidating those properties."

"You need to stop finding suspects for me. I've already got a team trying to track down where Vanessa Owen disappeared to." Spencer exhaled a deep breath and rubbed his hands up and down her arms, trying to keep the fear of her getting hurt pushed down deep where it couldn't distract him. It was one job he was discovering he wasn't very good at. "Look, B—it's one thing to try to lure this woman out. It's something else when you purposely go looking for trouble."

Bailey's hands settled at his chest and played with his tie. He recognized the little caresses as an attempt to soothe his concern. "I wasn't looking for trouble. I just want answers. Besides, I wasn't alone. The guard was right over there." She turned to prove her point, but the table in the foyer was empty. "Max?"

"Behind you." He limped across the marble tiles,

leaning heavily on his cane. "Detective Montgomery, we've got a situation."

"Not again," Bailey whispered beside him.

Spencer reached for her hand as the bodyguard pulled a green envelope from inside his jacket and handed it over. It had already been placed inside a clear plastic bag, preserving any trace for evidence. But the card was familiar and the message was all too clear.

I warned you.

Now you've ruined your mother's Christmas.

"When? How?" Bailey's fingers convulsed around his.

"We found it in the donation basket under the ballroom Christmas tree," Max reported. "We've been changing the basket out every hour so we can put the checks and cash in the safe. That means your suspect has been here in the past twenty minutes or so."

Spencer surveyed the number of guests and staff in the house. Maybe fifty in the foyer. Another two hundred in the ballroom. There were people in the dining room and game room. Staff in the kitchen and throughout the rest of the house. "She's probably still here. Any sign of a bomb?"

"Not yet. I talked to Mr. Zeiss and our people have begun a low-key evacuation. We're stationed at all the exits. We're telling guests in small groups that we've detected a gas leak and that a repair crew is on its way." Max unbuttoned his suit jacket at the same time Spencer did. Both men wanted quick access to their firearm if needed. "I'm on my way to inform Mr. Mayweather now."

"Have him make an announcement in the ballroom. We need to clear the estate in an orderly manner without anyone getting hurt." And without such a rush to the exits that their perp escaped, too.

"Nick, she's here." He alerted the task force members on his radio. "We're evacuating the house. But don't let any of the guests leave."

"Understood."

Spencer wound his arm around Bailey's shoulders and turned her toward the front door. "Let's get you out of here, too."

Before they could take another step, all the lights went out and the first woman screamed.

BAILEY FELT SPENCER pushing her against the wall beside one of the Christmas trees, shielding her with his body as several guests panicked and ran from the ballroom, bumping into and tripping over the people who were already there.

A violin screeched and the music suddenly stopped. She heard curses and cries of pain. A glass crashed and shattered on the hard floor. Someone was crying. There were more screams and people shouting for loved ones, the excited chatter of hundreds of people talking all at once. She heard footsteps running toward the back of the house, others shifting like restless cattle.

She heard Jackson's voice in the ballroom, shouting to be heard above the chaos. "Everyone, remain calm. Stay where you are." He hollered for Zeiss and his crew to get them some light and the sounds of worried voices swelled. "Please, people."

"If anyone gets hurt…" Bailey clung to the walnut paneling, hating the frightened sounds she could hear. "Did I ever tell you I'm afraid of the dark? That Brian Elliott put a hood over my head when he wasn't…"

"Shh." Firm lips warmed the nape of her neck. "Just focus on the sound of my voice." Spencer moved behind her. He pulled out his cell phone and punched up an app that lit up the screen with a bright light. "Here." Suddenly, there was a small beam of light shining at her feet. "See? We're not in the dark."

Following the illumination of his phone light, Bailey could see other guests and the Zeiss security guards turning on phones and flashlights, transforming the dark night of the powerless house into a dim twilight.

Still, Bailey didn't breathe any easier until Spencer took her hand and pulled her into step beside him. He stretched his long arm over his head, forming a beacon that several people came closer to. "I'm Detective Montgomery, KCPD," he announced. "I need everyone to stay calm. I'm going outside to see if my people can tell me anything about the power outage. Please stay where you are."

He slowly made his way toward the front door, but he'd made the mistake of announcing his authority and the frightened guests were following in their wake like lemmings to a seaside cliff.

"Stay put, people," he reminded them, but they were gathering around, closing in. From all directions now.

A man jostled Bailey's arm. "Spencer?"

Someone bumped her again and she lost hold of Spencer's hand. "Spence?"

"Bailey?"

She reached for him again, but suddenly she was being pushed back. More people were drifting into the foyer from the ballroom now, separating her from her savior like a deep, rushing stream.

"Bailey?" He swung his light around, illuminating her face in the crowd. But they were moving farther and farther apart.

He flipped his light in a different direction, back to the ballroom's second archway. "Duncan! Can you reach her?"

A second beam of light hit Bailey from behind. "I got her."

"Bailey, I'll meet you outside."

"Okay."

The burly bodyguard pushed aside the people in his way and closed his hand around Bailey's arm. "Let's get you out of here."

Bailey nodded, eager to stay with a light and a friendly face. "What about my wrap? It'll be freezing outside."

Max tugged out of the path of an elderly couple feeling their way along the wall. "Cloakroom's the other direction. I'll take you out the back. I'll loan you my jacket if we can't find something along the way."

The crowd thinned as they cleared the ballroom exodus and Bailey realized Max was walking at a quicker pace than he had earlier this evening. And he wasn't using his cane. "You must be feeling better."

He held up the cane and shrugged. "I kept tripping people."

She smiled, appreciating his attempt to alleviate her concern. What she didn't appreciate was his grip tightening around her arm. Any more force and he'd be leaving bruises. She patted his hand. "Hey, lighten up. I can keep up now."

The first tinge of disquiet hit when he didn't loosen his grip.

The second came when he picked up the pace, walking just as quickly as she could on two uninjured legs. "Max?"

This was wrong. Something was very wrong.

Be aware of your surroundings, Bailey.

She knew she was in trouble when he turned off into a smaller hallway before they reached the kitchen. She tugged against his grip, but he wasn't stopping. "I grew up in this house, Max. This isn't the way—"

He pushed open a secluded door and shoved her inside.

She tumbled off one of her heels, wrenching her ankle, but it wasn't enough pain to stop her from charging toward the door and pummeling the muscle-bound bully who'd put her here. "Damn it, Max, it's as dark as a closet in here. Where's your flashlight?"

"Here's your light." Another voice. A woman's voice.

Bailey spun around.

"What?" Suddenly, there was a bright light shining in her eyes, blinding her after the darkness. Bailey shielded her eyes against the sharp beam of the LED flashlight and squinted at the face that went with the woman's voice into focus. "You're…Regina Hollister." Brian Elliott's executive assistant. Always lurking in the background whenever her employer was around. The papers she'd brought for Mara Boyd-Elliott to sign had probably been fakes. She hadn't come to the ball for a signature. She'd come for her. "What are you doing here?"

"Cleaning up a mess. Just like I clean up all of Brian's messes. He needs me for that, you know. From the time we started building his company together, I've always taken care of whatever he needs."

The Cleaner.

Instinctively, Bailey backed away from the woman's cold, unsmiling stare. But in the small butler's pantry, she quickly bumped into Max. He hadn't budged when she'd struck a moment earlier, so she tried pleading. "Please call Spencer. Whatever this woman is holding over you, whatever she's paying—it's not worth it. I'll double whatever she's paying you."

"Max," Regina warned. "We have a schedule to keep."

Even in the dim tunnel of illumination inside the room, she could see the regret stamped on Max's bulldog features. "It isn't the money, Miss Austin. I'm sorry I have to do this."

"Do what?" The rustling of her long dress was the only sound for several long seconds.

Then a soft cloth came down over her head and she was plunged into utter darkness. Bailey screamed. The flashback to fear was instant and overwhelming. But she was a different woman now than she'd been that night.

She bit down on the hand that covered her mouth. Max swore. She pushed off the hood, but his hands were on her again. Bailey punched up, catching him in the throat. When he grabbed her by the hair, she clawed at his hands, clawed at his face. Her fingers fisted around those ridiculous sunglasses he'd worn tonight and she ripped them from his neck, tossing them away into the shadows.

"Damn it, Miss Austin, quit fightin' me."

"You're wasting my time. Give me that." Something long and hard struck Bailey in the back of the head, driving her to her knees and knocking her woozy.

"Spencer," she murmured, feeling the floor rush up to meet her. "I need you."

She was vaguely aware of her wrists and legs being bound, of the hood sliding over her face. Her head felt like a swinging cannonball when Max picked her up over his shoulder.

This was her nightmare all over again—struck from behind, bound—her world reduced to the blackness inside the hood. Only one thing remained in the re-creation of that horrible night.

The last thing she heard was Regina's clipped, matter-of-fact voice. "Bring her. He wants to see her before I finish her off."

Chapter Twelve

Spencer stood in the doorway of the butler's pantry holding a twisted pair of sunglasses and the midnight-blue heel of Bailey's shoe.

He'd known she was gone long before they'd gotten the power back on and had cleared the entire mansion. If she was here, she'd have been right by his side, right in the middle of things—asking questions, straightening his tie, adding light to his dark old soul, listening, loving, standing up to make a difference.

But it had taken twenty minutes longer for the Zeiss security guard to report the drops of blood on the rug back there. It wasn't enough blood to indicate a serious injury, but it was enough to know that she hadn't gone willingly.

Keep fighting, sweetheart.

Now he just had to get to her in time.

Losing Bailey the way he'd lost Ellen wasn't something a man could survive.

Spencer unhooked his tie and loosened his collar. Time to go to work.

"What do we know?"

Hans, the muscular German Shepherd who partnered with big Pike Taylor, was panting in the hallway. Pike rubbed the dog's muzzle and ears, rewarding him for completing his task. "Hans followed the trail to the staff parking lot where Max Duncan's truck was parked. He had enough of a scent to get us out to the highway. They turned east, into the city."

"The only prints are Max Duncan's on the door knob." Annie Hermann pulled a giant pair of tweezers from her crime-scene kit and plucked a tiny filament from the rug. "I've got a black thread."

"They put a hood on her." Spencer couldn't prove it, but he knew how to put together the pieces of the puzzle. The hood was part of the Rose Red Rapist's M.O. His stomach twisted into knot. The darkness? The disorientation? Bailey would be terrified.

Nick's gut had him sniffing the air at the back of the pantry. "Do you smell that? Perfume. Unless it's Bailey's?"

"No." Bailey was clean, fresh, citrusy sunshine. "It's hers. The Cleaner's."

Nick's phone buzzed on his belt and he read the information there. "Got a text from Sarge. Once we narrowed the search to Duncan, she got a hit. Apparently, Duncan has a past he'd like to keep in the past. That's how she got him to turn on Bailey." He flipped open the key pad and replied, "I'll tell Sarge to put an APB out on his truck."

Kate Kilpatrick waited in the hallway. "I talked to Bailey's parents and got a list of all the women invited to the party and any female press or staff who were on their checklist."

Pike stood up beside her. "But if Duncan's the guy checking her in at the door, he wouldn't put her on that list."

"Here's the kicker." Kate opened a manila file and pulled out a photograph. "Loretta Mayweather is a wreck with her daughter missing—but that woman knows her guest list. I had her look through the pictures the photographer took, to help us match names to faces, and she spotted this." She handed the photo to Spencer. "The one person here tonight she didn't invite."

"The one person not dressed for a formal occasion." Spencer brushed his fingertip over the image of Bailey in the middle of her conversation with Mara Boyd-Elliott and Gabriel Knight. But he was looking at the fourth person in that photograph.

The one wearing slacks and a jacket.

Regina Hollister.

The Cleaner.

Spencer handed the picture off to Nick and the others. "Let's go get her."

Fight. That's what you do. You fight.

Spencer's voice filled Bailey's thoughts when she came to on top of the plastic-covered mattress for the second time.

She rolled onto her side, facing the voices she could hear, hating the sound of the crinkling plastic almost as much as she hated the hood that had kept her in darkness earlier.

She wasn't quite sure how she could take care of herself with her wrists bound and her head throbbing from the knot on the back of her scalp. A long silk gown with one shoulder and too many stays wasn't exactly her regular workout gear, either.

But she wasn't giving up. Spencer would be looking for her. He was smart and observant and knew how to get the best from the people he led. He'd figure it out. He'd find her.

She wasn't going to be another tragedy weighing heavily on his noble heart.

Bailey tilted her gaze to the discarded leg brace and cane lying on the floor beside the stack of lumber where Max Duncan sat, guarding her. Meanwhile, Brian Elliott and Regina Hollister stood with their heads bowed together over the workbench in the far corner of the construction site—laughing and plotting and not looking anything much like a boss and his assistant.

The sun must be up by now, although there wasn't a single window in this demolished section of some floor in some old building that was being renovated by Elliott's company. He owned dozens of buildings across the city.

But Spencer would find her. He would be there for her.

The setting was disturbingly familiar. An old warehouse, stripped down to the studs, covered in layers of plastic. She sat on a plastic-covered mattress in the middle of the floor.

The only difference was that Elliott was allowing her to see her surroundings in detail this time. He was allowing her to see his face without any effort to disguise it.

She knew the only reason they'd let her take off the hood and see the details of her surroundings was that they had no intention of letting her leave here alive.

"Why are you doing this, Max?" she asked, needing to do something before the fear or helplessness got too strong a hold on her again.

"I've done some things in my past I'm not too proud of. They could cost me my job." He laughed, but it wasn't a pleasant sound. "Let's just say I haven't always made a living with my clothes on."

"Oh." She hadn't expected that answer from the tough guy she'd once vouched for with the police. But then she supposed she didn't much care about the choices he'd had to make, since they'd led to her being held prisoner. Surely, Brian Elliott didn't think he could get away with the star witness in the case against him.

But then, maybe that's exactly what he thought. As difficult as The Cleaner had been for Spencer's task force to identify and capture, maybe Regina had a plan that would allow Brian to get away without any blame. After all, who was going to argue his guilt but one dead victim and a weak man being blackmailed into silence?

"What about Corie?" Bailey ignored the ringing in her skull and the throbbing in her injured cheek when she pushed herself up to a sitting position. "She had a crush on you, you know. It wouldn't have mattered to her who you are or where you've been."

Max leaned forward, bracing his elbows on his knees and resting his chin on his hands.

Brace. He'd removed his leg brace entirely and tossed it to the floor near the edge of her mattress. Maybe he'd never been injured at all, and it had simply been a ruse to gain her trust and give him access to her mother's guest list last night.

"I'm sorry about your friend. She was a sweet kid." Bailey scooted to the edge of the mattress and dropped her feet over the side, gathering her long skirt around her legs. "She was spying on you, too. Between her and me we had eyes on you almost around the clock."

"I had no idea." Now that hurt. Two people she'd trusted. Two people who'd betrayed her.

Come on, Spencer.

Bailey dropped the hem of her dress down around her feet, letting the edge fall over part of the cane. "So was she killed because she looked like me and someone made a mistake? Or was she collateral damage?"

"Neither. Corie was getting cold feet." Max's attention drifted over to the far side of the room to the two conscienceless tyrants who didn't give a whit about anyone else's lives but their own. "I don't think she wanted to see you get hurt."

Bailey curled her toes around the cane and pulled it out of sight beneath her dress. "I don't suppose Regina lets you change your mind about helping her."

"If Regina wants something, she calls you. And if you don't do what she asks, she finds you." Max snorted a derisive laugh through his nose. "We're just pawns. It's all about Mr. Elliott for her. That is one sick relationship. She's lover, mother, caretaker, protector to him."

"What does he do for her?" Weapon? Check. The

cane seemed to have done a decent job on the back of her own head. Bailey stretched out her arms, making a show of flexing her fingers while she got her feet planted flat on the plastic tarp beneath them.

"I'm not sure. The money. The job."

Bailey reached down for the cane and came up swinging. Nose. *Pop!* She heard the cartilage give when she smacked it across Max's face. Holding his bleeding face, cursing, he pushed to his feet. Throat. She swung again, catching him in the Adam's apple and knocking him back to his seat.

"Max!" Regina shouted a warning.

"Stop her!" That was Elliott.

Gut. Max fell backward over the stack of wood and Bailey brought the cane down hard in his midsection, stealing the wind from his belly.

The split second she paused to decide whether to hold on to the cane or go for the gun in his belt was the split second it took for Brian Elliott to reach her.

She screamed when his arms clamped around her body, lifting her off her feet. He shook her like a rag doll until the cane dropped from her hands. After kicking it away, he threw Bailey back onto the mattress and was on top of her before she could scramble away.

"Get off me!" She scratched at his face, gouged at his eyes. "Get off!"

"Oh, yeah. This is what I wanted." He pulled at the folds of her skirt, shoving the silk and petticoats up to her thighs. Bailey twisted, screamed.

"Shut her up!" Regina yelled behind him. "Someone will hear."

Ignoring the warning, Elliott gave her a command. "Bring my kit."

Bailey heard Max moaning, footsteps running.

"You should have let me take care of her," Regina insisted. "I could have made this problem all go away."

"Don't tell me what to do!"

"Here." Regina dropped a toolbox beside the mattress. "I hear sirens."

"Spencer!" Bailey yelled in desperation. "Help!"

A hard slap across the face silenced her plea. Bailey felt her mind sliding back to that night. To this place.

She'd tried to fight. But her head hurt. Her arms were so tired.

Elliott rubbed his hands together and she realized he'd squirted some kind of disinfectant onto them. "Of all the women who have dared to defy me, you have been the most brazen." He covered the chemical smell with the wretched cologne that sent her straight back to that night.

"Stop. Please," she begged.

"Brian." Bailey saw Regina come up behind Brian and touch his shoulder. "The police are downstairs. You have to get out now."

Police? "Spencer!"

Fight. That's what you do. You fight.

"Not until I'm finished!" He shrugged off the warning and ripped at the seam of Bailey's gown. "Calling me out in the press? Picking me out of a police lineup?"

"You raped me!"

"You needed it."

Bailey had one move left. Groin.

"Brian!"

Her attacker fell onto the floor, writhing in pain, and Bailey rolled off the mattress on the opposite side, pulling down her clothes, pushing to her feet.

"Max, get up! Get rid of her! Brian?" Regina knelt on the floor beside the man she idolized. "Darling?"

"KCPD! We're coming in!"

A loud pop and the cracking of wood filled Bailey's ears as she lurched toward the door.

"Spencer!"

"Bailey!"

She caught sight of his red-gold hair. An army followed him through the door and fanned across the room, each targeting a different kidnapper.

"KCPD! Get on the ground! Now!"

A dog's fierce barking drowned out the words.

Brian Elliott cursed. "Get that slavering dog away from me!"

"You found me." Bailey rushed forward, needing Spencer's arms around her now. "Thank God, you—"

Bailey jerked back, stumbling at the sudden shift in movement, as Regina snatched the back of her dress. The taller woman wound her forearm around Bailey's neck and pulled her in front of her body to use her as a human shield.

Regina must have recovered Max's gun, or had carried one all along, because there was definitely a hard metal gun barrel pressing into Bailey's temple.

"Everybody, stop!" Spencer ordered. "B?"

His gray eyes flickered over Bailey's face, then hard-

ened when they met the threat in Regina's. But his arms
had frozen in the air, his gun cradled between his hands.

"I missed on purpose last time," Regina taunted.
"Thought I could scare some sense into your little girlfriend here." Bailey cringed as the woman pressed the
gun against her cheek. "You let Brian go—" Regina slid
the gun to Bailey's temple "—or I won't miss again."

Bailey's eyes stung with tears at the anguish that
lined Spencer's face. She could see the nightmare in
his eyes. But his first love had surrendered. She hadn't
trusted him enough to keep her safe. "I'm not Ellen,
Spence," she said simply, filling her eyes and her voice
with all the love and trust she had for him. "You aren't
going to lose me."

"Isn't that sweet? Don't worry, Brian." Regina
ground the gun into Bailey's temple, hard enough to
tilt her head to the side. Brian Elliott was already in
handcuffs. But Regina would clean up his mistakes right
up to the very end. "I promise Miss Austin will never
testify against you."

It was a promise Regina would never keep.

Spencer fired his gun. Bailey jerked at the first shot.
But Regina's grip on her went slack.

"Get down, B!" Spencer marched forward as Bailey ducked and Nick Fensom pulled her safely out of
the line of fire.

Regina pulled the trigger, but her shot went wide.
Spencer fired two more times and Regina Hollister
crumpled in a heap, dead.

Finally, he lowered his gun. "B?"

"Spencer!" Bailey ran to him. "Spence—"

He claimed her mouth in a kiss that was hot and hard and over far too quickly. But his arm anchored her to his side. She lifted her fingers to straighten the collar that was hopelessly twisted with the hanging tail of his tie. He leaned down to rest his forehead against hers. "We got 'em, sweetheart. The bad guys didn't get to win."

They stood there like that for several seconds, his eyes searching her face. Finally, he raised his head, although the arm around her remained. He looked to the other members of his team. "We need to clear the prisoners out of here and secure the scene. Get Annie up here with her kit and call—"

"We got it, boss," Nick teased. "We can handle a crime scene." He pulled Max Duncan to his feet and winked at Bailey. "Be gentle with this one, Bails."

"Out!" Spencer ordered.

Pike Taylor led Brian Elliott out the door and Nick followed.

Spencer started to say something. But with Regina Hollister's dead body in the room—or maybe because he didn't quite know what to say, either, now that the threat to Bailey had been neutralized and there was no need for a relentless cop to protect her anymore—he touched the cut on her cheek and sighed.

Next, he holstered his weapon and shrugged out of his jacket. Like the true gentleman he was, Spencer draped it around her shoulders and took her by the hand.

He led her down a flight of stairs and they made a bracing dash to his SUV. After killing the emergency lights, he turned on the engine, cranked the heat and pulled her into his lap so he could capture her mouth in a deep, potent kiss. Bailey wound her arms around his neck, riding the deep rise and fall of his chest— answering him touch for touch, kiss for kiss, until they were generating plenty of heat on their own.

When they came up for air, Spencer framed her face between his hands and looked into her eyes. "I know you want to change the world and doing something meaningful and take care of yourself. Those are mighty big dreams for a man to compete with. But I need you, B. Please let that be enough."

Bailey stroked her fingers across his lips, quieting the raw urgency in his voice. "You *do* love me, don't you, detective?" she asked, feeling one little bit of uncertainty. "Don't let me be the only one feeling this way."

Spencer pulled her back to his chest, tunneling his fingers into her hair. "Yes, I love you. I want to marry you. I know with the rape, you need recovery time. And then everything you've been through this week, and the trial to deal with. I'm a patient man. I'll give you all the time you need, all the space you want until you're ready to say yes."

"Yes," Bailey answered without hesitation, snuggling into Spencer's arms, feeling safe, strong, perfect. "Yes."

WHEN DWIGHT POWERS called her name, Bailey released her grip on Spencer's hand. She walked past the defense's table, looking beyond Kenna Parker's stoic expression to meet Brian Elliott's hateful, condemning eyes.

But Spencer's steady, granite-colored gaze was there

for her when she turned to face the courtroom. His engagement ring was on her finger. She stepped into the witness's stand beside the judge's bench and raised her right hand.

"Do you solemnly swear to tell the truth, the whole truth, and nothing but the truth, so help you God?"

Bailey answered, "I do."

* * * * *

Merry Christmas
& A Happy New Year!

Thank you for a wonderful
2013...

A sneaky peek at next month...

INTRIGUE...

BREATHTAKING ROMANTIC SUSPENSE

My wish list for next month's titles...

In stores from 20th December 2013:

❏ Cold Case at Carlton's Canyon – Rita Herron

& Dead by Wednesday – Beverly Long

❏ Wanted – Delores Fossen

& The Marine's Last Defence – Angi Morgan

❏ Unrepentant Cowboy – Joanna Wayne

& Gone – Mallory Kane

Romantic Suspense

❏ The Return of Connor Mansfield – Beth Cornelison

Available at WHSmith, Tesco, Asda, Eason, Amazon and Apple

Just can't wait?

Visit us Online

You can buy our books online a month before they hit the shops! **www.millsandboon.co.uk**

1213/46

Special Offers

Every month we put together collections and longer reads written by your favourite authors.

Here are some of next month's highlights— and don't miss our fabulous discount online!

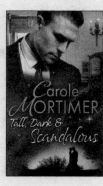

On sale 3rd January   **On sale 3rd January**   **On sale 20th December**

Save 20%
on all Special Releases

Find out more at
www.millsandboon.co.uk/specialreleases

Visit us Online

0114/ST/MB44

Come in from the cold this Christmas with two of our favourite authors. Whether you're jetting off to Vermont with Sarah Morgan or settling down for Christmas dinner with Fiona Harper, the smiles won't stop this festive season.

Visit:
www.millsandboon.co.uk

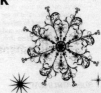

Join the Mills & Boon Book Club

Want to read more **Intrigue** books?
We're offering you **2 more** absolutely **FREE!**

We'll also treat you to these fabulous extras:

- Exclusive offers and much more!
- FREE home delivery
- FREE books and gifts with our special rewards scheme

Get your free books now!

**visit www.millsandboon.co.uk/bookclub
or call Customer Relations on 020 8288 2888**

FREE BOOK OFFER TERMS & CONDITIONS

Accepting your free books places you under no obligation to buy anything and you may cancel at any time. we do not hear from you we will send 5 stories a month which you may purchase or return to us—the choic is yours. Offer valid in the UK only and is not available to current Mills & Boon subscribers to this series. W reserve the right to refuse an application and applicants must be aged 18 years or over. Only one applicatic per household. Terms and prices are subject to change without notice. As a result of this application you ma receive further offers from other carefully selected companies. If you do not wish to share in this opportuni please write to the Data Manager at PO BOX 676, Richmond, TW9 1WU.

SUBS/ONLINE/l1

Mills & Boon® Online

Discover more romance at
www.millsandboon.co.uk

- **FREE** online reads
- **Books** up to one month before shops
- **Browse our books** before you buy

...and much more!

For exclusive competitions and instant updates:

 Like us on **facebook.com/millsandboon**

 Follow us on **twitter.com/millsandboon**

 Join us on **community.millsandboon.co.uk**

Visit us Online   Sign up for our FREE eNewsletter at
www.millsandboon.co.uk

WEB/M&B/RTL5